DESCENDANTS OF THE WOLF

JERRY AUTIERI

FOREWORD

You are about to embark on a rollicking Viking adventure. Before you do, be advised that this is a continuation of a previous series, Ulfrik Ormsson's Saga, which begins with the book *Fate's Needle*. There is absolutely no need to have read that series first. This series was written to stand alone. However, characters and history from the prior series do appear in this volume. Again, knowing that history will only enhance your enjoyment of this tale; however, without it you will do fine. These are new characters and new adventures.

Depending on when you are finding this series, it may either be just beginning or completely finished. Reading in chronological order is not necessary. However, if you want to follow a family history you can start with Ulfrik Ormsson's story and continue here. Enjoy the tales of Viking adventure that follow!

1

Yngvar crouched in the indigo shadows of the spruce trees that striped the field. He squinted against the late afternoon sun, then smiled. The sheep were as white clouds floating in their pen. The sweet scent of hearth smoke carried in the wind, rolling across his face. The sheep would not detect them downwind.

"We best move before the farmers herd them to the barn," he said. He belched and the honey taste of mead filled his mouth again.

Standing at his back, huddled in the same spruce shadows, Bjorn and Thorfast gave him a gentle push. He turned on them, his vision still wobbling from the mead.

"Don't rush this," he said. His voice was low and his hands were cold and trembling. He grabbed the hilt of his sword for reassurance, and hoped it made him seem more confident than he felt.

"What is it then?" Thorfast asked. His left brow arched in characteristic challenge that set Yngvar's hand itching to slap his friend's face. "Explain what you mean by slowly hurry. I'm confused."

"He never said that," Bjorn said. Though he was one year junior to Yngvar, and thus not yet a man, he was nearly as strong as one. Bjorn even had the start of a beard, and of the three of them he seemed more the raider.

Yngvar turned back to the sheep in their pen. He scanned across the field to the long house where white smoke twirled from the thatched roof. These Franks built square-framed homes from stone and timber. Some Norse had started to construct their homes after this fashion, and Yngvar regretted the change. His people did not need to lose their traditions to make this land their home.

"You're the leader," Thorfast said. "So how are we going to do this?"

Yngvar swallowed. He was no longer certain that this had been a good idea. They had all drunk too much mead and had soon talked themselves into a raid they were ill-prepared to conduct. But what could be done now? They had crossed the border, and Yngvar had led them this far. His mouth was filled with cotton but he straightened up. "My grandfather would have charged in and taken the whole flock for his own. The farm, too, if he had a mind for it."

Thorfast shook his head. His hair was so light as to be nearly white and his pale face was flushed red. "Your grandfather would've been dressed in mail and shield. We're wearing cloaks and shirts, if you didn't notice. And he'd have had an army with him."

"Grandfather was brave," Bjorn said. "He wouldn't be pissing himself in the shadows, would he?"

"All right, then," Yngvar was loud enough to cause all three to wince and look toward the farm. Nothing stirred, and Yngvar let out his breath. "There's only three of us. We each can carry one of the sheep back. Bjorn, you can probably take two. The stupid Franks won't miss them."

"Who cares if they miss the sheep?" Thorfast asked, his hands spread wide. "This is supposed to be a raid, isn't it?"

Yngvar closed his eyes and drew a breath. "Yes, this is a raid. Not much like the tales of old, but the best we can do now. One day, we'll be better than this. This is practice. One day, we'll take to the sea like our grandfathers did and we'll sail to glorious battle. Skalds will write songs of our adventures, I promise."

"That's right," Bjorn said with all the sincerity of a believer. Bjorn was Yngvar's cousin, and equally devoted to the ideals of the Norse warrior.

Thorfast's eyebrow remained cocked, but he said nothing. He made an exaggerated wave at the waiting sheep.

Without a word, Thorfast jogged from the protective shadows of the spruce trees. His steps were straighter now that the mead had worn off. In fact, the burning in his guts had chased off whatever remained of his drunkenness. This was a bad idea, he decided halfway to the sheep pen. His head swiveled like a loose mast, constantly watching for the farmers to appear. Bjorn and Thorfast stumbled behind him, crowding up against him as if he could shield them from their own foolishness.

At the pen, Yngvar unlatched the gate. His hands quaked as if the sound of the wooden bar would bring the cavalry of Frankia crashing down on him. The sheep bleated and huddled at the far end of the pen, clustering into a ball the color of millet.

"Be quiet," he said to the sheep as he slipped into the pen. The ground was soft from the constant tread of the animals and he skidded as he rushed toward the closest sheep. Bjorn and Thorfast followed, each seizing their own prize.

He had not actually carried an unwilling sheep before. For its small size the animal weighed more than he could have guessed. Thorfast could not hold his, and even Bjorn struggled to keep his under arm.

"Three bloody sheep," Bjorn said, his nose wrinkled. "And they all stink like shit. Is this all we get?"

"They won't follow us," Thorfast said. He snatched at a smaller animal, causing the rest to crash into the fence and bleat louder. "This is going to bring the farmers."

Yngvar's sheep escaped his grip and he twisted after it, cursing as it slammed into its fellows. "Odin's balls! This is a waste. Get what we can and go."

"I've got mine," Bjorn said, his head tipped back. "The two of you can't handle a fluffy little lamb?"

"We don't have time," Yngvar said. Thorfast spun in a circle as this sheep eluded him. "Forget it all and let's go."

"This isn't glory," Bjorn said, hiking his sheep on his hip. "We've got to take more."

With his sheep crushed to his side, Bjorn turned toward the other animals. He started kicking at them, forcing them toward the gate.

"That's just making more noise," Thorfast said.

Yngvar gave up on the sheep. He looked toward the farmhouse and knew what he would see. A dark shape had just ducked back around the corner of the house. Yngvar spit in anger. "We've been seen. Come on, let's go."

He took two strides to the gate and the shape reappeared. The farmer was tall, dressed in simple gray and black clothing faded from days under the sun. His black beard was thick and hid his face. Yngvar noted nothing more of the man.

All he saw was the bow and arrow on the string leveled at him.

"Put up your hands," the farmer shouted in Frankish. He drew the string to his cheek and Yngvar saw the arrowhead glint.

"It's just one man," Bjorn said. Yngvar dared not turn around, but he could imagine Bjorn standing with feet wide and head tipped back in challenge. He did that at the start of every fight.

"Not one," said another voice. Yngvar broke his stare and saw another figure emerge from the opposite end of the house. A second bowman had an arrow drawn to his chin and aimed at either Thorfast or Bjorn. The man was slighter with a light beard, probably Yngvar's own age. A limp quiver was slung across his hip and a handful of arrows rattled in it. They might not be war arrows, but they were enough to bring down all three of them.

"Put up your hands," the farmer repeated.

· Now the farmer's wife appeared, brandishing a wooden pitchfork in her fat hands. She was equal to her husband in size, and her dress and head cover did nothing to disguise her brutishness. She seemed less tentative than her husband, as if she could hardly wait to run at them with her weapon.

Yngvar raised his hands. "We'll do as you say."

"By Ran's rotten cunt! I'm not afraid of dying!" Bjorn bellowed his curse, and Yngvar heard the sheep bleat in horror as it fell to the ground.

A young boy now joined the rest of the family, and he hauled a black dog twice his size by a rope leash. The instant the dog saw them, the boy lost his grip and the dog charged with a snarl.

"For glory!" Bjorn shouted.

Yngvar spun toward his cousin, but he slipped in the mud. It saved his life, for he heard the arrow tear above his shoulder and thud into the barn wall. He nearly landed in a split, his thigh muscles burning with pain. He recovered, grabbing the fence.

The other bowman, likely the farmer's oldest son, released his arrow, but it seemed to vanish. Yngvar did not mark where is struck, but Thorfast screamed and ducked.

Only Bjorn was unmoved by the terror. He struggled with his sword, which still remained in its sheath.

Yngvar's guts blazed into fire. He grabbed his own weapon. The peace straps were still tied there, the leather bindings that men wore on their swords when in another's hall. Peace straps prevented an easy draw. They had all been drinking in Thorfast's father's hall, and so wore the straps rather than surrender their weapons. They had been so drunk when they set out they had not removed them.

The dog bounded the fence and landed on Bjorn. It was all black fur and snarling yellow teeth. Bjorn's scream belied his physical size. He sounded like a terrorized child as he blocked his face with his arms.

"Call off the dog!" Yngvar shouted. "We surrender!"

He dared to stand up. The farmer and his son were already nocking their next shots.

The dog yelped. Yngvar turned to see Bjorn driving his thumb into its eye.

"Come, Goliath!" the farmer shouted, lowering his bow.

The son did not lower and his aim was square on Thorfast, who ran at a crouch toward the gate. Yngvar yanked him down to the dirt in time for the son's hasty shot to pound into the fence post. The shaft quivered in the splintered post as if enraged for not having drawn blood.

"Goliath, heel!" the farmer repeated, then he pointed at his son. "And don't shoot again!"

The dog slunk away, whimpering and its tail hung low. However, Bjorn lay moaning on the ground and clutching his arm. Red blood stained his sleeve. The sheep had crushed themselves into a group so tight it now seemed like a single animal.

"Put up your hands," the farmer said. Yngvar and Thorfast did as asked, but Bjorn remained staring up at the sky and clutching his arm.

The dog now ran back to the farmer, prancing around his legs before the young boy gathered up the leash once more. Only the wife had not shifted her stance. The shadows filling her deep-set eyes seemed to reveal a droop that spoke of disappointment.

After a long stillness, the farmer approached. An arrow remained on the farmer's bow, and the son took aim at Yngvar.

"You're well dressed for thieves," the farmer said. Now that he had come closer, the deep lines and scars on the farmer's face became clear. He was a hard-bitten man, one who had seen battles before and survived to carve his livelihood from the land. Yngvar and his friends were not going to intimidate him. "And I bet those would be fine swords if you could draw them."

Bjorn finally roared, pounding the ground with the fist of his uninjured arm. "We forgot the peace straps."

"Throw those swords out here," the farmer said. "You can save yourself more injury if you behave."

Yngvar's face was on fire. He thought his ears might curl and fall off as cinders. He carefully unhitched his sword and threw it in the grass where the farmer had indicated. Thorfast did as well. Bjorn finally struggled to his feet. His face glistened with slobber and he clutched his forearm where the dog had bitten him. Blood dripped between his fingers.

"Can you help me remove my sword?" he asked. Yngvar pulled the baldric over Bjorn's head, then clanked the sword atop the others.

He gave his most defiant look to the farmer, narrowing his eyes. He ignored the wife and two sons who had converged on them.

The farmer scanned over the group, searching Yngvar head to toe. He frowned and blinked as if trying to clear his vision.

"I recognize you. You're Jarl Hakon Ulfriksson's boy?"

Yngvar did not want to admit it. The surly wife now lowered her pitchfork and the eldest son snorted a laugh.

Face beaming heat, Yngvar gave the farmer a slight bow.

"I am Yngvar Hakonsson. This is Thorfast the Silent and the one your dog attacked is Bjorn Arensson." Yngvar sighed and let his shoulders slump. "And we are your prisoners."

2

Yngvar felt the trek back to his father's hall had been twice as long as it should have taken. The springtime air had cooled by evening and raised gooseflesh on his exposed arms. He had given his cloak to Bjorn, who had left his in the sheep pen where it had fallen, and now wished he had not been so generous. The farmer, Ferdegar, walked in front of them and his eldest son followed up with the dog on his leash. The poor animal whimpered the whole way, its eye shut and weeping. Bjorn sneered at the dog, holding his bandaged arm like it would drop from his body otherwise.

Hirdmen from Jarl Hakon's hall escorted them now, seven men with mail and spears. They had given Yngvar sly smiles, glanced at Bjorn's wounds and the armload of captured swords Ferdegar carried. Again Yngvar felt his face going up in flames. This day could not end soon enough. Their trudge through the village drew out onlookers of every age. Most were wise enough to hide their amusement, but Yngvar knew they would snicker at him after he had passed. People liked him well enough, but everyone was happy when the jarl's son made a misstep. He did not understand why people took pleasure in such things. He did not laugh at their failures.

His father's hall seemed grander than ever now that he stood in its shadow, knowing Hakon Ulfriksson was seated at the high table waiting to receive his captured son. The hall seemed as high as the towers of Paris. It was all in shadow, and the hirdmen at the doors were equally black and indistinct like demon guardians of a hole into the underworld.

"No weapons in the hall," said one of the hirdmen. Ferdegar offered the swords to the waiting hirdman. "And the hound remains outside. You can tie him up to that tree."

The hirdman waved at a poplar tree that quivered with tender green leaves. He did not wait for Ferdegar's response, but carried the swords to the side of the doors. He then disappeared inside to announce their arrival.

"I'll let you explain this," Thorfast whispered from behind. "He's your father, after all."

"For once, then, keep silent," Yngvar said. He watched the farmer's son tying up his dog. He stooped to pet it, trying to get a look at its eye as it twisted away. Yngvar felt a pang of remorse for the poor dog. It had only been defending its home. He blamed himself for all the injuries to the dog and Bjorn.

"Don't forget to tell him I wasn't afraid to die," Bjorn added. "And that we wouldn't be hostages now if I could've drawn my sword."

Yngvar shook his head and filed into his father's hall behind the hirdmen and Ferdegar.

The hearth fire blazed, having been stoked for the evening meal that was now delayed from their imminent disgrace. Heat wrapped his face and the smell of sweat and smoke filled his nose. It was a familiar taste, one that made him feel oddly at ease despite being a hostage. The hall had been cleared of anyone other than hirdmen, who lined the walls on either side. Tables and benches had been dragged aside, scrapping paths through the straw covering of the dirt floor. Servants and slaves lingered in the corners, ready to answer a command.

Yngvar occupied his vision with every aspect of the hall other than the high table directly ahead. He looked at the weapons and hunting trophies lining the walls. From the rafters, banners of vanquished enemies waved in the current of air rushing up to the smoke hole. High above the stage was the green standard with black elk antlers. That had been his grandfather's standard. Ulfrik Ormsson had once been a great hero and master of this hall, which his son Hakon now ruled.

"Welcome to my hall." Hakon Ulfriksson's voice was as loud as a crashing wave in the silent hall. Yngvar turned his eyes down, but not first without glancing at his father.

Hakon sat on his bench, elbows leaning on the table to reveal his strong arms. His gray hair fell over his red cloak and his white beard was braided to his chest. Yngvar could not meet his father's icy gaze, but he saw the irritated expression etched into his hard face. Men said he looked like his father, and they said the same for Yngvar. He did not doubt his grandfather could wither an enemy with a single look.

"Jarl Hakon," Ferdegar said, then knelt. The son did the same. Though Ferdegar was a subject of the Frankish king, he was wise enough to show respect to the most powerful man in range of his home. "It seems your son and his companions had lost their way. I found them in my sheep pen, and thought to escort them home to you."

Yngvar perked up at Ferdegar's exceptional Norse. Most Franks had not bothered to learn the language, preferring the Norse to learn theirs. Yngvar, by dint of his birth in Frankia, spoke both with ease.

"So my messengers have informed me. I hope they did not cause you any grief."

Ferdegar paused and Yngvar noticed how the son's fist clenched, though both remained deferent to Hakon. Ferdegar licked his lips before continuing.

"They had drunk too much, lord. I startled them and they charged about the pen. I lost control of my hound and it fell upon the large fellow. I fear it tore the boy's arm. My wife has patched it up, but it will need better care. I think my hound was blinded in the confusion, lord."

"Confusion," Hakon repeated. "These men seemed to have surrendered their swords during this—confusion."

Ferdegar now raised his head. Yngvar saw sweat glisten on the farmer's brow. "Swords make confusion worse, lord."

Hakon's laugh was a quick bark, and he slapped the table. "Wisdom! How much better the world would be if more men thought as you, Ferdegar."

"You honor me," Ferdegar said.

Waving the farmer and his son to their feet, Hakon leaned back from the table. Yngvar saw the motion from the top of his vision, though he studied the base of the raised platform where his father sat. Small bones from old meals were shoved into the corners there.

"Now I would hear from my son and his companions. They are free to speak, are they not, Ferdegar? You make no demands of me before returning them?"

The farmer's son stared at his father, but Ferdegar shook his head. "Nothing, lord. As I said, I felt obligated to lead them home."

At least that much had gone better than Yngvar hoped. By rights, Ferdegar owned them as hostages. Granted he had no power to keep them and had he intended to do so he would not have taken them here. Yngvar did not understand why he had not sold them to a Frankish noble in Paris.

"Father," Yngvar said, meeting Hakon's gaze. The look immediately filled him with dread. Here was the face he had seen dozens of times before long-winded speeches on responsibilities and the life of a nobleman. Doubtless a tirade on their family honor would follow no matter what he said now. His father wore the face of a man who could never be persuaded. Besides, his father knew everything and had an answer for anything. This was going to be a pointless exercise in public humiliation.

"We'd been drinking all night in Thorfast's hall—"

"Stop." Hakon held up his hand. "Do not tell me why. That is for a discussion later. Tell me what happened. And it's not Thorfast's hall. It is his father's."

"Yes, Father." This was going to be a long night. "So we thought to steal sheep from the closest Frankish farmhouse. We set out drunk and with no plan. We were caught. They had bows pointed at us and by Loki's own luck their shots missed. The dog attacked Bjorn."

"I'd have killed it if I could've drawn my sword," Bjorn said. If

Yngvar had a sword he would have cut off Bjorn's tongue. He whirled on his cousin with an angry hiss. But his father laughed and stood up.

"What is this? You could not draw your sword?"

"Just shut up, Bjorn," Yngvar said, giving him the same deadly look he had learned from his father. Bjorn scowled but closed his mouth. Yngvar rubbed the back of his neck and turned to his father. "We left peace straps tied to our swords. It was too late to remove them when the dog attacked."

Hakon stared at Yngvar, his cheeks puffing out with suppressed laughter. At last he dropped his head and burst into laughter. The rest of the hirdmen joined in. Only Ferdegar and his son shared Yngvar and company's embarrassed silence. Yngvar glared at Bjorn, whose eyes now widened in comprehension of his blunder. Bjorn could always be counted on to speak without thinking.

When Hakon finally sat down, he wiped the corner of his eye with the back of his wrist. "You three must have been a sight. No wonder Ferdegar could not shoot you at so close a range. His laughter shook his aim."

Ferdegar held up both hands. "It was a warning shot only, lord. I did not recognize them until later."

"Peace," Hakon said, waving down Ferdegar's hand. "You did as you should. Any man would protect his home from thieves. I am grateful you returned these three to my hall. Now, it is a late hour and I have heard all that I can bear for one night. Would you and your son be my guests tonight? It will be too dark to travel and I promise you safety and comfort here. As for your troubles, I shall pay you in silver. For your hound, I cannot undo the hurt done to it. But I shall grant you a pup of my own. We have a new litter of fine hounds. Yngvar will select the best one for you before you leave."

His name was like a slap on his head. It roused him from his humiliated silence. "Yes, Father, I will choose the strongest among them."

"And you, Bjorn and Thorfast, shall attend our guests tonight. Serve them and keep their cups full. You three have already drunk enough for one day."

The uproarious laughter made Yngvar wish he had actually died as Bjorn so often repeated. He could look at no one, not even Ferdegar who simply nodded his way through the ordeal. He seemed as dismayed as Yngvar, and perhaps in that commonality they would find a way to repair Yngvar's stupidity.

"We are not servants," Bjorn said. Over the laughter most either did not hear or chose not to hear. Yet even while Hakon slapped the backs of his men in their laughter, he shot a dark look at Bjorn.

"Mind yourself," Thorfast said. "And learn from my silence."

"Just smile at whatever is said tonight," Yngvar said. "And get your arm looked at. No one wants you bleeding over their dinner."

Bjorn muttered another curse. Yngvar met his father's cold eyes, and behind the deep laughter lines he recognized the fury lurking there. The night was not done yet and neither was his father.

3

Yngvar's eyes throbbed from lack of sleep. He staggered through the field, the morning chill scraping his exposed arms. He still had not secured a new cloak. To warm himself, he clutched the puppy closer to his chest. Whenever he looked down at the dog it licked his face, leaving a swath of slobber to grow cold in the air. The dog was short-haired and tawny, only a few months old at most. The kennel master said the dog's name was Thor. Wasn't every dog's name Thor? Giving such a common animal away wouldn't be as hard as surrendering the best.

"This one likes to play," the kennel master had said. "But he doesn't lead."

"That's fine for where he's going," Yngvar said. "If my father asks, tell him I took the pride of the litter."

His father wouldn't ask, of course. He would be too hung over to care. Hakon had spent all night getting drunk with his men and the Frankish farmer. Yngvar's humiliation had become something of a celebration. Was it that men had nothing to celebrate anymore? With all the peace and prosperity, men had no glories in battle, no enemies to shame, no songs to sing, and no riches to flaunt. All had become farmers and tradesmen. No one raided. No one crossed the borders with the Franks. Were there even borders these days? One in three

Norse spoke Frankish and most had taken Frankish wives. Their half-Frankish children took pleasure in laughing at the foolish Northmen, as they so loved to call their ancestors. So now he had given them a reason to laugh and to congratulate themselves on being so much better at everything. They were real men, after all, and they knew what was best in life.

"Well, you're lost in yourself this morning."

The voice brought him back out of his head. The dog scampered up Yngvar's chest, licking his chin again and forcing his head back.

Three girls laughed at the dog's desperate affections. Yngvar had to weave his head side to side to avoid the puppy's increasing adoration. The girl in the lead was tall and well shaped. Platinum hair hung free about her shoulders, turning to fire at the edges from the sun rising behind her. Her smile was what Yngvar always admired the most. He loved the way it curled up into her cheeks, bringing a touch of mischief to even her most innocent look.

"Kadlin," he said. "I didn't expect to see you out here."

"Nor did I expect to see you." She placed a slender hand on the puppy's head and ruffled its ears. The pup nearly jumped from Yngvar's arms to Kadlin's hand, licking furiously. "He's so cute. This is the gift to the farmer you failed to rob?"

"News travels fast," Yngvar said, his voice flat. He surrendered the puppy to Kadlin, who cradled it like a baby and rubbed its belly. Thor whined with maniacal joy as he paddled his rear legs.

"They marched you through the village. Not much else anyone can talk about when the mighty Yngvar Hakonsson is led red-faced and weaponless before everyone."

The two other girls giggled, whether from petting Thor or from Yngvar's humiliation he did not know.

"Well, it's not less than what we all deserve." Yngvar sighed and joined the two other girls in petting Thor. "We were drunk when we came up with the plan, and we paid for it with our dignity. We could've paid for it with our lives. The Franks had arrows lined up to our necks."

Kadlin said nothing, and instead rocked little Thor in her arms.

The puppy was now fully mad with glee, twisting and jumping at all the attention.

"You're here to fetch Thorfast?"

She nodded. "Father is here too, you'll remember. Mother wants me to get both of them home. She spent all night shouting about what she is going to do to both of them. But as soon as she sees Father she'll be as meek as Thor here. And, of course, dearest son Thorfast could never anger her for long."

"Though I don't suppose she'll be as forgiving to me."

Kadlin shook her head. "If you weren't the jarl's son, she'd forbid either one of us from ever speaking to you. She thinks you're a dreaming fool."

Yngvar stared at her smiling at Thor. She was the most beautiful girl—no, woman; she would turn sixteen soon—he had ever seen.

"Send your friends away," Yngvar said, extending his arms to take back Thor. "I want to talk to you alone."

She looked up at him with a wry smile that vanished. He was earnest and she had to have recognized it. She let Thor kick and squirm out of her arms into Yngvar's, then dismissed the two servants that had accompanied her. "Go on to the hall and tell my father and brother I am coming."

They both watched the girls leave across the field to the long mead hall where inside men would still be facedown on tables or sprawled on the floor. The orange light of early morning turned the roof thatch to gold, a startling contrast the drab clothes of the two servants crossing toward it.

Kadlin turned to Yngvar and the two said nothing as the puppy squirmed in Yngvar's grip. He wished he could drop the puppy, but it would probably run off.

"Do you think I'm a dreaming fool?"

She raised her chin and cocked her thin, faint brow. She and her brother shared this trait. "And why do you care what I think?"

"A question is not an answer. Am I a foolish dreamer?"

She stifled a laugh and began to pet Thor. "I think my mother knows people. If that is what she says of you, then it must be true."

"So that is what you think? I'm a fool?"

"You didn't look like anything else yesterday, did you?"

Yngvar pulled Thor back, causing the puppy to yip for Kadlin's touch again. "Yesterday was a mess. I agree. But that was the last you'll see of such foolishness. I'm a man now."

"So you say."

"What does that mean?"

Kadlin's wry smile returned. "Wouldn't a man know what that means?"

"Don't mock me," he said. Unable to reach Kadlin, Thor fell back on Yngvar's chest and began nipping at his chin. "Your mother thinks I'm going to lead her son into trouble. Well, the other half of yesterday's mess was your brother's doing."

"Is this what you wanted to talk to me about?" Kadlin folded her arms and shifted her weight to her right leg. "You want me to tell my mother you're not a fool? That yesterday you didn't nearly get my brother killed? You're wasting my time, Yngvar Hakonsson. My father is expected home, and I must fetch him. Will you leave me to that task, please?"

How had this turned sour so fast? Yngvar's ears heated in frustration. None of this was what he wanted to say. Why did she always do this to him? He shook his head as if to clear it.

"No, not yet. This is not what I wanted to say." Kadlin remained with arms folded and brow raised. "I wanted to say that one day I will be greater than what you see now."

"Oh, yes, you will inherit all your father's lands and the oaths of his men, my father's included. I may be a woman, but I understand that much without explanation."

"No, I mean I will achieve greatness beyond this. I will lead men to glorious battle. I will raid the richest kingdoms of the world and bring the spoils home. Skalds in every hall will sing songs about me and my men. You cannot judge me on one drunken adventure."

Kadlin remained stone-still, no expression on her face. The breeze stirred her nearly white hair, the only motion from her.

"So all of that will be added to this." He wanted to stretch his arms wide, but filled with a squirming puppy, he could only rotate side to side to indicate the breadth of his father's lands. The gesture was less grand than he had hoped.

"Well, I shall congratulate you on that day." Kadlin still did not shift.

"It will not do for me to achieve so much without someone at home to make it all worthwhile." Yngvar's heart beat harder and his breath suddenly felt short. Even Thor sensed the tension and settled down. Yngvar took a step closer to Kadlin.

"Since we were children, you've known I've always imagined you as that woman. I know you have as well. Don't let yesterday's mistakes put you off of me. Don't let your mother's anger cloud your feelings. We are children no more, and the time for imagining is past us. You should be my wife."

Kadlin's eyes widened and her folded arms dropped uselessly to her side. She seemed unable to speak, blinking as she sought her words. Yngvar smiled with patience, realizing how shocking it would be to hear these thoughts given voice at long last.

"You wanted to know if I think you're a dreaming fool?" Kadlin flipped her hair from her face, blinking rapidly as she did. "If your foolishness was measured in height you'd stand taller than a frost giant. Good day to you, Yngvar Hakonsson. You've wasted enough of my time for one day."

Kadlin stalked across the grass toward the hall. Plumes of white smoke now floated above the golden thatch. Men must be rousing from their stupors and demanding food. Kadlin walked as if leading a charge to an enemy shield wall.

Thor began to kick and whine again, licking Yngvar's chin. He did not fight it this time, but watched his best friend's sister meld into the black rectangle of the mead mall. Only her brilliant hair showed against it.

"All right, boy," Yngvar said to Thor. "Let's have a run out here for a while, get out your energy."

Yngvar wasn't going to the hall until Kadlin left with her father and brother. He set Thor down and the puppy bounded in circles around him.

"She's going to take a bit more work than I thought."

4

By midday, Yngvar and Bjorn finally received their summons to the hall. The servant who delivered the message gave them both an embarrassed smile and was quick to retreat ahead of them. Yngvar stood facing the distant line of trees where the standing stone to his grandmother lay and where his grandfather died at the hands of a traitor. For a moment he considered running into those trees and never returning.

"This was what we've been waiting for," Bjorn said. He sat in the grass, his forearm now wrapped in a fresh bandage that still showed brown speckles. "Let's see what punishment Uncle Hakon has for us."

The walk back to the hall felt like an hour as Yngvar imagined all the humiliation his father was about to heap upon him. Even though the Franks had already left with their new puppy and blinded dog in tow, the village was still in a stir. At least a dozen dark shapes lingered at the edges of the village, looking up the hill toward the hall. No doubt they were imagining the same things as Yngvar, only they were getting a laugh from it.

The guards at the door gave them both solemn nods. Yngvar thought it patronizing, but Bjorn at least seemed to consider them genuine, thanking them as they passed into the dark hall.

Light spilled from the open smoke hole over his father's wide shoulders. He did not sit at the high table, but waited for them both at the center of the hall. He wore a heavy wolf fur cloak that enhanced his menace. His white hair glowed with the light, errant strands were like a halo of fire. The deep lines of his face pulled his expression in a sour displeasure. His numerous golden armbands glinted in the light.

"Don't hide at the edge of the hall," he said, extending his hand to wave them forward. "Come to me. No one else is here but us."

Yngvar swallowed. So it begins. He glanced at Bjorn who stood half a head taller than him. His sparse beard in comparison to Hakon's long, braided one now made him seem so young. Both stepped forward and lowered their heads.

Hakon nodded, studying each of them. He put his hands behind his back and began to pace as he spoke. Yngvar hated this. He was going to be in for a long, impassioned speech, at the least. Who could guess what punishment would follow?

"There was a time when we could laugh about such foolishness and credit it all to youth. But you, Hakon, are nearly eighteen years old. Bjorn, you are a year his junior. Do either of you know what this means?"

"That we are men, Uncle."

"Very good, Bjorn. Would you say that deciding to raid anywhere without first consulting your jarl is the action of a man?" Bjorn did not answer and Yngvar knew better than to speak unless prodded. He watched his father's deerskin shoes pace over the new straw spread over the dirt floor this morning.

"Since the answer escapes you, let me tell you such independence is strictly forbidden. I am jarl here, and any raid undertaken either drunk or sober must be first decided with me. Let me make it plain. Any man who defies this rule will be cast out from my protection. Yes, even my own kin, if it came to that."

Yngvar raised his head and found Hakon's blue eyes smoldering on him. His father would not throw him out, not for a run-in with a farmer.

"The two of you and that troublemaker, Thorfast, nearly set a fire I can ill-afford to combat right now. Thank all the gods that you were incompetent fools and Ferdegar had sense enough to recognize what danger you brought him."

Bjorn was about to speak over his uncle. Yngvar heard him inhale. So he cut off his cousin before he could dump grease into the flames.

"Father, you are right as always. We were not thinking clearly."

Hakon pulled up at the interruption, but since it was Yngvar's contrition he let his frown melt into a slow nod.

"Thinking is a warrior's greatest strength. Men make much of swordplay and ax-throwing. They admire the berserker's wrath. But none of that will carry a battle for you. You must always be thinking. Count on your enemies to do the same and you will have a chance for glory. Stop thinking, even for one detail, and you may have spent your life and the lives of your men."

"We just wanted to prove we could be raiders like the heroes of old," Bjorn said. Yngvar closed his eyes. His cousin never did learn how to keep quiet.

Hakon's light brows arched and his mouth remained frozen in an O-shape as he stared at Bjorn.

"Raiders like the heroes of old," Hakon said. "Do you understand what could have happened yesterday? Come, boys, show me the depth of your thinking. Consider the possibilities of your heroic raid."

Neither Yngvar nor Bjorn spoke, but glanced at each other.

"Don't look at each other!" Hakon snapped. His voice echoed through the empty hall, the banners on the rafters swaying as if blown by his voice. "Can you not imagine any other outcome from yesterday's disaster?"

"We could've been killed," Yngvar said. His father's fears were so predictable.

"Yes," Hakon agreed. "Two bowmen trained on fools wallowing in the dirt like pigs. You should have all been raked with arrows before you could cry for your mother."

"But they missed," Bjorn said. "And if I had got my sword drawn, they'd not have a chance."

"I'm sure you'd have batted the arrows out of the air with your flashing blade," Hakon said, tilting his head to the side. "Then in one stroke of your mighty sword you'd have cut the heads from all of the

Franks and their dog as well. It would've been the makings of a song. Only you were on your back with a hound tearing off your arm. So I suppose we'll have to imagine the glory instead."

Yngvar fought his smile. Bjorn deserved that.

"So going with the more reasonable outcome, all three of you could have been killed before anyone recognized you. Then the true problems would begin."

Yngvar's smile vanished and he furrowed his brow at his father. He expected to hear about his mother's tears and how no one would inherit his father' lands. But Hakon continued on without stopping on any of those clichés.

"Your deaths would have to be avenged. So, for your adventure where your spoils amounted to three sheep I hardly need, I would ride with twenty men and kill good Ferdegar's family. Mind you, it would have to be done in the most terrorizing way. I'd give his wife to my men while Ferdegar and his sons watched. When they were finished, we'd cut off her head and the head of her young boy and put them atop spears. Then Ferdegar would follow after we brutalized him to the point of madness. At last, we'd blind his oldest son and chop off his sword hand. He'd be sent to his lord as a warning of my wrath. I would do all of this, though I detest it. For this is how a man avenges his family, and what those who follow a jarl expect of him."

Yngvar lowered his head. He had not considered this. Yet Hakon was not finished.

"But that is only the start of the suffering. Now the peace is broken. The Franks will come to make their own determination on the justice of my actions. They will demand compensation which I will not pay. We will fight. More men on both sides die. Jarl Vilhjalmer Longsword in Rouen will be displeased, and I will have to answer for my aggression. I will plead vengeance for my dead son and nephew and he might understand. But politics demand a peace and he would force me into a humiliated truce. So I will be disgraced and poorer, and families on both sides will face the winter without fathers and sons they depend upon. All for your three fucking sheep and childish dreams. This is how a man weighs the possibilities of his actions."

Yngvar swallowed, not daring to raise his head. Hakon stood before them, his booted feet lined up directly before Yngvar. He let the quiet simmer until it grew uncomfortable.

"Go see to your arm," Hakon said, pointing at Bjorn's wound. "The bandages are still spotted. That is not good. I should have demanded that hound be put down, but I let anger distract me. Yngvar, remain with me a while longer."

Bjorn gave an astonished look. "No punishment?"

Hakon shook his head. "Unless you want one. No one was hurt and nothing actually happened. In the end, you have punished yourselves. You looked like fools, and admitting to raiding a farm with peace straps on your swords—well, you will be living down that stupidity for as long as men have memory."

"Thank you, Uncle." Bjorn bowed, gave Yngvar a bright smile, then backed out of the hall.

Hakon swept off his cloak and sighed. "I wear that so Bjorn doesn't think he's getting size on me. What have I been feeding him these years? His father will not recognize him when I send him home. Here, sit with me."

Yngvar took the bench his father dragged from beneath a table. It was odd sitting in the center of the hall with no one else. Even the servants had disappeared into the shadows or other rooms, though doubtlessly they listened to be called and to eavesdrop. His father rubbed his face with both palms, then smiled weakly.

Feeling encouraged, Yngvar sat up straight. "You did not ask us to think about what would have happened had we succeeded. Do you believe we could not?"

Hakon's smile strengthened and he shook his head. "Even had you got away with three sheep, they'd have fled you. You could never drive off the flock over such a distance without a dog and shepherd to aid you."

"But had we got back with the three, certainly it would not be a disgrace."

His father leaned back against the table. "Let me ask a question that I already have the answer for. I wonder if you know it. Had you not tied peace straps to your hilts, and had you the upper hand on Ferdegar and his family, would you have killed them?"

"There wouldn't have been need to kill them."

"You are raiding their home and destroying their livelihood. How do they know you will not return with others? They would try to kill you. Could you kill Ferdegar and his two sons? Would you enslave his wife, or kill her if she resisted? All for three sheep you have no real interest in or need to steal?"

Yngvar held his father's gaze, but faltered. This was always his problem. He saw Ferdegar as a man with a family. He had even felt bad for the dog's wound.

Hakon slapped Yngvar's knee. "You would not do it. Your face answers for you."

"Are you saying I'm a coward?" Yngvar thought to stand to the challenge, but his knees were weak.

"Not at all," Hakon said. "I know my son. You are smart, certainly smarter than what yesterday showed to the world, and you have compassion for your fellows. That is good, but such hesitation will get you killed. If you raid, then forget pity and forget compassion. You threw aside those ideals the moment you thought to take another man's property by force. I do not doubt had you drawn your swords Ferdegar would have killed you. He would have no hesitation. If that choice sits ill with you, then do not put yourself in such a position. You are not a raider, son. You are filled with foolish ideals of what raiding is."

"Grandfather was a raider," Yngvar said, glancing at the green banner with black elk antlers. "He came from nothing and created all of this by his own strength."

"He did not raid poor farmers," Hakon said. "At least, if he had a choice. I'm not certain what stories you hear, but there is no glory in raiding. It is the work of desperate men who have no other means to prosper."

"The strong take what they desire from the weak," Yngvar said. "Is that not true of these very lands? Didn't you and Grandfather take these lands from the Franks? Did you need them?"

"Of course we did," Hakon said. He folded his hands over his belly.

Yngvar noticed how it bulged now, where it hadn't in years past. Was his father getting soft in his age? It was hard to conceive. "But I am speaking of this free life on the seas you and your cousin imagine. It is a hard life and one for desperate men. You are neither disposed to a hard life nor are you desperate. You are my only surviving son. When the pox took my children, only you survived. That marks you as one the Fates left to a great destiny. You will inherit all of this when I go on to Valhalla. You will lead armies to glorious battle. You will have no need of raiding."

"But how can I lead men in battle if I have not tasted it? There is nothing but peace here. I have to go across the channel to where our people still fight for their lands."

Hakon's laugh shook his stomach. "You are too young to remember the wars we fought here. Peace? Could it be six years, not even? Hrolf the Strider broke his truce with Paris and sent us all grabbing more land. Now that his son Vilhjalmer rules after him, he will do the same. I've known Vilhjalmer since he was a boy. He will push south once more. There will be plenty of fighting here. No need to go overseas in search of it."

Yngvar folded his arms. His father could never understand what it meant to be trapped in a life of unwanted obligations. He had always been a jarl, and had his fill of adventure and glory before retiring to his easy life. Yngvar would have to accept a role made for him by his father, and inherit his responsibilities. Whatever wars he might fight would not be from any choice of his own, and the spoils would go to a jarl sitting behind the walls of Rouen.

"I wanted you to remain behind today because I have something to tell you," Hakon said. He leaned on both his knees. "Your mother and I have discussed this at length and we think a cure for your youthful dreaming is to take on a man's responsibilities. Yesterday just reminded me how long I have let this slip past. You are seventeen, by the eye of Odin. The years have sped like an arrow to the mark."

A fire lit in Yngvar's belly. He hoped his father was not about to say what he expected. But the twisted smile on his father's lips worried Yngvar.

"It is time you married," Hakon said. "We have been discussing arrangements with Jarl Flosi the Breaker. He has a daughter, thirteen years old, a good match for you. Jarl Flosi brings key lands on those southern borders where there will be the battles you so desire. It is a good union between our families."

Yngvar stared through his father. Kadlin was walking toward him across a field of golden grass, smiling, her platinum hair wreathed with brilliant sunlight. He carried an armful of riches to her, hard-won from a month at sea raiding fat merchants and gold-laden churches. She was breathless at the spoils and Yngvar's heart soared to see her so pleased.

"Yngvar? You've nothing to say to this?"

The vision faded. His father's eyes were lined from his smile. Yngvar shook his head.

"She's a fine choice, from what your mother says. A sturdy girl from a good family. They are Danes, not Norse, but we cannot ask for everything. Jarl Flosi still honors the old gods, too. You will be happy with her."

Yngvar's mouth was cotton. "Wh—when will this happen?"

"We've not set a date, but it won't be long. You're probably surprised, but you should've realized at your age you cannot remain unmarried. I met your mother later in life, but all was in chaos then. Otherwise, I'd have been your age when your grandfather married me off." Hakon slapped Yngvar's leg once more. "Well, that was all I wanted to tell you. Go think upon it. You will have more to occupy your mind than fantasies now."

Yngvar did not even remember leaving the hall. He was alone outside, the two door guards staring after him. He gave them an idle nod, then stumbled off without any direction.

"I've got to get out of this," he said. "Thorfast will know what to do."

5

"What do you mean you don't know what to do?" Yngvar's voice cracked high.

Fair-haired Thorfast shrugged. "He's your father and jarl. No one can gainsay him, least of all on decisions for his own family."

Yngvar looked to Bjorn, who seemed flatly disinterested in the discussion. He held his bandaged arm and studied the brilliant white wrapping.

They stood behind the forge wall, where Davin the Blacksmith hammered at his work. The clang reverberated through the rough wood. Burning embers filled the air with sweet smoke, and as Yngvar leaned against the wall, he felt the forge heat emanating through it. They all waited for the hammering to stop so they could continue. In the distance, farmers worked at whatever they did in their fields. Yngvar never had a clear idea of how they harvested, only that some years were better or worse than others. Farmers also never seemed to agree which field belonged to which farm, seeing how often these disputes came to his father's hall.

The bellows began to huff once the hammering stopped. Yngvar jumped back into the opening.

"Do either of you know Jarl Flosi's daughter?"

Bjorn frowned. He knew nothing. Thorfast scratched his head.

"I think my father had dealings with him once. Did your father say she was sturdy?" Yngvar nodded. His stomach churned and gurgled. He had not eaten yet, such had been the chaos of the day. Thorfast scratched his head harder, grimacing. "That sounds about right. She was a square girl. Short, dark hair, and a mole on her chin."

"Gods, stop joking. Did you see her or not?" Yngvar pressed his lips together, hoping Thorfast would laugh. He did not.

"I'm telling you what I remember. Sorry if it's not to your liking, Jarl Yngvar."

"He ain't a jarl yet," Bjorn said, then lowered himself onto the grass. "Maybe he'll never be. His fat wife will crush him to death before that day."

"This is not good." Yngvar ignored the other's laughter. The bellows stopped their heavy wheezing and Yngvar felt the heat immediately recede from the wall behind him. His thoughts were filled with Kadlin and the gifts he would bring her from afar. He could not envision bringing even a copper bit to a boxy wife with a mole on her chin. Did a hair grow from it, he wondered. He repeated his worry. "This is not good. My whole life will be ruined. I'll be chained to her, to a sow from what it sounds. And all my toil will be to bring glory to Jarl Vilhjalmer who hides in Rouen."

"Hey," Bjorn said, sitting cross-legged in the shade of the forge. "Maybe you should talk to my father. He's Jarl Vilhjalmer's best friend. Maybe they can find someone better for you. Someone as pretty as you are, cousin."

"No one is as pretty as the heroic Yngvar Hakonsson." Thorfast and Bjorn laughed again, but Yngvar gave a dismissive scowl.

"Did Kadlin mention anything to you this morning?"

Thorfast stopped laughing. "She said nothing other than mother was in a foul mood and I had to hurry home. Foul was not the word to describe her, either. She was in a rage, and I heard it from her until my ears were bleeding. She doesn't like you much. Seems to think you're going to get me killed. Da put an end to all the yelling, though. His head was still ringing from last night."

"Did Kadlin say anything about me?"

Thorfast studied Yngvar now, giving him an appraising eye. Bjorn began to rip up grass and let it blow from his hand.

"She said nothing. But she was quieter than usual. Did you meet her before she came to the hall? The servants arrived before her but did not say what had delayed her. I didn't think to ask, either."

Yngvar's face heated and thankfully Davin began hammering once again. The riotous clanging offered him a reprieve. Thorfast had long ago figured out Yngvar's fascination with Kadlin and used to tease him when they were children. Still, he had asked Kadlin to marry him this morning. It hadn't been in earnest. It hadn't been properly thought out, which had become his recent hallmark. If she had said nothing at all, did that mean she was considering his proposal? She had stormed off, but women were strange that way. If she had truly been as disgusted as she had behaved, then shouldn't she have said something to her father?

Again the clanging stopped, and now they heard the satisfying hiss of Davin quenching his work in a bucket of water. Yngvar decided he had best change the topic.

"Maybe I should do as Bjorn suggested. Uncle Aren is well connected. Maybe he can delay this arrangement while he works out something better. Maybe he could even convince Jarl Vilhjalmer to send us raiding overseas."

"I was joking," Bjorn said. "My father isn't interested in us. He never sent for me again after putting me with Uncle Hakon. He's too busy being the jarl's right hand to worry about who you'll marry. He didn't even want my mother."

"Don't say that," Yngvar said. But it was true. Uncle Aren was so smart as to be a strange man. Jarl Vilhjalmer prized his intelligence and kept him always at hand. Aren had his son, Bjorn, and satisfied with his duty to pass on his blood, he then divorced his wife and sent Bjorn to foster with Hakon. Yngvar enjoyed having what amounted to a little brother, but he did feel regret for his uncle's callous treatment of his own family.

"Bjorn is right," Thorfast said. "Your uncle is not going to interfere with your father's wishes, and I doubt Jarl Vilhjalmer would send three inexperienced men on any task of importance."

"Well, that just proves my point," Yngvar said. He clasped both hands to his temple and began to pace. "We'll never be of use to anyone if we don't all get experience. My father wants to keep Bjorn and me safely under his wing so he can pass on his hall to family. Your mother is just as bad, and I don't even know why. Your father is a hirdman, after all."

Thorfast frowned and nodded. "I don't argue it. My father is more concerned with marrying off my sister than seeing me properly made a man."

Yngvar's stomach lurched at the thought of Kadlin being married off to another. But with his father selecting a political marriage over one of Yngvar's choosing, there was no way for Kadlin to be his.

"If Uncle Aren can't or won't help me, then there is another choice."

Both Bjorn and Thorfast looked at each other. Yngvar paused, hands still on his head.

"You're talking about your uncle, Gunnar the Black," Thorfast said. "He frightens me."

"He's got a temper," Bjorn said. "But maybe that's what will do us some good. Get him riled up for Yngvar. Maybe he'll give Uncle Hakon something to think on."

"There's something to that," Yngvar said. "Uncle Gunnar has been actively going to sea until just a few years ago. His men are all named raiders."

"I think you mean to say they're all named madmen," Thorfast said. "Doesn't he have a berserker in his service?"

Yngvar shrugged. He knew his father and Uncle Gunnar had cooled off their relationship. From what he remembered, they ended up disputing many things after grandfather Ulfrik's death. His father always said Gunnar was too easy to anger and caused more troubles than he settled. Something had happened between them to cause a split so that they rarely spoke. Yngvar didn't even know his cousins well because of their rift.

"Uncle Gunnar will understand us," Yngvar said. "I'm certain of it. If anyone might speak out for me, it would be him. Even if he didn't care, he might be willing to try just for mischief's sake."

"I don't think old jarls like your father and uncle play those sorts of games," Thorfast said. "Besides, when was the last time you visited your uncle? How do you know he'd even take you into his hall?"

"He and my father are at odds, but they don't hate each other. He'd open his hall to us. He might even take us on raid with him. Now wouldn't that be something?"

Bjorn stood up and nodded, but Thorfast's frown deepened. "Isn't he a hundred years old? I doubt he raids anymore."

"He's not that old," Bjorn said, throwing his last handful of grass over Thorfast's head.

"That's settled," Yngvar said. "I'm taking this to Uncle Gunnar."

"Why is not talking to your father even a choice?" Thorfast brushed the grass from his hair, flicking errant blades back at Bjorn. "Maybe if he understood you better he would change his mind."

Yngvar laughed. "A fine joke. My father change his mind? My father is jarl. My father's word is law. He'd cast us out from his protection if we raided without his leave. He just told us that this morning, eh, Bjorn?"

"That is what he said. Uncle Hakon is a stubborn man," Bjorn said. "But I like him."

"It's not about liking him," Yngvar said, pacing once more. "It's about making sure we get what we want from life before we are all locked down forever. Our grandfathers did not worry for their freedom. They took to the waves and sailed where their hearts led them. They plundered the rich and made themselves fat on their spoils. They didn't fret about boxy wives with moles on their chins, or what the neighboring farmers thought of their lives. And all of them rose to great glory. They must weep to look on us from Valhalla and see us shoved along the safe paths of life. For how will we ever join them in the feasting hall if we live the lives of sheltered husbands on land won for us by greater men?"

"Well said!" Bjorn's eyes glittered as he stood tall before Yngvar. "I don't want to live a sheltered life."

"And you think I am the one gifted with words," Thorfast said. He too stood straighter after that talk. "It's a fair point you make. We must build a life on our own deeds, for there is no other path to glory."

"So are you coming with us to my uncle's hall?" Yngvar asked, and Thorfast clapped his shoulder in affirmation. It was a warm, hard squeeze.

Together they walked to the front of the forge where thin, balding Davin sat on an old stump mopping sweat from his brow. The forge pulsed beside him, as tired as he was after an afternoon of work. Davin broke into a smile, his few yellow teeth showing beneath his copper mustache.

"Secret meeting all done, boys?"

"You mentioned my Uncle Gunnar was late in shipping you something?"

"Not your uncle, but his traders promised me the leather I need to complete these swords. Not much use waving swords around by the tang. Need good leather for the hilts, and they're late in sending it."

"Could I take word to my uncle for you? I have not visited him in ages and wish to see him myself. So I thought I could help you."

Davin wiped his forehead again. "Don't make me seem too impatient. But I would appreciate it if you could hurry them along. Your father is eager for this order to complete."

Yngvar smiled at his companions. Now he had his excuse for visiting. Uncle Gunnar the Black would surely help him.

6

Yngvar rejoiced at his fortune. His father had not only accepted Yngvar's wish to help Davin, but was supportive of sending him and Bjorn to Uncle Gunnar. He assigned two men to escort them, and before leaving he took Yngvar behind the hall where no one else stood.

His father's eyes softened as he pulled Yngvar near. "Your uncle and I were not always at odds. We loved each other as only brothers could. I still love him, though he's a fool. Let him know we are both too old for the ice that has grown between us. Tell him you will be married, and that he should come to my hall for a celebration. He is welcomed here."

Hakon stared past him as if reliving a distant memory. "Yes, tell him I'm a fool as well. I would go with you and tell him myself were I not needed here."

His father's request dogged Yngvar's journey north, where Gunnar held a sliver of land that accessed the Seine and therefore the sea. Yngvar wondered what had divided the brothers. Crossing fields of dark pines and traversing the thin woodland tracks, he began to doubt himself. His father had asked for reconciliation yet he sought to exploit their division for his own benefit. With every step he took north he felt his heart sinking. Was he truly going to pit them against each other when his father sought peace?

They traveled in a thin column and on foot. Their escorts went before and after them, wearing heavy leathers and carrying spears and shields. Both he and Bjorn had rich clothes and fur-trimmed cloaks, but carried only their swords. Thorfast was the poorest of all, dressed in common clothes with a plain wool cloak he had removed during the day. His sword was shorter as well, more akin to a sax than a normal longsword.

"How did you get your father's agreement?" Yngvar asked him.

"I told him Jarl Hakon picked me for the role of escort. It seemed to make him proud. And he was drunk when I told him."

Gunnar the Black was not a rich jarl. Yngvar realized this was why he probably raided as he did. He needed income to keep his hall and hirdmen. Wisdom held that anyone with access to the Seine would prosper, but Gunnar the Black seemed to defy the notion. When pox had scoured Frankia, killing all of Yngvar's siblings and hundreds of others, Gunnar had also lost all but one of his children and his wife. The children of Ulfrik Ormsson and Runa the Bloody were too strong to be taken down by a pox. Yet their descendants had not been, and it was a hard blow to the wider family. Yngvar wondered if something that happened during that time had divided Gunnar from his father.

Gunnar's meager hall was visible atop a high, bald hill. As they drew closer, it flitted behind treetops with the rise and fall of the terrain. What he could see of it showed old, gray thatch and dark, rain-stained wood. Nor did it appear large, but without anything near it for reference, Yngvar hoped it was just a trick of his sight.

The surrounding village was no more than a handful of farms and ranches. Being proximate to the Seine and the traffic it produced between Rouen and Paris, people here did not scatter at the sight of a small band crossing their land. Nor did they hail them or otherwise recognize them. Their drab, thin forms continued at whatever duties commonfolk performed. Yngvar's eyes glided over them.

"Shouldn't escorts meet us?" he asked the guard in the front. The sandy-haired man was thin, not much taller than Yngvar, and spoke with a voice that sounded as if he had just been screaming. The entire journey the hirdman had said nothing beyond his name, which Yngvar had forgotten. He did not know all of his father's men. There were too many.

"No, lord, Jarl Gunnar does not patrol his lands or set a watch."

"Oh?" Yngvar glanced back at Bjorn and Thorfast as they picked their way through the last stretch of a light woods of gray-trunked trees. Dead leaves crunched beneath their feet. "You've been here before?"

"Twice, lord," the man paused to check his bearings, then continued without looking back. "No need for guards on Jarl Gunnar's lands."

"Why is that?" Yngvar asked. He actually did not know his uncle well. His father had preferred to talk of something else whenever Gunnar's name was raised. The sandy-haired man glanced at him. Yngvar thought he looked like a dog that had been caught shitting under its master's bed.

He looked around, and his friends were concentrating on their footing and the other hirdman was too far back to hear them.

"Why does my uncle not require guards on his land?"

They stopped and he pointed at the trees dotting the end of the woods. Dozens of skulls swayed from old, black ropes in their branches. The cheery new growth of spring contrasted with the brown and yellowed bones. Beneath one thin tree part of a rib cage rose out of the ground.

The rest of the column stopped, wondering what they looked at. Thorfast sucked his breath when he saw what Yngvar did.

"That's why, lord," the hirdman said. "Gunnar the Black has no patience for trespassers or fools. Neither live long in his lands. Small trouble avoids this place. Anything larger than that he could see from his hall."

Yngvar squinted at the vague shape of the hall atop the bald hill. It did command a view that left no hiding place. All the trees had been cleared off the hill and surrounding area. Judging from the stumps they skirted on the way up the hill, deforesting the area had to be the work of years. Yngvar knew his uncle was called Black not only for his dark hair but for his wretched temper. He would not treat his own family so poorly, would he?

At the hall, guards stood ready for them. Yngvar's escort raised his hand in peace. He also carried a smoothed piece of deer antler with Hakon's runes upon it to prove they came in his service. These men were craggy, stooped figures that used their spears like old men use walking sticks. It was a lazy display and they blinked at their approach like two sleepy cats by a hearth fire. Yngvar's escort motioned that they stay back, then climbed the rest of the distance to talk to the guards. The antler piece traded hands, then one man went inside while Yngvar's escort returned.

Yngvar waited, his stomach tightened and nostrils flaring. The air was cool for late afternoon, smelling of grass from the wide fields surrounding them. He searched for a good sign that he had done the right thing in coming here. Yet only a few clouds hung in the pale blue sky and any birds or other carriers of omens were far off dots. Thorfast and Bjorn huddled behind him. Thorfast's breath was hot on his shoulder as he leaned in.

"Do you think I should wait outside? This is family business, after all."

"Don't tell me you're afraid of my uncle?"

"I won't then. I'll let you figure it out yourself."

"It's just some bones," Bjorn said. "Probably bandits, is all. You worry too much."

The door burst open and a stronger, taller man exited. He had long golden hair cascading over his shoulders and a flowing beard to match it. His heavy brow pulled down over his shadowed eyes as he looked over the visitors gathered at his hall. He wore plain clothes of brown, and a large grease stain marred his shirt. Gold and silver rings decorated his strong arms.

"My cousins?" His voice was coarse and strong. "You're still alive?"

Yngvar swallowed at that. He expected them to be dead? He felt Thorfast step back from the powerful man who now marched down the hill. He was neither threatening nor welcoming. He carried no visible weapon, but seemed capable of danger with his knuckles alone. He pointed a thick finger at Yngvar.

"You're the very image of him, just like they say. It raises my neck hairs to see it."

Yngvar's stomach knotted and he inclined his head. "People say I look like my father."

"No, you look like our grandfather. You never saw him, did you? Well, look into a still pond one day. He'll be looking back at you."

Yngvar liked his cousin. His stomach unclenched and a warm glow drove off his fear. His cousin, Brandr, had once been a hostage to Jarl Hrolf the Strider. He could not have been but a child when grandfather Ulfrik died, yet he still seemed to remember him.

Brandr stood before them, hands on his hips, but still did not smile. His face was lost behind the silky beard and his expression remained hard to read. He glanced past Yngvar to the others. "Cousin Bjorn. Big for a lad your age, aren't you? What happened to your arm?"

"A war hound attacked me."

Yngvar turned at the comment. Bjorn had not flinched at his exaggeration and ignored Yngvar's dubious look.

"I hope you killed the beast," Brandr said. "The rest are your escorts, then. This white snowflake melting behind everyone? Who are you?"

"I am Thorfast the Silent, a good friend of your cousins."

"Excellent. Friends are good, and silent ones are best. Live up to your name and we shall get along fine." Brandr finally extended his arm to Yngvar, and they both gripped the other in a formal greeting. Brandr finally smiled and it was surprisingly warm. Up close he smelled of beer and sweat, and his grip was strong and sure. Yngvar decided his cousin was a decent man despite having only just met him. Brandr did the same for Bjorn and extended the same courtesies to rest.

"Come inside," he said, extending an arm toward the opened doors. "My father is preparing to receive you. I admit it is a surprise that Uncle Hakon has dared to send you here. Yet you are family, and so I promise you all the hospitality of honored guests. Come now. The hall is a modest place, not what you boys are accustomed to."

Yngvar wanted to ask about that division, but thought better of it.

Instead he rounded on Bjorn as they followed their cousin uphill. "Don't mention the troubles between my father and Uncle Gunnar."

"I was just about to ask him," Bjorn said, seemingly surprised at Yngvar's timeliness. Yngvar rolled his eyes and followed Brandr to the doors. Everyone surrendered their weapons, leaving them with the ragged men who seemed as likely to steal them as they were to safeguard them.

Transitioning into the hall, Yngvar's eyes failed to show him anything. It was dark with the hearth unlit and the smoke hole closed. Only low burning lamps shed illumination in thin puddles of yellow. Every hall was laid out the same, though, and Yngvar could navigate by that familiarity while he stayed close to Brandr. The cramped hall was filled with benches pushed to the walls and heavy with the scent of urine and smoke. Several hirdmen crouched in the corner tables, playing dice or drinking. All rose at their entrance, each one a hard man with scars and deep lines filled with shadow. No wonder fools were frightened of this land, Yngvar thought.

"My brother sends his son and fosterling to me for no reason. This is a surprise, though one I've expected for some time."

Yngvar followed the commanding voice to the front of the hall, where the high table had been pushed aside. Seated in a Frankish-style chair, Gunnar the Black leaned on his knees as if straining to see them. He began to cough and fell back with his fist over his mouth.

"Uncle Gunnar," Yngvar said, bowing before he had a chance to study the man in the chair. "I am Yngvar. Thank you for receiving me after a long journey."

"Couldn't send you by horseback or wagon." Gunnar stopped to cough again. "Made you walk, did he? Well, straighten up. You're family, don't act like a stranger."

Gunnar the Black was no longer a dark-haired man. His wavy hair remained full and long, but was now white with only telltale traces of the original black. His beard was short but not well groomed. It seemed he had just cut it square when it grew longer than he liked. He leaned back in his chair like a man who had run a long race and needed to catch his breath. He reinforced his name by wearing all black clothing that set off the armbands he wore.

Yngvar could not help but stare at the stump of his right hand, which rested on the chair. He did not hide it, and the old flesh was dark and ruddy with the cauterizing burns used to seal the stump. A Frankish warlord had cut off his hand in his youth. Yngvar did not recall the story other than that act had changed his uncle forever. He was legendary for fighting with a modified shield and ax, and for removing hands from his foes whether dead or living.

After greetings were done, Yngvar faced his first decision since leaving home. His father had asked him to carry a message of peace. Yngvar planned to fan Uncle Gunnar's anger with his father to get help in escaping his marriage. The two plans were opposed.

Gunnar coughed again, and Yngvar noticed how sunken and red Gunnar's eyes were.

"Are you well, Uncle? Did we come at a bad time?"

"I am well," he shouted. Yngvar jumped as did all the others. "Why does everyone ask after my health? When I'm dying I will tell you."

Yngvar bowed in apology. Brandr moved to his father's side and put a hand to his shoulder.

"We are all anxious to learn why you have come," Brandr said. "It cannot be an enemy at the borders, for we'd have known. Is your father well? Did something happen?"

"In fact, I was asked to remind you our blacksmith is awaiting leather he needs to complete his work." Both Gunnar and Brandr frowned at this. Yngvar decided he better give a good reason, and only the truth would do. He was not a skilled talker like Thorfast was. He could not come up with words he did not believe. The silence extended, and Gunnar's dark eyes glittered as he leaned forward.

"Your father needs leather? He sent the two of you here to tell me this?"

"Not exactly, Uncle. He ... well, I contrived to come on my own." He looked at Bjorn and Thorfast, who stared at him with wide eyes. Did that mean they disapproved? It didn't matter. He better not look at anyone but his uncle. "My father has arranged a marriage for me. I've no desire for his choice. I want freedom, Uncle Gunnar. I want to sail the seas as you and Grandfather did. I want a life of glory and adventure and not be a piece my father pushes along a game board. I thought I might use the anger between you and my father to gain your help in escaping my marriage. I see now how wrong that would be.

"My father did not know I came with this plan in my heart. He agreed to the trip and wanted me to convey a message of reconciliation. He said that he is sorry and—"

"Enough!" Gunnar raised his hand. "If your father wishes to reconcile then he would have come himself. This would not be the first time he sent apologies through another, and it's no matter you are kin."

Yngvar cringed at the wild anger he read in Uncle Gunnar's eyes. Whatever had transpired between father and uncle had left a deep wound. Yngvar did not know where to take his request, having scuttled his plan. But Gunnar was not finished. He seemed to regain himself, then started coughing. This lasted an uncomfortable time where Yngvar felt as if he could crawl between a loose stone in the hearth and hide. At last his uncle accepted a horn from Brandr and guzzled beer to drown his cough. Foam spilled down his beard onto his shirt. He threw aside the horn when finished and wiped his mouth with the back of his hand.

"As for your desire to remain free," Gunnar said, his tone softer now. "I understand how you feel. But I have no place to tell your father what he should do with his son. He does not tell me what to do with mine, after all. So stay tonight. We will feast and celebrate better relations with my nephews. For long has it been since family has laughed beneath this roof. But tomorrow you must return home and to your future life."

7

The hall was bright with roaring hearth fire and echoing with the laughter and boasts of dozens of hirdmen. Yngvar was crushed against Bjorn, who in turn leaned against Thorfast. Across the high table, their two escorts sat between red-faced men from Gunnar's hird. The hall doors hung open to let in air that could not penetrate the smoky room to the back of the hall. It was as if all the drunken revelers between the door and Yngvar sucked up all the air.

"Your cup is empty," Brandr said, sitting on his opposite side. His formerly intimidating cousin was not an agreeable drunk, and he sloshed beer out of his dark wood pitcher. Half of it missed Yngvar's cup. It ran off the edge onto his lap, a cool relief from the humid heat of the room. It was the third spill this night, and Yngvar had ceased reacting to it. Brandr, however, found each subsequent spill more humorous than the last. He threw his head back in laughter and slapped Yngvar's back.

"Now this is a feast," Bjorn said over the din, leaning into Yngvar's ear. "If only they had more women here."

"What would you do with a woman?" Thorfast shouted. "Show her the wound you got from that war hound?"

Bjorn smiled, red-faced, and said nothing.

From the high table, the hall seemed much longer than it did when on the floor. He had not often sat at his father's high table, being too young to enjoy such revels as this until only the last few years. It seemed there had been less feasting since he became old enough to attend. Yet another sign of his staid and boring future married to a hag with good political ties.

"Here, does your father allow you to sulk at the table?" Uncle Gunnar, rheumy-eyed and haggard from a long night, still managed to smile. He sat next to Brandr and leaned behind him to regard Yngvar. "Is my beer so poor?"

"No, Uncle, your beer is fine." Yngvar realized he had been a poor guest. He had not even presented gifts. He had left them in his pack which was still at the front of the hall with his sword. "Excuse my rudeness. I have prepared a gift for you. I am a poor guest to have forgotten it for so long. Please let me get it from my belongings."

"Fine manners," Gunnar said. "Must have learned them from your mother."

The jibe got confused laughter from most of the hirdmen. Only Brandr smiled weakly and moved aside to let Yngvar leave for his gift. He squeezed along the wall, passing the men falling over each other at their boards. The floor was wet with beer and scraps of the meal. The few serving girls were not much to behold, but nonetheless none of them could travel five feet before a drunk pulled her onto his lap.

Finding his pack, he removed the sax his father had selected to send to his brother. Gunnar was to take the credit for the gift, but it came from his father's belongings. The sax was a short sword used for fighting in tight shield walls, something Yngvar doubted he'd ever see now. It was usually worn at the lap for an easy draw. This sheath came with no baldric, and was plain, leather-wrapped wood. What made the blade special was the green gemstone set in the pommel. It flashed and winked in the hall light, and was probably worth more than the blade.

He swam his way across the hirdmen back to his uncle who waited with his chin resting on the stump of his right hand. Yngvar held the weapon in open palms, so none could mistake his intent with it. As he approached the table, Gunnar sat up with interest. The men around him parted for Yngvar to give his gift. He offered the sax to his uncle.

"My father and I selected this sax for you. I know you prefer an ax to a sword, but I hope you will find this gift suitable for your hospitality."

Gunnar stared at the blade without a word. His reaction brought silence to the men closest to him. Yngvar felt his face heat up at the prolonged stillness. At last, Gunnar reached out with his only hand and took the blade. He stared at the pommel, holding it up so that the hearth light made it blaze.

Were those tears shinning in his eyes? He held the blade high so that the wrinkles of his old neck stretched as he looked up at it. More men quieted as he held it there, until only a few hopeless drunks at the back of the hall watched him.

"Your father picked this?"

"He did."

Gunnar nodded and lowered the sax, placing it on the board before him. He coughed several times, then cleared his throat. He spoke louder than needed for Yngvar to hear him.

"You say you want a life of adventure. Is there a man here who does not desire such a life?" Those close and sober enough to understand pounded their tables and shouted agreement. Gunnar smiled slightly. "As I thought. Glory is all a man lives for, and there is no glory sheltering in a hall. He must go into the world and find it."

Yngvar nodded, agreeing but not understanding the sudden change in his uncle's demeanor. Was he drunk? He had not seemed to drink much all night.

"This gift reminds me of that need." Gunnar's one hand reached to the sword and touched the green gem on the pommel. His expression became thoughtful, and as he lingered on it, his inebriated audience began to drift back to their drinks. Brandr, however, watched his father carefully.

"There is great treasure hidden in the world," Gunnar said with a loud suddenness that recaptured the men's attention. "This is but a part of what lies hidden. This is a warning to me that my days are short, and if I am to ever make good on my promise then it must be now."

Brandr leaned back from his father. His fog of drunkenness had seemed to blow away. "What promise?"

"When your mother died," Gunnar said. "She left the world without the jewels and riches I promised when I courted her."

"You're drunk," Brandr said. "You should rest now."

Gunnar exploded from his chair with violent speed seemingly impossible for a man of his condition. He whirled on Brandr with his face pulled tight like a snarling wolf.

"Do not treat me like a doddering old man! I know of what I speak and you know nothing."

Turning to his men, now commanding the attention of the hall, he straightened himself. If he had given the impression of an ill and aged man, now he was a warlord in black. Fierce strength pulled him upright and his eyes raked the hall. Yngvar could only imagine what he must have been like in his prime. His glare alone would turn a shark back to the depths of the sea.

"I am Gunnar the Black, son of Ulfrik, son of Orm the Bellower. My mother was Runa the Bloody. I come from strength and power. My father ruled the Faereya islands before he helped the ungrateful Hrolf the Strider earn his kingdom. He had won his treasure long before coming here, and he was as wise as he was wealthy. Rather than carry a fortune aboard ship and under the nose of the greedy Hrolf, he buried it on our ancestral family lands in Grenner, back in Norway."

The hall began to mumble at the claim. Brandr stared at his father as if seeing him for the first time. Yngvar wished he had brought a trinket for a gift rather than something to drive his uncle mad. He gave a desperate look to Bjorn and Thorfast, but they were staring open-mouthed at Gunnar.

"This is the first time you've ever mentioned this," Brandr said.

"Of course, you fool! Treasure would not remain hidden long if revealed even to one's kin. I was sworn to secrecy. Besides, Norway is under the boot of Harald Finehair."

"Erik Blood-Axe," shouted someone from the middle of the hall. "His son rules now."

Gunnar waved his stump in dismissal, frowning. "No matter who rules, I let the jarls of Norway delay me all these years. My father told me the location of his treasure. It was meant to be saved for when he needed it most. But he never had a chance to retrieve it. For like me, he waited until he was too old to make the journey and died before he could reclaim the riches he had won for his family."

Yngvar looked around at a quiet hall, blurry eyes trying to focus on Gunnar. No matter how much they had drunk, none of them were so far gone that they did not smell the gold lust in the air.

"What good has it done buried in Norway?" Gunnar asked. "Before I die, I will reclaim it. I will share it with those who aid me. There can be no more delay."

Brandr spoke, but Yngvar could not hear him over the shouts of the other men. From his frown, it seemed he disagreed with his father. Gunnar ignored Brandr and lifted the sword off the table. He held it by the sheath so that the green pommel gem extended toward the gathered men.

"Will you come with me on this final journey to glory?"

Every man in the hall stood, hollering their pledges. Yngvar was suddenly crushed between two sweaty men with body hair like wire. Both had surged forward to shout their oaths. Only after he had squeezed from between them did he realize his uncle stared directly at him.

Did he mean to take him on this adventure? Panic caused his stomach to burn and he again looked to Thorfast and Bjorn, who were both as stunned as he. Thorfast's platinum hair glowed in the dim light. It made Yngvar think of Kadlin. If he went with his uncle, he would delay or even avoid marriage to Jarl Flosi's beastly daughter. If it was a family treasure, then perhaps his uncle would be generous in sharing it with him. He could afford to take Kadlin away and start a life together. Of course, Kadlin would come to her senses by that time. So being away for a time might help as well.

A dissenting voice broke into the general celebration. Yngvar looked to Brandr, but found he was sitting with arms folded and face lost to shadow. The shouting continued until Yngvar heard it right behind him, just before the owner of the voice shoved him aside.

He piled up against the sweaty man with wiry hair that grated on his exposed arm. The man roared in dismay, and shoved Yngvar aside only to have him collide with another man. When he at last regained himself, the dissenter was poised beneath the high table.

The man was tall and thickly built, with a deep chest of tense muscle. He wore his black beard in a long braid and his hair was thin and flowing, such that it shimmered in the light. He sported a silver armband over his plain gray shirt and golden rings glinted on his fingers.

"Jarl Gunnar, I'm as eager as any man to claim treasure. But your own son does not seem convinced."

"Bregthor, always challenging me at every turn." Gunnar put the sword down on the table, letting in thump against the wood. "Brandr is rightfully hurt I have not shared this with him before revealing it to everyone else. That is why he sulks."

"Is that true?" Bregthor asked of Brandr.

Gunnar flipped the table aside, sending mugs and plates and their contents showering down on everyone below him. Yngvar caught a spray of Bjorn's mead before the man in front of him leapt back from the falling table and knocked him aside. Gunnar pounced down to stand face-to-face with Bregthor, that wolflike snarl returned.

"Nip at my heels again, pup, and I will break all your teeth," Gunnar seized Bregthor's shirt with his single hand and pulled him close. Despite being older and smaller, Gunnar was certainly the more ferocious. Bregthor seemed to shrink in Gunnar's grip.

"I only wanted to ask—"

Gunnar wrenched him closer. "You challenged my word before everyone. Do not try to talk your way out of it. Cover a pile of shit with lilac and it is just shit-stained flowers. Now answer me clearly. Do you challenge my claims?"

Bregthor shook his head. Gunnar was so terrifying Yngvar found himself shaking his head as well.

"That is good." Gunnar released his grip and stepped back. "You never before doubted the gold I put into your hands. So do not doubt me in this."

Bregthor stepped back and went to his knee. "Forgive me, lord. I have drunk too much tonight."

Gunnar was not swift in bestowing his forgiveness. He let Bregthor hang until at last he waved him to his feet. Yngvar noted several men had held their breath for Bregthor's fate and received him back into their company. They escorted him toward the hall entrance, as if he could not find it without their help.

Now Gunnar turned to Yngvar. His smile was smug. "And you would be welcomed on such a journey as well. After all, it was your gift that roused me to this. Will you join your uncle and reclaim your grandfather's treasure?"

Yngvar could think of nothing else to say. Despite all that had happened, he was getting exactly all he had asked for. "Of course, Uncle Gunnar. It would be an honor!"

Gunnar swept him into a bear hug, and Yngvar smelled the beer. Perhaps he was drunk. But when he fell out of his uncle's embrace he looked up to Thorfast and Bjorn, both equal parts stunned and delighted.

A memory came to Yngvar as he navigated over the ruined table to rejoin his friends. He had been with his father returning from a hunt with a huge boar in tow. He hadn't been on the hunt, but joined his father as he returned to the hall. On the walk his father had seemed happy for his catch. It was expected to be a hard winter and the boar would feed the hall for a good part of it. But Hakon suddenly turned grim and knelt beside young Yngvar, putting his hand on his shoulder as he spoke. "When the gods grant all that you desire without a struggle, you must worry. They are planning mischief. The Norns, who weave the fate of all men at the foot of the World Tree, will gather their black threads and weave them into your life."

Yngvar set the memory aside and embraced both Thorfast and Bjorn, who were now as excited as everyone else in the hall. Even Brandr had seemed to warm to the thought of adventure. He now helped Gunnar back up the ledge of the stage and patted his father's back. Yngvar laughed and reveled at his prospects.

He tried to suppress the rest of his memory. After the winter when his father had caught the giant boar, a plague had spread among the sheep and cattle. He remembered field upon field of dead animals and the men who lingered hopelessly over the corpses.

8

Yngvar lifted his head from the rolled cloak he used for a pillow. His eyes pounded from the drink of the prior night's feast. He was still on the stage of the high table, the table itself still overturned on the floor below. Dozens of men still snored, filling the hall with a low hum. Bjorn was next to him, his mouth hanging open as he slept. Yngvar wanted to tug his sparse beard and silence his thunderous snores. But light filtered through the smoke hole and a square of faint illumination showed in the dark frame of the front hall. He would awaken soon enough.

Wiping his eyes and smacking his dry mouth, Yngvar sat up. Thorfast was slumped against the wall. For a moment it seemed as if he had died there, but his cloak neatly covered his lap and his feet twitched from beneath it. It seemed a strange way to sleep. Extracting himself from between his friends, he noticed his uncle had left. He had private rooms in the back of the hall. Brandr was gone as well. Several men noticed him rousing and gave weak, knowing smiles. Everyone had drunk too much.

The scent of ashes and beer mixed with the urine scent that clung to the walls. Yngvar himself would normally piss on the outside walls, but most men did not care to go so far from the beer. Not to mention, drunken men wandering outside sometimes did not make it back in.

Every hall smelled like piss, but Uncle Gunnar's hall was the worst in his limited experience. His stomach churned and with the hirdmen laid so cramped about the floor, he dared not risk vomiting here. He picked his way outside.

The air was bracing and the pink stain of dawn was just filling into the eastern horizon. From the hill, Yngvar could see every approach and beyond. Twirls of hearth smoke showed behind dark trees where villagers were preparing for their day.

"You can see the Seine from the hall roof." Brandr's voice surprised Yngvar, making him step back. There were no guards at the door, something Yngvar's father would never had allowed no matter the celebration, and he had thought himself alone. Yet Brandr leaned at the corner of the hall.

"I suppose we will be seeing the Seine much closer now." Yngvar tried to smile, but it was all balanced on the fragile hope that last night's drunken proclamations would hold up in a sober dawn.

Brandr shrugged, lifting his left foot to press against the wall. His gray cloak fell aside to reveal his arms folded over his chest. "You may be right. My father seems convinced he must do this thing before ..."

Yngvar waited, but Brandr stared off at the horizon. He judged it best not to push Brandr on what he intended to say. He was now glad he had not woken Bjorn, since he would go after that unfinished sentence like a hound to a bone.

"Will he really take me and the others?"

"My father never says anything he does not mean. Ever. And he detests those who cannot do the same. So know that much about your uncle. If you will go raiding with him, then if he vows to kill every woman and child he sees then you can be sure of it."

Yngvar laughed. Of course Uncle Gunnar was not about killing women and children, but fighting enemy warriors or church guardians to get at their hoarded gold. Brandr continued to stare ahead.

"Who was the man that challenged Uncle Gunnar last night?"

Now Brandr laughed. "A fool and a braggart, that's who. Bregthor Vandradsson is his name. He's served my father these few years. He's good in a fight, but not much use in anything else. Thinks he knows more than anyone, and some fools believe it. I'd get rid of him, but my father has accepted his oath. So he has no choice but to keep him."

While they spoke the sun lifted above the trees and the sunlight strengthened. Brandr pushed away from the wall and gave Yngvar a smile. "If we're going to sea, then there's much I have to prepare yet."

"Of course, do you have a family?" Yngvar's voice was small, since Brandr was his cousin who lived only a day away and yet he knew nothing of him.

Brandr shook his head. "Dead. Pox got my sons. My wife died of a broken heart. I warned her not to get too attached to them until they were strong enough to stand on their own. Remember that when you have your own children. Don't put too much into them in the early years."

Yngvar nodded sagely, as if he had received deep wisdom. He hoped he would not have children soon. Certainly not with Jarl Flosi's daughter. Brandr walked downhill, his sword slapping at his hip as he went. It reminded Yngvar to re-equip his. He'd have to pull it out of the pile himself, since no guard was in sight. Was Uncle Gunnar's reputation so powerful as to not even require a guard at his door? Even the great jarls of Rouen posted guards. Yngvar returned to the hall and its human scents.

"Good morning, lord."

Yngvar walked into the sandy-haired escort and his companion. The two men were lined up like a wall blocking entrance. Yngvar wondered if it was purposeful, so rather than greet them he frowned.

"Am I not allowed back inside?"

Both men smiled and parted for him. The sandy-haired man spoke. "Of course. We were just headed outside to see where you had gone. Your father was clear in his instructions to remain close to you."

"Hopefully not so close that we are all sleeping under the same blanket."

"You slept comfortably last night?" asked the other man. He was darker haired and had eyes like a sad dog's. "We did not sleep under the same blanket, did we?"

"And you have my gratitude for it," Yngvar pushed between them.

The pile of weapons at the front door was a haphazard mess. His sword remained at the top of the pile.

"As for last night, lord," said the sandy-haired man. "That was quite a feast. Your uncle is very generous."

The dog-eyed man clucked his tongue at his companion, then turned to Yngvar. "Look, are you honestly going with your uncle?"

Yngvar felt his face heat. Were these two going to prevent him? He straightened up before retrieving his sword. "He invited me, didn't he, and I accepted? Were you two so drunk that you did not hear?"

"No, lord," said the sandy-haired man. "In fact, to best perform our duties to your father we did not drink as much as the rest. So we were very clear on what was said. We both think Jarl Gunnar was a bit ... sudden ... in his plans. Do you think he will sail for Norway?"

"My uncle never says anything he doesn't mean."

The two hirdmen exchanged worried glances. The dog-eyed man picked his nose while the other seemed to think of what to say.

"You two are going to try to prevent me from going?" Yngvar put his hands on his hips. "That's not going to happen. I am a man and I make my own choices. You were to guard me and add numbers to boost the safety of our traveling group. That was all."

"But he did tell us not to let you out of our sight." The sandy-haired man stared at the floor in deep thought.

"But we're sworn to Jarl Hakon," said the dog-eyed man. "We can't leave him to serve another jarl, even if it is his brother."

Yngvar huffed at the two fools. This was not his problem to solve. He pointed to the sandy-haired man. "What's your name again?"

"Bresi Kettilson," he said, clearly taken aback. Yngvar figured he had to get the man's name now.

"Bresi, you come with me to keep your promise to my father. I'm sure he will be glad to know one of his finest is protecting me. You," he said pointing to the other, whose name he no longer needed to know. "Go back to my father and tell him what happened."

"What should I tell him? I think he would want you returned home."

"Stop thinking so much," Yngvar said. "You don't get to think for me or my father. Unless he told you to restrain me should I try to

52

leave with my uncle, you've not broken any oath to my father. He wasn't that complete in his orders to you, was he?" Both men shook their heads. "Good. Then you can tell my father what you saw last night. And you tell him that all of us decided to go raiding without his leave, which means we have lost his protection. So we're saving him the trouble of throwing us out. That's what you tell him."

The man swallowed, his dog eyes wide. Yngvar doubted the man had the guts to deliver the message. Perhaps it was best he didn't hit those angry notes that Yngvar had infused into his words. His father was not a bad man and was not trying to harm him. But he was interfering in his life and setting up an inescapable future. Even if it meant he had to disobey his father, Yngvar had to take this chance now or be lost forever. Even if he declined Uncle Gunnar, eventually his father would learn of this temptation and would hurry the proceedings to lock Yngvar to his fate.

The two hirdmen seemed settled to this agreement.

The rest of the morning was slow to start as men were thick with drink. But by afternoon when Uncle Gunnar reappeared, he was more enthusiastic about this adventure than last night. He entertained Yngvar and the others with old stories, pausing at times to cough or wheeze. Later they were given heavy leather jerkins and better shields. The rest of his men prepared the ship for travel. Again they feasted that night, but not as extravagant as the prior night's. Then by morning of the following day Yngvar went down with thirty men in their war gear to the Seine River. Women and children were there to see them off. Yngvar thrilled at the departure. Unfortunately, he only had the dog-eyed hirdman to wave at.

As the sun burned off fog from the surface of the muddy river, Gunnar's ship pushed out into the current.

Yngvar was now on his first raid, and he could not wait to claim his treasure.

9

Yngvar shivered, his breath fogging around his nose as he wrapped his cloak tighter. The fog rose up with the dawn and never burned off. The sun failed to show itself for days, and the spring weather had turned wintry. Today was the worst it had been in all the days they had progressed north. The ship rocked on the waves and men grumbled about the bad omen. Yngvar wondered at taking to the waves in such fog. How would they spot land? Yet Uncle Gunnar was eager to reach Norway's shore.

"We are close now," he barked. "Don't show your bellies to me. Man the oars! I can steer us by the sun."

Thorfast and Bjorn moaned in pain at the order. Yngvar's shoulders and back burned from the stress of rowing, and his hands were blistered. He stuffed back his complaints, not wanting to catch that evil eye from his uncle whenever he caught them complaining.

They had sea chests, mostly empty now and awaiting treasure, which served as their rowing seats. Thorfast and he worked an oar while Bresi and Bjorn sat in front of them on theirs. Brandr walked the row to encourage men however they needed it, either with an encouraging word or a thump on the head. Bregthor and his friends got most of Brandr's attentions. Yngvar wasn't certain they needed it as much as Brandr gave to them.

"How does he make anything from a bright spot in the sky?" Thorfast asked.

"It's not as hard as it seems," Bresi answered. "As long as there is a patch then you can find your way. It's when the sun is completely lost to heavy clouds. Then only a sun stone can help."

Bjorn asked about the stone, as Yngvar expected, and the two fell into conversations he could not hear. He and Thorfast began to haul on their oar, moaning as they did. Once they had a rhythm they tried to keep up with the songs the crew sang to pass the boredom. Yngvar laughed at his mistakes, as well as the men nearby, and he rowed until sweat poured down his face. It turned cold in the air and stung his eyes as it dripped from his brow.

"This is the day," Gunnar said from the stern where he held the tiller. He had altered it for use with his stump, but Yngvar had not been given a chance to study it. "We will be ashore before the sun sets. Then we travel inland to where my father's treasure is buried. We will face angry Norsemen, but do not fear them. Gunnar the Black will—"

He fell into a coughing fit and Yngvar never learned what Gunnar the Black was going to do to his enemies.

"What is that shape?" Yngvar asked. "It's too small to be an island. It's not a rock, I hope."

All the men on the port side followed Yngvar's gaze. The fog was clear enough past their oars, but soon the world shaded off into a circle of white-and-lead-colored sea. It seemed impossible that any other ship would be foolish enough to join them in this cloud. Yet the vague shape seemed to have a long-necked prow.

"A ship!" shouted one of the crew.

"That can't be good," Thorfast said. "Merchants wouldn't risk their cargo in this fog."

"That's a long boat," Gunnar shouted. "Shields!"

The men around him drew in their oars enough to prevent them from falling into the ocean. Yngvar stared at the swiftly approaching ship. Its long neck resolved out of the white, its naked mast like a shark fin cutting the fog behind it. Dark shapes leaned over the sides of the ship as the sea split over its hull. The crew was silent and watchful.

Gunnar's ship leaned hard to the side, and the jerk roused Yngvar to his senses. Gunnar's crew pulled their shields off the racks, then slung them over their backs before returning to their oars.

"Get your shield," Brandr yelled at Yngvar. "That ship's been hunting us."

"You knew it was there?" Thorfast asked.

Brandr frowned at him, giving a brief nod before moving off.

"He couldn't have known it was there," Yngvar said. "It's almost on us. Why wouldn't we try to outrace it?"

"To capture it, of course," Bresi said.

Gunnar's ship was long with high sides. No common long ship would challenge it without great risk, or so Gunnar had claimed. Yet here was a ship of equal size bearing down on them with a crew as silent as the dead. Yngvar wished they would make some noise or give a war cry. Anything to make them less spectral than they appeared. Now they had drawn close enough that shadowy faces emerged from the fog.

"Shields up!" Gunnar yelled.

The crew pulled up their shields, creating a canopy. Yngvar knew what to do, but could not believe he had to do it. This was it. A real attack from a real enemy. He checked his sword, ensuring it was not strapped into its sheath.

"Fool! Get your shield up and hug the gunwale!" Brandr tore at Yngvar's arm, hauling his shield up and shoving him at the gunwale.

Uncle Gunnar had steered his ship to point directly at the enemy boat, cutting down the angle for enemy bowmen. Yet just before Yngvar ducked behind the gunwale, he saw the enemy point their arrows at the sky.

He didn't recognize the first two or three wooden thuds as arrows. Right behind these dozens more rained down on the deck. Thorfast shouted as a bodkin broke through his shield, fortunately remaining stuck inches from his face. The clatter and thud of the falling arrows brought the screams of men. From beneath the shadow of the shields, Yngvar glimpsed someone tumble on the opposite side of the deck.

"Hooks!" Gunnar shouted, and the canopy of shields disappeared.

Yngvar's heart slammed against the base of his throat and his ears roared with his pulse. A man writhed on the deck with an arrow in his neck, brilliant blood pulsing onto the boards. Men danced around him as if he were nothing more than one of the sea chests they had been sitting on.

The enemy ship had maneuvered alongside them and was a spear's throw away. Warriors stood atop the rails on both ships, spinning hooks before letting them fly. Bowmen took aim and shot. Men on both sides screamed and fell into the water.

"Take their ship!" Gunnar shouted. "Leave no one alive!"

Yngvar stumbled as the ship lurched toward the enemy. They had more bowmen and so continued to shoot at the fools who made themselves targets. He watched as these men let fate decide life or death. Surely no man died before the Fates had chosen his time, but these fools seemed intent on taunting them. One man went tumbling overboard. What purpose had that served? Where was the glory? He didn't even make a sound as he died.

"Lord, draw your sword," Bresi shouted at him, rushing to his side. Both Thorfast and Bjorn were close behind him. "Stand with me and we will make a shield wall. Do not board the enemy ship. All of you, drop your cloaks or the enemy will use them to drag you down."

Yngvar steadied himself as the two ships slewed at each other. He pulled out the antler pin at his shoulder to let his cloak drop. "How can we take their ship if we don't board it?"

Before he got his answer, the hulls slammed together as the men hauling on their ropes howled in triumph. The impact sent water into the air and men flying backward from their perches. Yngvar caught Bresi for support. When the rocking steadied, he drew his sword.

Gunnar held his ax high in his left hand. A black shield made to fit the stump of his right arm guarded him. Brandr stood by his father, sword and shield ready and as ferocious as a wolf. Both stood on the rails, hanging onto rigging for support. Their men surged beneath them and gave a throaty war cry. The enemy, once so silent, now roared as a gritty, sweaty mass that swarmed over the sides to pour onto Gunnar's men.

A fierce pride grew in Yngvar's heart. "Bjorn, do you see that? The son of Ulfrik goes to battle, and we his grandchildren hide in the rear."

"I'll not stand at the back," Bjorn shouted, his face red with shame. "I want to kill the enemy."

"For glory!" Yngvar shouted, raising his sword high. Bjorn also raised his sword and Thorfast followed.

"No, wait for an opening," Bresi said. Yngvar felt him snatch at his shoulder as he charged toward the whirling fight at the seam of the joined ships.

Yngvar crashed into the rear of the fighting men, hoping to push his way to the center where his uncle and cousin fought. The enemy had easily half again as many men as Gunnar's crew and had shoved them back from the rails onto their own deck. A rudimentary shield wall formed, though no one locked shields. Through those gaps the enemy thrust their long swords and spears.

Cold and bloody sea water sluiced at his feet as he slid back against the crush of men. Thorfast joined his right and Bjorn was on his left. They also vainly sought a way toward the front, cursing and shoving with their shields.

Men screamed and swore. Spear points flashed in the diffuse light, darting into the press and coming away bloodied. Axes rose and fell, bringing the crash of wood or the howls of agony. Salty, hot blood drizzled down Yngvar's exposed head and ran to his mouth. He spit it out in disgust, looking up at the man he pushed against. He was dead but still standing as both he and Thorfast shoved. The man's head hung back with his throat and face gashed open. Yngvar had not even seen him die.

"Push into their backs," Bresi shouted, joining next to Thorfast. "Our shield wall has to advance, or the enemy will get around us."

Yngvar tried to see his uncle, but could not from so close behind. The noise was deafening and the ship hulls beat out a shuddering rhythm as they bumped against each other. He shook the blood out of his eyes. What had his father told him about the rear of the shield wall? He had not paid much mind to that training, always assuming he'd be in the front and center of any battle.

"We can lap around their flank," Yngvar said. "We can pull them off the front lines."

"They outnumber us," shouted Bresi as he pushed his shield in the small of the man's back before him. "We can't let our line thin."

"We're doing nothing here," Bjorn shouted.

Yngvar's feet continued to slide back. The water sloshing over his boots was now as red as Frankish wine. If one lapped the enemy's flank only when outnumbering them, he thought, then the enemy crew would do it now.

"We can't let them get behind us," Yngvar shouted. "Thorfast, Bjorn, follow me!"

When he relented, the dead man he propped up thumped to the deck. The next man slid back and stumbled over the body.

"You've started a chain," Bresi shouted. "We're all going to fall."

Bresi was correct, but not because of what Yngvar did. He swung out from the rear toward the prow. The enemy crew had crumpled the line of Gunnar's men and they were stumbling and falling all along the railing. The enemy piled up, thrusting spear and blade into the collapsing men.

Gunnar now emerged atop the fray. His white hair and beard were stained with blood. His ax head was slick with gore as he raised it high. He shouted, "For glory!"

The war cry cut short.

An enemy spear shot from below, sliding under Gunnar's shield and into his side. His back arched and eyes widened, then he sank into the mass of hacking and stabbing weapons.

"Uncle!" The cry escaped Yngvar without a thought. He searched for the enemy he had expected to lap them. There was not enough room, their foes taking the brute force approach of crushing their opposition.

"We're going to be defeated," he said, his voice thin beneath the crash and thud of battle. He could see it even if none else could. The enemy were almost entirely aboard their ship. Gunnar had fallen. Brandr was lost amid the fighting. Men were stumbling.

"We'll become slaves," Thorfast said. "This can't happen."

"I'll die before that happens." Bjorn flung toward the melee, but Yngvar caught him. Bresi joined not far behind.

"No one's on the other ship," Yngvar said. "We've got to get away."

"You can't sail off with their ship," Bresi said.

"Of course not, we sail with ours," Yngvar was already stepping up to the prow. He held out his shield for balance, not daring to but glance at the gray water slapping the hull beneath him. He leapt to the enemy deck. Thorfast was right behind.

"What are we doing here?" he asked, as Bjorn and Bresi made the same leap.

"Destroying their rudder," Yngvar said. "Bjorn and you cut the ties between our ships. Bresi, help me dump the rudder into the sea."

Yngvar moved with a coolness and assurance he did not actually feel. He had to appear strong or his friends would not listen. In fact, he wanted to lie down on the deck and die. This was nothing like he expected. His first battle and he would end it enslaved or executed.

The enemy was too consumed with their push for victory to mind Yngvar and his companions. He and Bresi began hacking at the binding at the top of the rudder. Yngvar tore away the tiller and flung it into the sea.

"Work fast," Bresi shouted. "We'll not remain unchallenged for long."

The top broke free, but the rudder was primarily secured through a hole in the hull where a wooden rod held it. It now swung free, but did not fall.

Glancing over his shoulder, Bjorn and Yngvar were hacking at the ropes, throwing them aside as they broke. One man challenged Bjorn, but fortunately one of Gunnar's crew picked him off.

"We've got to shove this through," Bresi said. "We can't chop it, not without an ax and not in time."

Yngvar gave the rod a test chop, but it was strong wood meant to withstand the stress of the ocean. Only a giant could hack it off in a single blow. What had he been thinking?

"We're not trying to preserve the fucking thing," Yngvar shouted. "What are we doing? Kick it!"

He jumped on the rail, then nearly pitched overboard. Bresi grabbed him by the hem of his pants. He drove his heel at the rudder. It twisted and bent, but did not snap. It was firmly anchored to the hull. If he could pull up the deck boards and get below, he could shove the rudder out. But he had no time. With Bresi holding him, he kicked again.

"The ships are freed!" Bjorn shouted. Both he and Thorfast stood framed against the enemy. Yngvar closed his eyes in disgust. Where the enemy had not noticed before, those in the rear turned around and began to point at Yngvar and Bresi.

"He could've at least yelled that in Frankish," Bresi said.

"He doesn't think before he speaks," Yngvar said. "Lower me down onto this rudder. It's our last chance."

Bresi did not argue, but held him by the shoulders as he slid the short distance down the hull to stand where the rudder attached. He was only as low as his waist, but the water lapped below him as if hungry to take him into its dark, frigid depths. Bresi's hands were like cold iron on him. Yngvar still held sword and shield, which now unbalanced him.

"I've got you," Bresi said. "Do what you can, but this is it."

Yngvar braced against the hull, placed both feet on the rudder, then kicked.

The satisfying snap thrilled him. The rudder broke over the rod, rendering it useless. The fat blade beneath the water did not break, still being attached to the hull. But no one would be able to use this to steer now.

He hopped back aboard the ship, face wide with a smile. But Bresi and he did not have time to celebrate. A half-dozen enemies from the rear were converging on them. Their barred teeth were red and their swords dripped blood.

"Run for the ship," Bresi shouted, and pushed Yngvar. "I'll block them."

"You can't—"

Bresi shoved Yngvar forward and it gave him a running start. The ships were already drifting apart.

Screaming, Bresi flung his shield at the man closest to Yngvar. The rim caught him full in the face, knocking him aside into the man next to him. Yngvar dashed past them, and leapt the rails to land on his uncle's ship.

Bjorn and Thorfast along with a handful of other men were using oars to push away from the enemy ship. To Yngvar's shock, the enemy streamed back to their own deck.

"Bresi," Yngvar yelled. "Take my shield."

He made to throw it across to him, but Bresi was already surrounded. His typically calm face was flushed and full of rage. He struck like a badger at the men converging on him. The two he had taken out with his shield were still dazed.

Yngvar watched with his eyes stinging as the ships drifted apart. Bresi cut one man in the throat, killing him. But it was a pointless victory. The three others brought him down like an old tree, then encircled him as they hacked Bresi to death.

"Row!" Brandr's hoarse voice boomed out across the deck. He stood with Uncle Gunnar cradled in his arms. "Row, you bastards!"

Yngvar jumped on an oar and threw himself into it. The few enemy that remained aboard tried to surrender, but Gunnar's crew had been told to let none live. Enemies knelt before their surrendered weapons, but they died with split skulls.

The crew of the enemy ship roared in anger, powerless to follow as Brandr took the tiller and cut hard away from the enemy. The fog was welcoming now, like a gentle hand that would ease the pain and terror of battle.

Gunnar lay at the center of his ship, hand over the wound in his side. He was laughing.

10

Men grunted and cursed as they rowed. The deck creaked and rocked over the fog-shrouded waves. They sailed into the wind, so that the enemy could not pursue using their sails alone. For even without a rudder a ship could still be given a general heading. Brandr had steered his ship while every man had rowed, heedless of the wounded moaning and bleeding out on the deck.

Yngvar's mind held nothing. The world around him appeared flat and meaningless. His uncle's bloody coughing was punctuated with bouts of laughter. As Yngvar rowed he stared at his uncle's blood-soaked white hair. Sweeping his gaze around the ship, he found gaps where once rowers had sat shoulder-to-shoulder. Bjorn was alone on his oar. Bresi was dead.

That thought repeated over and over. Bresi had died to save Yngvar's life. He died keeping his oath to Hakon. Without a doubt he died in high honor and in great glory. He had challenged six men to battle. Not even the heroes of songs could lay claim to such bravery. With every stroke of the oar, Yngvar remembered the ferocity in Bresi's face and how he died taking a foe with him. He promised to retell Bresi's story to anyone who would listen. When he returned home, he would tell his father of Bresi's deeds and his family would enjoy the glory he had earned.

Brandr strode past Yngvar, waking him from his thoughts. He stared at his cousin, who had passed the tiller off to another, as he crouched by his father. Perhaps Brandr had proclaimed them safe from being overtaken, for others were either getting off their oars or slowing their pace. Most turned inward to stare at Uncle Gunnar. Yngvar had been so lost in thought he had not heard anything.

"I'm going to see my uncle," he said to Thorfast. His friend, face flecked red, nodded. He seemed as if he had lost all of his blood, turning his already pale face to snow white.

Yngvar stumbled as the waves rocked the ship. The fog was thinner now but still clung to the sea. Everything smelled like blood and salt, and seagulls had begun to trail their ship. They were close to land, though Yngvar had lost all his bearing in their flight from the enemy. He wondered if instead of fleeing they had sailed directly onto the enemy's shore. Brandr would know. But now he knelt beside his cousin, who was holding his father's stump. He leaned over Uncle Gunnar's face, head turned so that Gunnar could speak directly to his ear. Yngvar leaned forward to get a better look at Uncle Gunnar's wound.

His old hand remained clamped to the puncture in his side. Dark blood seeped steadily into a thick pool beneath him. Gunnar's face had aged thirty years. His eyes were rheumy and sunken and his cheeks were hollow. His lips were blue and his teeth were yellow with bloodstains. He gave Yngvar a weak smile.

"Yngvar, come closer. Where's Bjorn? Bring him to me."

Calling Bjorn over, he saw other men converging on them. Brandr whirled on them. "Get back to your oars. We're not stopping."

"He's our oath-holder. We've a right to see him." The man who challenged Brandr cast his shadow over all of them. Yngvar looked up into the face of Bregthor Vandradsson. Seeing him up close, Bregthor had a drifting left eye that made his gaze challenging to meet.

"Get back," Brandr shouted. "Give a dying man his time."

Bregthor leaned back and muttered as he turned aside. "No comfort for the others dying on this ship."

The words struck Yngvar like a slap. He glanced again at Uncle Gunnar's wound. It was deep and just beneath his ribs. The spear had been thrust up, and so doubtlessly had slipped behind the rib cage to cut his vitals. Across the deck, four other bodies of their crew were sprawled out. The enemy dead were mingled with them.

In the time it took for Yngvar to take all of this in, Bjorn had come to Uncle Gunnar's side.

"I'm sorry your first adventure did not have a happier ending." Gunnar began to cough, blood spraying his reddened beard. "But you are men now, yes? You've sailed with Gunnar the Black on his final journey. You saved his crew with quick wit and bravery. You are heroes."

"It doesn't feel like I did anything," Yngvar said. "I never drew blood. I let another man die to save myself."

Gunnar's laughter gurgled in his throat. "If one day you will lead men, learn to accept you will kill many of them. Sometimes lives must be sacrificed for the benefit of others."

"It was to save myself alone," Yngvar said. He did not want to feel better about Bresi's death. "I should've died with him."

Gunnar closed his eyes and swallowed. He remained breathing heavily as if asleep until Yngvar wondered if his uncle had passed out. Then Gunnar's eyes opened once more.

"I have been dying for a long time now," Gunnar said.

"Father, don't ..."

"They should know, Brandr." Gunnar's words were followed again by more violent coughing. After it subsided he looked at Yngvar with sad eyes. "I have hidden it as long as I could, but others began to suspect my weakness. When you arrived I had already been long considering how I should spend the last days of my life. A hero does not die in his bed, but yet it seemed so it would be. Your plea to find adventure and your gift of the sax put the whole plan together in my mind. I thought to sail in search of a worthy enemy. Not a dirty Frank or a half-breed Dane. I wanted to come north again, to the land of my ancestors, and find real warriors worthy of claiming my life. I thought it would give you the adventure you sought and along the way we might find treasure worth taking."

Yngvar glanced at Bjorn, who looked to him as if expecting an interpretation. Instead he turned to Brandr, who continued to hold the stump of his father's hand and stare expressionless at him. Yngvar licked his lips.

"So Grandfather left no buried treasure?"

Gunnar closed his eyes. "None that I know. It was foolish of me to lie, of course, but I was not going to live long. Nothing motivates men to action like the promise of gold."

"What did he say?" Bregthor's voice roared out behind them, and Brandr sprung up with a snarl.

"I told you to get back to your oar," he shoved his chest into Bregthor's. Yngvar did not watch them, but crawled closer to his uncle.

"It's all right," he said. "We will find other treasures."

Gunnar's smile barely held on his lips, falling away as he gasped. "I am so cold. You two, my nephews, tell your fathers I am sorry we were all not closer in the end. It seems foolish now. Yngvar, your father extended the hazel branch to me and I pushed it aside. Tell him I was the fool. Tell him I love him as my brother and I will be waiting in the feasting hall with our father. I will embrace him there and we shall never quarrel again. You'll do that for me?"

"Of course I will," Yngvar took Gunnar's cold, blood-slicked hand from holding his wound closed and put it on his chest. Then he drew his uncle's sax, the same one he had gifted him days ago. "Hold this sword as you go to Valhalla."

Gunnar nodded, putting his trembling hand on the hilt. "Where is my son?"

Behind them, Brandr had finished screaming the crew into submission. Bregthor was seated now, but stared hatefully at everyone.

"Your father wants you," Yngvar called. "Hurry."

Brandr rushed to kneel beside Gunnar, but his father's eyes were already staring into another world. Blood dribbled from the corners of his mouth, and his labored breathing had stopped. Brandr put his ear to his father's chest, closed his eyes, then sat upright. He brushed his father's lids closed.

Gunnar the Black, son of Ulfrik and Runa the Bloody, had gone on to the great feasting hall of Valhalla where he would celebrate with all the great heroes until the end of days.

"I'm sorry," Yngvar said. His words sounded like thunder in the silence. Only creaking boards and complaining gulls gave any sound.

Brandr shook his head. "He died as he wished. Not every man can make such a choice."

Bjorn had retrieved a brown cloak from the deck, one with the least blood upon it. He extended it to Brandr, who then laid it over his father's body. The deck creaked and the waves thumped the hull, but nothing else made a sound, not even the gulls that had followed them. The birds had vanished.

After a thoughtful silence, Brandr went to the prow of the ship. He stared into the fog before turning on the crew. "My father has passed on to Valhalla. Your oaths to him are fulfilled. For now, I lead this crew and I claim my father's lands and property. You all know he has left them to me. Does anyone dispute this?"

Yngvar shook his head, as if his opinion mattered in the least. He was mesmerized with Brandr's commanding presence. His cousin's hard gaze withered anyone who challenged it. Even Bregthor, who Yngvar guessed would oppose him, turned aside. Brandr folded his arms to finalize his claim.

"When we return home, I will hear oaths of loyalty from anyone who wishes to remain with me. You are free to choose who you will serve. But for now, as crew of my ship, you answer to my commands. I'm not confident we have shaken our enemy. Those were not raiders but hirdmen of some Norse jarl. I did not note their standard, but they flew one from their mast. They will bring more men seeking vengeance. So we will not stop rowing. We sail through the night in shifts. I'll organize the groups, but for now take care of our wounded and break out the beer. We've earned a rest."

The men shifted on their benches, secured their oars, and started to stand. Brandr called out to Yngvar before everyone dispersed.

"We've got your wits to thank for our lives today. Crippling their ship was both wise and an act of great bravery." From his burly arm,

Brandr worked free a silver armband. He held it up for all to see. "You earned this today. Let no one deny it."

The crew mumbled agreement and several clapped his back. Yngvar accepted the band from Brandr with both hands, amazed at the warm, blood-flecked silver band resting in his palm.

"You did well, cousin," Brandr said with a smile. "Wear it with pride. Also, put your young strength to work on the oars. You'll get us through to the night."

Yngvar rowed with Thorfast and Bjorn in his group. Bjorn remained thoughtfully quiet while Thorfast chattered endlessly about Yngvar's achievement. He wanted to silence Thorfast, to tell him that his achievement succeeded only because Bresi had sacrificed himself. Also, had Thorfast not noticed Uncle Gunnar had died? His corpse remained shrouded beside three others at the center of the deck. Could he not be silent long enough to respect the dead? But Yngvar did not voice his thoughts and continued to row.

By nightfall every muscle of his back and shoulders burned. Even Bjorn, as strong as a bear, or so he claimed, stretched out on the deck when his shift ended. They had their sealskin sleep sacks in a single chest and pulled them out to bed down for the night.

"It was an amazing day," Thorfast said. "What do you suppose tomorrow will bring? Are we close to home?"

"Can't be close to home," Bjorn said. "Took us how many days to get here? Can't row back in one go. Where are we, anyway?"

Yngvar ignored both of them as they continued to chatter. As he pulled the sleep sack up to his neck, he peered at Brandr. He remained on the tiller, working it effortlessly even as the seas roughened. The deck swayed and rocked, and the creaks and pops were loud against his ears as he drifted to sleep, exhausted.

He awakened again after what must have been hours.

The deck was all blue light from the moon above. Dark lumps that gently rose and fell were strewn across the deck. The hum of snoring competed with the sound of the wind filling the sails. Yngvar blinked away his sleep, eyes throbbing in protest as he awakened. No one rowed now that the sails propelled them. Yngvar guessed Brandr had let everyone sleep once the wind turned favorable.

Twisting his head toward the tiller, he saw Brandr's silhouette leaning over it and staring out to sea. The fog and clouds has vanished to reveal stars floating through the dark. Yngvar thought to join his cousin, but then let his head settle back to the deck. He had just lost his father. He deserved some peace and time to reflect. With this surly crew, he would need to be rested. As the day had progressed, Yngvar overheard grumbles about being cheated of treasure. Some felt Brandr would make good, others thought the cost in lives had been a foolish waste that could never be repaid. Yngvar was in between. The men had died gloriously and guaranteed a seat in Valhalla, but ultimately they were pursuing nothing on this journey to Norway.

As he watched, something stirred in the deep shadows of the gunwales. At first Yngvar considered it a trick of the night. Rigging swayed and cast strange patterns over the deck. Perhaps that was all he had noted. Then a human shape emerged, followed by another.

Swift as lightning, the two men each seized Brandr by a leg and threw him overboard.

His cry was brief and faded with the dim splash that receded as fast as the ship sped over the waves.

The two figures circled about, and in the sharp blue light Bregthor Vandradsson revealed himself.

Yngvar started to scramble to his feet, but a hand restrained him.

Thorfast stared at him, eyes wide and gleaming with fear. His hair was white in the stark light of the moon as he shook his head.

He fought to rise, but Thorfast tugged him down again, his arm extending from the sleep sack. His whisper was harsh but low.

"Do you want to join Brandr? They'll kill us both."

Yngvar stared at Thorfast, then checked on Bregthor and his accomplice. Both seemed satisfied they had not been caught and returned to the darkness. The tiller remained tied to the course Brandr had set.

"We can defeat them," Yngvar whispered back. "Wake Bjorn."

Thorfast shook his head, and withdrew his arm back into his sleep sack. Yngvar also fell silent as Bregthor and his shadowy companion walked among the sleeping men. Blue light flashed from their drawn swords as they carefully stepped between sleeping bodies, peering down at each man.

Yngvar ducked his head into the sack, and bit his lip as the footfalls drew nearer.

11

Yngvar held his breath as either Bregthor or his murderous accomplice hung over him. His side tingled with the imagined plunge of a sword into his body. In the black of the sleep sack, where all smelled of his own sweat and wet breath, he waited until the footfalls continued past. He remained hidden a long time, constantly reimagining Brandr's black shape in the blue moonlight. He heard the faint splash of water a hundred times before he peeked out of the sack again.

No one stirred on the deck. The whole crew was asleep now. Had Brandr not set anyone to help him? Even if he had been fine to take the tiller, he would have had a second man with him. If Bregthor had not killed that man, Yngvar thought, then whoever had remained to aid Brandr was a traitor as well.

Yngvar met Thorfast's eyes in the indigo darkness. His whites were as bright as his hair. The two remained still and staring at each other until dawn began to stain the horizon. Yngvar repeated Brandr's murder over and over in his memory. Filthy Bregthor would try to cover up his crime, but Yngvar and Thorfast had witnessed it. He would not cheat justice. Yngvar just needed dawn to come, when he would enjoy the safety of numbers to support him.

As the first men stirred, Yngvar was quick to sit up. Again, Thorfast pulled him down, daring a louder whisper.

"Don't be the one to discover this. Let another do it or Bregthor will suspect you."

"I don't care," Yngvar hissed back. "He murdered my cousin."

"And he'll murder us when he finds out we know," Thorfast said. "When we get home, we can tell your father what happened. He will avenge his brother. Don't risk our lives."

Their harshly whispered exchange seemed to awaken others close to them. Though Bjorn was close enough to touch, he remained on his back with his mouth open and snoring.

The first men to discover the ship had been drifting were those closest to the tiller. Yngvar narrowed his eyes at Bregthor, who was among the small number of men gathering at the steering board.

"Awaken!" shouted one of the men. "Brandr is missing!"

The news seeped across the deck, rousing men in small groups from their weary slumber. Yngvar kicked at Bjorn, who rolled over with a snort. "Go away."

Yngvar pulled him out of the sleep sack and rolled Bjorn onto his back. He pulled his cousin's eyelids open. "Brandr was murdered last night. Bregthor and another threw him overboard."

Bjorn pulled Yngvar's hands from his eyes, then blinked at him as if he had not understood. The moment those eyes widened in comprehension, Yngvar clasped his hand over Bjorn's mouth.

"Don't say or do anything until we know what's going on," Yngvar said, leaning close to Bjorn's face. "We don't know who is on our side yet."

Nodding agreement, Yngvar let his hand off Bjorn's mouth. Thorfast, now also standing, tipped his head in agreement with Yngvar. He had said the words but did not feel them in his heart. He stared over his shoulder at Bregthor pantomiming how Brandr must've fallen overboard. Yngvar realized silence was prudent, but more than anything he burned to stick a dagger through Bregthor's neck and toss him overboard. Let him drown in his own blood.

"He must've drunk too much," said one man. "Probably leaned overboard to puke and then a wave took him. I've seen it before."

"He didn't drink anything," countered another.

"Could've been a swell that knocked him off balance," offered another.

Yngvar now joined the crowd at the steering board. He noted how Bregthor had draped himself across the tiller as if assuming possession of the ship. He couldn't help but glare at him, and lazy-eyed Bregthor straightened his back at the challenge.

"What happened?" he asked. To his own ears, the falseness of his question was plain. Yet many men cast him a condolent smile.

"Brandr must've fallen overboard," said one man with a thick red scar beneath his left eye. "I'm sorry, boy. You lost two kin in one day."

"How did it happen?" Yngvar's question was flat, and several of the crew glanced at him with raised brows. He didn't care if they wondered at his reaction.

"No one knows," Bregthor said. "Best guess is he either leaned too far over the rails and fell or a swell caused him to stumble overboard."

Staring at Bregthor, Yngvar held his question until he felt every eye upon him. "Why do we have to guess? Surely Brandr would not have steered all alone. Who was with him?"

This caused a stir among the crew. They were too surprised or sleepy to have thought this through. Yngvar, however, had been brooding for hours. Soon men were turning to the shorter man at Bregthor's left. His eyes protruded like a fish and his scraggly hair was the color of iron. Yngvar noted he seemed as trustworthy as a viper, and the cords protruding from his neck only enhanced his cold-blooded appearance. Whatever this person said would be a lie.

"Davin, you were to tend the rigging," said the man with the red scar. "What happened?"

Davin, his bulging eyes suddenly jittering as if he searched for an escape, only let his mouth open.

So here was the second man who had followed Bregthor around the deck looking for witnesses to silence.

"I was exhausted like all of you," Davin said, finding his story. "I dozed off. That's when Brandr must've fallen overboard, otherwise he'd have woke me."

"I didn't know my cousin for long, but he didn't seem the type to let anyone doze off. He gave me this armband then put me on an oar. No time for me to doze off."

Bregthor now stepped from behind the tiller to face Yngvar. His gaze was unfocused but no less furious for it. "What are you saying? Are you accusing Davin of throwing Brandr overboard?"

Yngvar could not keep his smile down. "I wasn't speaking to you, Bregthor. Nor did I accuse anyone of such a heartless murder. Do you think my cousin was murdered? No one else has said anything about murder."

That was the step over the threshold Yngvar should not have taken. The fury in Bregthor's face drained away. He stepped back and let his tensed arms relax at his side. Behind his unfocused, black eyes there seemed a growing comprehension that he and Yngvar were going to be enemies. Yngvar had essentially admitted to witnessing the murder. He regretted this, glancing at Bjorn who had dutifully restrained himself. Gods know keeping his mouth shut must have been a colossal battle waged across his raging heart. Yet Yngvar had been the one to give away their safety.

"I'm sorry," Bregthor said. "I'm as shocked and tired as everyone else. I misspoke. Davin is a good friend, and I took offense too easily. You'll forgive me?"

"Of course." Yngvar had to speak the words, but in his heart he added forgiveness will come when Bregthor is drowned in a bucket of horse piss.

"Friends, no one can know what happened to Brandr." Thorfast now stepped before Bregthor, addressing the wider crew. "That secret has gone to the sea grave with him. It is a tremendous loss for all of us. But it must have been the time the Fates had set for him, and we mortals can do nothing about it. Let us remember him well and as the man who guided us away from our enemies. Now, we have the dead to attend. We've many days at sea ahead of us, and that's if Thor is as kind to us as he was for the journey north."

"Well spoken," said the man with the red scar. "Wisdom from one so young."

"Does anyone know where we are?" asked one man from the edge of the gathered crew. "We are not headed south, not as I reckon."

Heads turned toward the sun at the horizon, which was now fat and orange over a clear sky. The winds had shifted again, and with the tiller tied in place it now seemed they had been pushed onto a western course. The seas rippled morning light over the waves in the gentle wind.

"We can get back on course," said another man. "But we're at least a day off in good weather, more if it turns against us. We have to bury our fellows at sea."

The crew called out their agreement. Yngvar went along with them and tried to ignore Bregthor. Yet he could not help notice that of the remaining crew, a large number of them seemed to congregate by Bregthor. Yngvar tried to tell himself this meant nothing. But their glances at each other were too reserved to be coincidental. Where others were trying to console each other with a promising word, a smile, or a laugh, these men seemed to be calculating something.

Yngvar's mood worsened as it seemed of the twenty or so men left, these silent men around Bregthor were the majority. Well, of course they would be. Bregthor and his cronies would've hid at the back of any fight. So they would survive. The sincerest and bravest would've thrown themselves into the enemy and therefore more of them would've died.

"Good work," Bjorn said to Thorfast. Yngvar's face heated up. It was quite a thing when Bjorn could chastise him for speaking out of turn, even if he did it indirectly.

"How's your dog bite?" Yngvar asked. "Healing up, I hope. We're going to need a strong fighting arm before this voyage is done."

Bjorn pulled off his bandage, which was now brown with splashed blood, and threw it on the deck. The bite was dark red and scabbed, all good signs of healing. Thorfast took Yngvar by the arm and led him from the dispersing crew.

"It's not as bad as you might think," he said. "Though you all but told Bregthor you saw him do it."

"I couldn't help it. He jumped right on the bait and nearly admitted it himself. Do you think anyone else suspects him?"

"How can I know what others think? Listen, you and Bjorn are the sons of great jarls. He's not going to risk killing you."

"Last night you were certain he'd kill us. Can't you make up your damn mind?"

Thorfast clucked his tongue. "Last night he could've killed anyone and covered it with lies. Today, if you and Bjorn die then he'll have a problem. The men will know Jarl Gunnar's family was targeted by someone. This is not a big boat. Someone is going to realize Bregthor's evil, and then he'll have to kill most of the crew to silence them. But that won't happen, will it? He'd be risking his own life in a straight up fight. So even if he kills you and never returns to Frankia, when your father eventually learns what happened he will have revenge. Your father could pay handsomely for Bregthor's head. So he's better off letting you live."

"You assume he's not a fool," Yngvar said.

Thorfast smirked. "I assumed as much about you, and look what that has gained me?"

Yngvar rebuffed the kidding with a wave of his hand. He went to crouch beside Uncle Gunnar's shrouded corpse. He pulled back the cloak to place his hand on his uncle's frigid arm. It was like touching cold, wet wax. Gunnar's hand was clamped to the small sax. The green gem on the pommel blinked at Yngvar, as if it invited him to take the sword. The idea lingered and he felt deep shame for thinking it. He had gifted it to his uncle. To take it back ... yet he wanted it. Somehow he felt the sword would be better in his hand than in a dead man's at the bottom of the ocean.

The sword came free after three hard tugs. Two men watched him without comment. Yngvar now drew Gunnar's own sword and replaced it in his uncle's frozen grip. All the while he kept the face covered.

"You want me to take this," he said to the corpse. "I don't know why I know this, but I feel it in my blood. I will wield it with honor and gather glory to our family with it. Thank you, Uncle."

He replaced the sword in its scabbard. He would have to oil and sharpen it soon, since it had sat exposed all night with only a cloak to protect it.

No one challenged him when he took the sax, which now rested across his lap like any other man's short sword. Bjorn simply glanced at it and returned to brooding atop his sea chest. Thorfast raised his brow and smiled. The morning passed as men resumed control of the ship and set a new course.

Yngvar realized he should've been more active in this, but he chose to let it pass. Bregthor and his men seemed content to handle the details. Well, no one could challenge that this ship belonged to his family and Bjorn's as well. Others had no right to it.

By late morning the bodies had been prepared for sea burial. Bjorn and Yngvar had attended their uncle's body, wrapping it in two cloaks and ensuring his hand remained wed to his sword. Four corpses in total, all wrapped tight in faded cloaks, were now laid on a board over the starboard railing.

"Someone should say something for these men," said the man with the red scar under his eyes. Friends spoke in turn for the three others, but when it came to Gunnar, eyes shifted to Yngvar and Bjorn. Bjorn's face reddened and he extended his palms toward Yngvar.

"I'll say a few things," Yngvar said. "I hardly knew my uncle. But I've heard the great stories. He overcame the loss of a hand to lead men as hard and demanding as you. He died as he lived, fighting on the deck of his ship. Whatever his mistakes, he was true to himself. He died in glory and has gone on to the feasting hall of Valhalla. He will be waiting for us there with my grandfather and cousin. Farewell, Gunnar the Black. We'll keep your memory alive in songs of your deeds."

Yngvar touched his uncle's wrapped hand a final time. Bjorn did the same. He had tears in his eyes, which shocked Yngvar. He hadn't known Uncle Gunnar any better, yet he seemed moved by his death. Bjorn just shook his head and stepped back.

Without further ceremony, Yngvar helped tip the board up so the bodies slid over the side. The splash of the water was unnaturally loud and haunted Yngvar with memories of last night.

Go find your son in the sea grave, he thought. Come back for revenge, Uncle. If anyone can, it must be Gunnar the Black.

Yet he knew to rely on a revenant to take revenge was foolish. That would have to be done by mortal hands.

"That's done," Bregthor said. "Now we have to decide on who leads this ship. I'm making my claim for it."

Yngvar's hands went cold. What had Bregthor said?

"Anyone opposed to it can save me the trouble and throw himself overboard now."

The crewmen that had seemed so skeptical and nervous now gathered around Bregthor. His lazy eye only enhanced the wickedness of his smile. He had the majority of men behind him. This was his play, to steal the ship? Did he expect the crew to do anything but rebel?

"You can't take the ship," said a weak voice from behind.

"Who says I can't?" Bregthor set his foot on the rail. "Jarl Gunnar lied to us about this treasure of his. He promised us wealth, and he led us into a trap that killed ten of our friends. All so he could die like he wanted. Fuck him! We claim this ship as our share of treasure. We earned it with our blood."

Bregthor's gaze settled on Yngvar, such as it could with only one eye to focus. His smile quivered like a worm, and Yngvar wanted to carve it off his lips.

"What do you say to that, boy? Unless you have something better to offer us on behalf of your lying family, we're taking this ship."

"You murdered Brandr. You and that snake, Davin. You fell upon him from behind and shoved him overboard. Then you walked the deck to make sure no witnessed you. I saw it all and so did Thorfast, you dog-fucking bastard!"

Bregthor's sword hissed from its scabbard, and he leapt forward with a roar.

12

Despite the indolent cast of Bregthor's drifting eye, he was much faster than it made him seem. Yngvar scrambled back over the deck, bumping into men that shouted as they stepped aside. He grasped the cold leather of the sword hilt at his lap and tore it free in a smooth pull.

The deck rocked and moaned with a sudden wave, causing Yngvar to spread his feet for stability. The same rocking put Bregthor off his strike. The air snapped beside Yngvar's ear as Bregthor's sword missed.

Yngvar's shorter sax, however, stabbed up beneath Bregthor's overstretched arm and drove at his gut.

But something hard caught his arm and the strike shuddered to a halt. The point dipped into Bregthor's chest, right beneath his sternum.

"Stop this!" A man dragged Yngvar backward, where more hands grabbed him. Surprisingly, Bregthor's men did the same. They intercepted him, pushing him back into their thick numbers with shouts to stop on both sides.

Thorfast wrestled with Bjorn, whose arm was folded across his body as he tried to draw his sword. Thorfast kept him pinned and off balance.

"You little bastard," Bregthor called. "You think I fear you because of your father? Where is he now? I'll gut you like the kitten you are."

Strong, hairy arms interlocked around Yngvar, holding him as tight as chains. "Everyone watch yourself around this liar or he'll slip you overboard like he did Brandr."

"Enough!" The man with the red scar beneath his eye now interposed himself between Bregthor and Yngvar. Most men fell silent, but Bjorn and Thorfast both collapsed to the deck in their struggle. Bjorn howled like an injured dog while Thorfast rolled around the deck to keep him restrained.

"Someone get those boys off each other," the scarred man said. "That's embarrassing."

"Who are you to give orders to me?" Bregthor shouted at the scarred man. "I've made my claim, and I'm the leader here. You want to challenge me, Ander?"

Ander held up a hand to Yngvar, his expression pleading for cooperation. Since he had seemed a reasonable man, Yngvar complied. He ceased struggling, though the strong hands on him did not relent. Ander then turned to Bregthor.

"I'm doing you a favor, you fool. You know who these boys are?"

Bregthor spit. "The pretty one is a dead man, that's sure enough. They're all turds, as far as I can see."

The cursing did not sit well with most of the crew, including those on Bregthor's own side. Someone behind Yngvar spoke up.

"They saved our lives. Without them, you'd have no ship to claim. You'd be dead or a slave."

The arms around Yngvar loosened, then pulled away. He stepped out, amazed that his short sword was still in hand. It seemed that Uncle Gunnar had left it for him to take vengeance for his son's murder. Yet Fate had decided otherwise. The scarred man, Ander, pointed at the sax.

"Put away your weapons, both of you. Let's hear Yngvar's claim again."

"It's lies!" Bregthor raised his sword, rather than put it down. Yet he paused, realizing that a dozen other men were reaching for their own. It made Yngvar's heart beat faster, and a brief smile lit his face. Bregthor shoved his blade back into its sheath.

Thorfast and Bjorn finally popped back up from the deck, both of their shirts pulled up and their hair disheveled. They were breathless and red-nosed, like two naughty boys caught fighting behind the mead hall. It made Yngvar smile even more.

"We'll hear your accusation again," Ander said. "Now tell us clearly and calmly what you saw."

Feeling confident he was about to get Bregthor nailed to the mast, he recounted everything he had seen. Ander and the rest of the crew remained quiet, each man staring into his own thoughts as Yngvar explained. When he was finished, Bregthor's face was as red as an ember and his mouth bent in a violent curve.

"And only your friend, Thorfast, saw this? Bjorn was asleep?" Ander pointed at Thorfast, who now, with his mussed hair and sniveling nose, looked far less respectable as a witness. "Did anyone else see this?"

Of course, no other man stepped forward. Yngvar had hoped another witness had been biding time for the right moment, but Fate had decided only he and Thorfast would witness the heinous deed.

Ander circled around but no one else came forward. At last he turned to Bregthor. "Your story, then?"

"There's not a fucking story! I was asleep and woke up to find him missing." Bregthor threw up his arms. "Do you want to know what I dreamed about?"

He drew a sycophantic chuckle from a handful of his own men, but Ander just shook his head. "And Davin? You've been accused as well."

The bulbous-eyed Davin stood up from where he had been squatting. "I fell asleep, like I said. That's my only crime, if it is one."

"But the two of us witnessed this," Yngvar said. "It doesn't matter that no one else did. What other proof do you need? We'd both swear it on our honor. Besides, why would I accuse two men I don't know?"

"Maybe you did it," Bregthor said. He stood straighter now, apparently pleased at discovering this twist. "You're in such a hurry to make me the murderer. Why is that? Can you prove you didn't shove Brandr overboard?"

Yngvar's mouth fell open but was unable to make a sound. He blinked at Thorfast, who returned his stunned look. At last he regained himself. "Me kill Brandr? Why would I do that?"

"To steal the ship, of course." Bregthor folded his arms as if he had just proved everything. "Brandr was taking you home. But you're trying to escape a marriage you don't want. You said it before everyone the night you arrived in Jarl Gunnar's hall. That's your reason to kill him. Take the ship and sail away from whatever hag your father picked for you."

Yngvar again blinked in utter shock, unable to think of what to say. Bjorn instead came to his defense. "That's stupid. Yngvar wouldn't murder our cousin. He's better than that."

"But he was ready to pit brother against brother to get his way," Bregthor said, tilting his head back. "Now that his situation has become desperate, who knows what he might do? Like he said, he hardly knew Brandr. And we hardly know Yngvar and Thorfast."

Heat radiated from Yngvar's cheeks into his eyes. He wished he had been more circumspect in stating his mind. His father had warned him that being forthright was admirable but oftentimes fatal. He was beginning to understand why.

"None of what you say changes the facts. You and Davin shoved Brandr overboard because you are greedy and plotted to seize this ship for yourself. Thorfast and I witnessed it."

"Two boys," Bregthor said. "You're not men yet. Your words count for nothing. Nor do I need to prove anything. I say you two murdered him."

"All right, this is pointless," Ander said. "Fact is Brandr is gone and there's no way to know who's telling the truth or not."

"You think I killed Brandr?" Yngvar grabbed Ander by the shoulder, who brushed his hand off.

"Bregthor makes a good case against you," Ander said, lowering his eyes. "But I'm willing to believe after saving us yesterday that you are telling the truth."

"I'll point out he was saving himself as well," Bregthor said. "Let's not give him more credit than he deserves."

"Let the gods decide who is telling the truth."

Yngvar did not see who spoke. The voice came from behind, small and hesitant.

The idea caught on with Ander, who smiled at the suggestion. "Yes, a duel to first blood. Whoever wins has the gods behind him."

"No, that's not what duels are for," Yngvar said.

"Of course they are," Bregthor said. "If you refuse, it must be due to your guilt."

"It's because you're stronger and more experienced than me," Yngvar said. "This is a foolish way to prove anything other than who is a better fighter."

"I'll be Yngvar's second," Bjorn said, slapping him on the back. Yngvar gave an astonished look to him.

"No," Ander said. "I will be Yngvar's second. That will make up for some of Bregthor's advantage in experience. This is a fine idea. The gods will judge who is truthful and we shall live with that judgment. We will take the first landfall we can find to hold the duel."

Bjorn patted Yngvar's back. "Let the gods decide, then we can't lose because you're telling the truth."

"The gods have their own plans," Yngvar said, turning in disgust from the satisfied crew. "They care not for justice, but only their entertainment. Isn't that what grandfather was supposed to have said?"

"It is," Bjorn said. "And according to what your father has said, if we entertain them well they will favor us. So this can't go wrong."

The rest of the day Yngvar sat apart from the others with only Thorfast and Bjorn for company. He rubbed the silver armband on his left bicep, unable to imagine that yesterday he had been lauded by these same men as a hero. Now he got dark looks from others, as if he had slit Brandr's throat in front of them.

"I think you are too quick to give out nicknames," Thorfast said. "You should really be called the silent and not me."

"Now's not the time," Yngvar said, turning to watch the ocean slipping past. The crew did the work of rowing and steering, and while he was under suspicion he declined to aid them. They asked nothing of him, either. A gull appeared in the sky as a black dot. Landfall would be nearby. The men called to each other against the wind, and he leaned to the side as the ship turned.

"Try to cut the back of his hand or his brow," Thorfast said. "You just need first blood to drip upon the mat. Either of those spots bleed a lot, and if you get him sweating the blood will fall faster."

"He won't be sweating," Yngvar said, resting his chin on his fist. "We're just going to stand there and hack at each other. This is foolish."

"He'll be sweating," Bjorn said. "He knows what he's done. The gods will punish him."

Landfall came too soon, and Yngvar found himself on an uninhabited island of dark pine trees and dirt. The grass was lush and green, and they had a long search for a flat patch of dirt. When they found it, men began to mark the square boundaries by carving into the ground with sticks. The sail was taken out and folded into a square, then laid down with stones to hold it.

He had seen a duel once, but had not paid much attention to the protocol. This was a holmgang, a duel with specific rules he was sure none of this lot understood clearly. Their dueling ring looked nothing like he remembered. Ander Red-Scar, as Yngvar had begun thinking of him, oversaw the preparations to the final detail. Yngvar avoided looking at Bregthor, who had selected a young, wiry man with hair as light as Thorfast's to be his second. The two of them leaned into each other as they spoke, probably deciding how to cheat.

At last Yngvar was summoned to the duel. The sun was low, casting deep and long shadows from the nearby pine trees. Birds were singing gleefully as their day ended, but Yngvar thought only of what was to come. Bregthor and his second waited at their side of the dueling area, a pile of three shields stacked by their feet. Yngvar had a similar pile by his.

Ander nodded to him as he retrieved the shield. "Strike true, boy. Make him bleed."

Yngvar expected a ceremony or grand words. But instead, both he and Bregthor came to the center of the mat. Each had both hands wrapped around their swords. Each of their seconds selected one of the three shields and held these up to block.

Bregthor swept his lazy gaze over Yngvar and sneered. "You know the rules? If you step outside the cloth you forfeit. When your shields are gone, you must block by sword alone and your second steps aside. You can only use whatever weapon you've taken to the ring. Whoever drips first blood on the cloth loses. I won't bother with the rest, since this won't take long."

He struck with sudden force, but Ander slammed the sword aside. Yngvar hesitated, unsure that the duel had begun. Bjorn roared his name from the edge of the ring, and all the crew started calling for their favorites.

"Don't give him a moment to gather himself," Ander said. "Keep this fast. Break all his shields if you can."

He swiped hard at Bregthor's smirking face, and the light-haired second easily knocked aside his blow. Bregthor's return strike came over head as if he planned to split Yngvar like a log. Ander used both hands to brace the shield, easily stopping the strike. However, the shield wood thudded and cracked, and a plank fell out, rendering it useless. Ander threw it aside to grab another.

Yngvar struck low, hoping he would pull Bregthor's second out of position. The shield slammed down, but Yngvar could not reverse his strike with any conviction, all his power being dispersed in the block.

They traded exchanges like this, circling, hacking, grunting with each alternating strike. Ander caught Bregthor's sword in the second shield and tried to bend it before Bregthor's second knocked it free. Some men called it cheating and hissed, but Bregthor did not pause.

Yngvar's shoulders burned with the effort of holding up his sword, worsened by all the recent rowing he had done. He was simply not used to this. Bregthor, however, was smiling. His first shield endured, but the wood of Ander's second shield rattled and shivered as if ready to fall apart.

When Ander screamed out as Bregthor shattered the second shield, he followed up with a fast strike. Rather than slash, he stabbed in under the shield Bregthor's second hastily threw in front of him. He aimed for Bregthor's exposed thigh, just above the knee. He felt the flesh give and heard Bregthor shout.

They paused, for Bregthor's knee now ran with blood down his shin. If he stepped, he would certainly drip blood onto the cloth. Yngvar was about to shout in victory.

Bregthor's second crowded Ander, interfering with raising his shield. Yngvar saw a flash of white slash at his face and he yanked his head back as Ander batted away the strike with the rim of his shield.

He felt the hot sear of a line drawn over his left brow. Warm blood ran into his eye socket.

"Watch carefully now," shouted one of the onlookers. "Blood will fall soon."

Yngvar's eyes blinked uncontrollably as the superficial cut steadily ran blood into his eye. He was slick with sweat from the unexpected effort of this duel. It was his turn to strike.

"Try to go easily," Ander said to him. "He may drip blood before you, but not if you are too vigorous."

He gave a lazy stab that drew angry shouts from some. He barely tapped the shield. Bregthor did the same, and Ander shoved the sword aside.

Yngvar watched the cut on Bregthor's knee slow. It was also a marginal cut, and the blood ran down into his doeskin boots.

He, however, felt blood dangling from his chin.

The drip pattering on the cloth was as loud as a boulder falling into the sea.

"I win," Bregthor said, stepping back to embrace his second. "The gods have sided with me."

Yngvar blinked, looking down at the two spots of blood that had splashed at his feet. He spoke softly to Ander. "I saw him do it. He and Davin threw Brandr overboard. This proves nothing."

Ander seemed ready to agree, but as Bregthor drew closer and shouted his victory to everyone, he shook his head. "The gods have sided with Bregthor."

Thorfast and Bjorn rushed to his side. Thorfast dabbed at his brow with the cuff of his shirt. "This is not fair."

"You want to argue with the gods?" Bregthor said, snatching

Yngvar away by the shoulder. "You've lost. You killed Brandr and tried to blame me for it. Now you get what you've earned."

Yngvar wiped out the blood from his eye and pulled out of Bregthor's grip. He had not put down his sword. If Bregthor and the others thought to have so-called justice for Brandr, he was going to kill as many of them as he could before he died.

Bregthor's crooked gaze settled on Yngvar's sword and his smile widened.

13

Bjorn stood shoulder to shoulder with Yngvar against Bregthor and the crowd at his back. Yngvar felt a swell of pride as his cousin gave him a slight nod and settled his hand upon his sword. His sparse beard no longer made him look so young. He simply appeared fierce in the low light of the day. On this empty island of pines and chattering seabirds they would die together if such was Fate's plan. The wind whipped the grass toward the sea, and the dark shape of their long ship on the beach was visible over Bjorn's shoulder.

"Hold on," Thorfast said, moving between them and Bregthor. "A holmgang is to settle disputes between two parties. You were aggrieved by our accusations."

"By the truth," Bjorn shouted, causing Thorfast to pause and wince.

"No matter, you have won the duel and can now settle your grievance. You cannot demand justice for Brandr's death, for his murder and the murderer have not been proved to everyone's satisfaction."

"The gods have shown I speak the truth," Bregthor said. He spoke patiently, as if Thorfast was as child, but his drifting eyes flashed anger. "You and Yngvar are his killers and have tried to lay the blame on me."

Snatching up Thorfast's lead, Yngvar stepped forward. "If the gods have shown anything, it is that they desire to support your version of the story. I've no idea what the gods plan in this. It is the work of Loki, if ever there was. But a spot of blood on the cloth does not make me Brandr's killer."

This dampened the crew's bloodlust, as many of the erstwhile fervent supporters of the duel now scratched their heads. Even Ander, the originator of the duel, stared at the grass and probed his cheek with his tongue. Yngvar continued to build on their doubts.

"So what will you do now? Hang me and Thorfast from a tree? Will you abandon us to starvation or slavery? What do you plan to tell my father when you return home? Would you accuse his son of murdering his nephew, and then tell him you killed me or stranded me to die slowly? Have you considered you'll never return home if that's the news you bring? If you believe Bregthor over me, then return me to my father for trial by the whole community. That is what's right."

"I agree," Ander said. "Let him be judged by his own family."

"I won the holmgang!" Bregthor's face was now dark red and his teeth flashed in the low light.

"So you won the ship as compensation," Yngvar said. "You defeated me, and by rights I am to pay you in silver. I have only this armband, but I suppose you would like the ship better. As this was my uncle and cousin's ship, by rights it should stay with the family. My father would claim it, and he would gladly deliver it to you if it meant ending this nonsense and getting everyone home. Take the ship. You'll have no argument from anyone."

Yngvar had been over-generous but could think of nothing else to assuage Bregthor. His lazy gaze grew distant as he considered the offer, and his cronies looked on. Of course he had wanted the ship all along, and to give it over under the pretense of legality must have appeal. Yngvar was not certain the ship was his to give away.

"If that is your offer, then I accept."

"The offer comes with one condition that you must swear before everyone on your honor."

"I won the holmgang!" Bregthor shouted again. "There are no conditions."

"Well, then you can have this armband as compensation. It is enough, considering your innocence is in more doubt than mine. I at least have a witness to my claims. The ship remains mine." He began to remove his armband, deliberately taking his time so Bregthor would have an opening to change his mind. He did not disappoint.

"You little bastard," he said. "What is your condition?"

"You will take me, Bjorn, and Thorfast directly home and guarantee our safety to the best of your ability. Anyone wishing to return with us, you will let return as well. Then you can take this ship and sail for whatever glory you might find. Will you swear to this on your honor?"

Bregthor's indistinct gaze seemed to sharpen, as if he were straining to detect the trap in the offer. Yngvar had set no trap, other than he was certain between his own father and Bjorn's father, Aren, they could catch Bregthor again before leaving the Seine for the open sea. He would pass through Rouen, right under Uncle Aren's nose. Both of them had the ear and lifelong friendship of Jarl Vilhjalmer Longsword who was sworn to the King of Frankia himself. Bregthor could not sail fast enough to escape.

"I do swear," he said. "May the gods forgive me for letting this murderous pair flee justice, but I see no way to prove what I know you have done. Let us be done with each other."

Ander gave a slow nod to Yngvar, as if he was unsure of what had just transpired. Most of the honest crew seemed mollified at the settlement, yet Bregthor's men began to grumble. Davin, his fish-eyed accomplice, spared no shame in airing his own quarrel with the outcome.

"The ship was to be compensation to all of us for the lies Jarl Gunnar forced us to accept." He ran both his gnarled hands through his iron gray hair as he yelled. "You can't just take it. What are you going to do for the rest of us? I didn't help—"

"I hear you," Bregthor said, cutting off Davin. Yngvar had leaned forward expecting Davin to reveal his part in Brandr's murder. Bregthor had likely expected the same, and now pulled his lap-dog to heel. "Truth is we can't always have all we want. The ship is mine now, and I'm satisfied with it. For the rest of you, though, your loss is still real. I will need a crew for my ship, and to attract a crew I need gold. So, we are off course to the west of where we want to be to return home. There are rich islands to the west, the Hebrides. We shall raid there and take all Jarl Gunnar had led us to believe we would earn. For my part, unless we stumble upon great treasure in excess of the value of this ship, I will take no share. It will all be divided evenly among you."

The men raised their fists and shouted their agreement. Thorfast began shouting over them, but Yngvar could not hear his complaint.

Bregthor turned to the three of them, sneering at Thorfast. "You've got something to say to this?"

"You just swore to protect us," Thorfast said. "And to take us home. Yet you're taking us miles out of the way and possibly endangering us as well."

Bregthor leaned back and laughed, joined by almost all the crew. He had both hands over his gut as he recovered. "Weren't you just crying in Jarl Gunnar's hall about going on a raid? Well, here's your chance and you're afraid of getting hurt. Don't worry, little boys, I will keep you safe at my side if you're that cowardly."

"We're not afraid," Bjorn said, his brow drawing tight. "You've sworn to take us home, that's all."

"And I will," Bregthor said, spreading his arms wide. "I'm not an oath-breaker. I just never said when I'd take you home, and you never specified a time."

"I said to go directly home," Yngvar said. He now stood between Thorfast and Bjorn, his heart beating faster. He had left Bregthor a crack to slip through. He should've realized such a worm would have no troubles using such a low gap to flee. "You are twisting words."

"That did not mean time, but the path to take. When the day comes to return to Frankia, I will go directly there. Never fear, Bregthor keeps his word."

Yngvar and Thorfast looked at each other, then to Ander Red-Scar. He shrugged as if this were no longer his problem. Not all of the crew seemed at ease with the indefinite plans. Some leaned into each other to speak hushed words. It did nothing for Yngvar now. The majority of the crew had been raised to the prospect of plunder once more, and Bregthor fanned that enthusiasm.

"Come now, boys," he slapped Bjorn on the back, who yanked back with a snarl. "You were so brave the other day. Surely you want a taste of raiding before going home to hide behind your fathers once more. We will not leave those islands without the riches we deserve. There are good churches there, I'll wager. Where there are churches there is gold, plenty of gold for all."

The men cheered and Bregthor dismissed Yngvar with a wave of his hand.

Blood still seeped from his cut brow, and Yngvar wiped it away with the back of his arm. Thorfast and Bjorn folded in with him, the three of them huddling together.

"I thought it was a great plan," Bjorn said. "Until he gave us that shit about not picking a time to return."

"It's my fault," Yngvar said. "I should not have left him the room I did."

Thorfast clucked his tongue. "He's bending your words like a hot iron rod. Besides, he can't keep us at sea forever. We're not provisioned for it, and we're not strong enough to stay at sea alone. He has to keep moving or someone will learn a lone ship is operating nearby, then we'll become prey."

"He'll have to take us home," Yngvar said. "Or he'll be an oathbreaker, and no man will follow him then. I just wish I had been more direct. What's my problem? I say too much when I should say little and then say half as much as I should when more is needed."

His companions looked at each other, then Bjorn smiled. "I guess that means you're stupid. Try to be smarter."

They all laughed, putting their arms around each other's shoulders. Yngvar hung his head in shame. "I swear to you, I will be. Until then, I'll rely on you two to carry us through my mistakes."

"It seems you're resigned to marrying Jarl Flosi's daughter," Thorfast said.

"I'll worry about that later. We must escape Bregthor's grasp as soon as possible. Getting home without slit necks is the goal now."

Thorfast shrugged as if the possibility was a detail. "We did want to raid. Our leader is a deceitful, murderous snake, but otherwise this was what we have been seeking."

Yngvar thought of Bresi dying under hacking, bloodied swords. He gave a wan smile. "We've no choice but to go along. Once we find enough plunder to satisfy the crew, we will push hard to return home."

"Comforting your friend after his loss?"

Bregthor appeared with his wiry second and fish-eyed Davin. All of them wore smug smiles and pushed into their midst with careless ease.

"Get axes from the ship and collect us firewood for tonight," he said. "We're making camp here and sailing at dawn. You three are going to stay close to me, since I've got to protect you."

Yngvar glanced around. The rest of the crew were dispersing to their tasks or in conversation. He narrowed his eyes at Bregthor. "All of us know you murdered Brandr. I expect you've got a dagger planned to slip between all our ribs. But unless you kill everyone on this ship, word will get back to my father and you'll have nowhere to hide."

Bregthor chuckled. "Again with your father. You've made your point, boy. And I didn't kill Brandr, no matter what you say. I'll take you home, as I promised. But until then you and I are going to be close, and you're going to work hard."

He leaned in, turning his head like hawk sizing up its prey so that one of his eyes met Yngvar's. "You're going to work hard enough to wish you were dead."

14

Yngvar kicked the door open with the heel of his foot. The bar gave way with a crack and the flimsy boards shattered. The gray wood collapsed into the darkness of the shack. He didn't hesitate to charge inside, sword and shield at the ready. All around him women were screaming. Such a small village yet they raised a noise like an army being drowned in a thunder storm.

More screams met him inside the house.

"Did all the men run off and leave the women to defend the village?"

He lowered his sword, but not his shield. A thin woman with dark circles under sunken eyes and fly-away brown hair stood before her young daughter. She flung something at him, which he knocked aside with his shield. The shack was so small that whatever struck his shield thumped into the packed dirt wall to his left.

"Come on out," he said. He was not screaming like everyone else. The rest of Bregthor's crew ran through the village as if assaulting the walls of Paris, shouting and waving their swords. There could not have been more than a dozen buildings here, and one had collapsed long ago into a mushy pile of rotted thatch and earth.

The woman screamed something in her strange language, then picked up something from the table at her side. She flung it at him, an earthenware mug. It broke over his shield again, probably her most priceless possession.

"What's taking so long?" Davin poked his sweaty face inside. His bulging eyes roamed the small space until he saw the woman, and then he smiled. "Thought to have something for yourself, did you? Well, no taking prizes until we've all seen the loot."

He barged past Yngvar toward the woman. She slapped at him wildly, but he bashed her on the head with the hilt of his sword. The girl behind her screamed as the mother crumpled, either dead or unconscious.

"Take the brat," Davin said. "We've got everything else collected outside. We're waiting for you."

Yngvar stared at the girl, as thin as a wilting blade of grass with a dirty face dominated by owl-wide eyes. There was nowhere to let the girl escape. Davin turned in the doorway, the mother slung over his shoulder like a sack of grain.

"She's too young for what you're thinking," he said. "Not as fun as a grown woman. But every man has his tastes, I guess. Now come on!"

The thought of raping a child made Yngvar feel sick. Never once had something so revolting ever been made into a song. None of what had happened this morning had ever been made into a song. This was murder and robbery. Just like his father had warned him.

"Come, girl," he said. "You're not going to be hurt."

The girl either did not understand or did not believe him. He didn't believe himself. Taking the girl by the arm, he dragged her outside. He took a quick look, and no one was facing them. Davin was directly before him, and the woman swayed lifelessly across his back as he carried her toward a group at the village center.

He let the girl free. "Run. Or you'll die or worse. Go."

The girl stared after her mother, shaking her head. She had light hair that reminded him of the serving girls in his father's hall. When she didn't run, he shoved her away. She stumbled, got to her feet, then began to flee.

Then he bit his wrist and screamed, more from frustration than pain.

"Here, what's this?" Davin asked, turning around. "Where's the girl?"

"She bit me and ran off."

Davin's fish-eyes stared into his, but he said nothing. They joined the group at the village center, where Davin plopped down the mother with no more care than he'd spare for a sack of rocks. "I hope I didn't kill her. She put up a spirited fight."

Bregthor stood triumphantly amid the pathetic village. Thorfast and Bjorn had both already been gathered up. Both looked as if they had seen their own mothers killed, which said much for Bjorn who had never known his mother. They refused to meet his eye but looked at the ground.

The village, a sorry collection of mud and thatch homes huddling on an endless grass plain broken by lonely stands of spruce trees, had been ransacked. Eight men had offered resistance, and all had died beneath Bregthor's better-armed men. Yngvar had faced one such defender, a gray-bearded wildman wearing an animal skin and waving a notched sword that looked as if it had not been sharpened in the man's long lifetime. Knocking the man flat with his shield was an embarrassment. He was prepared to bypass the defender in search of a better foe. But the man behind Yngvar followed up with a spear thrust to the defender's gut. The seven other men were now corpses around the small village, all having met the same merciless demise.

Gathered in the center were twelve women of various ages, all clinging together. An old man was evidently blind and shouting in his strange language. A number of children were in the center of the women. The few dogs of the village had been killed, and now someone threw two protesting chickens into the center. Other so-called treasures included cooking pots, striking steels, half-filled sacks, and a single shield that seemed it might have once been painted green.

Glorious treasure.

This was what they had rowed two days to find. Bregthor's promise of nearby islands were the Nordreyar, the islands that clus-tered north of Scotland. Yngvar had thought the Norse had settled these islands, and perhaps they had, but these folk were clearly something else.

Bregthor shouted, holding up something he had pulled from the old man's neck. Others strained to see it. The morning light flashed off metal as the old man jumped at his stolen necklace.

"A cross of silver," Bregthor said. "These are Christians, my friends. So there must be a church nearby. And where there is a church, there is gold."

Davin wasted no time and started pulling women from the group. Bregthor showed them the cross and gestured at the wide plain surrounding them, then pointed the cross toward the land.

When the woman stared at him as if he had gone mad, Bregthor backhanded her. "Tell me where the church is, you sow."

This process repeated until they decided the woman was too dumb. Yngvar watched in mute anger as Davin dragged another woman before Bregthor who then beat her to the ground. It wasn't until the fourth woman that they began to understand what Bregthor wanted to know. The woman started to prattle in her language, mixing in Norse words that were of no use. They started scratching lines in the grass and others joined. Soon everyone was pointing out the church location. At last Bregthor smiled.

"We know where to go now, men." He looked over the women. "None of these are to my taste, the rest of you take your turns with whomever you want. Then it's back to the ship. I want to sack this church before sundown."

Bregthor drew a dagger and plunged it into the old blind man's neck. It did not kill him immediately, being an ill-laid strike, and the man gurgled on the ground while his blood poured through his fingers. Bregthor ignored his death, as did most others who were busy selecting their women.

"I'll go ready the ship," Yngvar said, not wanting to watch the rape. He understood this is what happened on raids. He was not surprised that Bregthor would do this. Yet he could not watch the defiling of these simple, desperate women who had awakened to the madness of attackers out of the dawn that killed their men and destroyed their homes. Both Thorfast and Bjorn joined him, as did a few others.

Yngvar was disappointed Ander Red-Scar was not among those returning to the ship.

"Carry some of this loot back," Bregthor said. "I had no idea you all enjoyed men better than women."

He laughed at his own joke then ignored them. As Yngvar bent to gather the shield and a small sack, Davin seized his arm. He pulled his wrist up to examine the bite.

"Little girl had big teeth," he said. He smelled like leather and sweat and his bulging eyes narrowed in accusation.

Yngvar ripped his hand away. "Like horse's teeth. Now get away from me, you fish-eyed dog-fucker."

"More fight now, I see." But Davin did not take up the insult and slunk back toward the group of men surrounding the women. Their shrill screams and squeals set Yngvar to hurrying back toward the ship.

He flung the shield and sack onto the deck with a thud, then pulled himself aboard. He found his sea chest and sat on it, Thorfast and Bjorn gathered around him. They sat quietly, flinching occasionally at the scream of a woman who had not resigned herself to her fate.

"Well, we would've done this to that Frankish farmer, right? I mean, that was a raid," Bjorn said at last. His cheeks were bright red, as if he had been slapped.

Yngvar slowly shook his head. "That was three drunk boys acting half their age. My father was right. I'd never do anything like I've just seen done. Good thing we didn't all get killed that day. This is nothing like the stories of my grandfather. Where are the lines of warriors? The mail coats and thickets of spears? There's no enemy banner to tear down. No arrow storm to shelter from. What is this? What songs will be written from this?"

"I think we took the stories too much to heart," Thorfast said. "My father said I had no idea of what really happened, and that skalds always made everything brighter and bigger than reality. He was right, of course."

They remained in tense silence. Yngvar discovered the others who had passed on the rape had done so not from any sense of humanity but because they "could never have a woman after another man had used her." He sensed Bjorn wished he could join in. He seemed to gaze overlong at the village and covered his mouth as if trying not to speak. Thorfast at best seemed indifferent to the screams and laughter wafting across the distance. Yngvar slumped forward on his knees, thinking. Was he not a man, then? Were his friends just following him to ease his awkwardness?

The doubts shattered when the men returned with Bregthor in the lead. A younger woman was hauled aboard, her torn skirt revealing a white patch of belly and a good portion of leg. Yngvar certainly felt like a man at that moment. One of the men grabbed the woman by her waist and shoved her down to the gunwale. No other woman came aboard, and the village was eerily silent.

Bregthor plucked Yngvar's shoulder. "Sitting on your ass does not ready the ship to sail. Get out and help shove us off. Come now, all three of you."

Yngvar did not look at Bregthor's eyes, noticing instead all of the blood splattered across his feet and pants.

He jumped onto the sand with the others and joined three more men to shove the ship back into the cold waves. He waded through the water, letting it slap him side to side as he reached for the railing. He half expected to be left behind, but Ander Red-Scar and his friends helped them aboard. Yngvar pulled off his boots to dump the sea water, not speaking to anyone. Bregthor was not done with him.

"Here's your share," he said, sticking out his palm. Two bits of silver no bigger than a fingernail glimmered on his hand. Yngvar noted the dried blood gathered in the lines of Bregthor's palm.

"I'll not take anything from the man who murdered my kin."

Bjorn and Thorfast now joined them, leaning over to see the silver.

Bregthor snorted. "Come now. It's only fair you take your part of the spoils. Most of it was in goods to trade later. So I'm paying you hacksilver now. Take it."

"I don't want it."

"You're part of my crew while aboard this ship, so you've earned it. I want you to have it."

Yngvar finally looked up, and Bregthor had an earnest almost worried expression. The absurdity left him speechless. He could commit murder without flinching, but worry for the fairness of his gold-giving.

"You two get the same." Bregthor turned his extended palm to Bjorn and Thorfast.

Bjorn gave Yngvar a sheepish look, but then tilted back is head. "Don't want it either, murderer."

"But you must take it." The exasperation in Bregthor's voice turned the heads of other nearby. "You've earned it."

"How about you two award your shares to me?" Thorfast asked, extending his opened palms to Bregthor. "I'll have mine and theirs, unless they disagree."

Yngvar shrugged and Bjorn walked away. Bregthor grunted and dumped the bits into Thorfast's palms. He retrieved the other shares from a pouch and pressed them neatly in Thorfast's hands.

"Fair is fair, boys," he said, regaining his swagger. "Now we're off for greater treasures than this."

After Bregthor abandoned them, Thorfast shook his head at Yngvar. "Don't look at me like that. Refusing silver won't change what happened today. Besides, we're not home yet. Having a little silver in our pouches might be useful."

Thorfast cocked his eyebrow, his pale hair blowing across his face as the wind raced over the deck. The sail unfurled above them with a boom.

"You're right, of course." Yngvar leaned on the rails. "But I still cannot accept anything from his hand."

They both sat in silence, staring at the beach fading away. Nothing moved and no sound came from the distant village. It was as if no one lived in this place.

"Get to your oars," Bregthor hollered from across the deck. "I want this ship to fly like an arrow across the water. We've got gold to claim."

And murder to commit.

Yngvar spit over the rail into the foamy sea, then took up his hated oar.

15

They arrived at the church after traveling overland from the beach. They had sailed down the coast and landing at whatever landmark the doomed villagers had provided Bregthor. Yngvar scanned the barren coastline and could not guess what had been the indication to land here. A heavy patch of spruce trees, dark and swaying against the deep gray of the sky, perhaps had been the sign. This place was a world of grass and little else. The wind smelled of rain and foul weather, reflecting Yngvar's mood as they tramped inland.

He had offered to remain as a guard for the ship. Bregthor nearly doubled over with laughter, accusing him of planning to steal the ship. Yet Yngvar had merely hoped to avoid repeating the mayhem of earlier in the day. He had not even considered stealing the ship. He would not have enough men to pilot it anyway.

"You're under my protection, boys," Bregthor said, then shoved Yngvar forward. Ander Red-Scar had looked on with a slow shake of his head. Yngvar had no idea what it meant, but Ander seemed less friendly as the day wore on. Well, he did not need friends among this rabble. He was headed home to his father's hall, where the men had honor and fought real enemies and not toothless old men.

The church was surrounded with spruce and pines, and a well-trod path wended across the grass. It would likely trace back to more hapless villagers. Yngvar hoped the church would be guarded by men worthy of carrying their swords. He would welcome a clash with a real warrior. He thought back to the attack on Uncle Gunnar's ship. The terror and bloodshed of a true battle had sharpened his wits and revealed the best in him. The killing of women had simply turned his stomach.

"Here's what we'll do," Bregthor said, stopping the line of almost twenty men by raising his hand.

"We will rush the front entrances." Bregthor swept his hand across a group of dark-faced men, including Ander Red-Scar and his lot. "You will circle around back to where the priests will flee. Kill anyone that gets away from us. We don't want them warning the area that we're here."

Yngvar's stomach burned when Bregthor's lazy gaze encompassed him and his companions. Three others were given the task as well.

"Looks like there's more people in there than priests," said Davin. He pointed over their heads, where all turned to see men entering the front doors. Almost everyone flinched down, as if being caught in the open was dangerous. Yngvar did not move. This place was poorer than any he'd ever seen, which admittedly wasn't much. Could these people even possess a single sharp sword among them? It seemed unlikely they'd face anything worse than being pelted with the parchment books priests so loved.

Yngvar and the others began jogging at Bregthor's command. Bjorn laughed as he ran, and Thorfast's smile was wide. Yngvar trotted with the group, feeling as though he were watching everything happen to someone else. The grass swished across their feet, and Yngvar felt a cold prick of a raindrop strike his cheek. Would Thor send a storm to show the Christian god his power? That also seemed likely. Thunder rumbled in the distance.

They looped around the church in a wide arc. The sparse trees offered no cover to them. Had the priests posted sentries with bows, the massacre would've been the opposite of what Yngvar expected. In Frankia, the priests commanded men like jarls and protected their gold with bloody-minded jealousy. These priests huddled in their stone building, oblivious or cowering.

Or they had nothing worth defending. Yngvar bit his lip at that thought. With no spoils, Bregthor would keep them at sea longer. As he completed the loop to the rear of the church, he found himself hoping for success. It would be his fastest route home and away from this madness.

A steep hill fell away from the back of the church. It hid the thicker growth of pines from the forward approach. The top of a small woods stretched out into the ever-darkening horizon.

"Looks like there's plenty of places for the priests to hide down there," said Thorfast. "We should spread out in case they scatter."

Yngvar nodded. Both Bjorn and Thorfast exchanged glances. Thorfast lowered his voice. "Look, we have to kill whoever runs this way. We don't want to give Bregthor any excuse to be dissatisfied with us. He'll figure a way to use that to break his oath to return us home."

"I'll gut anyone that crosses me." Both Thorfast and Bjorn widened their eyes and flinched from Yngvar. He must have spoken harsher than he had thought. He dropped his voice. "I know what we have to do here. Don't worry for me."

They ranged in a wide arc so that anyone fleeing toward the safety of the woods downhill would have to run between a pair of them. No unarmed priest would escape that trap. Yngvar watched the squat stone church. A wooden door sat in its stained rock walls. Rain drops tapped his cheeks and hands, cold and infrequent pricks as if the sky were trying to keep him awake. His sword trembled in hand, and he squeezed the hilt to steady himself. He did not mind sending priests to their deaths. They worshiped death, as far as he knew, and were always ready to go to the hall of their dead god. He hoped none of the others inside the church were like the victims from the morning.

Muffled shouts and screams announced that Bregthor had stormed the front. He saw Thorfast glance at him from the corner of his eye. Bjorn had set himself at the center and was out of sight. Yngvar put aside what they thought. He only had to pass these next moments.

The door slammed open against the wall, wood clapping raw

stone. Yngvar jumped as if someone had shouted from behind. Now men in brown robes tied with rope belts streamed out of the church. The howls of Bregthor's raiders chased them out of the door. The priests scattered in every direction, some sprinting like heroic runners and others prancing like young girls. One priest lifted his legs so high as he ran that it seemed he was trying to not touch the ground.

At first it seemed no one was coming his way. Most were making a direct line toward the woods. Bjorn and the others now shouted and charged at the fleeing priests. Yngvar thought it unnecessary for him to join, as these unarmed men were as lambs.

A white-haired man in the same brown robes fled with a smaller man leading him. The smaller figure pointed to where Thorfast, Bjorn, and the others were running down the priests, then he snatched the older man's hand and began running toward Yngvar.

He raised his sword and charged at the pair. Time to show he had the nerve to kill the innocent. Surely his father and grandfather had done the same. It is a rite of passage, and Yngvar had to pass it.

The pair of priests spotted Yngvar's charge and pulled up short. But neither turned to flee. Instead the old man fell to his knees and threw his arms wide. He started calling out in a strange language.

Yngvar didn't slow. So the priest wanted to die on his knees. He could oblige him.

As he closed the distance, sword raised and shout rising in his throat, the old priest pulled the other to his knees. The shorter one was no man. He was a boy, perhaps four or five years younger than Yngvar. Both knelt in the grass as the old man called out strange words. The boy simply knelt with his wide, smooth face bloodless and moon-bright.

The roar burst from Yngvar's throat. He shuddered to a halt, sword raised. The old man's eyes streamed tears. His hair was thin and flying away in the breeze. His nose was bulbous and scarred, reminding Yngvar of one of his father's friends who enjoyed singing in the hall. The boy had squeezed his eyes shut and tucked his head down.

His sword hovered over them.

No. He had set sail to find real battle, heroic adventure, and glory. Hacking apart an old man and boy behind a time-weary church was none of those things. If Bregthor would use this mercy to break his oath, then Yngvar would not hesitate to fight Bregthor to the death.

"Yngvar!" the shout came from Thorfast. His sword was already pointed at the ground and he could not look at his best friend, not now. Instead, he watched the boy dare to open a single eye. He had perfect skin, smooth and unblemished, so striking that had he met the boy in a forest he might've thought him an elf. His hair was cut short, and shimmered between brown and copper.

"Yngvar!" Thorfast shouted again. Yngvar hovered over the priest, who continued to babble as his milky eyes stared up at the cloudy sky. Was he calling his god?

"What's this?" Bregthor's voice was loud across the short distance to the church. Crashing and screams followed Bregthor and his men as they exited the church. "What did I tell you to do?"

All the other priests had disappeared, and only Bregthor's men remained. Yngvar absently realized they had not disappeared, but were now lying dead and hidden in the grass.

"Kill those two!" Bregthor shouted, now only a spear's throw away. "What are you waiting for?"

More crashing and smashes echoed from the church. Rain continued to patter over Yngvar's shoulders. The priest continued his stream of words, maybe a spell or a curse, and the boy had opened both eyes but remained perfectly still.

Bjorn and Thorfast joined him. Fresh blood dripped from their swords. A line of blood had splashed across Bjorn's cheek. So they had the nerve, but he did not.

Ander Red Scar now arrived with Bregthor and several of his closest men. Davin, the fish-eyed bastard, swept forward with his bloodied sword.

"You've no stones at all, do you?" Davin grabbed the priest by his wispy hair and put his sword to the old man's neck. The priest squealed, but continued to spout his nonsense.

"Wait," Bregthor said. "Maybe he'll find his courage yet."

The laughter of the crew brought heat to his face. Men who were only just complimenting his bravery now derided him because he wouldn't murder innocents for no reason other than greed. Perhaps the praise of men was not worth as much as he had thought. Did it not take more bravery to hold to one's principles than it did to follow the group? These so-called men would never see that. Even Ander Red-Scar glowered skeptically at him.

"Yngvar?" Thorfast's whisper had said volumes more than he had spoken. He heard the compassion in his best friend's voice. Thorfast knew what conflicts raged within him. But he also heard the reproach, the plea to take action, the frustration at risking their lives for his beliefs. Yngvar could not look at him, but stuck his sword in the earth.

"I'm taking these two as my captives. That is my right."

"What foolishness is this? I ordered you to kill anyone fleeing out the back."

"Have a care," Yngvar said. "I am of noble blood, far nobler than whatever bitch's cunt dropped you on this world. I take orders from you that are necessary for the safety of our crew and ship. That is all."

"You whelp," Bregthor said, pointing his blood-splattered sword at him.

"Put that down," Yngvar said. "Do not mistake me for fearing to battle you again. For I will gladly, and this time it will be to the death. No constraints of the holmgang to keep my sword from your neck. Shall we see who the gods love more? Look at my family, and I think you will see who they favor."

"Yngvar." Again Thorfast's single word spoke much more. It told him to not get carried away, to step back from the edge he had taken them all toward, and to refocus on the immediate problem.

"These are my captives," Yngvar said. "You gave a woman slave to one of your men this morning. I take these two for my slaves."

"He took her for a wife," Bregthor said, lowering his sword. "And you can't take two slaves. That's more than your share."

Yngvar glanced at Thorfast. "He'll take one as well."

"What? I don't—"

"No," Bregthor said. "One slave. If you defy me in this, then I will fight you to the death. You've tried my last nerve, boy."

106

Bjorn and Thorfast both pleaded with their eyes. Yngvar knew he had gone too far, and likely all three of them would accidentally fall overboard now. Probably with help from the rest of the crew, too. He nodded his agreement.

"He let a girl escape him this morning," Davin said, putting his sword back to the old man's neck. The old priest closed his eyes, but continued to mumble his prayers. Yngvar hadn't noticed he had quieted. "I don't think he has it in him to kill. He made it seem he was saving us when our ship was attacked, but he was just helping himself flee. He let his guard fight and die for him. He's a coward and should give back that armband."

Every eye turned toward him as if he were expected to explain. He shrugged. "She bit my wrist and got away. I guess I'm not as bold as Davin to run down and kill a child. I just let her go."

"She was my property," Bregthor growled.

"I didn't see any other—property—come back to the ship. So what does it matter that one got away? If you're so concerned, we can sail back and you can show me your battle prowess against the little girl. I'm sure she's a challenge for you."

Bregthor again lifted his sword. "One slave. You kill the other. You kill the other, or I say you are no man and I owe you nothing. I will leave you here to die. I will sail to your father's hall and tell him myself that his son was an embarrassment to his name. He'll reward me for it."

There was no choice, of course. Yngvar smiled and raised his sword. The boy blinked at him, then looked at the old man. When the boy started speaking fluent Norse, Yngvar nearly fumbled his sword in surprise.

"Please, lord. He is an old man. Send me to God."

"Sorry, boy, but for a slave you're more useful than an old man."

The sword slid through the priest's neck. His eyes widened and blood gurgled from his mouth like dark wine. His pulse throbbed up the blade into Yngvar's palm. He flicked the blade to the side, so that it tore the skin and severed the artery. A geyser of bright red blood shot over everyone's heads, sprinkling them with a mist of gore. The old priest's babbling faded and he collapsed on his back.

The artery jetted blood in time with the slowing beat of the priest's heart.

"I claim this one as my slave," Yngvar said, pointing his bloodied sword at the boy.

"Then it's done," Bregthor said. "That's your share of the treasure. And you take no extra food or water for him. You feed your slave from your own bowl."

Yngvar looked at Thorfast and Bjorn, who wore no expressions. Ander Red-Scar seemed to consider the events, but gave no hint of his opinion.

At last the clouds released the rain they had harbored, and thunder rumbled close by. Thor was victorious. But was he pleased? Yngvar did not know.

16

Yngvar pulled his cloak tighter against the wind blowing from the sea. He huddled with Thorfast and Bjorn against the hull of their beached ship, the hard wood shielding them from the worst of the cutting wind. The sky remained rolling with gray clouds from two days of rain, the sun nothing more than a vague brightness behind it. Yngvar's stomach growled and he looked up the long, rock-strewn slope as if expecting to find food there. Bregthor and his raiders had left them with scant supplies. No doubt they were plundering meals for themselves and gorging over the bodies of their victims. But he saw nothing but rolling folds of grass that in places fell away into ditches. It was a bleak and hard land.

"What if he doesn't come back?" Thorfast asked. The flat light turned his hair nearly white, and he brushed it out of his face as the wind gusted around the hull. "Do you think we can get the ship back to sea?"

"He'd not leave us with the ship if he thought we could sail it," Yngvar said. He continued to scan the long, shallow slope of grass dotted with white rocks. "Let's hope they return before our supplies run out."

"I'm sick of salted fish," Bjorn said. He leaned against the hull, his gray hood and cloak wrapped around him so that he seemed like a baby in swaddling. "Ale is running low, too."

Yngvar nodded. Of course he felt the sting of having added to their burden. The young boy he had taken as a slave remained on the ship, where the other woman captive stayed tied to the mast by a rope that let her roam the deck. It was like tying a hound to a post. Yngvar let the boy go unfettered. In fact, he hoped the boy would flee during the night, but each morning he awakened to find him curled up like a cat under a cloak.

Bregthor had decided the storms made sailing too dangerous, and so chose to continue to search the area for more valuables. Yngvar was glad to have been given guard duty for the ship. Yet he was frustrated the others appeared to think he was undependable. Their opinions should not have mattered, he knew. Soon he would be rid of all these men. Still, there were many among the crew he considered competent warriors. He hoped those men understood he was not weak, but instead standing for what he believed in.

"If Bregthor does not return, then we are stuck without a crew for this ship." Yngvar put his hand upon the green gem on the pommel of his sax. It was cold and hard against his fingers as he considered what to do next. "With just us three and two slaves, we have no way to make it home. I'm not even sure I'd know how to get us there. It's not like my father spent much time with us aboard ships."

"Well, it's a long walk home," Thorfast said. "We could hire a crew."

"Bregthor's got all the gold with him," Yngvar said. "And my armband won't raise us enough men to crew this ship for so long a journey. Anyone finding us will likely take the ship and add us to their count of slaves."

"Not me," Bjorn said. "I'll die before I'm captured. No way I'll ever become a slave."

Yngvar nodded. "But we will not be so fortunate. Bregthor has Loki on his side, and his mischief is not done. He has somehow caused men to forget Brandr's murder. I even gave him this ship, which is what he wanted from the start."

"Not your best idea," Thorfast said. "I'd have bargained for more.

You gave him an ocean-going ship—and for what? For the insult of revealing him as a murderer?"

"What would you have me do? He wanted to claim our heads, if your memory can go back so far. For this ship, he was like a dog begging food from the table. I just gave it to him, and he shut up. Do you think my father will really let him sail off with it?" Yngvar kicked the hull with a dull thud. "If Bregthor thinks this is his ship, then he's a fool."

"Which is why he is never going to take us home," Thorfast said. "He won't have to fear your father if he never gets near him again, does he?"

"He swore before all his crew. If he breaks his oath, so will his men. He's not such a great leader that they'll stay with him if he is faithless."

Bjorn grumbled and spit into the sand. "This is giving me a headache. He's got us standing around doing nothing for days, while he's probably in a warm hall and having fun."

Yngvar closed his eyes. "When he returns, I'm going to demand he take us home."

"Remember, he doesn't have a time he must take us back before," Thorfast said.

"I'm giving him one, or he and I will fight again."

Both Bjorn and Thorfast exchanged glances. He knew they didn't believe he could best a seasoned warrior. Who knew the future? Bregthor was older and more experienced, but was also arrogant and evil. Yngvar was certain justice would carry him to victory. The gods loved to bring men high only to cast them down. That was their plan for Bregthor, Yngvar was certain. Let him have his ship, raid like a sea king, kill women and children like a beast. Then they would let Yngvar carve out his heart and crush it over his face.

"I'm serious," he said. "He meets my demands or I will kill him in single combat."

"Master," the voice was thin in the blustery wind. Yngvar stepped back from the hull to see his slave leaning on the rail. His face was pale and pure, and his short, coppery hair stood up with the wind. He pointed up the slope. "There are men coming."

From his lower vantage, Yngvar saw nothing at first. Yet in a moment a dark line of bobbing heads appeared above the grass on the horizon. A distant cry seemed to follow them as well. In a blink, Yngvar realized these men were running. Not as in a charge, but as in fear.

"They're being pursued," Yngvar said. "That's Bregthor and the others."

The mob of nearly twenty men ran as if the wolf Fenrir himself was chasing them. As they crested the rise, one man stumbled from the group while the rest wheeled their arms for balance coming down the other side.

Both Thorfast and Bjorn stared with their mouths open. Yngvar, too, wondered what could cause them so much fear. Yet the cause did not matter. They had to escape whatever pursued them.

"Everyone, we've got to get this ship launched," he said. He looked up at his slave. "Get down here and help push."

The ship was beached well, dragged ashore by ten men with ropes to aid them. The surf had eroded enough of the path back to the water to make it easier to relaunch the ship. But not with three men and a slave as the sole crew.

They grunted and pushed, and to everyone's surprise the ship began to slide. But it was not moving fast enough. Yngvar's shoulder pressed against the cold, hard prow as he strained. The calls behind them grew louder, both the shouts of fear from Bregthor's men and a crazed knell from whatever pursued them.

"We can't do this," Thorfast said through clenched teeth. "It's too big and too far from the water for just the three of us."

Yngvar realized he had wasted precious moments. Both Bjorn and Thorfast were wide-eyed with panic. The young slave continued to push when all had stopped. The woman tethered to the mast leaned over the rails, laughing and crying tears of joy.

Not a good sign.

Yngvar turned to see Bregthor's men stumbling their way down the slope. They had traveled the clear path up, and so had picked the same route to return. Behind them were about an equal number of men in pursuit, though in the lead were a half-dozen men on small ponies. They wore furs but nothing else, their white flesh stark against the gray of the sky. Patterns in blue paint adorned their bodies, and their swords flashed overhead.

"Forget relaunching the ship," Yngvar said. "Bregthor's men will smash it back into the sea. We've got to draw away the ponies and hope others will follow."

Thorfast cocked his brow and narrowed his opposite eye. "When did you learn magic?"

Yngvar did not explain. He grabbed the young slave and hauled him up on the deck. "There's a horn on the mast. Bring it to me. Also gather as many spears and helmets as you can carry. Hurry."

"What are we doing?" Bjorn asked, his face now bright with anticipation.

"You're the strongest of all of us," Yngvar said. "Get one of the bows strung and kill the ponies as they come after us. Don't worry for the warriors. Kill their mounts."

Bjorn nodded and climbed back on deck. Yngvar grabbed the horn from his slave, and Thorfast took four spears and two leather helmets.

"Run with me," Yngvar said. The beach sand offered slippery footing, but desperation drove him clear to the grass. Bregthor's men were turning on their pursuers, realizing they had no chance to escape. But they were undisciplined and panicked. Some of their number continued to flee.

"What is this?" Thorfast shouted from behind. "Where are we going?"

A sharp dip in the rolling slope was thankfully close. Yngvar praised Odin for its placement. Once behind it, he could barely see the fight over the top. He plunged the first spear in the rain-softened earth, blade up, and topped a helmet on it. He pointed Thorfast down the line of the ditch. "Do the same there. Keep your other spear ready for whomever comes."

He took his own cloak and pinned it to the top of another spear. The ruse would not fool a careful observation, but men in battle did not think. They reacted. Yngvar counted on it.

As soon as Thorfast set his spear, Yngvar sounded the horn. It was a clear, powerful note so loud to his own ears he guessed it could be heard at the top of the world.

"War cries," he said to Thorfast. He began to shout and raise his own spear over the top of the ditch. Thorfast did this same. If the horn had been powerful, the two of them sounded like children playing in a field. He blew the horn again.

The pounding of hooves responded.

"They're coming," he said, smiling at Thorfast. "They've taken the bait."

"Wonderful," Thorfast said while he thrust his spear overhead. "What now?"

He hadn't thought that far. He glanced back for Bjorn. Where was he? The ship seemed empty but for his slave and the woman bound to the mast.

The first pony flew over the ditch. It was a sandy brown projectile as it launched overhead. Yngvar had time only to note its wide, rolling eyes before throwing himself flat. The beast crashed behind them, screaming in pain as its bones broke. It had no rider.

"Come on," Yngvar said, dragging up from the mud. "We've drawn off some men. Now we've got to get back to the ship."

They sped across the muddy ditch the way they had come. Another pony mounted the crest, this one under control of its rider. He was nothing more than a dark figure in a shaggy fur hide. He held a flashing blade low in one hand, and the other hand gripped the mane of his mount. An arrow hung loose from his fur cloak.

The rider pointed at them and shouted in his strange language.

Yngvar spun, spear held level at his shoulder, then sent it flying. The spear caught the warrior in his torso, knocking him from his mount with a grunt of pain. Thorfast sped past him, bearing their last spear.

As they emerged from the cover of the ditch, Yngvar saw more of Bregthor's men streaming away and the enemy in retreat up the slope. It had been a short, decisive clash and the enemy had decided not to fight a desperate enemy. Perhaps his ruse had broken the enemies will to fight? A warm pride spread through his chest, but then he heard fast approaching hoofbeats.

The pony riders, two of them, were bearing down along the edge of the slope. Their riders held swords high and gave high-pitched war cries.

The ship was already sliding into the water, a dark cluster of men shoving it into the unfolding waves. Men clambered aboard, turning to pull up their companions.

Thorfast looked over his back, shouted, and redoubled his run. Yngvar turned to see both men nearly upon him.

Bjorn's bow hummed and an arrow hissed overhead. It grazed one of the men, and he yanked his pony hard to the side.

"The ponies!" Yngvar hoped Bjorn heard him. He crashed to his knees as the second rider swooped past him, sword whipping through the air beside Yngvar's head.

His heart thundered in his chest and the pony seemed to slow. Clods of dirt flung up from behind its hooves as it sped past him. The rider already raising his blade again to strike Thorfast. Bjorn placed another arrow on the bowstring.

The deflected rider had corrected himself and now bore down on Yngvar. The short sword at his waist, the sax his father had sent as a gift to Uncle Gunnar, drew easily into his hand.

He dove on his back beneath the pony. The stink of the animal covered him as it passed over him. A flare of white hot pain erupted on his left thigh.

Striking up, the fresh and sharp blade of his short sword eviscerated the pony. Hot blood rained over him, but the animal screamed and fell past him. The rider threw himself clear, landing in a heap.

Bjorn's bowstring snapped again. He struck the other rider's pony, but the animal was riderless now. Thorfast was circling the enemy clad only in furs and a loincloth. His spear kept the man at bay.

Yngvar rolled onto his feet. The ship was headed to sea and the last men were leaping aboard.

"They're leaving us," he shouted. "Get back to the ship!"

Bjorn looked aside as the pony he shot ran in a circle then collapsed on its side. Thorfast jabbed with this spear, only to buy himself a glimpse over his shoulder.

Bregthor was abandoning them to the enemy.

The rider that Yngvar had just dismounted sprung to his feet, scrambling to recover his sword. Up the slope, the dark cluster of enemies had turned now. He heard their cries as they spotted three potential captives on the beach. They raised their weapons and charged.

The enemy dueling with Thorfast tried to grab the spear but missed. Bjorn had three arrows in the ground beside his foot.

They were trapped against the ocean as their enemies rushed down the slope, swords and spears raised for blood.

17

The ocean waves rolled out a droning beat against Yngvar's back. The dismounted rider had now retrieved his sword and danced it between them. He crouched low, blood streaming from his nose across his golden beard. He had a scar across his left cheek that enhanced his wicked smile. Yngvar, slathered in blood from the dead pony, stepped back and his left leg fired pain up to his hip. The pony had clipped his flesh, tearing away a hunk of it and his pants. Thankfully it had not broken his leg.

Thorfast and his attacker suddenly broke into a twirl of motion. When Thorfast struck, his enemy rushed inside the spear. None of them were especially practiced with a spear, and Thorfast's inadequacy was plain to everyone. Yngvar screamed, expecting his best friend to be gutted.

Then his own attacker leapt.

And he staggered back, a gray-feathered arrow vibrating in his chest as he collapsed.

Bjorn had two arrows left.

Thorfast remained standing. He had abandoned his spear and both hands were wrapped around his attacker's sword arm.

Both Yngvar and Bjorn barreled into the enemy at the same time.

All of them collapsed into a pile, the enemy cursing and biting at them. The press of bodies on the surf smelled like ocean, sweat, and blood. Elbows rammed into ribs and faces. Nails dragged into bare skin. Bjorn finally hauled the enemy onto his back and slammed him into the sand.

Yngvar spun, his short sword still in hand, and rammed the blade into the attacker's inner thigh. He howled, and blood gushed into the sand. He did not die immediately, but such a wound was fatal. He turned back to Thorfast.

"Are you hurt?"

"You're kneeling on my arm."

Yngvar pulled Thorfast to his feet, then looked behind. The enemy's charge had slowed, but they were still approaching. Yngvar then turned to the sea. His heart flipped in his chest at what he saw.

"They're coming back for us!"

The ship lurched across the rolling waves, its sail now unfurled and fat. The ship glided at an angle, so that their few bowmen lined up on the rails.

"They can't risk the shallows," Yngvar said. "We'll have to wade out to them. Hurry."

The cold water slammed against their legs. When Yngvar's injured thigh submerged, fire crawled up his hip and around his back. He clenched his teeth.

Something splashed the water. He thought it might have been something he or the others dropped as they pushed against the tide. The muck beneath his feet slowed him as the water reached his waist. He held his short sword high, but his long sword was already wet. It would likely be ruined after this.

Another splash, and this time he heard the unmistakable hiss of an arrow.

Glancing back, the enemy had lined up along the beach. They raised their weapons and shouted challenges. Yngvar did not need to understand their language to hear the curses and insults shot at them. But none of them had bows.

The arrows came from their own ship.

"You can't reach them," shouted Bjorn, his voice booming across the waves. "Stop shooting."

Now in water up to his chest and walking on his toes, Yngvar feared he'd slip and drown. Some men were preparing ropes to throw to them. The waves bobbled the three of them like so many planks of wood.

A definite hiss and splash hit just before him. He saw the white trail of the shaft as it bent and turned in the water. Had the shot been a fraction higher, the arrow would've planted directly in his chest.

Bregthor stood with one foot on the rails, bow in hand and hesitating to draw again. Yet others were calling for the shooting to cease. Though they were separated by distance and the water, they both remained still and staring at each other. Yngvar was only being pulled from one enemy to the next.

He grabbed the rope the crewmen tossed a second time. He wound his arm into it, using the other to keep his sax clear of the water. Both Thorfast and Bjorn were already being dragged up the hull like two dead seals. Men reached down and hauled them aboard. Yngvar let them drag him across the current to bump softly against the hull. He struck his nose against the strakes as they pulled him up. Water drained away, pouring through his clothes and making him feel lighter with every pull on the rope. Finally warm hands grabbed him and dragged him onto the dry deck.

Cheers went up among the crew. Yngvar lay facing the gray sky, an ever-widening pool of chill water spreading beneath him.

"Master, you have been saved." His young slave appeared above him, bringing a dirty cloth to pat the water from his face.

Yngvar blinked at the boy. He could not be much younger than him, for he acted with the precision and decisiveness of a man, but he was so small as to seem almost childish. He lifted Yngvar's head and slipped the cloth beneath it.

"What is your name?" he asked. He had told himself he would not learn this slave's name. He had nothing to bring back to Kadlin, and a slave was hardly treasure worth delivering to the young woman of your desire. So he would sell the boy and give Kadlin the gold she deserved. Yet this slave had been so obedient and accepting of his lot. Yngvar had to learn his name.

"Alasdair," the slave said. Then others crowded in, pushing him back.

"That was some good work back there." Yngvar stared up at Ander Red-Scar, his eponymous scar wriggling as he smiled. "It was just enough to make them doubt our numbers. You gave us the break we needed to slip away."

"It was all of us that did it," Yngvar said. He sat up with Ander's help. The crew surrounded him, most of the men smiling but others appeared to offer a grudging acceptance and no more. Bregthor, Davin, and his attendant cronies returned to their duties as if nothing had happened. It was not quite half the crew now. Yngvar smiled. He had converted some to his side.

"Don't mind them," Ander said. "They're angered at having you three save their hides at every turn. Most of us are grateful you're with us."

"I suppose it was you few who forced Bregthor to return for us," Yngvar said. Ander nodded, but said nothing more.

Alasdair appeared through the small group surrounding Yngvar. He held the sax that Yngvar had dropped the moment he had been safely aboard ship. When Bjorn saw it, he frowned and snatched it away.

"A slave don't carry a weapon." He turned to hand it to Yngvar, who took it gratefully. Blood had stained the grip and the blade had still got wet. He had to tend to it soon or it would rust. "Did you see what he did to that horse? Jumped under it and cut its belly open. Amazing!"

Ander and the others looked at him, brows raised and heads cocked. Ander shook his head. "I was too occupied fleeing for my life to see."

"It's how I hurt my leg," Yngvar said. "Lucky the beast didn't step on me directly or I'd probably be dead. And it was a pony, not a horse."

A murmur of agreement circulated, and Ander nodded to the

sword. "The blade did not break or bend. That is a fine weapon. It should have a name."

Yngvar smiled at the thought of owning a named sword. Every hero carried a named sword, for their weapons were indestructible and magic. His was perhaps not magical, but it was special. He stared at the green pommel gem which glittered in the flat light. Suggestions were called out: Life-Drinker, Leg-Biter, Foe-Killer. They were good but common names. Nothing that spoke to what the sword meant.

"How about Pony-Bane," Thorfast suggested. Everyone, Yngvar included, laughed. Yet it did suggest the name to him. He held the sax so the point faced the sky and his shadow fell across the blade.

"It's a sax for close fighting, and I did get close to that pony's belly. I'll call it Gut-Ripper."

"A fine name!" Ander slapped Yngvar's back and Thorfast nodded at the better choice.

Amid the congratulations and expressions of gratitude, he saw Bregthor, Davin, and the rest of his dark crew scowling and sulking. Bregthor was at the tiller, guiding the ship out to sea so that the coast faded with every moment. Ander noted the looks and pulled Yngvar aside.

"We lost everything out there," he said. "All the treasure from the church, gone. Seems you got the most treasure with the slave you claimed."

"What happened?" Thorfast asked. "Who was that chasing you?"

Ander explained how after the first day they had come to a larger village led by its own jarl. The village men were away for some reason but returned to catch them looting. A fight broke out, and they traded their loot for safe passage out of the area. But they were betrayed and were ambushed in the rolling plains by the men Yngvar had fought. Their pony riders were herding them onto the enemy spears. They had used the terrain to make an escape, but were about to be caught before Yngvar's ruse spooked the pursuers.

"So no one has anything except what they might've hidden in their cloaks." Ander shook his head. "We lost three more men too, and a few others took wounds. We're beaten now. Nothing to do but return home. We don't even have supplies enough for the journey."

Yngvar's heart lifted knowing he would head home. While he had to face his father and find another way to avoid Jarl Flosi's daughter, he was glad for it. He had learned how misguided his dreams had been. Raiding and sailing the open seas was only for the desperate. His father had told him so, but he chose to believe stories instead. Such a fool he had been. Real heroes were not found pillaging helpless villagers, and true adventure was not making one desperate escape after the next. The raiding life as he imagined it existed nowhere but in songs and his own imaginings.

"There's something more," Ander said, his voice dropping. He pulled Yngvar closer and guided him toward the rail. Others took the signal and left the two in peace. "On that first night of raiding, we had captured ale from a farmhouse on the way into the village. There was plenty of it and we got drunk. That night, Davin's tongue loosened and he bragged about killing Brandr. Not everyone heard him, and I'm not sure his drinking companions even remembered it the next morning. Bregthor certainly did not hear. But I was not so dizzy that I misheard him."

Yngvar's eyes narrowed as he stared at the sea. He saw nothing but Brandr falling overboard with a lonely splash to mark his passing from the world. He heard it again and again while Ander continued to mumble in his ear.

"Why did he do it?" Yngvar did not expect an answer, but Ander lowered his head.

"Bregthor challenges everyone who tries to lead him. He is a strange man that way. He thought Jarl Gunnar old and crazy. Perhaps he was both, but he was still jarl and still had our respect. I think he saw a chance to claim a ship and make his own way in the world. What greater mark of power is there than a ship of one's own? Rather than raise the gold or the manpower to build his own, stealing one was more to his liking. That's the best I can guess."

Yngvar nodded, then turned to lean back on the rail. Bregthor stared at them across the deck as if he knew what they discussed.

"I will have justice," Yngvar said. "When we go to my father's hall, you will vouch for what you've said?" Ander gave a slow nod. "Then his days are marked. I will drag him to the hall myself."

"After this disaster, you'll have my support and more than a few others. Bregthor's ambitions have ruined us." Ander turned with him to face Bregthor.

Handing the tiller off to another, Bregthor swaggered to the middle of the ship and leaned on the mast. The female captive recoiled from him.

"Listen, all of you," Bregthor said. He stared directly at Ander and Yngvar. "If you've got complaining to do, you do it to me. Don't cry like women at their looms, gossiping away from my hearing."

The crew fell silent. The deck creaked and the sail snapped. Yngvar narrowed his eyes at Bregthor, daring him to go further. Bregthor obliged.

"I think I've had enough of the trouble-making Yngvar and his friends have brought us. His continued life has offended the gods. They had decided to cast him down in the holmgang, but we defied them. You see how it has cost us? We lost everything because we bear this cowardly, slave-loving fool on our decks."

"Cowardly?" Bjorn jumped forward, and two men behind Bregthor reached for their swords. It did not dissuade Bjorn, who raised his fist at them.

"You ran like a rabbit while we covered your escape. Every man on this ship is a coward and fool. So if anyone's sick of anyone, it's me that's sick of all you fucking stupid fools. Fuck you and your mother, Bregthor the Craven. You and all your gutless, murderous, pig-loving bitches should throw yourselves overboard and save me the trouble."

Yngvar's brows touched his hairline and he blinked at his cousin's tirade. Bjorn's neck pulsed and his face flushed. Yngvar knew Bjorn was prepared to back up his curses. Bregthor's face had also turned red.

"What he's saying," Thorfast said, jumping to Bjorn's side. "Is that you're acting a bit ungrateful for all that we've done to help everyone survive."

Bregthor put his hand on his sword. "Gratitude? We've got nothing to show for our blood because of you three fools and your family. Men died out here. We started with a crew of thirty and are now almost half, all because of Jarl Gunnar and his fool son and his even more foolish kin. What's to be grateful for?"

Yngvar's own neck pulsed. He drew Gut-Ripper and stepped forward.

"Time to cut that vile tongue from your mouth." He raised his sword and pointed it at Bregthor.

18

The ship swayed on the waves as the sail rippled above the deck. Yngvar held his newly named sax, Gut-Ripper, level at Bregthor's chest. He stepped carefully to the center, beside Bjorn and Thorfast who were both red with fury. The sword felt light in his hand, and a touch of cooled blood from his last defeated enemy rolled onto his fingers. It was as if he were being assured he would spill more blood this day.

The entire crew dropped whatever had occupied them, straightening up for the confrontation playing out beneath the flat gray sky. Yngvar's left eye twitched and his lip curled.

"Put down that sword," Bregthor said. His dark eyes, drifting in different directions, narrowed. "Son of a jarl or not, no one threatens me aboard my own ship."

Yngvar snorted. "It's not your ship. You murdered Brandr to claim it for yourself. You and Davin. I saw you do it."

"Enough of these lies," Bregthor roared. His voice echoed off the water, and in the distance a gull called in answer. They were still not far from shore.

"Davin bragged about it while he was drunk. Ander and others will swear to it." Yngvar glanced at Ander, who now lined up with him and folded his arms.

"That's true," he said. "Davin told how the two of you slipped him overboard while he was unaware. He was proud to be part-owner of this ship with you."

Bregthor's split gaze fell on fish-eyed Davin, who looked as green as if he had swallowed a bucket of sea water. The two murderers regarded each other, and Bregthor began to smile. Then he turned one malevolent eye at Yngvar.

"You were never going home, you fool," he said. "Looks like we'll have to do this the hard way. It's all for the best. We don't have enough food left for a journey to Frankia."

Bregthor's men drew their swords. Those behind Yngvar stood blinking in shock, heads swiveling as if trying to decide which side to join.

Bjorn and Thorfast drew their own weapons. Thorfast put his arm across Bjorn's chest to stop him from charging straight into Bregthor.

"Is this the man you will follow?" Yngvar said to the crew that had gathered behind him. "He risked your lives, gambled your treasure and lost it, and now will ask you to murder your friends. None of you have broken any laws other than those of decency and clear-thinking. You side with a murderer and you stain your honor with his crime. Step back from him, and let Bregthor and Davin face justice alone."

Half the crew was arrayed against Yngvar, and their dark, hard-lined faces offered little hope they would see reason. The other half, if they had wavered, now drew their weapons and stood at Yngvar's back. A true mutiny was at hand. He had heard the tales of such disasters, but had never expected to find himself at the heart of one.

"The men know you are weak and accursed by the gods," Bregthor said, drawing his own sword with deliberate care. "You are what stains them and this ship. The gods love might and cunning, which you lack. You play tricks and use words like daggers. Are you a woman? No, you are not even old enough. You are girl. No real warrior would stand with one who cannot fight fairly."

Yngvar cocked his head. "Who twists words better than you? So, I see you are all intent on becoming masterless pirates, no better than flotsam on the waves. You once were sworn to a noble jarl, and could be once more. If only you will choose wisely. Bregthor will keep you searching for gold in a land where men eat grass and mud. How rich will you become? What glory will you find? This is your last chance."

"Last chance for what?" Bregthor said. "There are more of us than you."

"He has saved our lives twice," Ander said. "All of yours as well. Bregthor murdered your lord."

"Brandr wasn't our jarl," said one of the opposite crew. "And we've nothing waiting for us in Frankia. Time to take our own freedom. No more oaths to old jarls who sit on their gold in their beautiful halls."

Bregthor's men grumbled and nodded. Davin turned his bulging eyes to the others behind Yngvar. "And we don't have enough food for everyone. So some of you have to go anyway. Looks like you choose sides poorly. We could have scraped by if we got rid of the boys alone."

The madness of this scene made Yngvar shake his head. These men had rowed shoulder-to-shoulder and stood in a shield wall against enemies, or at least so he had thought. Perhaps Uncle Gunnar's men had always been so divided. But without a strong leader, the men fractured and now courted their own deaths at sea. Whoever emerged victorious, even if it was him, would be faced with a food shortage for the journey home. They would be forced to raid, and in small numbers raids, would be even more dangerous.

"This is your last chance," Bregthor said, mocking Yngvar's offer. "Lay down your swords or you will not hold them in death."

Yngvar glanced at Bjorn and Thorfast. Without a word, Thorfast let his arm drop from Bjorn's chest.

The three of them charged forward, screaming for blood. Bregthor's men surged around him and both sides joined in a clash at the center of the deck.

Bregthor hid behind others, shouting curses and taunting Yngvar, yet remaining away from danger.

Without shields, this was going to be a bloody business. Iron clanged together. Men cursed and screamed. Yngvar's short sword availed him nothing against the longer weapons. With shields all on the racks, he had nothing to defend him as he got close. He danced away from a half-hearted swipe.

Neither side fought with any zeal, despite Bregthor haranguing his crew.

"Face me, you coward," Yngvar called.

Bjorn wove between blades with fluid dodges, then brought his sword down atop one man's unarmored head. The skull cracked with a dull, liquid thud and the man collapsed to the deck. He had drawn the first causality of the battle and both sides peeled away from raving Bjorn. The suddenness of the death seemed to quell the fight. Fortunately for everyone close, Bjorn's sword remained wedged in the victim's skull. He struggled to pull it up.

"Sails! Two straight ahead!"

Yngvar saw one of Bregthor's men point, but he did not face away. This ruse was worse than a child's. He remained hunched and ready to strike, glancing at the shields racked over the rails. In this pause, he might grab one.

Yet others did turn, and they shouted the same warning. Bjorn had his foot on his victim's head, trying to wrench his blade from the dead man's skull. Thorfast, however, stood tall and pointed. Yngvar followed the line to where two ships with their sails furled and oars digging the water had glided from behind an island of rocks and pine trees. It was nothing more than a pile of stone for birds and seals, but it had easily hidden the two ships.

The fight ended. Even Bregthor paused to lean over the rails for a better view.

Yngvar's vision was sharp. His father had always relied on him to read the distance, and so he did now. His stomach fell at what he saw. Neither ship had shields on the racks. This meant the shields were strapped to the arms of their owners, ready for battle.

"How did they know we are coming?" Yngvar asked, more to himself than anyone else. But Ander Red-Scar, who had stood beside him in the fight, tapped his shoulder.

"Look to the shore. The third ship must have signaled them."

A third ship sped straight for them. The square sail of this one was full and the oars rose and fell with measured intensity. This was the hammer to drive their ship against the anvil closing from the front. Their only escape was the open sea and a bid to outrun them.

No one moved, each man realizing they were not escaping this time. Yngvar knew it too. They had lingered too long raiding, letting word of their violence spread. These ships were not from the petty jarl that had chased them into the sea. These were either raiders themselves or the real power in the local islands.

"We've got to row," Yngvar said. Waking to the danger, he pushed to the bow of the ship, where he confronted the slack-faced crew. "We've got a lead on these slower ships. If we reverse into the wind, we might row out of this trap. But we have to act now. Hurry!"

Bregthor seemed to awaken to the challenge to his authority. "That's right. Row, you bastards."

Men took in the sails and everyone else jumped on an oar, including Yngvar. Men who moments ago were prepared to kill each other now worked to save themselves from a common enemy. Nothing good could be approaching on those ships.

Bregthor now stood in what served as the bow as they rowed straight away from the on-coming vessels. He steered a straight course. Yngvar sat beside blood-flecked Bjorn, who rowed with powerful and deliberate strokes. His stared ahead, looking at nothing.

"This cannot get any worse," Thorfast said from behind. "It's like we knocked over a beehive."

"We did," Yngvar said. "These are dangerous waters. We should have went to a shore more welcoming of our people. We should've went home. Now unless we slip these ships ..."

Men were listening to him, he realized. His father had often told him that men needed confidence in their leaders to be of any worth. Even if the leader felt hopeless, he had to show a strong face.

"We will escape," Yngvar said, forcing his confidence. "We've got the lead. We can succeed."

Yet even as Yngvar rowed until his arms grew leaden, they could not increase their distance. The three enemy ships were faster and sleeker. The crew around Yngvar began to slow their effort, realizing they had lost to a lighter, better built ship. Bregthor had not steered a true course, either, but had still keep the land in sight. Perhaps it was inexperience or force of habit that told him to keep land on one side. No matter, their only escape had been straight to the heart of the ocean and Bregthor had not steered the course. He remained at an angle to the land, and the fast ships easily closed the distance.

The first ship to reach them pulled alongside Yngvar's row. The ship was full of crew, at least thirty men, all with spears and mail. Again, these were professional warriors and not raiders. Their shields were freshly painted and their helmets gleamed. They defeated Yngvar and the crew with their beauty alone. Here were glorious warriors.

A man with wavy gold hair flying in the wind and full beard braided and held with a gold band stood atop the rails. He wore a mail hauberk, but seemed to dance lightly on the edge unworried for falling into the sea. He waved at them and called across the distance.

"Hail, friends! Where are you going with my ship?"

Heavy thumps hit the hull on the opposite rails and Yngvar jumped in his seat. The second ship had pulled up and threw hooks to snare them.

He drew his oar in and let it fall on his lap. He gave Bjorn and Thorfast a desperate look. The two seemed resigned to capture.

"Well," Thorfast said. "Things just got worse."

Yngvar turned toward the corpse of Bjorn's enemy lying face down on the deck, his brains and blood spilled like an overturned soup bowl. Bjorn's sword still remained lodged in his skull. Perhaps he had been the lucky one this day.

19

Yngvar let his feet dig into the cool beach sand as he stood waiting for his masters to disembark their ship. He was tethered to the man before him by a rope around his throat. The line of five men included Ander Red-Scar directly behind him. Two other ships disembarked their captured crew in the same way. He spotted Thorfast's near-white hair among the captives. Bjorn, despite swearing to die before becoming a slave, walked down the gangplank of the closest ship. He too was bound by the neck to a man, and his face was folded up in disgust. Alasdair was too short to be picked out of the crowd from a distance, but he had to be among the dozens of people lining the beach.

The evening air was crisp, and birds circled the docked ships seeking scraps. Yngvar watched the mad flock squawking and dueling with each other as the crew herded everyone ashore. He cast one last glance at his uncle's captured ship. She was a good ship, a match to the ones that had overtook her, but she had been poorly crewed. No ship could save a fractious, half-strength crew. Unlike the ships that had towed her, she remained floating at sea while her new owners shuffled across the deck tightening rigging and otherwise inspecting her condition.

Crowds of onlookers came to the beach to marvel at the catch, mostly women in plain blue dresses and white head covers. These were all Norse people, Yngvar noted. His captors were Norse and they had mocked the accents of Yngvar and his fellows. In Yngvar's case, everyone here sounded like his father and his friends. In a strange way he took comfort from the harder accent.

A bare-chested man yanked on their rope and snarled at them. "Get moving, scum. Don't stand there with your mouths open."

They marched up a track inland. Yngvar was not certain of exactly where they had been taken, but it was far from where they had been captured. It was still the Hebrides, only the far south. Spruce trees were more abundant here and these waved a lazy greeting alongside the track stamped through ankle-high grass. The women followed, chattering to themselves. Children ran alongside them, making claims on which of Yngvar's companions they would take as slaves. Yngvar apparently would be owned by a girl with golden curls and an upturned nose who was no older than seven. His chores would be combing fleas from her dog's coat. If only his real master would be so adorable, he thought.

Once away from the shore they came to a thriving village, as big and full of life as anything he had seen in Frankia. The buildings here were new as well, built from fresh logs and bright, tightly woven thatch. The tangy scents of life overwhelmed him and the clamor of so many people confused him. Every strange face seemed to search his as their captors pulled them through the village. He kept his eyes focused ahead.

At last they came to a long set of buildings, barracks from their appearance. The man leading Yngvar's group opened the door and pointed them into the dark beyond. "In there for now, you Frankish dandies. None of you are lovers, I hope? King Erik doesn't have a place for man-lovers."

Others of their captors laughed as if this were the pinnacle of humor. Yngvar raised his head at the name. Though they had been at sea for a day with these men, he had no idea who they were. "King Erik? Where are we?"

"Ack, your accent hurts my ears, boy. Get inside and don't let me hear you again." The bare-chested captor shoved them all through the door. Inside was spacious, more than what was needed for five men. Pallets lined the walls and fresh straw covered the dirt floor. The door slammed shut, and a bolt or spear rattled against the other side. One of the men with Yngvar, a fool who had sided with Bregthor, shoved at the door immediately.

"I'm sure they'll let you out if you ask," Ander said. They were still all tied by the necks. Yngvar decided to pull the man back, and he fell away with a yelp. He was the only one who had sided with Bregthor. The other two men had stood with Yngvar and Ander.

They all sat in a row on the pallets. They remained silent a long time. Yngvar had resigned his fears after being captured. The first moments when these enemies boarded their ship filled him with terror. His newly named sword, Gut-Ripper, was pulled from his hand and thrown on a pile with all the other weapons. At that moment, fear left him and defeat filled its place. But now, after his sea journey and march through the thriving town, he had found a new purpose that left no room for doubt or fear.

He had to figure a way to escape this place. This King Erik was obviously taking them as slaves, either to sell or for his own use. So Yngvar had to determine where they were, how they could escape, and where they could escape to. He swallowed at the prospect. It was too soon for definite plans, but he had to keep his wits sharp and be on watch for opportunities.

After about an hour of uncomfortable silence, Bregthor's man sitting as far as his tether would allow, they had all begun to doze. They had been fed, barely enough, and Yngvar was both tired and hungry. He soon leaned on Ander, who pushed him back with a twist of his shoulder.

"Do you want some advice?" Ander asked, looking down at Yngvar.

"You sound like my father. He never cared if I wanted the advice or not. He just gave it."

"Smart man," Ander said. "You needed to build your relationship with the crew more than you did. You let Bregthor beat you at that game, and so the men believed him more than you. You were an outsider to us and spent all your time with your two friends. Yes, you saved our lives and we were grateful. But you were not one of us. That's important, you know."

Yngvar bit his lower lip and thought. "I can see that now. Thanks for the timely advice. I'm sure it will do me good as a slave."

Ander nodded. "Slaves need leaders too."

Yngvar shifted on his seat, the hard wood making his back sore. "You served my uncle for a long time?"

"Since before you were born. I knew Brandr as a small boy."

He looked at Ander, and his beard was still dark for a man of his age. "Do you know what happened between Uncle Gunnar and my father? I never understood why they did not get along. No one in my father's hall ever spoke of it, even in private. I tried to learn more but only ever got rumors."

Ander leaned on his knees and let his breath go in a long stream. "I was just a warrior under Jarl Gunnar in those days. He never confided anything in us. But I know the stories. They're just rumors, nothing more."

"The stories of Ulfrik's children were always that they worked together. But I've never known them to speak to each other. Uncle Aren, Bjorn's father, never leaves Rouen. It's as if he is not family. My father said he is only a half-brother, that he was born when my grandfather was thought dead. I don't know what to believe, but I guess it doesn't matter."

"He is Jarl Vilhjalmer's favorite man," Ander said. "Consults him for everything, as I hear it told. But what happened between the brothers, I don't know for sure."

He bent his mouth at Yngvar, as if he wondered whether to continue. Yngvar nodded. "I want to hear what you know."

"It was a terrible scandal." Ander leaned back and rubbed his legs. "After Jarl Gunnar's wife died from the pox that killed so many, he became inconsolable. Apparently, Jarl Hakon's Frisian wife tried to comfort him and I understand it went too far. Jarl Gunnar denied it. Your mother denied it as well. But your father accused them both. I don't know what he based his suspicions upon. From what I saw myself, your father later regretted his accusations but there was no forgiveness from Jarl Gunnar. He did not go so far as to break family ties, but he made it clear no one from Jarl Hakon's hall was to be given any special treatment. I guess he never forgave his brother, until the moment of his death, at least."

Yngvar had heard a similar tale, but had never believed it. He stared at the straw beneath his feet, trying to imagine his mother at the center of such turmoil. She was so timid, Yngvar could not see her imbued with any passion strong enough to sleep with her husband's brother. But what did he know?

"Thank you for telling me. What was the timing of that?" Ander frowned at him. Yngvar pulled at this rope collar and cleared his throat. "Was I born yet?"

Ander laughed. "You're Jarl Hakon's son. Never doubt it. I never knew you, of course. I just knew she had a baby boy and was accused of sleeping with Jarl Gunnar. The scandal was all kept away from us and I've told all I know. But the sons of Ulfrik never did cooperate again after that. A sad fate, I say."

"It's a shame," Yngvar said. "My grandfather left all of us a fortune and a kingdom. Now here I am tied up in a foreign hall, enslaved to some strange king. It seems all of us have squandered what he built."

"Well, rebuild if you can." Ander fingered his own rope, likely understanding that neither of them would live out the year to make rebuilding possible.

The door rattled and voices mumbled beyond. Yngvar shoved the man at his side to awaken him, and all five were alert when guards opened the door. They were square-jawed men with cold, determined eyes. They wore helmets and leather hauberks, four of them all together, and carried spears. The lead man handed his spear off and began to untie Yngvar.

"You're to go before King Erik," he said, roughly untying the loop around Yngvar's neck. His flesh rejoiced at the cool air when the rope lifted over his head.

"Where are we?" Yngvar asked. "Who is King Erik?"

The man took back his spear and stared at Yngvar if he were mad. Another of the guards answered.

"They're not from here, so they must not know." He turned to Yngvar, a gentle smile on his hard face. "You are in the lands of King Erik Blood-Axe. We are his hirdmen."

Ander and Yngvar shared a glance, and the others drew a sharp breath. Yngvar risked the question, "Isn't he king of Norway, after Harald Finehair?"

The first man shook his head. "He no longer rules there. For now. He has moved his kingdom here. Enough questions. Get outside."

The remainder of Yngvar's crewmates were already gathered in the field between buildings. Most were rubbing their necks in relief at having their ropes untied. Bregthor stood with Davin across the field, and the two sneered at him. Yngvar glided past them to where Thorfast, Bjorn, and small Alasdair gathered. Thorfast raised his hand for Yngvar's attention.

Twenty of King Erik's guards, all in heavy leather coats with full cloaks, surrounded them. They rested on spears and some carried torches. The sun had vanished, leaving a night of perfect black without stars or moonlight.

"This is hopeful," Thorfast said as Yngvar joined them. Ander Red-Scar had followed, along with the other two. But Bregthor's men gathered around him.

"Do you know we are prisoners of Erik Blood-Axe?"

Both Thorfast's and Bjorn's eyes went wide, but Alasdair brightened. "He was king of Norway once," Alasdair said. "But he became a sea king. I did not know he claimed these lands for himself. The Norse have ever claimed these lands as their own."

"Shut up," Bjorn said. "You're worse than Thorfast, and he never stops."

"I don't think I deserved that," Thorfast said. "Besides, this little one has better things to say than you. What've you done but grumble about killing everyone before you die? At least he taught us something."

"I'll teach you to live up to your name, Thorfast the Silent."

Yngvar waved them to silence. "If King Erik wanted to kill us, our heads would be on spears by now. But our guards told us we're to be summoned before him. So that means he will either sell us or keep us as his own slaves. We can't let that happen or we'll never get back. If we're sold to slavery, we won't remain together."

That thought seemed to strike both Thorfast and Bjorn hard. They both leaned back and frowned.

"I'll kill King Erik before that happens," Bjorn said. Thorfast rolled his eyes.

Yngvar paused at Bjorn's boast. "Right, well, he was king of Norway. He is probably well guarded. What we must do is make ourselves too valuable to be sold as slaves." He avoided Ander's gaze, since he had no plan to help him directly. "If we can do that, then perhaps he'll ransom the entire crew."

"Do we claim to shit gold, then?" Thorfast said, his eyebrow cocked. "We'll be lucky if he blinks before he decides to either enslave or sell us. When do we have time to impress him with our value?"

"We have to let him know we are the sons of wealthy jarls who can pay more for our release than he can make by selling us." Yngvar gave a hopeful smile to the blank expressions he received from the others. "He might have even heard of my father and grandfather."

Thorfast grimaced. "Will he believe us? What can we show for it?"

"What can any man show to prove who he is?" Yngvar said, hoping the aggravation he felt did not reach his voice. No one else was offering a plan to escape this mess. "The crew can vouch for us. We just tell him the truth of how we came to be here. Otherwise, we're not fighting our way to freedom, and King Erik is not going to allow us to sail off. So what other hope do we have? A ransom is the best way to get us back to Frankia and away from the slave markets."

Bjorn and Thorfast both looked at the ground. If Alasdair had any hope of freedom for himself, he said nothing of it. Ander nodded. "We will vouch for your story. Hopefully he'll believe the whole crew will be better ransomed than sold."

"The king is ready," announced one of the guards. The rest of them lowered their spears in the direction they intended everyone to march.

Yngvar swallowed. He had this one chance. As he followed the rest of the crew, he realized how lowly he appeared. His cloths were limp and torn. White patches of sea salt obliterated the color of his clothing. His hair was tangled and matted, and his thin beard felt like an old cloth over his chin. He hadn't groomed himself in weeks. He would have an easier time convincing King Erik that he was a slave.

Perhaps soon he would become one in fact.

20

Yngvar roused from his thoughts as a guard prodded the back of his arm with a spear. The cold sting got him moving faster. Torchlight gleamed in the guards' spear blades. Yngvar shared a nod with all of his companions as they followed the rest of the crew. He would press their case with King Erik and pray to the gods for aid. If he had time to make a proper sacrifice, he would have gladly offered up his silver armband. It was the total of his wealth now, and the best he could give. He had to entrust the Norns were not weaving a fate for him to die in slavery.

Their crew came shoulder to shoulder as the guards forced them together. Bregthor had worked his way to the front, as if he were leading this sad procession. In fact, two men carrying torches led them through the town where more shadow-filled, quizzical faces stared out of doorways as they passed. Yngvar suddenly felt how small their number had become. Their guards alone outnumbered them. The proud war band Uncle Gunnar had hastily assembled had whittled down to a fractured, diminished rabble. Had Bregthor not murdered Brandr, no one would be prisoners. Yet another reason Bregthor deserved hard justice.

At last they came to a steep hill topped with a large hall. Constructed from the same fresh timbers and thatch as the other dwellings of this village, it was by far the tallest building here. The double doors hung open and cheerful bright light and laughter tumbled out of it. Shadows flickered in and around it, imparting an air of festivity. Yngvar's heart lightened for it. Perhaps King Erik Blood-Axe was a good man after all. As if to confirm the thought, two men emerged from the warm light laughing each with an arm over the other's shoulder.

The guards pricked any stragglers with their spears as they all filed into the hall. Thorfast yelped when a spear blade touched him, and Yngvar laughed. Everyone else glared at him.

"Remember who we are," he said, keeping his voice low. "We are not frightened by this. We are noble sons of mighty jarls."

The hall was warm and bright, the hearth fire blazing as if it were the dead of winter. The familiar scents of home greeted Yngvar, further setting him at ease. Sweat and smoke battled the pungent odors of men who had feasted over-much. The hall had been cleared of tables and benches, leaving scrapes in the old straw and dirt of the floor. Hirdmen in full war gear filled the hall. Their helmets had faceplates that looped around their eyes, making each one's stare shadowy and inscrutable. That they bore spears inside the hall made Yngvar's chest tighten. No one carried weapons into the hall without good cause. Perhaps King Erik would have them all killed rather than deal with them. Would such a thing be possible, he wondered. Everything else seemed so welcoming.

"Kneel before your king," a guard shouted, emphasizing with a prod of his spear to another man's back. Bregthor went to his knee so fast Yngvar thought he had fallen. Others did the same, their cloaks sweeping behind them as they knelt.

Yngvar did not instantly take his knee. Instead he regarded the man who must be King Erik Blood-Axe, sitting on an unadorned but high-backed chair at the rear of the hall.

King Erik remained unmoving, like a man carved from wood. His eyes were bright and fierce, almost glowing beneath a tangle of golden hair that flowed freely over his broad shoulders. He relaxed against the back of his chair, but the muscles of his thick body radiated power like a viper ready to strike. His clothes were plain but fastidiously clean, and on both thick arms and heavy fingers gold and silver winked in the firelight.

Yngvar dropped to his knee the moment those smoldering eyes drifted over the heads of the others to meet his. He lowered his gaze a moment, but looked up again to find the king still lingered on him. He smiled like a man who was about to spoil the end of a long and carefully told story.

"King Erik Blood-Axe," announced one of their guards. "This is the crew of the captured ship we delivered this morning."

The hall had grown silent. Yngvar focused the ground before him. He felt the heat of the bodies close to his, Thorfast on his left and Bjorn on his right. Behind him Ander's breathing sounded labored, as if remaining on his knee was a great strain. Yngvar chanced a second glance around. The guards along the wall remained as still as their king, strong hands wrapped around their readied spears. Between posts throughout the hall more guards stood with swords at their sides. At least two men for each of Yngvar's own were ready to strike them dead if King Erik wished it.

Two imposing hirdmen in chain shirts and faceplated helms flanked King Erik. Yngvar wondered at the show of strength. Wearing a mail shirt in a stuffy, crowded hall was more a punishment for the man wearing it than anything else. Did King Erik believe Yngvar and his companions warranted this display of might, or did he always surround himself with a show of power?

"Is the leader of this sad crew alive?" King Erik's voice was powerful and smooth, but not as deep as his thick chest suggested. Rather than the roar of a bear it was the growl of a wolf.

"I am." Yngvar and Bregthor said at once.

A smile flickered on Erik's face, but he did not move other than to lift one finger from the armrest of his chair and point at Bregthor. "You speak to me on behalf of this crew."

Heat flushed through Yngvar's guts as Bregthor subtly turned his head as if resisting the chance to leer at him. The king let him hang for long moments as his smoldering eyes shifted from man to man. When he came to Yngvar again, the subtle smile returned. At last he shifted on his chair, raising his left hand to support his head as if he were so bored it might fall off his shoulders.

"You've done a shit job raiding. One woman and two cooking pots? I'm told you've come all the way from Frankia in search of treasure. I wonder at the point of all your effort."

"Luck was against us, lord," Bregthor said. "From the beginning, we have had an ill run. Your ships overtook us at our lowest moment."

"Indeed." Erik's single word hung over Bregthor like an ax. Yngvar had never heard a word more packed with meaning. His tone and wry smile said he knew of the conflict among the crew and perhaps even more. Could he have coerced one of the others to say more? What would they say about him, Yngvar wondered.

"Well, I ... I am in command of this crew, lord, such as it is. They need a strong hand to guide them."

Bjorn's face had turned red and he had closed his eyes. Yngvar gave him a slow nod, though his cousin couldn't see it. He knew the struggle, for it was his as well. Yet to speak up now would invite Erik's wrath. Whatever cozy feelings Erik's hall had produced had merely been relief from weeks at sea. This king and his hall were full of threat.

"And you are that strong hand," Erik said, tapping his finger against his temple. "Well, you bore me. All of you bore me. I had expected more entertainment from you, after what I had heard about your crew. Someone had brained a man just before my men captured you. Where's that fighting spirit? You're just a groveling lump of shit that washed up on my shores. I've no need for that."

Bregthor snapped his head up, turning it side to side like a frightened pigeon. He had reached the limit of his ability and Yngvar resented him even more. The gall of this fool, to assume he could treat with kings. He was a liar and murderer, indeed a lump of shit. But he did not represent Yngvar and never would. If he had any chance to sway King Erik, now was his moment. He stood and every head turned to him.

"King Erik, this man is not my leader. I am the son of a mighty jarl, captive to this man. I—"

A bloom of cold pain sprouted across the back of his head and his eyesight turned white. He staggered forward, tripping on the man before him and sliding to the dirt packed floor. Echoing laughter bounced around his ears while he shook his head until his vision returned.

"You don't stand or speak without the king's leave," a man shouted from behind. A spear butt struck him on the shoulder, flattening him down to both knees.

"That is a small improvement," Erik said. At last he put his hand down and leaned forward on his chair. "This one may stand and speak to me."

Yngvar paused for someone to help him up, but realized no one would aid him. He slowly built up to his feet. The heavy blow left his head throbbing and his vision blurry, but after a moment he was composed enough to make his plea. King Erik's eyes search him as he smiled. He was like the alpha wolf with his pack at his back, leaning over its defeated prey.

"King Erik, I am Yngvar Hakonsson. I come from Frankia, where my father is jarl over forty farms and five ships." He paused to see what impression he had made on Erik. Nothing, of course, He had once been King of Norway where he would have had jarls with larger estates beholden to him. "Here is my cousin, Bjorn Arensson. His father is the right hand of Vilhjalmer Longsword, son of Hrolf the Strider. We are both grandsons of Ulfrik Ormsson."

He declared his grandfather's name with great pride, and it stung to see no change in anyone's expressions. King Erik raised his brow at the pause and Yngvar continued.

"The ship you captured belonged to my other uncle, Gunnar the Black, who was jarl of twelve farms in Frankia. He was killed on raid in Norway." Here Erik sat up straighter. He could not still be king of Norway, could he? "This man who claims to lead us has only recently grabbed power for himself. He does not represent me nor those who are still loyal to my family."

Erik pursed his lips and gave a slight tilt to his head. "Thank you for the family history. Those names mean nothing to me but for Vilhjalmer Longsword. Perhaps I've heard of your grandfather, Ulfrik, for it is an uncommon name. No matter. Why have you consumed the short time I've given you to tell me all of this?"

"You will either enslave or sell us," Yngvar said. Erik's smile widened. "But we are more valuable to you as hostages. Our fathers will pay well for the return of their sons and men. Do not waste your time haggling with slavers, who will only undersell our value. Send us back to Frankia for a greater reward."

Erik tilted his head back as if considering the possibilities. His smile deepened as he seemed to arrive at a conclusion. "You speak well, though with a horrible accent. No lying about where you hail from. But are you truly a jarl's son? You allow lesser men to abuse you?"

A chuckle circulated among Erik's men. Erik himself stared down Yngvar, a wicked smile quivering on his lip.

Whirling on the balls of his feet, Yngvar faced the man who had struck him. He was the same height, draped with a gray cloak and wearing a helmet and faceplate. Yngvar had time only to note the neatly trimmed, reddish beard of the man.

He struck the guard in the face, clipping the faceplate and skinning his knuckles. The hard bone of the man's cheek crunched against Yngvar's fist, and he staggered back in surprise. The hall erupted in laughter and applause.

Yngvar did not let the man recover, but followed up with a weak punch from his left to topple the man over those kneeling behind him. He crashed the floor, cloak fluttering over his head and his helmet falling off. Yngvar's hand throbbed and stung where blood raised from the broken skin of his knuckles. But he ignored it and hovered over the man.

"You will treat me with more respect from now on. Do not think to lay hands on me again unless you wish to lose both of them."

He turned back to King Erik, who smiled but did not laugh as hard as the rest of his men. The two hulking guards at his sides gave no reaction at all. Yngvar flexed his sore hand and stood straighter before Erik.

Bjorn's whisper was harsh over the laughter. "You should've gutted him with his own sword."

"I'm more convinced of your claim," Erik said. "But now you have done violence in my hall. I cannot abide that."

More laughter, and Yngvar's stomach burned. He hoped his fear and surprise remained hidden, but Erik now finally leaned back in wicked laughter. Nothing he had done made any difference. Perhaps it was as Thorfast had said, and they had no hope from the start. He had just been a toy for King Erik to paw and bite.

"Like I said before, you are all shit." Erik waved his hand in dismissal. "We'll sort out who's to be sold and who's to be kept. Get this rabble out of my hall."

A hand like iron clamped over Yngvar's arm and spun him around. The guard he had floored smirked at him, a trickle of blood running from his mouth.

Yngvar swallowed, meeting the man's cold eyes shadowed beneath his faceplate.

"What are you going to do if I lay hands on you again, oh mighty son of whore?" He smiled. "I think you're going to be too broken to sell. Such a pity."

21

Yngvar stared at the guard who gripped his arm. All around the brightly lit hall, helmeted guards laughed. They leveled their spears at Yngvar and his crew, and anyone who might have considered resistance blanched before the gleaming blades. Erik sat unmoving on his chair, hand once more supporting his head in boredom. His fierce eyes fixed on nothing, as if he had forgotten everyone assembled before him.

"Bjorn Arensson is no one's slave!"

Bjorn spun on the guard closest to him, too near for spears to be of any use. For all his rage and wildness, Bjorn was the best fighter of all three of them. King Erik's men had been overconfident in carrying their weapons into the hall. Bjorn tore away the guard's sax, which hung at his side without any peace straps to restrain it, and flicked off the sheath.

Yngvar leapt for his cousin, but pulled up short in the grip of his captor. Thorfast also tried to grab Bjorn, but was likewise already restrained.

The blade flashed, and Bjorn cut up with terrible if inaccurate force. He shaved a line of blood along the guard's arm, causing him to flail back with a scream.

Laughter turned to shouts of anger, and a cluster of spears

converged on Bjorn. The rest of the crew either fell flat or danced away to avoid being skewered. But Bjorn was howling his rage, reversing his grip on the short sword to deliver a mortal strike even as a dozen spears would pierce his body in reply.

"Stop this!"

King Erik's voice was thunder in the hall. Everyone flinched, both Yngvar and his captor as well. Even Bjorn paused in his red-faced rage. But when he saw the spears ranged against him, he snarled.

"Get fucked, you whoresons!" He pulled back to strike the injured guard.

King Erik exploded through the throng, so fast and powerful that men bowled aside of his charge. Bjorn had only an instant to look up before the mighty king had driven his ring-crusted fist into Bjorn's jaw. As he doubled over with a grunt, Erik brought his knee up into Bjorn's ribs. Yngvar watched his cousin stagger and fall. King Erik stamped on Bjorn's sword hand, pinning it to the ground.

The room became as cold and silent as an ice cave at the top of the world. Erik had defeated Bjorn even without a weapon of his own. Bjorn, now winded and pinned, panted like a red-faced dog. Yngvar's stomach knotted imagining Bjorn's demise.

Thorfast struggled to get before the king. "My lord, he—"

King Erik kicked Thorfast aside like an aged hen that had wandered into his path. The king retrieved the short sword from Bjorn's grip, never raising his pinning foot.

Rather than plunge the blade into Bjorn's throat as Yngvar expected, the king released him. A dozen spear points drove within a hair's breadth of Bjorn's face, and he remained still beneath them. King Erik rounded on the wounded man, holding up the blade.

"Cut with your own sword in my hall? You dishonor yourself and disgrace me. I've no place for a weakling like you, who would let a boy disarm and nearly kill him."

King Erik braced his palm to the pommel of the sword and with both hands drove it like a spike through the man's gut. He had not moved, and barely whimpered as he collapsed at his king's feet.

"I've returned your sword," King Erik said. "Put it to better use in Niflheim, you shit."

King Erik turned back to Bjorn, his lip curled. He did not speak, but raised his hand to signal his men to pull Bjorn to his feet.

Yngvar again strained against at his captor, who despite his horrified expression had not relented. So Yngvar did the next best thing he could for his cousin. He shouted at King Erik.

"We are the sons of great jarls, whether we look it or not. Treat us well and you will be repaid for it. Sell us to slavery, hang us from your walls, or anything else, and you have squandered the prize your men have brought to you. Are you so rich as to throw away gold?"

King Erik remained silent, his back to Yngvar, and the blaze of hearth fire cutting him to a silhouette. His head imperceptibly turned to Yngvar.

"How wealthy are you, King Erik?" Yngvar squared his shoulders, knowing all his men were watching—even Bregthor. He had to be their example. If his words led to a cruel death, then he would accept it. Someone had to take action, and he was their leader.

Murmurs circulated among the crowd. The eyes of guards shifted behind their faceplates, each man seeking the reaction of his companions. Yngvar knew he had hit Erik in his ribs. He boasted wealth and strength because he lacked them. He had been King of Norway, and now he had lost it to become king of these lost islands of grass. Of course he was poor.

"Our fathers will pay all you ask," Yngvar said. "I guarantee it with my life."

Erik did not move, and his voice was full of threat. "Who is your father again?"

"Hakon Ulfriksson," Thorfast said. Erik closed his eyes and lowered his head.

"Hakon," he repeated. "Is there a name I hate more? Is there a name that better fits a man full of lies and guile. No, there is not."

Yngvar had no answer for Erik's sudden anger at his father's name. He sought to divert that anger before it ruined his chances.

"My grandfather should be better known to you. Ulfrik Ormsson was jarl of the islands not far to the north. He sailed with Hrolf the Strider to attack Paris."

"That is why I've heard his name," Erik said. He looked up now,

148

seeming to shrug off his anger. "Have any of you heard of this man, Ulfrik Ormsson?"

Yngvar smiled as a dozen men nodded. Several confirmed what Yngvar had said. Erik seemed to relax, then faced Yngvar and Bjorn both.

"Perhaps it would do well to keep you on as hostages," Erik said. His smile had warmed, but it did not reach his eyes. Yngvar wondered if King Erik knew what a genuine smiled looked like. "Yet Frankia is far and I've no inclination to travel there myself or send men of my own. I can send word with traders, and your father can seek me out."

Yngvar gave Bjorn a hopeful look, but his cousin was shifting his jaw and prodding his tongue against his cheek.

"Not just us two," Yngvar said. "Our whole crew is to be ransomed. It will only bring you more gold."

Erik's warm smile faded. "And I'll be feeding them until I can reach a deal with your father. I must profit from this, and these men are of no account."

"We will work for you," Yngvar said, not letting his voice falter. In fact, he wanted to ball up beneath Erik's ferocious gaze and hide. "All of us can care for ourselves. In time, you will find us as good as your own men."

Erik turned his head in thought, and his eyes revealed his mental calculations. "Very well. You will all earn your keep. If you prove yourselves, you can have your weapons back. If any of you are fit enough, you might sail with me."

He waved at his guards and the corpse at his feet. "You men show them to the barracks until we can find a place for them. And someone clear away this fool and give his family whatever blood-price they ask. If they still have complaints, send them to me."

When Erik swept from the hall to his rooms in the rear, the tension in the air dissolved. Men who had moments ago leveled spears at their guts now treated them cordially. Bjorn received a number of scowls. Yet Yngvar had no chance to worry for it. His own crew converged on him.

Ander Red-Scar embraced him. "I owe you my life once again. I'm thrice beholden to you now."

"I was saving myself too," Yngvar said. "And this time it's not a lie to say so."

He cast a glance at Bregthor and his staunchest cronies. He still had Davin and five or six men standing with him, sullen and defeated. Did they prefer slavery to this? Some fools could never be saved, and he abandoned hope for them. Even those who had once sided with Bregthor now crowded Yngvar to pat his back.

"It's just another kind of slavery," Bregthor said, pushing forward into the group. "We will all be made to work for nothing, own nothing, and have no freedom at all."

"You ungrateful pig," Ander said. "You'd rather have your head shaved and a slave collar fastened to your throat? Better yet, how would you enjoy a slave brand? You think we'd fare better being sold in Dublin? You're a fool."

Yngvar smiled, unable to imagine any finer rebuttal. Thorfast, true to his reputation, had the better twist.

"Slavery suits Bregthor and his ilk. For they have ever been slaves to greed and lies. That slave collar is fast around their necks, even if we cannot see it. A slave cares little how many collars he wears."

Bregthor sneered, but rather than fight, he gave himself over to the guards to be led out of the hall with his small band.

Thorfast slipped his arms around Yngvar's shoulders. He then reached out to Bjorn, who was still working his jaw, and pulled him close.

"We're together still," Yngvar said. "That's something to be grateful for."

They had no more time for celebration, for Erik's men were impatient to end their night. They herded them off toward the barracks they had occupied earlier. Someone had the wise idea to divide them, and astutely kept Yngvar and Bregthor apart.

As the night wore on, Yngvar's jubilation soured. Bregthor had been right, and it pained him to accept it. He took up a pallet with Thorfast, who had already spread himself across his side. His eyes were closed and his chest rose and fell in time with his breath. The barracks were dark, and men were mumbling off to sleep.

They had believed in him. It had felt incredible. Today he had become their leader. He had never experienced such a weight. These men actually thought he knew what he was doing, but he did not. Would they discover this? Would they go over to Bregthor when they did? Would they shame him? Probably all of that and worse. Yet no one else would lead. Bjorn was also Ulfrik's descendant, and his father Aren was renowned for his sharp mind. But Bjorn had inherited only stubbornness, loyalty, and fighting prowess from his ancestors. He was not a leader. Yngvar had to be that man.

So what now? The thought gnawed at him. He had managed to make them all hostages. But what was the next step? His philosophical patience from the earlier night had vanished. He had not time to wait and see how things developed. He had to agitate for a swift return to Frankia, otherwise they might all be absorbed into King Erik's ranks and never see home again. Not seeing home again had seemed an adventurous, daring choice to his foolish mind only a few months ago. How much he had learned since.

He lay down on the hard pallet. Thorfast was already lightly snoring next to him. Yngvar tucked his hands behind his head and searched the gloom before his eyes. He had no choice but to see what developed and exploit any chance he uncovered. He hated to believe it, but he was well and truly out of choices.

He and everyone else were, in all ways that mattered, slaves to King Erik Blood-Axe.

22

Yngvar wiped sweat from his eyes as it rolled off his brow. His back and knees ached from crouching in the hull of his ship for hours on end. He enjoyed standing on the beach, letting the cool air wash over his naked torso. Their ship was not far from the shore, where gentle waves lapped the rocks on this sunny day. The ship rested on a frame that held it straight while Yngvar and others repaired and improved it. He drew a deep breath, letting the salt air scour out the scent of pine pitch that had clogged his nose

Three other ships were laid out on the beach, the last of these being carried into place by a crew of two dozen men. Their shouts were distant as they lowered their burden onto its frame.

"Here's more pitch," Thorfast said from behind. Yngvar had smelled the heavy pine scent of it. Thorfast set one bucket beside his foot, and carried the other past him to where Bjorn and two other men waited against the hull.

"And wool," said Alasdair. The young, smooth-faced slave dropped a basket of wool beside the pitch.

"So my rest ends," Yngvar said. "We've got all these ships to caulk yet. Look at my hands. They're like wool mittens."

"Mine as well, lord." Alasdair held his hand up to Yngvar's. Both were covered in spilled pitch and errant wool, so that they looked more like lamb legs than human hands.

Erik had put them all to work on various tasks over the last several weeks. Yesterday he announced that ships need to be re-caulked and assigned Yngvar and a dozen other men to the task. Yngvar's former ship was the first one to receive the honors. He had spent all morning pulling up the deck boards and crab-crawling through the hull with a bucket of pine pitch and wool to fit between the strakes. It was tiresome work.

"This is better than clearing trees," Alasdair said. "I'm glad King Erik relieved us of that work."

Yngvar chuckled. "You were worried one would fall on you."

"God protects me, lord." But Alastair's eyes unfocused as he likely imagined a tree trunk crushing him to the ground.

Yngvar retrieved the heavy bucket of pitch. Thorfast and Bjorn were already atop the deck, both of them also naked to their waists and glistening with sweat. Thorfast put down his bucket to reach for Yngvar. Once he pulled him over the rails, Alasdair followed. The other men were already working at the opposite end of the ship.

"Looks like your admirer is here again," Thorfast said, trying to pretend he had not noticed anything. "She's got an eye for you."

Bjorn's laugh was like a seal barking. "You think it's him she fancies? She likes strong men, and I'm the strongest here."

"And the one with the thickest skull," Thorfast said, flinging a basket of wool to Bjorn's feet.

Thorfast casually glanced over the rails and across the field of grass that led to Erik Blood-Axe's hall.

Erik's wife, Gunnhild, watched him from across the distance. Her servants followed her and a hulking brute of a man trailed behind all of them. He wore a mail shirt and helmet that had been scoured to gleam with the slightest light. In the bright sun, he burned like a candle flame.

Gunnhild reminded Yngvar of Kadlin. Her hair was not as white, but she was tall and winsome as Kadlin. She bore herself with pride and dignity, and even from this distance Yngvar felt the power she radiated. He had not seen her up close, but from afar she seemed fair and clear-skinned with a rose-red bloom to her lips. She always seemed to show up wherever Yngvar was working and lingered in the distance before moving on. At evening meals where Erik had his men gather in the hall she never acknowledged him. Granted, Yngvar and the others sat by the front doors, the seats of least honor.

"Do you know, I learned why he is called Blood-Axe," Thorfast said. He and Bjorn were already down in the hull, painting their pitch along the strake they planned to caulk.

"Ain't it because he breaks skulls with an ax?" Bjorn asked.

"No, it's because he killed all his brothers to become king of Norway." Thorfast cocked an eye at Yngvar. "He only has one brother left now, and he chased him out of Norway. You know what his name is?"

Yngvar shook his head, distracted with Gunnhild and her troupe. They were turning to leave, but the blazing guard headed toward the ship.

"His brother is Hakon the Good. They call him that because he's a Christian."

"Praise be to God," Alasdair said, drawing an angry growl from Bjorn.

"Spent time in Wessex," Thorfast said. "And it turned him against the old gods, I suppose. But that's why Erik hated the name so much. Hakon the Good stole his throne and now he's trying to bring Norway back together. So Erik killed all the wrong brothers, and he must be bitter about that."

"How do you know so much?" Bjorn asked.

"I just learned all this last night. Unlike you two, I talk to the others. If we're going to find a way out of this mess, we're going to need a lot of friends."

Yngvar remained at the rails, watching the tall guard approach. Alasdair stood with him and looked up with a frown.

"Are we in trouble, lord?"

"I don't know. I'll go down to meet him." Yngvar pointed at the wool and pitch. "Get to work on this. I won't be long."

Yngvar landed in the soft beach sand, clapped his hands together to knock away loose wool, then approached the guard. He stood a head taller than Yngvar, his massive body intimidating at such proximity. Sunlight beamed off the rings of his chain shirt.

"You are to come with me," the guard said. He did not even meet Yngvar's eyes, but scanned up to the ship. "Tell them you will be back later. Don't make me wait for you."

He nodded at the commands. Both Bjorn and Thorfast now stood beside Alasdair along the rails. Yngvar put his hand on the back of his head, squinting up into the sun.

"I've got to go with him. I'll be back soon. Just keep working on this so we don't get behind."

The guard and Yngvar then marched across the grass in total silence. Yngvar looked back, but no one was watching him from the shore. The largest group were the men who had carried the last ship ashore, and they were now seated in the grass at rest.

Rather than follow a track into the village, the guard led him east away from the settlement. Yngvar waited for an explanation, but finally he could stand no more.

"Where are you taking me?"

The guard did not break his stride, but gave a small smile. "You will enjoy where you are going."

Glancing back at Yngvar, the giant man had eyes like clear water. Despite his smile, his gaze was predatory and cruel.

"Remember, I'm a hostage. If you harm me, you are defying your lord's will."

The guard nodded. "Any harm to you will be done of your own will. You'll understand soon enough, if you haven't figured it out already. Are you so witless to not understand where we are going and why?"

He thought of Gunnhild and swallowed hard. His breath suddenly felt short. Could she really be arranging a meeting with him?

They passed through whatever spruce trees had remained from their tree-clearing exercise of the prior week. At the bottom of a low rise was a small home. The thatch was bleached nearly gray and the log walls were black with water stains. A thin curl of white smoke raised over the roof, where two black crows turned their heads at their approach.

"In there," the guard said, raising his strong arm toward the house. "I'll wait here."

Yngvar stared at his clear, mirth-filled eyes, but when the guard said nothing more he descended the slope to the home. The door was rickety and open. A single push sent it creaking into the yellow light beyond. A feminine voice, husky and warm, called to him.

"Enter, Yngvar Hakonsson. Do not keep me waiting."

Gunnhild left no doubt for her intentions. If there were features in the room beyond a small hearth and furniture decaying in gloomy corners, he did not see them. A bed dominated the single-room home, and it was piled with furs and wool blankets. The frame and posts of the bed were fresh hewn from logs, unlike anything else inside. She sat on the edge, her bare calves extending from the bottom of her blue skirt that had caught on the bed. Yngvar's pulse quickened at the sight of her shapely flesh. When had he last been with a girl? That maid he had chased into the forest more than a year ago? She was nothing compared to the full-bodied woman enticing him. Her hair was unbound and flowing over her shoulders, light gold that shimmered in the light. Her cheeks were high and her red lips full.

"You are a handsome man." She slid over on the bed, and patted the space beside her. "I have enjoyed watching you at work."

If he fled now, perhaps she would leave him alone. Yet if he rejected her what form might her vengeance take? Her smile was inviting but twisted with a hint of wicked pleasure. Did she know the dilemma she had placed him in? Yngvar swallowed hard and lingered in the doorway.

"Do not defy your queen," she said. "I cannot wait any longer."

He had no choice. Sliding up beside her, Gunnhild wasted no time. He was without a shirt, and soon without his pants. She guided his hands in revealing more of her milky skin. He trembled both from anticipation and the terror of taking what belonged to Erik Blood-Axe, the man who had murdered all but one of his brothers. The thought nearly vanquished his lust, but in the end Gunnhild was a skilled woman.

Yngvar had not counted the hours he had dallied with her. At first tenuous, he soon abandoned restraint to his base instincts. No matter how tired and sore his body had been, the time with Gunnhild had rejuvenated him. Even the remaining pine and wool on his hands no longer troubled him. As they lay intertwined on the bed, Gunnhild examined his fingers and idly pulled bits of wool from what still clung to him.

"Your husband will kill me if he finds out," Yngvar said, his reason finally restored after his lust had exhausted.

"Very few get a taste of royal flesh, and many would gladly die for that chance." Gunnhild put his hand between her soft, warm bosom and smiled. "Besides, my husband is not a jealous man. He has his women to entertain him. I have my young men. We do not question each other's indulgences."

Yngvar had no answer for that. It soothed his fears to believe it, so he chose to accept her claim. They lay still for a short while longer, then she got up and dressed. Yngvar admired her full curves and thin waist. Her gooseflesh was obvious in the flickering light of the hearth. After dressing, she combed out her hair. "I will leave first. You will wait until I'm gone and then return to your companions. We will meet again." She kissed his forehead. "Soon."

It was nightfall when he stumbled back to the village in time to make the evening meal. To his shock, Gunnhild was present with her clear-eyed guard. She doted on King Erik at his table, never troubling Yngvar with a second look. In fact, both Erik and Gunnhild seemed happier than ever.

Alasdair had greeted him merrily, but Thorfast and Bjorn acted much cooler. Throughout the meal of flavorless barley soup and an over-salted mutton, neither had said more to him than they had completed the first ship and started the second. Finally Yngvar took a deep gulp from his ale and let the mug thud on the table. The other men filling the hall did not bother with him, but Thorfast and Bjorn both stared at the mug.

"What choice did I have?" he whispered harshly, wanting to

scream but realizing eyes and ears were always ready to pick up gossip. "What would you have me do? Could you imagine the revenge? We're talking about a woman used to having her way. Do you think we'd ever get home if I refused?"

Thorfast cocked his head as if to speak, but instead shook it. Yngvar noted a tuft of wool clung to his white hair. Bjorn spoke up instead.

"We're just jealous, is all. I'm better looking than you, so why do you get picked for the fun?"

Thorfast turned on Bjorn. "It's not jealousy, you oaf. It's the danger we're all in now."

"It's just him waterin' his man root," Bjorn said. "Why make it our problem? And you are too jealous. Your face turned so red when Yngvar went off this afternoon I thought you had burned it in a forge."

"That's true," Alasdair said. "You even called master Yngvar a horny git."

"For once the boy and I agree," Bjorn said. Thorfast's mouth opened in outrage, but he said nothing.

"Enough of this," Yngvar said. "What's done is done. I doubt she'll call on me again, and if she does I'll try to discourage it."

They completed their meal, arguing over how upset Thorfast had been. By the end of the night they had so many laughs at Thorfast's expense that all of them were in a better mood. When the evening crowd broke up, Thorfast clapped Yngvar's back and offered his apology.

The next day they returned to work caulking ships.

Gunnhild's warrior appeared and Yngvar left with him, giving a sheepish look to his companions.

The pattern repeated three or four times a week for weeks, always at the same abandoned house. The weather was steadily warming and his trysts with Gunnhild had left them both covered in early summer sweat. Yngvar came to anticipate the days, for Gunnhild was skilled and passionate. They did little more than satisfy themselves in each other's bodies, and Gunnhild did not linger in idle conversations. Yngvar surprised himself as being the one who longed for something more personal.

All the while King Erik continued on as if he did not know of their encounters. He had even visited Yngvar and the others at work, and praised them for their efforts. Thorfast had pressed him on a date to ransom them, but Erik had only offered a gusty laugh before leaving. That same day, Yngvar laid with his wife and took additional pleasure in making her quiver beneath him.

Their swords had been returned as promised, but Yngvar did not receive Gut-Ripper. He immediately suspected Bregthor had grabbed it for himself, but as far as he could tell the sword had simply vanished. Bregthor and his men were now so separated that Yngvar hardly saw them. Erik always gave them tasks out of the village and away from Yngvar or his friends. In the end, Yngvar settled for his longsword and hoped he would find Gut-Ripper.

One night Yngvar returned late from an encounter with Gunnhild while Erik was gone. He slipped into the barracks without anyone caring where he had been. But as he made to lie down for the night, Thorfast spoke up.

"You've got to use Gunnhild to make Erik keep his promise to ransom us. We've been gone for months, and summer is here. No better time to travel south. It has to happen soon or we'll never see home again. We'll be caulking ships and clearing fields for the rest of our days. Is that what you want?"

"Of course not. I've not forgotten what we've dreamed of all these years."

"Good," Thorfast said. The barracks darkened as the last candle extinguished at the far end. Men were already snoring, so Thorfast whispered. "And don't forget Bregthor. He's becoming Erik's man. Since your face is always buried between that woman's legs, I guessed you wouldn't have noticed."

He sat up on the pallet, trying to make out Thorfast's face in the gloom. Yet there was no moon and he remained little more than a vague outline.

"Oh yes," Thorfast continued. "We might've got our swords back, but we're still shoveling shit for Erik. Bregthor, Davin, and his other fools are worming their way into duties that look much like those given to hirdmen. Wouldn't he be much safer in King Erik's service rather than returning to Frankia to be tried for Brandr's death? You've not forgotten Brandr, have you?"

"Loki's tongue! What's crawled up your ass tonight?" Yngvar collapsed back down and rolled over.

The pleasant rhythms of the last few weeks had mesmerized him. He was failing as a leader to the men who relied on him to get them home. None had said aught to him, but then they were not given to speaking their minds. They trusted to him, that was all they needed. Yet he had not only lost sight of his goal, but allowed Bregthor to quietly slip from justice.

Worse still, if Bregthor was gaining favor with Erik, then how much longer before that became trouble for Yngvar and all the others?

He clenched his fist, wishing to strike himself in the head for his foolishness. Tomorrow could not come soon enough, for he burned to correct his course.

If it was not too late already.

23

Yngvar rolled off Gunnhild's soft, warm body. Salty sweat trickled over his lips and down his back, absorbed into the sheets as he faced the rafters above. The sun filtered through holes in the thatch roof, slivers of yellow light in the gloom. He was still flush with pleasure and his thoughts floated free. Staring at the holes in the ceiling, he guessed that when it rained the house would become unsuitable for continued use. There was already the vague scent of mold upon it. Perhaps he should thatch the roof himself.

Gunnhild sighed, then turned on her side and slipped toward the edge of the bed. "We will not meet for a while yet. Erik has returned from his trip, and last night he was demanding of me. I can't keep up with both of you."

Yngvar chuckled, wiping the sweat from his face. "The king's needs come first."

She said nothing more. Yngvar watched her combing her golden hair, admiring the curve and unblemished skin of her naked back. She was years older than him, though by how much he did not know. Not enough to matter in most ways, but in bed she far outstripped him in experience and skill. How lucky he had been to take up with her.

"I will call you again when I am ready," she said, slipping her green dress over her head. With both hands she flipped her hair out of her collar and over her shoulders. "Be ready for me, my young warrior."

He smiled. Then his stomach burned with fear. He had forgotten his resolve from two nights before, where he vowed to press Gunnhild for aid. Just seeing her and the promise of her sweet breath on his face had caused him to forget.

"Wait, there is something I must ask." He stretched to brush her skirt, but she recoiled as if he had struck her. The reaction caused him to snap back as well. "Sorry, I just want to discuss something with you."

She stared at him, her bright eyes narrowing. "Make it quick. I'm expected at the hall soon."

He had never asked anything of her before, and was stunned at her sudden change. He smiled in hopes it would soften the edge her gaze had assumed, but she continued to look at him more like a thief than a lover.

"King Erik has taken us as hostages, but the longer he waits to ransom us the less he will earn for our release."

Gunnhild's lips curled in a smile. "How so? Does your father love you less each day?"

It was a good question, particularly since Yngvar had not considered what he had planned to say. He had blurted out whatever came to mind. How he hated battles of words. That was for Thorfast and not him. He had best stick with the truth.

"I fear King Erik is absorbing us into his ranks rather than treating us like true hostages. Summer is here and the time to travel is now. Frankia is not so far that a trip will need more than a few weeks. I hoped you could lean on him to send us back."

Gunnhild's expression softened into a smile, and she at last looked aside from him. She gathered her brown linen cloak and flung it around her shoulders. "My young warrior, what if I want to keep you here for myself?"

Gods, would she do that? Why hadn't Thorfast or Ander Red-Scar warned him of that possibility? This was a disaster.

She began to laugh, covering her mouth with her pale hand. "Your expression is worth a wagon of gold. You are a terrible liar and even worse at hiding your thoughts. I won't keep you here, but I am not eager to see you leave. I've not tired of you yet."

Tired of him? Another thought that hadn't occurred to his naive mind. What then? Gods, what trap had he set foot in? No wonder Thorfast considered them all in worse danger than if Gunnhild had never took an eye to him. He wished he could be as smart as his friend, then maybe he wouldn't find himself in so many binds.

"Your friend has made an impression on the king, though. What's his name, the one with the lazy eye?"

"Bregthor." Yngvar slumped, pulling a wool blanket into his hands. He began twisting it as he thought of the man. Gunnhild continued on, fixing her cloak with a silver pin as she did.

"Yes, he presented King Erik with a gift, a fine sword with an emerald in the pommel."

Yngvar leapt up, naked, and flung the blanket aside. Gunnhild stepped back, hands at her throat. "Is an emerald a green stone?"

She nodded and seemed to be considering calling for her huge guard, a man called Hrut. Yngvar let his breath go and sat back down on the bed, hopefully putting Gunnhild at ease.

"That was my sword," he said. "He must have stolen it when we were getting our weapons back. The bastard made it a gift to the king, then."

Gunnhild also relaxed. "So it would seem. He is an ambitious man, this Bregthor."

"He murdered my cousin, who was our leader before me. When Erik's ships came we were about to settle that debt for good, but now we are here."

Everything was as Thorfast had said. Nor had he learned his lesson from what Ander Red-Scar had told him. He had not befriended anyone outside his small circle of friends, leaving himself distant from Erik's men. Bregthor had done the exact opposite and now prospered. He would be outplayed by this fool at every turn.

"Murder is a strong charge," Gunnhild said. "Can you prove what you say?"

"You doubt me?" He looked at her as if he had met her for the first time. Had they not been making love for hours at a time, day upon day and week after week? She could wonder if he would lie about the murder of his cousin?

"Don't stare at me like that," she said, the sharp edges returning to her face. "It must be more than your word against his."

"I have witnesses. You needn't be worried for that, " Yngvar said, letting his indignation show. This seemed to rile Gunnhild, who straightened her back and glared at him.

"It's not me who has to worry." Yngvar wondered at what she meant, but the frosty edge of her voice disappeared and she adjusted her cloak pin. "If you are confident, then take your accusations to my husband. He will give you justice."

Yngvar remained quiet, thinking through how to phrase his concerns without raising her ire. "King Erik has a reputation for, well, they call him Blood-Axe."

She stared at him flatly. "He was a great king of a great land. He will be that king again. Men are ever jealous and say a great many things that are not true. Do you think Erik is cruel?"

Remembering the man whom Erik killed in his own hall, he had to concede he was. Instead, he held his mouth shut. She seemed to take his silence as affirmation, nonetheless. She clucked her tongue.

"Erik is in a hard situation. His brother forced us from the throne of Norway, and he has to hold men together with strict discipline. Do not mistake that as having no love for justice. If Bregthor is a killer, then my husband will grant you justice."

The thought of bringing Bregthor down held great appeal. How often had this snake escaped the consequences of his evil? Yngvar should drag him back to Frankia and let his father pronounce judgment upon him. Yet if given the time to travel, the crafty bastard would find a way to slip justice once again. His victory in the holmgang was one example of how he could twist things to his favor. Yet here, trapped on this island and in the center of Erik's military power, Bregthor would have nowhere to go. Vengeance for Brandr might not come from the hand of his own kin, but at least it would be fulfilled.

"I will do it," he said. "I will take my witnesses and bring the charges against him."

Gunnhild smiled, small and fleeting. "Good. Now I must leave."

Rather than kiss or even touch him as she normally did, she spun around and strode out the door. Yngvar lay back down on the bed. He had to give her enough time to reach her destination before he left the house. While Bjorn, Thorfast, and Ander may have thought all this time away was given to pleasure, in fact much of it was spent waiting. He occupied his wait with thoughts of Bregthor's final defeat. While he might not have succeeded in securing Gunnhild's aid in speeding up their ransom, at least he had found a means of extracting revenge on Bregthor.

He had not even considered charging Bregthor in public and demanding justice from Erik. Yet, of course this had always been a possibility. He was a hostage and not a slave, though sometimes the distinction was negligible. Erik was a law-giver and any complaints among his people were judged according to his decisions. Even as a hostage, Yngvar was one of his people. Bregthor himself must have realized this earlier and worked to ingratiate himself with the king. Well, Yngvar had ingratiated himself with the queen. She could prove just as powerful an ally, and perhaps more so. Gunnhild seemed to exert a control of Erik that no one else did. With a word from Gunnhild, everything would turn in Yngvar's favor.

When he had judged his wait finished, he raced back to the village where he found Thorfast and Bjorn hauling empty casks from the ships back to the village. Alasdair filled in for Yngvar's absence, and he alone seemed happy to meet him. Such a strange slave, Yngvar thought. Hadn't he murdered Alasdair's master? After explaining what had happened, he looked to Thorfast for confirmation. His friend held his hand over his mouth as he thought. Bjorn spoke first.

"It's not as good as cutting Bregthor's head off myself. I was Brandr's cousin, too. I could still do it."

Thorfast shook his head. "That'll just make you a murderer in Erik's eyes. I think Yngvar is right. Bregthor is worming into Erik's good graces, both to protect himself and to sow trouble for us. If he gets in too deep, we might never see home again. Bregthor has no care to return, nor do those following him. We have to stop him now."

Satisfied that a more devious mind than his approved the idea, Yngvar set out to gather his supporters. Ander Red-Scar and a half-dozen other men promised to stand behind him in the accusation. Yngvar's heart was fluttering with excitement. The stain of shame for not having avenged Brandr had been a shadow over his heart for so long he had not realized how it had affected him.

That night, they drank and ate in the hall as usual. Yngvar found everything tasted like cloth and he had no appetite. Rather than let his gaze drift to Gunnhild as it did every time she was near, he instead sought out Bregthor. Indeed, he had moved closer to Erik's table than the rest of the crew. He laughed with men from Erik's hird, raising his mug again and again with his fellows. How nice that he should live a life of celebration while Brandr's corpse was devoured by scavengers at the bottom of the sea.

When the evening meal finished, Yngvar looked at all his supporters. Thorfast's face was whiter than usual. Bjorn's had flushed with anger. Only Alasdair seemed positive. "I will ask God to serve justice tonight, master."

Yngvar gave him a lopsided smile and patted his shoulder. He'd take any god's favor tonight.

Now was the time for men to bring their glories or their worries to the king. It was not an official moment, but one that all men understood was available from their lords. Yngvar stood up from the bench, and forced his way through the long hall toward the front.

He looked straight ahead, but the corner of his vision followed Bregthor. He was as acutely aware of Yngvar as he was of Bregthor.

Standing before his king and captor, Yngvar cleared his throat. Gunnhild was filling Erik's mug and gave him the barest glance. Her hulking, clear-eyed guard, Hrut, did not even look down at him. Erik himself remained embroiled in conversation with the burly man beside him. Finally, Yngvar summoned the will to call for attention.

"My King Erik, I have a complaint to bring to you."

Some at Erik's table put down their mugs and bowls in astonishment. Erik himself continued to drink as if he had not heard.

Yngvar squared his shoulders and spoke louder. "I demand justice for the crime of murder."

The hall stumbled to silence, so that the crackle of the hearth fire was the loudest sound. Men pushed away from Yngvar as if he had suddenly developed an odor. Perhaps he had an odor of doom, but he cared not. He tilted his head back and waited for Erik's response.

The king's mug clacked on the table, and he gave a long belch. He spread both hands wide along the board and finally met Yngvar's eyes. His gaze was the steady beam of a wolf hovering over its kill. The gold adorning his arms and neck glittered as he spoke.

"Why do you trouble me at my meal?"

"You are law-giver here, and I am your subject while under your protection. You hear the complaints of your men after the meal. I have witnessed this myself, lord. Am I wrong to speak up now?"

Erik's eyes seemed to narrow, but he did not move. Gunnhild faded into the darkness behind him, and Yngvar silently hoped she would whisper to him from behind. Erik remained still long enough for the entire hall to hold its breath. At last he tipped his head and extended his palm. "Speak, then."

"One night at sea, months ago now, Bregthor and Davin both fell upon my cousin, Brandr Gunnarsson. It was late at night while he worked the tiller and rested a moment at the rails. They each grabbed a leg and dumped him into the sea. He barely had a moment to shout before his voice was only for sharks to hear. Then they walked the deck to kill any witnesses, but he did not find me nor Thorfast. We both saw the crime happen. So I ask that Brandr be brought to justice for the murder of his oath-holder."

Brandr had not actually taken anyone's oaths, but Yngvar thought it a nice twist. Perhaps it would make Erik hesitate in accepting Bregthor as one of his own. He felt a warmth of pride in his chest for having thought of that detail.

"Lies!" Bregthor roared, shoving his way to where Yngvar stood. He stared up at Erik, more to see what Gunnhild might do. Yet it was too early for her part, and she remained impassive behind her husband.

Erik held up his hand to silence Bregthor, who inhaled to

continue his protest. So Erik slammed his fist on the board and set every bowl and mug jumping.

"You have witnesses? Thorfast, you say. Why is he not here beside you?"

Before Yngvar could think of a reason, Thorfast leapt to Yngvar's side. "I was not certain of how to act, my lord. Forgive me. It is all as Yngvar said."

"And the crew will vouch for me," Yngvar said, vaguely waving behind himself and hoping he was pointing at Ander and the rest.

Erik nodded, as if he began to take an interest at last. "And Bregthor, you deny this?"

"As I've told you before, my king, this one is a liar and a cheat. He thinks he's better than anyone else. He hates me because I had the strength to lead the crew when he did not. I know the crew will support me in this."

Yngvar's heart leapt. So he had been working against him with Erik. At last he faced Bregthor, who glared at him from the one eye he could bring to focus.

Erik sighed, leaning back from the table. He spoke wearily. "Who supports Yngvar?"

Turning to the crowd, Yngvar saw all he expected with raised hands.

"And support of Bregthor?"

Hands went down and the expected hands went up. It seemed to Yngvar that some who raised their hands were not even part of the crew. Had Bregthor prepared for this? Before he could count, Erik began laughing.

"So it would seem each side of this argument is equally represented. How unhelpful."

Erik sat with his arms folded. Yngvar watched Gunnhild, for now a word from her would turn everything. But she was staring off idly, not even watching the proceedings. One of her serving girls knelt at her side, holding a cup.

"Well, I have a way of getting to the truth," Erik said, his voice brightening. "And it will provide us some entertainment on this dull night."

Animated murmurs circulated around the hall. Yngvar's heart pounded harder. Gunnhild stood up and walked back into the darkness of the rear, not glancing at him.

Erik stood and gestured to his guards. "Take Yngvar and Bregthor outside. Strip them to the waist and tie them to posts. You two will be whipped until the truth is told or one or both of you die."

24

Yngvar staggered out of the hall, a guard shoving him through the door. The open ground between the mead hall and barracks was now filled with hundreds of faces, leering white orbs in the gloom of the night. A fierce bonfire threw its heat across the muddy ground, and shadows of children danced around it. Intermittent shouts of protest defeated the loud chatter of excited spectators. Yngvar wandered toward these voices, head spinning, but something yanked him back.

"This way, you fool."

His guard pulled him by the waist of his pants. Nearly an hour had passed since Erik declared this event, and the entire time he had sat without his shirt as a prisoner in the hall. He and Bregthor, both with their hands bound at their laps and guards surrounding them.

"This is not law! This is a crime itself!" Thorfast rushed toward him, but a score of guards had him, Bjorn, and all his other supporters held at bay. Whatever else Thorfast shouted was lost behind the wall of spears that warded him away.

A series of posts had been sunk into the earth, and Yngvar had never paid them any attention until now. Today he realized their cruel purpose.

The guard hauled him to the post where he unbound his hands.

A sharp, cold point in his back warned him that another guard had a spear ready to impale him. The guard then pulled his arms around the post and tied them anew.

Opposite the posts, King Erik's chair had been carried out to the yard. He sat sprawled in it as if relaxing for a night of riddles and song. Hirdmen and servants surrounded him. Next to him, Gunnhild sat in a second chair. She looked directly into Yngvar's eyes.

She blinked slowly and looked away, smiling.

"He's innocent! It's all lies." These calls came from Bregthor's camp.

Yngvar's face pressed up against the cold, rough wood and he turned aside so he would not have to see Gunnhild. Had she led him to this on purpose? Why not just have Hrut cut his throat after their last tryst? Did she have to kill him in such a public, humiliating way?

The guard tugged hard on Yngvar's bindings, making his hands go cold. He gave Yngvar a pat on the shoulder and winked. "I've got silver against your name, boy. Pull through for me and I'll share it with you." He laughed as he strolled away.

Beside Yngvar, Bregthor was similarly tied to his post. The bonfire light shined on his naked back and his eyes were wide with fear.

"This is where the gods show who they love most," Yngvar said. "I will feel no pain. But, you murdering bastard, they'll pour fire into every stripe you get."

A loud clap from King Erik silenced most of the crowd, though the villagers' excitement hummed in the background. Yngvar twisted his face along the post, bending his nose, to face Erik. The king stood up from his chair to address the gathering.

"One of these men has accused the other of the gravest crime I know, murder of his oath-holder."

"Untrue!" The faint shout was so far back that Erik merely blinked at the interruption and continued.

"The truth of the claim cannot be proved. One of these men is lying to me, and I detest liars. So for the last time, in the interest of sparing an innocent man from the torture, I ask you both to speak the truth."

"Bregthor Vandradsson is a murderer," Yngvar shouted. "He and

Davin the Shit-Eater threw my cousin overboard in the dead of night. I witnessed it."

The crowd laughed at Davin's name, for Yngvar did not know what else to call him. He closed his eyes and prayed Bregthor would have sense enough to surrender now.

"I'm innocent. I don't know what he saw, but it was not me who threw Brandr overboard." His voice dropped and pitched at the back of Yngvar's head. "And the gods love me. They chose me once before."

Erik smiled as if genuinely pleased. "I'm so glad both of you can stick to your convictions. But a man cannot be innocent and a killer at the same time. So we will let blood decide who is honest. Is everyone ready to see blood?"

The crowd roared. From the corner of Yngvar's vision he saw fists and spears raised in the night, flashing orange light at him. Gunnhild sipped demurely from a cup as if bored with everything. He wished it was filled with poison. Erik raised his hands to the crowd like a master entertainer, turning to face all of his people. At last he worked off a gold armband from his bicep, one of three that adorned each arm. He held it aloft.

"For the honest man, I will bestow this gold band from my own arm. For the liar, if the gods do not kill him first, I will pronounce judgment once he confesses. If neither confess, then the gods have called these men to their own judgments. They will be whipped until death."

A second roar of approval shook Yngvar's eardrums. Erik Blood-Axe was a worthless king. He loved violence before law, spectacle before justice, and cruelty above anything else. His wife was his pet viper. Never had Yngvar ever imagined something as heinous as this happening under any jarl in Frankia. There was law in that land, and good kings who respected their people. Here, if any man accused another of a crime he would be whipped. Who would dare ask for justice under King Erik? Escaping Erik's grasp had to come at any cost.

His hateful thoughts had stolen Yngvar's vision, but a sudden flurry before Erik awakened him again.

Alasdair had prostrated himself before the king, and men were running with spears lowered.

"Don't hurt him!" Yngvar shouted.

King Erik held up a hand and his guards stopped short of impaling the small slave. When he seemed to realize he wouldn't be skewered, Alasdair raised his head. His dirty, torn brown robe made him look like a miniature priest. Yngvar realized it was barely any covering at all for the poor boy.

"Please, great king, take me instead of my master. He spared my life and saved me from the priests who kept me prisoner."

Erik's head tilted back in laughter. "You look like a Christian priest. Makes me want to cut your belly open right here. But you can't take your master's place. That would serve nothing. But I promise you this, if your master is a liar, then I'll have you buried with him. Now get away from me."

Three men hauled Alasdair off the ground and threw him back into the crowd like a fisherman throws a poor catch back into the water.

Erik returned to his seat and gestured to someone behind Yngvar. The crowd grew quiet. He twisted his head aside to face Bregthor again. Now all that mattered was the competition to endure the pain longer. He would not be whipped to death. Bregthor would crumble because in his deepest heart he was a liar and a criminal. He had no resolve, nor fire for justice. He would beg for his life. Bregthor's drifting eyes settled on nothing, but his back was slick with sweat.

Yngvar heard a hiss.

A crack shattered across his back and he felt a cold stripe cross from shoulder to waist. Before he felt anything more, he startled at the snap next to him. A strong man with a bright white shirt and leering face lashed a leather whip across Bregthor's naked back.

Another crack and Yngvar felt a second cold stripe atop the other. Bregthor's tormentor followed on this one as well, though he seemed to withhold his full strength.

A cold, numb sting began to spread across his back. Yngvar gritted his teeth, but was intent on watching Bregthor suffer.

Both sides traded whips back and forth. At first the crowd remained silent, but soon murmuring started again.

As this grew, so did the pain.

The cold numb now dissolved into fire. Yngvar's hard back grew softer with every whistling strike. Each one came faster as well, some cutting into his buttocks or the backs of his legs. His calves took several poorly aimed lashes.

He pushed his face directly into the post and screwed up his eyes against the pain. Fire now poured across his back, running down his legs like hot oil.

The crowds jeering grew louder, and the lashes intensified. The torturers had been pacing themselves, preparing for a long night of dealing torment. Yngvar clenched his teeth, determined to make the torturers tire before he ever let a whimper escape.

Each crack was like thunder. Each lash was like fire. He crushed his face to the post, felt his calves stinging and burning, but he did not let out a sound. Beside him, the same crack and snap surrounded Bregthor.

Finally, he heard a cry. He was so encompassed with pain now he feared it was his own. A second lash broke over his shoulder, splashing a hot drip of blood into his face. But he did not scream. When Bregthor's whip cracked, he let out a yelp.

Yngvar turned his head. Bregthor hung against the post. Blood rolled off his back. When the whip broke over him again, bloody sweat sprayed and he shuddered.

Another lash, and Yngvar's vision turned red. He also pressed to the post, but the sight of Bregthor's collapse buoyed him.

"The gods ... love me," he said, so breathless he wondered if Bregthor could hear.

If he could not, the crowds certainly could. A shout went up at Yngvar's taunt. He thought he heard Bjorn shouting his name. He forced himself to stand, sliding up the post now greased with blood and sweat.

The cracks were swift and clear, each one a bright white stripe of fire on the jelly of what had been Yngvar's back. But he was going to prevail.

Bregthor was now openly screaming with each lash. The crowd cheered in glee at his suffering. Yngvar smiled.

At last, he heard what he had waited so long to hear.

"I did it," Bregthor said. "I planned with Davin to kill him and take the ship. I killed Brandr. Please, stop this."

No more lashes fell, and Yngvar closed his eyes in satisfaction. He wished he could savor the moment, but all he could do was hang against the post in agony and exhaustion.

"Cut them down," Erik shouted over the roaring crowd. Yngvar felt his bonds loosen then snap free, letting him collapse to the dirt. He lay there a moment, unsure if he could hang on to consciousness any longer. He had to witness Bregthor's fate and prove it had all been worth it. He turned his head against the bitter dirt.

Bregthor was in a sobbing, bloodied heap. The sight of him made Yngvar's back burn hotter. Did he look as bloodied and defeated? Erik was now standing over him, holding his hand up for silence. When the cheering diminished, he prodded Bregthor with his foot.

"You killed your oath-holder," he said. "That's a crime I cannot tolerate. Society breaks down when men do not obey their oaths. For you, Bregthor Vandradsson, I pronounce you and all those who supported you outlaws as of this moment. You no longer have my protection, and I cast you out of my lands."

Yngvar smiled, wishing he had the strength to sit upright and laugh in Bregthor's face. This was a better fate than he deserved, but Yngvar could do nothing for it.

Now two muddied deerskin boots filled his vision. His neck and back raged in fiery agony as he twisted to look up. King Erik's impassive face stared down at him. He held out the gold armband as if he intended to drop it on his prone body.

"You have suffered for the truth. There is nobility in that. For your valor I award you this gold armband."

To Yngvar's surprise, the king knelt beside him and gently tucked the warm band under his hand. Yngvar suddenly realized he was shuddering uncontrollably, and his eyes were fluttering open and shut. King Erik then unhitched a baldric at his shoulder and placed a sword next to the armband. It was Gut-Ripper.

"This was yours, was it not? I return it to you now. Wield it for glory, young warrior."

Before he could speak, he was swarmed with dark shapes. A face was familiar, lined with worry and wet with tears. He could not think of who this man was, but the near-white hair was the clue that reminded him.

"Thorfast?" he asked, hanging on to the last burning shred of his consciousness. "The gods preserved me. They favored us."

His friend nodded, choking back tears. One landed on Yngvar's chest and it burned like a bee sting.

"Take my armband," he said in a hoarse whisper. "Hack it up into equal bits and give one each to all the men who supported me. And get Alasdair proper clothes. Can't have him looking like a drowned priest."

The words exhausted him and his head flopped back as he lost his grip on the world. Thorfast shook him back to consciousness, making him cry out for the first time since the ordeal had begun.

"You'll want to see this," Thorfast said, then propped up Yngvar's head in the crook of his arm.

Bjorn and Ander Red-Scar held Davin between them, dragging him beside the pile of bloodied flesh that had once been Bregthor. The fish-eyed bastard scrambled against them to no avail, and the crowd was howling with delight.

"Brandr was my cousin," Bjorn said. "And his murderers are outlaws. I want justice for Brandr. Let me take it, King Erik!"

Erik was out of Yngvar's sight, but the impatient, lazy response was clear. "They are as rats to me. Do with them as you will."

The crowd leapt in excitement. Bjorn, his face red and eyes wide with madness, screamed out to the crowd. "An ax! Give me an ax!"

He let Davin fall, and Ander wrestled him still. A half-dozen men produced axes and Bjorn took the one with the longest haft. Wasting no time, he straddled Bregthor's ruined body.

"Eat shit in Niflheim, you gutless bastard! This is for my kin!"

The ax landed with a miserable crack in Bregthor's skull. He was just looking up when the blade shattered his forehead, spraying blood and brains. The roar of the crowd and the gory scene was too much for Yngvar. The pain coursing over his back made his own brain throb with every beat of his heart. He watched a screaming, crying Davin forced onto his hands and knees while Bjorn wrestled the ax from Bregthor's head.

Yngvar smiled with satisfaction. Thank you, Bjorn, for setting our cousin's soul at peace. He will thank you himself when he greets you in Valhalla.

He heard a meaty chop, but then Yngvar's world faded to muddy, cold black.

25

Yngvar had begun to believe he might never lie face up again. Though a week had passed since his ordeal, his back felt no better than it had on the first day.

"It's healing, lord," Alasdair said. "By God in heaven, your body regrows before my eyes."

"Then why do I wish for death with each breath?" Every time Yngvar's ribs expanded with anything more than a shallow breath, his entire back lit up in flames.

He lay in a room given to his recovery at the front barracks. This had been a place for honored men and visiting jarls. The room was warmed with its own hearth and the floor was smoothly beaten dirt with fresh straw. Soft down-filled mattresses covered his bed. Sometimes the feathers poked his exposed flesh, and even that was painful. The smoke hole was either obstructed or not wide enough, and so a thick haze hung the air. Beyond the wall at his head he heard muffled laughter of others passing by the barracks.

He stared at Alasdair for a short time. His elfin slave had not left his side except when called to other duties. Now in fresh clothes of gray and white linen and sporting a brown cloak of good wool held with a wood pin, he seemed like a young Norseman. His coppery hair was an unkempt mess, otherwise he could pass for a noble.

"You said priests kept you prisoner." Yngvar did not remember everything of his ordeal, but the moments before and after were clear. The gods had blessed him with forgetfulness of the horror of the actual whipping. "You didn't seem a prisoner when I found you. In fact, you were ready to die for the priest."

Alasdair's prefect white skin reddened at his cheeks. "He was not as bad as the others. But honestly, if I died for a priest I would go directly to heaven. That would be better than life, lord."

"Better than life?" Yngvar raised his brows. "If being dead is best, then why not fall on a sword or jump from a cliff?"

"God forbids it. A man who takes his own life will be denied heaven." Alasdair's eyes were wide and clear with sincerity. Yngvar could not understand that logic, and was glad he was not troubled by such a contrary god. Odin and Thor demanded sacrifice, boldness, and glory. Their laws were simple enough for anyone to understand and follow.

"What about for me?" Yngvar asked. "Would dying for me send you directly to your god?"

"I can't say, lord." Alasdair studied his hands. "You spared my life when all the others were killed. I feel a great debt to you."

They sat in silence while Yngvar considered the boy. He knew little of this bold child. But was he a child when men twice his age had none of his guts? He could not be much younger than Yngvar himself.

"I will give you freedom," Yngvar said. Alasdair looked up, eyes wide with surprise.

"Where would I go, lord? My father sent me away to the priests. I can't go back to either."

"I would be glad for your company, but as a free man." Yngvar managed a smile. "I only claimed you as a slave because I had no other way to spare your life. You are worth more as a friend than a servant."

Alasdair's smile took over his young face. "Thank you, lord. I will not forget this."

The door creaked open and two women entered, one old woman and her young attendant. The old woman had a bent back and a nose like a gnarled root. She at least smiled and hummed as she attended Yngvar, even if she hardly spoke. The other girl was one of Gunnhild's maids and carried a wood basin of water and white cloth bandages over her arm. She had a cute, upturned nose that made Yngvar think of Kadlin. Kadlin made him think of home, and that saddened him.

"I will wait outside," Alasdair said. Yngvar did not enjoy anyone seeing him cry with agony as the old woman worked her magic and medicine.

Yngvar turned his head aside to face the opposite wall. He could see light between the planks that blinked out as someone passed by. He wondered when he could walk again.

The old woman's voice matched her gnarled face with its labored and raspy tone. "You will have to be carried to the hall today. King Erik wishes to address all of you."

Yngvar snapped his head around, letting it drop half-buried into the soft mattress. The old woman's red-rimmed eyes were bright with anticipation. Did she enjoy his pain while she worked?

"The king wants to see me and the others? Do you know what for?"

If she replied, he did not hear it. When she tore away the first bandage, his back blossomed with fire and he screamed. Pressing his face into the mattress to muffle his shouts, he endured what felt like hours of torment as bandages were changed, wounds cleaned, and salves applied. Everything was fire. She could have piled snow from the top of the world onto his back and he would swear it was flames.

When she finished, Yngvar remained heaving and sobbing with his face in the pillow. He heard the gentle trickle of water as old bandages were dipped and wrung out.

"You are doing fine," she said in her frail voice. "But I wish the king would not move you. A few of these cuts are deep but healing nicely. I'd hate for them to open again."

"We agree on that," Yngvar said, keeping his face buried. He heard other voices and sensed others had joined. Turning aside, he saw the old woman hobbling out with her assistant and both Bjorn and Thorfast standing in the doorway.

Bjorn entered first. "Erik called us back. Says he's got news for us."

Thorfast entered and sat on the bed beside Yngvar. He was eating an apple, its snap and crunch making Yngvar's mouth water despite the burning residue on his back.

"Your back looks like a shark puked on it," Thorfast said. "But at least it's a match for your face."

"How does it look? All Alasdair says is God is being kind to me."

Thorfast glanced at Bjorn, who shrugged. Thorfast crunched his apple and held out the eaten side that had browned. "It looks like this only with more yellow and black mixed in with red lines. If this is God being good, then someone needs to tell God what a man's back looks like. He's not doing a good job with yours."

They all laughed, even Yngvar though it hurt his sides. When they settled again, Yngvar became more thoughtful. "My mother would weep to see me now."

"Whose mother wouldn't?" Thorfast asked.

"Not mine," Bjorn said. "Anyway, now that your back's a mess maybe you'd be a better match for Jarl Flosi's daughter. Your back'd match her face."

"Don't make me laugh anymore," Yngvar pleaded. "Say, do you think Erik wants to ransom us at last?"

He refused to refer to him as King Erik whenever he could. Erik was no king or jarl to Yngvar's mind.

Ander Red-Scar ducked his head into the room. "Hey, we're summoned to see King Erik. I'm here to help carry Yngvar."

Yngvar dreaded being moved. The old woman had him sit upright at least once a day to avoid sores forming on his stomach and chest. The pain of those brief vertical forays had been unforgettable. To remain upright now while in the king's presence made his guts turn to water.

Ander and Thorfast both positioned themselves at either side of Yngvar, both unsure of how to grab him. Alasdair showed them how the old woman raised him by reaching beneath his arms. They did the same, hauling him upright. Yngvar grimaced and clenched his teeth. It was like a sheet of burning oil had slid down his back. He had a few stripes on the backs of his thighs, but that pain was nothing in comparison to his back.

Once they got him upright, Yngvar realized no one could move him without touching his wounds.

"I'll walk," he said through his clenched teeth.

"That's right," Bjorn said. "He's as tough as boar hide. Besides, the bottoms of your feet weren't whipped. You can do this, cousin."

Ander and Thorfast had him supported beneath his arms. Even still, they still rubbed up against him to his increased agony. By the time he had entered the main barracks, sweat was forming on his brow.

All of the men who had supported Yngvar now occupied this single barracks. Yngvar had noted how Erik had built more buildings than he had people to house. He either once had more followers or expected an increase. The men offered encouragement, forming a pack around him as they exited the hall. Erik's messenger was one of his hirdmen, who waited with hands on his hips. He squinted at Yngvar, then turned toward the slope that led toward the main hall.

The walk was tortuously slow, and Yngvar had to stop to gird himself for more. Alasdair stood by with a cloth to wipe his brow at these pauses. Erik's guard would turn around and demand they all move faster. Yngvar took heart that all his companions walked behind him. After what seemed like hours, they arrived in the hall.

Erik again sat still and emotionless on his chair. For a moment Yngvar imagined that Erik was not alive at all, but only moved and spoke when someone was there to see him. It was a strange thought, likely induced by the fiery pain broiling his back from neck to heel. Erik's hulking bodyguards flanked him. Yngvar stopped wondering why they wore chain shirts like other men wore linen ones. He guessed these two enjoyed getting their hair and beards tangled in the chain links. For any man wearing chain all day would be bound to tear out most of his hair. Yet these cold-eyed, immobile giants were plainly uncaring.

"Yngvar," Erik said, finally animating. "I had forgotten you are still suffering. How cruel of me to make you walk here."

Forgot? You were nearly drooling as you watched the flesh being whipped off my back. Bastard.

"I am here now, lord. I am glad to hear what you have to say." This was the extent Yngvar could speak without his voice cracking. He gave Thorfast a pleading look, and his white-haired friend nodded. He would speak for him now.

"You're all here?" Erik sat up straight as if to count their number. His cold eyes ran over the gathered crew. "Well, a lot less of you now that Bregthor's dogs have fled. Though we might see them again, as slaves for sure this time."

Yngvar and the others exchanged concerned glances. King Erik leaned back with a sly smile, idly twisting the gold rings on his fingers.

"You must wonder at why I've gathered you. Well, you are all my hostages and I've got information on that worth sharing."

The burn in Yngvar's stomach equaled that of his back. He had managed to keep himself and the others out of slavery through this pretense of becoming hostages. Now he would find out if this was the passage home he hoped it would be.

Erik stopped fidgeting with his rings and leaned forward on his chair. "I've learned about Jarl Hakon Ulfriksson and Aren Ulfriksson. Your fathers enjoy quite a reputation, particularly yours, Yngvar."

Yngvar inclined his head. Could Erik be leading up to the ransom he would request? His father would pay anything, he knew it.

"I imagine your generosity with your gold must run in your family's blood. Your father has squandered his on his men too liberally. So he has nothing to offer me that I can't earn selling you all off at the slave market. No need for a long, fruitless trip to Frankia."

"That is not true," Yngvar said, but his voice was hoarse and dry. Thorfast jumped in for him.

"My king, your sources must be wrong. I am certain both Jarls Hakon and Aren have great wealth. You have not been told the truth."

"I've been told by men who served under Hakon. And Aren is no jarl, but a hanger-on in the so-called court of Vilhjalmer Longsword. He doesn't even have ships. So your lies have bought my hospitality for several months now. I imagine you enjoyed eating my food and drinking my mead."

And fucking your wife, you dumb bastard. Yngvar's teeth ground hard enough for him to taste salt at the back of his tongue. Bjorn's face was turning red as well. Thorfast, however, remained calm for all of them.

"My king, we have been productively helping you in every way possible. It is true your generosity is famous and we are ever grateful for it. But we have surely taken the edge off our presence here through the work we've done. Not to mention, you have captured our ship which is worth a considerable amount. More than what we've cost you."

Erik's smile widened and he shifted on his chair. "Your fathers do not interest me. Your grandfather, Ulfrik, now there was a man I could have dealt with. His children? They are not worth my time. As for what value you represent, that is for me to decide. Right now, you seem fit for the slave blocks."

Conjuring Ulfrik's memory made Yngvar's chest expand with pride. His grandfather would've carved this overgrown fool in half. Even if in pain, Yngvar had to speak out. He pulled himself straighter in Thorfast's and Ander's grips.

"My grandfather is alive in me," Yngvar said, meeting the king's eyes. "I am no slave and never shall I be. Sell us if that suits you, but you are mistaken. The gods will mock you for such arrogance."

"I don't doubt your ill-tongue comes from your grandfather. I hear he was an onerous, foolish man who had more luck than sense. But those are just stories. What do I know of the facts? Well, I know this much, your very life is in my hands. Perhaps I don't sell you. Maybe I can line my shores with your skulls as a warning to enemies. Think before you speak, or you will find you've crossed to my bad side."

The crawling burn on Yngvar's back made him wonder how horrible Erik's bad side was.

"Now, in your time here you've all seen that I am in need of good men. My—disagreement—with my brother will have to be addressed, and soon. I need men and gold to complete that goal. At first, I believed you might be a source of gold, and now I know that was a false hope. But as your more even-keeled friend has noted, you have served well. If you do not want slavery, then you may swear an oath to serve me. My ships need crews for rowing and spear men for fighting. You all will do well."

Yngvar sank between his friends. An oath was for life, and to break it was to fall lower even than a slave. Erik Blood-Axe was not the lord Yngvar wished to serve. Not even a ghost of such a man. Yet here was his choice, one kind of slavery over another.

"Can we take time to decide?" Thorfast asked.

Erik sprung from his chair, screaming. "Think on what? Slavery or service to me. Could it be so hard to decide? I thought you the smart one of the bunch. Fool!"

Eyes turned to Yngvar, and he felt their burn like the whip that had marred his back. Yngvar licked his dry lips. "Slavery is forever, and once sold into it there is never guarantee of escaping it."

"Come now," Erik said. "Some owners treat their slaves like family."

Ynvgar's father had treated his slaves either with indifference or kindness, never cruelty. But most people thought of slaves as property and did not weep for them any more than they wept for a cracked bowl or torn shirt.

"I cannot speak for everyone," Yngvar said, knowing that in fact he did speak for them. "But I will swear my loyalty to you."

"A wise choice." Erik looked neither pleased nor upset. He held out his palm for a sword, which one of his mighty guards gave to him. He held it forward. "Place your hand upon it and we shall bind our fortunes together."

Led by Thorfast and Ander, he stood before Erik and placed both hands on the cold, smooth iron blade. They helped him kneel as he swore loyalty. "I will serve unto death."

Erik nodded and completed the oath. "I shall offer you protection, shelter, and honor for your service. Should either of us be faithless, then let this oath be forgotten and forfeit the life of the trespasser."

So it repeated with every man. When Alasdair finally stepped forward, Erik withdrew his sword.

"This one is a slave," he said. "I need no oath from him."

Alasdair looked back to Yngvar hopefully.

"I granted him freedom this morning," he said.

"Do you have witnesses?" Erik returned the sword to his guard.

"Without witnesses he remains a slave. My men do not own slaves. I do. So this one becomes mine now."

"I witnessed it," Thorfast said. He glared at Bjorn, whose sullen face hinted he was paying no mind to anyone.

Erik laughed, slapping the arm of his chair. "Of course you did. You are the witness to everything, it seems."

"I witnessed it as well," Ander Red-Scar said. "Yngvar granted Alasdair freedom just this morning."

Erik's eyes narrowed. "I detest liars. You were sent afield this morning."

"I swore loyalty," Ander said. "I am your man. Yet you already question me?"

The curl of Erik's lip revealed his yellow teeth. He stared at Ander a long while, finally extending his hand for his sword once more. He held it out for Alasdair to swear his oath.

When all was done, Erik approached Yngvar hanging between Thorfast and Alasdair. "Is my healer caring for your back?"

Yngvar nodded. Erik walked behind him and pulled away a fresh bandage. The cool air stung his tender flesh. He grunted and patted the bandage into place.

"When you heal, you will make sure my youngest warrior knows how to handle himself in battle." He circled around to Yngvar's front and hovered over him. "I'm in a fine mood today and willing to indulge my men. But always speak the truth to me, or your back will never heal and you will spend your days weeping for your mother. Do you understand?"

Yngvar nodded. He understood.

He was sworn to a tyrant for the rest of his life and had no hope of seeing home again.

26

Yngvar leapt into the cold shallows, his naked feet plunging into the muck. One of the crew flung a rope down to him, and he took it up with Bjorn and several others. Bracing the rope against his shoulder, he pulled for the shore. A dozen other men leaned into other ropes, dragging the ship onto the beach. The high-sided ship held thirty crew and as many captives. All along the beach King Erik's other ships were going through the same process.

The sky had darkened and they had beaten a storm back to shore. Summer was done and autumn ascended, but it was warmer here than Yngvar would have thought such a northern land could be. A balmy, salty breeze washed over him as he sat on the grass with the others who had pulled the ship ashore. His shoulder ached from the stress. At least now his back no longer hurt him. The thick, raised scars were like another cloak on his back. With his clothes on, it was as if he had never been scarred.

Thorfast and Alasdair staggered over from another rope crew and sat with him and Bjorn.

"I'm glad to be back here," Thorfast said, looking up toward the village. The wind caught his white hair and blew it across his face. Women were already descending the slope to greet the returned men.

"This place is shit," Bjorn said. "What a fucking waste of a summer. Chasing down old men and women. This is what Erik calls glory?"

Yngvar shook his head. He agreed with every word. He watched ship after ship disgorging droves of slaves. Women and men, boys and girls, all collected from Scotland, Ireland, and a half-dozen other nameless islands where hapless people scratched their livings from the rocks. The slaves were why Erik had prepared so many buildings. He needed gold to finance his army, but there wasn't enough of it in these lands. So he stole defenseless people from their farms and homes and would sell them for the gold he required.

"There's got to be three hundred or more slaves here," Thorfast said.

"You can't count that high," Bjorn said. "No one can."

"I can," Alasdair said. "I learned writing and numbers from the priests. God has blessed me with a memory for it, too."

"Great," Bjorn said. "When we meet a real enemy, you can write letters and numbers. See how long that keeps your head on your shoulders."

Everyone stared at the clusters of slaves. They huddled together as Erik's warriors pulled them into groups like they might sort spoiled fruit from a basket. Children screamed to return to their mothers. Husbands tried to hold on to their wives. Resistance was met with the butt of spear in the face of the transgressor. Their screams were distant and shallow against the purr of ocean. Yngvar had hardened himself to this after a summer of raiding. Slavery was a fact of life, and slaves had their place in the world. Yet he had never had to witness the making of one. These were families, not captured warriors. Fate had woven a terrible destiny for these people.

Bjorn growled and turned aside. "Better them than us. A man is free only as long as he's strong enough to protect his freedom."

After a summer at sea, Yngvar still felt the sway of the deck even as he sat on dry land. It seemed impossible that only a few months ago he was still on his stomach. Throughout the recovery, he had mostly spent days idle in his private room. That room turned out to not be from Erik's thoughtfulness—which he did not possess in any measure—but from the scheming of his wife, Gunnhild.

One day after the old woman treated him, he discovered that Gunnhild had arrived. Yngvar wanted nothing to do with her, but she remained after the old healer left. She had her way with him no matter how he protested, no matter how he cried out from pain. She wrapped her legs around his torso, heedless of what it did to him. She was a beast that could never be sated. This continued for weeks, then suddenly ceased. Throughout the entire ordeal, she never spoke more than commands. When she dropped interest in him, he was neither warned of it nor explained why. The old woman and her maid continued their work until they pronounced him fit again, which was just a week before Erik decided to set out for summer raiding.

"Yngvar!"

He roused from his thoughts and turned toward the voice. One of Erik's picked hirdmen, Grimkel, approached. He wore a heavy wolf fur cloak and still wore his helmet. The faceplate lent a fierceness to him that belied his smile.

"Oi, Yngvar, we are starting celebrations early tonight. Come with me to the hall where we will have the first of the summer mead."

"You're popular," Ander Red-Scar said. "But I don't know why."

"I did everything I could to be as useless as possible all summer," Yngvar said. "Yet Erik and his men seem to favor me."

Grimkel stood with hands on his hips, his smile bright in his dark face. "Come on. You've spent enough time with these fools for one day."

As they had progressed in their raids toward home, Yngvar had discovered a rising popularity that made no sense to him. Erik's men spoke to him as an equal. They praised him for his bravery under the whip. They admired his generosity. They said King Erik did as well. He found himself among their number more and more, as if they hoped he would become accustomed to their better drink and food.

Thorfast shrugged at him. "Go on. Maybe now that we're back you can set that cunning mind of yours to finding a way out of Erik's service."

"It's not a difficult plan to imagine," Yngvar said as he rose to his feet. "Just steal a ship and sail. Hope no one catches up to you."

He fell in with Grimkel, who slapped his back. In truth, it still hurt him, but it was no longer a burn but a dull ache. He wondered if he would ever be free of that pain.

Once they passed the crowds of gathered slaves, he decided to probe Grimkel. "I'm flattered you'd invite me to your drinking. But honestly, you've no reason to be so friendly with me."

Grimkel laughed. He had roguish good looks that set women swooning. Even some of the girls taken as slaves had stared overlong at him.

"You are a brave and cunning man," he said. "We need men like you to defeat Hakon the Good and win back Norway. It's true Erik asked us to bring you into our fold. But we enjoy your company."

The mead hall, for all the horrible memories of the place, was a welcomed sight. Inside was warm and dry, and coals of the hearth breathing red light. A fat, black, iron pot hung by a hook over it. Savory scents of lamb flowed from it so that Yngvar's mouth watered. Nothing like a clean hall compared to life aboard ship and camping on strange shores. For whatever faults Erik possessed, he knew how to live in comfort.

"Is it wrong that we should be here before King Erik?" Yngvar set his swords aside at the door next to Grimkel's. Only a half-dozen servants hustled around the main room and attempted to disappear when Yngvar and Grimkel wandered in. Together they pulled a table and bench from the side. Apparently Grimkel had no worries of King Erik's dissatisfaction, since he hadn't bothered to answer.

"Bring the best summer mead," Grimkel yelled at one of the servants. "Leave one cask for the king, but the rest are for his men."

He winked at Yngvar and soon they were drinking warm, sweet mead. They had relied on looted ale and beer for most of the summer, and the delicious sweetness of a crafted mead made Yngvar forget his worries.

Before long, others filed into the hall. All were Erik's picked men and all were veterans of dozens of battles. They sported gold and silver armbands that matched their battle scars. They laughed with the easy camaraderie of men who have faced death together and survived. Yngvar felt insignificant among them. Yet they crowded him on the bench and invited him to their conversations.

Most uncomfortable of all was giant Hrut, whose clear eyes glossed past him without a trace of hinting at what he knew. He was Gunnhild's guardian and apparently more loyal to her than Erik. He did not speak with Yngvar, but listened attentively when he spoke and treated him well.

"The slaves will be sold before the week is out," Grimkel said. "They're going to traders who will take them to Dublin."

"The traders know to come?" Yngvar asked.

Grimkel held up a hand while he guzzled his mead horn dry. He wiped his mustache with the back of his hand. "It was all arranged in advance. We got the number of heads promised, so we can count on the gold we'll be paid."

"So where will he buy more crews?" Yngvar asked. "We've got maybe two months before snow falls, I'd imagine. Can we raise enough men for an attack in that time?"

The veterans exchanged bemused looks, and finally Grimkel laughed. "He's got more settlements than this under his rule."

Yngvar blushed. Of course he had not seen everything Erik could muster. While he commanded an impressive fleet, he would have had other leaders, so-called hersirs, who commanded their own hirds to come to his aid.

"Erik will call all his jarls together," Grimkel continued. "And maybe pay for some Irish mercenaries. We will be enough to grab Hordaland on the west coast. That will divide the jarls and put a spear right through Hakon the Good's heart. From there we can subdue the west and that is all we need to topple Hakon."

Grimkel slapped the table and his brethren did the same. Yngvar did not understand the nuances of battle plans, but the general cheer around the table seemed premature to him. Hadn't this same force been driven out of Norway? It seemed simplistic to shoot headlong into the heart of enemy territory with nothing but battle lust to carry the day. Erik's men were fighting for gold and glory only. The folk of Norway would be fighting for their homes. Yngvar's father had spoken at length on attacking men in their homeland. With nowhere to run, such men fought ferociously and to their last breath.

Throughout the day they drank until nightfall arrived with a storm behind it. The hall was overcrowded with celebrants. Yngvar was drunk by the time he tried to explain to the others what he had learned. Thorfast said something about disappearing during the upcoming battle in Norway, but Ander seemed against the idea. Yngvar did not care by that point.

More days passed and Yngvar eventually faced Gunnhild once more. She had no eyes for him, which was as he wanted it. Yet he also wanted to scream at her and tear away that careless, false smile she wore. Hrut resumed his duty following her everywhere. Yngvar wondered who was now being dragged off to her bed. It didn't matter.

After a week, the mood in the village was changing from celebration to sterner attitudes. The slaves had been sold. Erik spoke after every night's meal on the coming battles and the glories awaiting his men. He even promised gold and riches that had to be out of proportion to what they would find in Norway. Yet no one questioned this.

"Well, they're all from Norway," Bjorn said one night. "They should know what's there for the taking. Maybe it won't be so bad."

"At least we won't be chasing old women out of their homes," Thorfast said. "Or at least that won't be our entire purpose."

Yngvar nodded. His head was swimming from the noise and the drink. Everyone had come to regard him as a favorite of Erik and his closest men. So his drinking horn was never empty as warriors toasted him.

"Our ship is still at dock," Thorfast said. "I'd have thought Erik would've sold it. It's not as grand as his ships."

"Small but fast," Yngvar said. "I think that's what both Uncle Gunnar and my father preferred in a raiding ship. Erik wants to bring war to the west coast of Norway. That's a different ship altogether."

They spent a long night remembering how things were at home. Ander Red-Scar told them stories of Gunnar and Hakon, and bits of what he knew of Ulfrik Ormsson. It was a pleasant night. Yngvar sneered at Gunnhild as she left with Erik, much earlier than usual which raised Yngvar's spirits. But as more men began to snore or leave, Yngvar yawned and declared they should also sleep.

"After all, tomorrow is another day of listening to Erik's boasts and waiting for the real action to begin," he said.

They tottered off to the barracks. Yngvar was so tired he couldn't be bothered to change from his clothes. He lay on the pallet, no longer needing to share one with Thorfast, and arranged his boots and swords against the wall. The night was bright with a half-moon that dusted silver light through the outline of the doors. Alasdair slept to his left, and Thorfast to his right. Bjorn preferred a spot closer to the hearth, which had gone cold. Despite the early autumn weather, the night was still not so cold.

He drifted off to sleep.

Then he awakened.

He didn't understand what was happening. Something hard and smelling of mead clamped over his mouth. It was a hand. Next, a cloth was driven into his mouth. He was still in the dark, unable to see anything other than silver-lined forms hovering over him.

A sack slipped over his head and at least three sets of hands lifted him off the bed. He heard men snoring all around, and heard a muffled curse from one of his captors. Something clanked to the floor and the men carrying him paused. But other than some broken snoring, no one called out.

Yngvar bucked and tried to spit out the cloth in his mouth. Yet the sack over his head pressed it tight against his face. His nose bent flat against the pressure.

He bumped through a door and then the set of hands heaved him onto a wooden platform. He thudded head-first against something, then felt others piling in behind him

Someone clucked his tongue and a horse snorted before Yngvar felt whatever he was in lurch forward. He rolled onto his side and tried to stand. His abductors pressed him flat and he felt cold iron points at his side.

A low, familiar voice spoke to him. "No sound and no moving, or we clean your guts out right here."

He went still, realizing he could not fight his way out now. Someone grabbed his arms and bound them behind his back.

They were headed uphill, and the horse picked up speed as they progressed.

Yngvar remained still, struggling to figure out who had captured him and why. But no one made a sound as they carried him away.

27

T hough Yngvar remained still, his heart raced like he was sprinting across an open field. The depth of night was like a knife against his exposed flesh. In a strange way he was grateful for the body heat of the men who surrounded him. He guessed there were three, and one driving what must be a wagon. He heard the wheels crushing the grass and sometimes bouncing over a hidden rock. More than once he experienced a jolt as the driver hit some hidden rut. The passengers cursed him in low voices whenever this happened.

The speakers were familiar, but he could not place them. These were Erik's men, for certain. This set Yngvar's hands running cold. Why would King Erik do this? Everything had seemed to indicate Yngvar was a favorite of his. Of course, he knew better. Did Erik realize Yngvar and the others were plotting ways to escape him?

The others. He suddenly realized he might not be the only victim. Thorfast and Bjorn both could be meeting similar fates. Same for Ander and Alasdair and all the others who had been loyal to him. Perhaps Erik had decided to dispatch them separately without witnesses.

A man who could murder all his brothers would have no

compunction killing more than a dozen men because they had somehow irritated him.

His escape was paramount, but he also had to ensure the others did as well.

Yngvar had forgotten most of the surrounding areas after being away all summer. He could not think of where the cart was headed, but from the bouncing and multitude of rocks they struck he guessed it was not on a path. When his break came, he would have to orient himself quickly. Otherwise he could run back into the swords of his enemies.

The cart rolled to a halt and one of the men with him grumbled. "Glad to be done with that foolishness. Now, let's be about it. Hurry, lads."

Strong hands gripped his ankles and hauled him to the edge of the wagon.

"Get him on his feet," said the familiar voice. "Leave the sack on his head for now."

He held still, straining to see beneath the sack that had cinched at his neck. He was in a world of utter black that smelled like well-used leather. Hands grabbed his arms at either side and dragged him forward. He stumbled and smashed his toes on stones. Without boots, each step cut into his feet. He heard twigs snapping and his captors breathing. Something caught his cloak, perhaps a branch, and nearly pulled him out of his captor's hands.

"Here we are," said the familiar voice.

They shoved him forward, so that he crashed to his knees. The blackness flashed white with pain as his left knee drove into a stone. A rough hand seized his head and pulled it back, tearing away the sack.

The rush of night air was cold and refreshing. However, in an instant a blazing torch both drove off the cold and blinded him once more. He threw his arm across his eyes, and another familiar voice spoke.

"Don't burn his face off. I can see him just fine."

The torch retreated and Yngvar at last saw his captors.

Grimkel held the sack that had been cinched over Yngvar's head.

He gave a quick wink, before he threw the sack into the hay cart. Three other warriors surrounded Grimkel, all Erik's men who had been acting as Yngvar's dearest friends for the last month.

"Shocked to find yourself here?"

Yngvar turned to the familiar voice beyond the blazing torch. He recognized him now.

"Erik, what is this about?" Yngvar squinted past the man holding the torch aloft. Erik was wrapped in a black cloak, a contrast to his blond hair glowing with the torchlight. Dark shadows ran into his eye sockets and hollows of his cheeks, casting him as an evil skull. He stood with arms folded against the cold, holding the cloak across his chest.

"That is King Erik to you, but no matter now." Erik looked to Grimkel and the others. "You have done well. Await me at the edge of the woods. This won't be long."

Grimkel and the others hopped back into the wagon, with one assuming the driver's seat. Yngvar glared at them, but they just waved and flashed their evil smiles as the cart pulled away. A quick glance around and Yngvar determined he was in a pine woods, both from the thick scents in the air and the density of the surrounding trees. The crescent moon barely topped the serried black edge of the woods. He had no idea where this place was in relationship to the village. But it could not be too far for Erik to have arrived at this place ahead of time.

"You can never be too sure of who your real friends are," Erik said. "If it helps, I do think they respected you for your endurance under the whip and your generosity. It was a noble moment."

"The respect of rats is nothing to me. Why am I out here? What about the others?"

With his arms tied behind his back and his feet bleeding from scrapes and cuts, he struggled to stand. Erik watched him with an amused smirk. The torch bearer's face was lost behind the golden light. When Yngvar did stand, he staggered to gain his balance.

"You're just going back on your knees again," Erik said. "I do admire determination in a man. It's too bad you did not work out."

Yngvar stuck out his chin in defiance, but now that he had moved he saw the torchbearer and realized what was happening.

Gunnhild's giant bodyguard, Hrut, stared back at him with his passionless, clear eyes. He held the torch as if lighting the way through a tunnel to the underworld. Perhaps he was. For now Yngvar understood Hrut had remained loyal to Erik all along.

"You'll remember Hrut, of course." Erik unfolded his arms, letting his cloak fall aside. In his mighty grip the iron head of an ax glared with the torchlight. Erik Blood-Axe he was called. Yngvar was about to feed his own blood to that foul weapon.

"She said your prick was too small for her." Yngvar could think of nothing better to say. Tied up as he was, lost in darkness, the situation was as hopeless as it could ever be. At least he would not die groveling.

Erik's brows raised and for a moment it seemed he believed it, then he smiled. "I'm sure she said many things. I can't blame you, honestly. In fact, let me be clear, I don't blame you. When a queen calls you, what can be done? You cannot resist, for you will offend. And if you wondered at what offending Gunnhild would be like, I assure you it was wise not to do so. She makes me seem a kitten. So you see? I understand everything."

Yngvar struggled against the ties at his wrists, hoping they had loosened. Instead, he found them as tight as ever, and his hands were filled with a numb cold.

"You understand nothing," he said. "Nothing but cruelty and anger. So you will kill me for laying with your wife. But you can't even do it like a man. You have to tie me up and kill me like a dog. You are too frightened to untie me and face me as a warrior."

Erik's smile widened. "You are determined and brave, but you're not original. Every man who has found himself here has said nearly the same thing. They believe me so easily gulled into freeing them and providing a weapon as well. Really, do you think I can be shamed into untying your bonds?"

"You do not understand shame."

"I do not," Erik said. "I have never experienced a reason for shame in my entire life. I am as the gods want me to be. I live as the Norns have decided. No shame in that. But you, you have slept with another man's wife. You are the one who should know shame. Yet where is it in you, my young warrior?"

The pet name stung him. How much did Hrut know, or had Gunnhild herself surrendered him to Erik?

Erik nodded as if reading his thoughts. His voice assumed a more paternal note. "Gunnhild has a shameful secret of her own. She likes young men, perhaps even younger than you. Her interest can be passing or, as in your case, it can consume her thoughts for days on end. I've learned that her secret shame can never be curbed, and so must be indulged if only to keep the peace in my own home. She will give me heirs one day, and she herself is of noble blood. So I must endure the inconveniences of her moods. The unfortunate in all of this is the young object of her affections. She is fickle, and when she is finished, her young lovers don't always understand."

He raised the ax and pointed it at Yngvar. This served as Hrut's cue to shove Yngvar to his knees. Crashing back into the ground, his knees again went cold with pain.

"You are what's left of Gunnhild's shame. So tonight I will erase it for her as I always do. Your head and body will be thrown into a bog. Men will ask where you have gone. No one will know, but some men claim to have seen you drunk and mumbling about late at night. Perhaps you became lost in the dark woods. Maybe you returned to your ship and fell overboard to join your dear cousin in the sea grave. Who knows? What we will all know is Yngvar Hakonsson has left and will never return. And those who look too deeply will meet the same fate. Soon, no one will ask and you will be forgotten."

Yngvar glared up at Erik, struggling against his bonds. Tears stung his eyes. "At least let me hold a sword and die a warrior."

Erik seemed to consider, then grimaced. "Another expected request. But of course I would never put a sword in the hand of a man I intend to kill. One day when I get to Valhalla, I will tell your father you died on your knees, crying like a baby, and that is why his son is being eaten by worms in Niflheim instead of feasting with heroes. He died groveling."

Hrut put his foot between Yngvar's shoulder blades, forcing his head down. Erik took the ax in both hands and stood aside of him.

Yngvar grit his teeth and felt the back of his neck tingle, expecting the bite of the blade.

28

Yngvar stared at his own shadow stretching out before him. It was stark against the earth as Hrut held the torch directly behind him while pressing Yngvar lower with his foot. The cold earth still clinging to Hrut's boot seeped into Yngvar's back, eliciting a dull ache from his still-sensitive flesh. His arms, bound behind him, tingled with cold numbness. The final moments of his life were being counted in heartbeats. His mind flooded with thoughts, his entire young life splattering across his vision.

His father teaching him how to sharpen and oil a sword.

Kadlin laughing and dancing in a circle with her friends, her pale hair on fire with golden sunlight.

Him falling to the ground as he played with a dog that tried to wrestle rope from his hands.

Thorfast as a boy crying with a bloodied lip as his mother dabbed his mouth with a cloth.

Too many other disjointed and pointless memories flashed through his mind. Were the Norns dispersing the threads of his life so that each one flew away on the wind? Were they determined to show him he had achieved nothing with his life? Now he would die with a handful of memories that the gods would scorn. Would he have nothing to show at the doors to Valhalla? No great glories to earn him a seat among the heroes and a feast until the final battle of the gods at Ragnarok.

But he had earned glories. He had defeated enemies with bravery and guile. He had courage to defend his beliefs. He had the fortitude to endure pain that crippled a strong man.

He was not one to die on his knees.

Yngvar craned his head over his left shoulder. Erik's ax hovered in the air. It was as if the gods had frozen him in place. Now those shadow-filled eye sockets were alight with bloodlust, and the so-called king showed himself as no more than a debased murderer. Torchlight rolled along the freshly sharpened edge as the ax began to descend.

You did not bind my legs, you arrogant bastard. I will not die this night.

Erik stood beside Yngvar now for a better angle at his neck. His legs were braced against the heroic blow he planned to cleave Yngvar's neck. Hrut's foot held him down with less attention than one would give to a lamb. They expected him to comply with their plans and die obediently.

Instead he rolled into Erik's legs with all the force he could gather.

Time broke from the slow drip it had been. Now Yngvar's heart thudded against his breastbone and his pulse roared in his ears. Erik's massive swipe, one that certainly would have sheared Yngvar's head from his neck, slammed into the ground with a metallic thud.

Yngvar pushed through the king's legs and the momentum of Erik's swing carried him headlong into the dirt. Hrut's foot now stamped forward, ironically driving Erik's head into the ground.

It was all the confusion Yngvar needed. Like a cornered rabbit that had discovered a bolt hole, he snapped to his feet and began to flee.

If he was as fast as a hare, then Hrut struck as fast as a viper.

Yngvar had taken a single stride before Hrut had tossed aside his torch and tackled him by the legs. Hrut's hand was like an iron band around Yngvar's ankle. He slammed into the ground, his shoulder taking the brunt of the impact. With both hands tied at his back, he had no way to bounce up without both of his legs. Hrut was already drawing him across the dirt while his other hand sought to draw his sax, the perfect sword for close quarters killing.

Both paused at cries that came from all around the night shrouded trees.

The dark wood was suddenly alight with torches. Men were shouting as the points of orange light bobbed closer.

Hrut growled and turned back to Yngvar.

Then he received Yngvar's naked foot directly in his face. He screamed as the foot stamped his nose. Yngvar felt the bone shift and heard it crack, then warm blood and snot gushed onto his flesh. He pulled back and drove his heel a second time. This time he met fleshy, wet softness.

To his amazement, Hrut absorbed the blows with nothing more than a single scream. He never released his grip, and instead of drawing his sword now got up to his knees.

The shouts were clearer now. King Erik remained on hands and knees, recovering from having eaten dirt when he had been expecting a spray of his victim's blood.

Yngvar seized his chance. He kicked up into Hrut's crotch, locking his toes to drive deeper into the softness there. Yngvar's big toe bent on bone, but the giant man only grunted as he fumbled for his sax. The sword had swung around his back and was not where he expected it. Yngvar used the delay to drive another kick into Hrut's crotch.

"I'm going to pluck out your eyes!" Hrut had certainly felt that kick. He released Yngvar, just so he could at last draw his weapon. Blood flowed down his beard onto his chest.

Yngvar pumped back as men began flooding in from every direction, torches alight and spears flashing.

"There they are! Hurry! The king is in danger!"

Men converged on the dying light of Hrut's discarded torch. Erik was staggering to his feet, his black cloak making him seem no more than a floating white head from this vantage. Yet the dozens of men outlined in jagged black and orange shapes from their torches all seemed to see him. They streamed toward Erik with spears raised.

"Save King Erik! Hurry!"

Hrut glanced at the approaching men, but was not dissuaded from his purpose. He drew his short sword with a hiss of iron.

Yngvar was already shoving away, but he could not retreat far enough to escape Hrut. He failed to gain his feet fast enough as the giant lumbered toward him, his bloody beard glistening in the moonlight.

"I'm going eat your heart." He voice was thick with mucus and blood, but was surprisingly even for the chaos that swirled around them. Erik had raised both arms and was shouting at the oncoming men.

Hrut suddenly found himself faced with three spearmen who charged from behind. He had to choose killing Yngvar or preventing the attackers from skewering him.

Yngvar did not wait for the outcome, but flipped on his stomach then wormed onto his knees. He castled up to both legs and then leapt toward the darkest patch of forest he could see.

"Halt, you fools!" Hrut's bellow was as nasal as it was furious. Yngvar had no chance to admire his work, but stamped barefoot across the earth. He landed on a stone, absorbed the stab of pain and kept running. Whatever was happening was a gift from the gods and he would not squander it.

Something darted from the side. It was a ball of white and flashed out of nowhere. Yngvar had no chance to avoid a collision.

A strong, warm body slammed him aside and they stumbled. With his hands tied, Yngvar had no way to balance himself and slammed onto his side. He had already run so far that Erik and the mass of men around him were too distant to see clearly. The bright light of torches gathered in the center of the field, and other points of light flew toward the others. He did not see who had knocked him down.

The attacker was atop him, his face lost in shadow. No torches to aid him now, Yngvar only saw the outline of a thin man whose long hair burned blue with the moonlight. He was on him now, a blade glinting in his hand.

Yngvar threw a low kick, but the man was crouched down. He struck his attacker's side but did not knock him over.

"You ungrateful prick. It's me."

The shadowed man rolled Yngvar over without another word. He drove his dagger into the binds at his wrists and cut them free.

Precious warmth flowed back into Yngvar's hands, followed by a vicious torrent of needles. He remained still and blinking, uncomprehending of what had happened. His pulse throbbed in his neck as his arms fell gently to his sides.

"It's not going to take them long to figure out what we did," Thorfast said. He grabbed Yngvar's shoulder and rolled him back to face the sky. Thorfast was still lost in shadow, but Yngvar imagined the cocked eyebrow and skeptical expression nonetheless. "I won't mind if you spend the rest of your life being grateful to me, but right now we've got to run."

"How did you know? What is happening?"

"Later," Thorfast said. "I'm not wasting my breath now if we're just going to be cut to bits by vengeful hirdmen. Get up. I think Erik is taking control again."

Yngvar sat up, glad to have both hands restored to him. Across the field, the cluster of men and their bobbing torches seemed less frenetic. Erik stood at the center, like the hub of a wheel of fire. His shouting was indistinct from this distance, but his outrage was clear.

"Through the woods," Thorfast said. "Then to the shore."

Yngvar's feet throbbed in protest. "I can't run through the woods in the dark, not without sturdy boots. I'll put a branch through my foot."

"Compare that to an ax through your head."

Thorfast hauled him up. Yngvar saw he had almost made it to the cover of the trees when Thorfast had tackled him.

"At least tell me how you found me."

They both ducked down as they sped across the short distance to the trees. Thorfast led the way, speaking in a hushed voice over his shoulder. "Finding you was as easy as looking for the fight. You're always at the middle of one."

"I mean, you were waiting out here for me. How did you do it?"

They entered into the woods, Yngvar's feet immediately encountering the sting of twigs and underbrush.

"I just ran beside you as you fled Hrut. I was only able to close the gap between us here."

Yngvar tripped on a branch and stumbled against a fallen trunk. He muffled a curse.

"This is going to be impossible. I need boots."

"Boot won't help you see where you're running. But Alasdair has them for you, and your sword."

"Alasdair is here?"

Thorfast shook his head as he helped Yngvar stand again. "He's on the ship, or I hope he is. Otherwise, we'll both be dying with our backs to the sea. At least that'll be heroic, won't it?"

He turned to run again, but Yngvar caught Thorfast's arm. "What do you mean by on the ship?"

"The plan, remember?" Thorfast said. "Steal a fast ship and hope no one catches up with us. Bjorn, Alasdair, and all the others should be bringing it around for us. My task was to make sure the hirdmen distracted Erik while I got you away. Your constant questions are interfering with that, if you didn't notice. Now let's get running. They have torches to help guide them through these trees."

Yngvar glanced back through the lace-like gaps between trees. True to Thorfast's prediction, the collection of torchlights were dispersing. A good number were heading directly toward them.

They both began to run without another word, Yngvar biting his lip against every rock and branch that assailed his feet.

29

Yngvar's flight through the woods left him cut and bruised worse than if he had been in a real battle. Branches had slapped his face and stabbed his feet. Stones and roots had hammered his toes into bloody nubs. His body stung with scrapes and throbbed with bruises from the dozens of falls he had endured. Now he flung himself into the cool grass on the opposite side of the woods, where the crescent moon spread its reflection across the gently lapping waves of the sea. He snorted the pine scents from his nose, and shook out needles caught in his hair. Some needles clung around his shirt collar, combining with the sweat pooled there to create a fierce itch.

He stared up at the dark sky and stars that winked through the patchwork of clouds. His chest rose and fell with the effort, and his body throbbed with every beat of his heart.

Thorfast collapsed beside him. The two remained wheezing and speechless.

Shouts echoed through the woods behind them. Yngvar let his head drop to the side, expecting to see orange balls of light bouncing toward them. Yet he saw nothing but the blue light of the moon painting the pines and spruce trees they had just plunged through.

"I've saved myself only to become a cripple," Yngvar said, closing his eyes against the pain pulsing in his feet.

"Running through a forest at night is like diving into a pile of spears and hoping for the best." Thorfast curled up from prone and gathered his knees to his chest. "I suppose that we survived shows the gods are with us tonight."

"Unless they're saving us for something better." Yngvar sat up with Thorfast. The ominous shouts out of the darkness warned that they had no time to delay. "Where's the ship?"

Craning around, Thorfast pointed out to the water. "Over there somewhere."

Yngvar rotated on the ground to follow Thorfast's pointing hand. He looked out on a calm sea that rippled with the faint light of the crescent moon.

"Tell me they're delayed," Yngvar said. Thorfast shrugged. "Exactly how were they going to steal the ship?"

"We raised the alarm, got everyone in a panic over Erik's disappearance. In the confusion, Ander and Bjorn went down to the docks to prepare for when most of the hirdmen left to find Erik. Amazing how a number of them knew where to look first. Anyway, they would've overcome any guards there and be waiting for the rest of the deserters to join them. I hope I told them the right place to meet us. But we couldn't be sure where he had taken you when we divided up. So they might be anywhere on the coast."

Yngvar rubbed his face and stared at the purring waves. "It was a cunning plan, right up until the part where it had to actually work."

"We didn't have much time to consider the particulars. We had a wee bit of pressure to make sure your head stayed on your shoulders. I seemed to have got that just right."

"Of course, sorry, that was well done. We will have to guess where the ship is. Do we follow the path north or do we go south? They could have overshot our location or fell short."

Thorfast scratched his head and stood. "I don't have a good guess. South of here would take us closer Erik's hall. I doubt they would linger there."

"If they didn't find us, the best thing they could do is head out to sea and let us hide. Then they could comb the coasts for us later on."

"Bjorn is with them, remember? I'd not be surprised if he tried to sail the ship directly through Erik's mead hall."

They picked up and headed north. Neither spoke the choice aloud, but both knew it was their likeliest chance to find the others.

The brief rest actually worsened the pain in Yngvar's feet. Standing again sent a roaring flame of agony through his toes and up his shins. He had to hobble with Thorfast's help until they found the softer beach sand. "To think I used to curse running through this," he said. "I'd take beach sand over woods any day."

The strand's width fluctuated as they proceeded north. At points they were walking single-file. Huge rocks dotted the beach, obscuring the way ahead and forcing them to skirt around. Shouts of their pursuers had faded into the background, though the dark wood was always at their left. Yngvar kept expecting torches to flicker into view, but nothing ever appeared.

"There they are," Thorfast said, stopping to point out to sea. A large rock inhibited their view, but the square sail of Uncle Gunnar's ship was clear and full. Without shields on her racks, she looked like a raiding ship searching for a landing. "By the gods, they really did this!"

"I admit, I wasn't expecting success," Yngvar said, still brushing pine needles from his clothes. "Bjorn couldn't have had the patience for this."

"Ah, he's not that bad," Thorfast said. "He's just direct. Now come on."

Both were in high spirits as they skirted the boulders that jutted toward the sea.

On the other side, six men with spears and a torch were also staring out at the ship cruising through the night. They lined up on the beach at the edge of the surf, leaning on spears and talking in a low mumble.

Yngvar's hands went cold, and Thorfast reached for his sword.

"Are you mad?" Yngvar grabbed Thorfast's hand and pulled him back to the opposite side of the rock. They leaned against its cold hardness, staring at each other. Thorfast let his hand fall and Yngvar released his grip. "Gods, man, even my grandfather wouldn't charge six men with one sword."

"Well, what are we going to do? More will come."

Yngvar shook his head. He gestured for Thorfast to stay against the boulder, then peeked out at the men. They had pulled together in discussion, one man holding his guttering torch above all of them. He slipped back to Thorfast.

"They must've just seen the ship and now they're discussing what to do. My guess is they will leave men behind to track it while others go to fetch Erik."

"So we can attack when that happens?"

Yngvar nodded and put his finger over his mouth, then he gestured that they should get atop the boulders to observe. The moon was not exceptionally bright and both wore dark clothes. Thorfast's hair was bright, but from a distance it might not seem important. They clambered up onto the cold, smooth boulders and lay flat.

As expected, two men were already tramping away while four others remained. The torch went with the two who were leaving. The ship, however, was executing a wide turn as if to stay in this area.

"They are trying to guess if it is us on the shore," Yngvar whispered. "Did you work out a signal?"

"I thought we might be running and screaming when we got here. That was the signal, I suppose."

"Four men," Yngvar said, more to himself than Thorfast. "That's a horrible chance when we only have a single sword, and a bad chance even if we had two."

"But we have surprise, right?" Thorfast said hopefully. Yngvar waited to hear the plan, but Thorfast just smiled at him as if he had provided the key to all their problems.

"We're better off slipping away. We can't get past them on the beach. We can retreat to the woods and let Bjorn return for us tomorrow. In fact, we might have to wait a day or two before it will be safe to show ourselves."

"You realize I don't even know where to find drinking water," Thorfast said. "It's not like either of us has any wood craft to our name. That's the trouble with being the jarl's son and his son's best friend. We got to live an easy life."

"Well, I won't argue that anymore. What I thought was hard was nothing at all, and what I thought was fun has turned into a fever nightmare. But we've got no other choice. We'll be killed here if we fight."

They slid down the rock.

Coming up the beach behind them were a half-dozen torches. The men trudged ahead in silence, like a grim procession coming to claim Yngvar's and Thorfast's souls.

"So about fighting," Thorfast said.

"We can chance a run back to the forest, but someone will see us. Your damn hair is like a beacon in the moonlight."

"All right, how about surprise then?" Thorfast put his hand upon his sword hilt and cocked an eyebrow.

"Let me gather a few rocks first."

Yngvar pulled up the largest rocks he could fit easily in his hands, stuffing them in the crook of his left arm. With each rock he gathered, he checked the approaching enemy. They were in no rush, but soon they would find footprints in the sand.

"For gold and glory," Yngvar said. Thorfast smiled in answer.

They crouched low and circled the rocks. Thorfast held his sword in its sheath as he glided through the grass. One of the four men sat back from the others, relaxing. The remaining three huddled close in conversation. At least none wore mail. In fact, most were in sleep shirts of plain gray cloth.

Yngvar prepared his rocks, waiting for Thorfast to get into position opposite of him. Without word between them, they had created a plan. Yngvar would attack with rocks and draw them forward. Thorfast would ambush from the grass. The rest was for the Norns to decide.

Do I die today after all? If I do, then it is better than dying on my knees with my arms bound.

He glanced at Yngvar, now like a cat ready to pounce. They nodded at each other.

Yngvar stood and let his first rock fly.

30

Yngvar pitched his rock with all the force of Thor throwing his hammer. As it sailed from his hand, he was already preparing another. The man sitting in the grass, leaning back on his arms as if relaxing at a summer festival, caught the stone on the back of his head. He screamed out as the stone thudded against the back of his skull. He toppled to the side and remained still.

Heart racing as if he were charging uphill, Yngvar slammed another rock at the next closest man. He tried for the head, as he still had time to aim. The rock struck the shocked man in the mouth, but the strike was at an angle and so bounced aside. Still he grabbed his face and staggered back.

The remaining two men did not know where to look. Yngvar pelted the third man with a stone, striking his shoulder with a meaty thud. Now they both had him.

"You little bastard!" One lowered his spear to charge, but the other foolishly cocked his arm to throw his spear.

The rock struck as the man's spear sailed through the air, landing far to Thorfast's left.

Now he had a weapon in reach. He dropped his remaining rocks and dashed for the spear. It jutted from the ground, the shaft still wagging with the force of the throw.

Spinning around, he slashed out with his spear. The man who had wisely kept his spear now charged at him.

He leapt aside just as Thorfast sprang on the spear-thrower. Yngvar had only a moment to see the blue flash of iron and Thorfast's streak of white hair. He had his own opponent.

They circled each other with spears flashing, batting tentatively at each other's weapon. Yngvar smiled at the frightened expression of his opponent. He was older and more experienced, but he was also without shield or armor. A man came to depend on his war gear to lend him courage in battle. He was fighting in a night shirt. Yngvar, however, had no such experience to draw upon and was unencumbered by worry.

A scream came from behind, but Yngvar did not turn. It was not Thorfast's scream. Yet Yngvar's opponent let his eyes slip past to whatever had happened behind.

Yngvar plunged along the edge of the enemy's extended spear. It was like a guide that slid the blade straight into the man's heart. Yngvar felt the spearhead catch on bone, then plunge through for the kill.

He shoved the man off his weapon, not hesitating to watch him fall. Instead, he whirled on the man whom he had struck in the mouth with a rock. He was backing to the sea, his own spear keeping Thorfast at bay, while blood flowed from broken teeth.

Never throw away a good weapon, he thought, except in the greatest need.

Yngvar hurled the spear, sending it in a wobbling arc to impale the final man through his thigh. He screamed and collapsed into the surf. He would bleed out in moments, but Thorfast dispatched him with a sword flick across his throat.

"They're coming," Yngvar said. Thorfast looked toward the sea, but Yngvar pointed him up the beach. "I mean the others are coming."

Torchlight bobbed and shook as the approaching enemy struggled to run across beach sand. Their shouts were distant but angry.

"Good thing Bjorn is also coming." Thorfast pointed to sea and the ship was heading straight for the shore. The square sail had been trimmed and oars rose and fell in a steady beat.

Both he and Yngvar leapt into the cold water and fought through the waves. Yngvar's feet burned up in the salt water so painfully that tears filled his eyes. Were it not the threat of death at his back he could never have endured. The cold muck was no relief to him. He and Yngvar were now waist deep when ropes from the shallow-draught raiding ship landed within reach. He coiled one around his arm as he pulled himself toward the ship. Thorfast did the same.

In moments the two of them were lying on the deck in an expanding pool of sea water flowing out beneath them. The night sky showed patches of stars above. Someone called to lower the sail, and it seemed to be falling right on Yngvar's face as it dropped.

Thorfast's head was close enough to touch the top of Yngvar's. His friend reached over and patted his leg. "We're getting lots of practice at this."

Bjorn and Alasdair appeared over him. The cherubic face of Alasdair was filled with worry, but Bjorn wore a satisfied smile.

"Now this is the adventure we've been seeking. You two have fun running around the woods? Did you hold hands like two lovers at yuletide?"

With help from Alasdair, Yngvar sat up. Water rushed from his shirt. He tried to avoid looking at his feet. To see the blood and bruises would only enhance the pain. Instead, he scanned the men at the oars. He counted his old crew plus several others who had apparently decided Erik was no longer their king. Including himself and Thorfast, the ship now had a nearly full crew of at least eighteen men. He wasn't sure of his count. Ander Red-Scar guided the ship at the tiller and raised one hand briefly to wave. The rest of the rowers sweated over their oars, but also spared him a welcoming smile.

"Lord, your feet." Alasdair crouched over his feet. Bjorn stood over him as well, hands on his hips.

"Did you run through a carpet of nails? Looks like you kicked an anvil a few times as well."

"Something like that." Yngvar extended his hand for help, and Bjorn pulled him up. Straight into a bear hug that lasted longer than

Yngvar felt comfortable. When they did part, Bjorn's carefree face had transformed to profound grief.

"I never thought I'd see you again. Thought you were done for."

Yngvar nodded, feeling a lump in his throat. He glanced over the rails, watching the cluster of torches wavering along the shore. They would find four bodies left behind by two men. An evil, satisfied smile bloomed on his lips.

"So how did you get me out of this mess?" he asked, turning back to Bjorn. Thorfast was now standing, sloughing off his cloak. He flashed a smile at Yngvar's question.

"It was this one that saw the whole thing," Bjorn said, pointing at Alasdair. "Soon as you were out the door, he was waking us."

Alasdair's face turned red and he pointed at the mast. "I placed your boots and sword and some of your other things by the mast, lord."

"When will you stop calling me lord? You're a free man."

"But you are noble born, lord. I've told you I can't ignore that. It's not what my parents taught me. The priests too. Respect and obey your betters, they always said."

Yngvar wiped away the sea water that trickled from his hair into his eyes. His cloak had come free on the deck and was sopping. He wished he had something to dry his head. He looked to Bjorn. "So Alasdair woke you. But all this? Plus how did you know what was happening?"

"Thorfast's the smart one. He's in everyone's business, talking about what they know and what they think. He asked a lot about you. So he figured out what Erik was up to early on. He'd just been waiting for something like this."

"And you didn't say anything to me?"

"Why?" Thorfast shrugged. He sat against the gunwales, letting his legs go limp. "It would've just made you do something foolish. I wondered why you were suddenly so admired by Erik and his men. Seems like that happens a lot to people who later disappear. I had no proof, of course, but guessed Erik used that false admiration to either put his victims at ease or to cover his hand in the disappearances. You'd been plowing his wife for a good while. That'd have to come back to you in one way or another."

"So Thorfast started talking to the men," Bjorn said, clearly anxious to tell his part. "Just stuff about wanting to leave and whatnot. Ander Red-Scar and the others were in. A couple more of Erik's men were not decided, but they came after all. You see 'em here. My job was to get our ship back and ready to sail."

Yngvar shook his head. "Why not tell me all of this? Why hide it?"

"Because maybe I was wrong," Thorfast said. "And we'd never be capable of stealing a ship unless there was a distraction."

"So this is the best part," Bjorn said with a moon-bright, smiling face. He stood before Thorfast so he disappeared from view. "As soon as they took you away, we went right to the hall and got Gunnhild out of bed. Used the hirdmen on guard for it too. We made such a fuss when we found Erik was away, and one of Erik's men who was now on our side said someone had captured the king and was going to hold him for ransom. Someone said it was you, and of course you were gone too!"

"Hey, this is my part of the story," Thorfast said, still hidden behind Bjorn, who continued on oblivious.

"That bitch knew what was happening, but she couldn't say nothing. Of course, the hird had to guard her so she couldn't go after us. So Thorfast gets everyone following him out to hunt for Erik. Every man was ready to be the king's hero. Dumb bastards must've been half-asleep and still drunk. It was beautiful, it was."

Bjorn clapped his hands and laughed. Thorfast now stood and pulled Bjorn aside.

"So you were the distraction. I knew Erik would want to kill you himself, and I was right. He loves murder too much to leave that up to another. No one is too small for him to kill. I bet he tormented rats as boy. Anyway, I figured the only place for a murder was the woods. Anywhere else you could all be seen. The rest you know."

"So you gambled my life on a few lucky guesses?"

"But I was right, so you can thank me instead of staring at me like I just pissed on your feet."

"I do thank you, with all my heart. You saved my life. You all did."

He spoke louder so that the rest of the crew could hear him. He stepped before the banks of rowers. "I owe you my life. Without your bravery, I would be without a head by now."

"You were giving a good fight when we caught up with you," Thorfast said. "I bet Hrut won't be able to walk for a week."

The chuckles raised everyone's spirits. Soon someone started up a rowing song, and others joined in. They sped out to the endlessly dark and colorless circle of the sea, shooting across gentle waves like a spear thrown across the water.

Yngvar had to sit. His feet were too painful. Two brushes with death in one night were too much for him, and he began to fade into weary sleep.

His final thoughts before sleep overwhelmed him were that while they had escaped, they had nowhere to go and no supplies to carry them.

They had a victory this night, but in truth had merely won the chance to starve themselves at sea.

31

Yngvar stared out at the blank, gray water behind them. The sky was dark and the air cold. The sea bristled with white caps and not a seabird followed them. It was a bad omen. He hobbled away from the rails, his feet now protected in his boots but still horribly burning.

The rest of the crew tended the business of sailing, but without the need to row many had little to do. Most sat huddled with their thoughts, as did Yngvar. His cloak had still not dried since the previous night, and he wished he had something against the biting wind. The full sail snapped and the mast creaked. A ship at sea made a hundred different noises, each one telling the pilot its own part of the greater story. Yngvar was glad Ander understood the language, for to him it was all shuddering groans of wood.

"Is it wrong to say I'm disappointed no one chased us?" Thorfast joined Yngvar and gestured him to sit at the prow, where Bjorn and Alasdair huddled under cloaks against the gunwales.

"We are not important enough," Yngvar said. "Besides, we just stole back our own ship. He's not out of much except pride."

Thorfast swept his white hair out of his eyes as the wind blew it around his face. "I hope we never see him again."

Yngvar's fists clenched at the thought of Erik's cruel, arrogant smirk. "I do hope we will meet again. My back is scored with a dozen scars that will never leave me, and the bastard was going to butcher me like a pig. I've got revenge to take."

"You were fucking his wife," Bjorn said, his cloak drawn up to his nose. "Can't fault him for wanting to geld you for it."

"No, it was different. I think he knew all along and the reward for indulging his wife was supposed to be murdering me."

Alasdair made that Christian gesture where he touched his forehead and shoulders. "Praise God that lord Yngvar was delivered from Satan's claws."

"Lord," Bjorn repeated, then rolled his eyes.

They sat together and retold the highlights of their adventures. Each one embellished his part a bit more than the last telling, and even Yngvar described himself in a far more desperate fight with Hrut than reality.

Ander Red-Scar had handed off the rudder to another and joined them.

"This weather is making me nervous," he said. His sword hung at his hip and his shirt was stained with rust colored spots. Yngvar recognized that he and his friends had not been the only heroes in this tale. "Smells like a storm coming."

Yngvar squinted up at the dark sky. It did not take any imagination to see it brewing. "But we need supplies. Are we headed toward the closest settlement?"

"Closest ones are in Northumbria, at least ones far enough from Erik are." Ander spit on the deck for luck. "We could try Scotland."

"We talked about it already; decided to keep moving." Yngvar wiped his eyes against his fatigue. "Too many cliffs, not much to pick from, and they're good fighters. We learned that this summer."

Ander nodded. "Erik picked over everything nearby. We've got to go farther afield than he took us. We've got enough mead. If the rain is gentle enough, we can collect fresh water to keep us going. But we're going to be hungry soon."

"I'm hungry now," Thorfast said. "Do you think we should pull ashore ahead of the storm?"

"You mean if a storm is coming. It's not a certain thing," Ander said. "We would be wasting time. If Erik did send someone after us, they'd close the gap."

"No one is following," Yngvar said. But Ander frowned.

"He's a petty bastard, and he thinks this is his ship. Even if he doesn't directly send someone, others will want to impress him and come after us."

"No," Yngvar insisted. "He's preparing for the big raid on his brother, Hakon the Good. He'll want everyone with him on it. He's only got so many days to raid Norway before the weather closes that down. He's not going to hold his forces all winter. He's going to want spoils and good Norse winter stockpiles to carry him. That's his plan. He's letting Fate deal with us instead."

The ship rocked and creaked. The crew mumbled among themselves, leaning in to hear what was spoken between Ander and Yngvar. The true leader of the crew had not been decided yet. Yngvar assumed he should be the one, yet Ander was indispensable as a man who knew the way. Only Ander and a few others could sail them home with any certainty. Yngvar did not know the landmarks along the coast. He'd get everyone lost. So the crew would likely follow Ander, at least while at sea.

Ander put both hands on his hips and sighed. "I think it wisest to put as much distance between Erik and us as we can. It's a hardship, for certain, but it's better than being recaptured."

Yngvar scanned Thorfast and Bjorn for their reactions. They looked expectantly at him. Alasdair simply smiled.

"What does your god say about a storm?" Yngvar asked.

The smile vanished and Alasdair's brows wrinkled. "God doesn't speak to me, lord. I'm as a speck of dust in His eyes."

"Let me know when your god can do something useful." Yngvar scratched his head. Would Thor see them and guide his storms elsewhere, or would he hurl his hammer upon their ship? Perhaps a sacrifice was needed? He could throw his silver armband into the sea in offering, but it was a paltry thing for a god so mighty.

"You are more experienced at sea than I am," Yngvar said. "We should do as you say."

Ander smiled and the crew seemed relieved.

"It's probably for the best," Thorfast said softly.

But it was not.

As the day passed in an endless stream of gray water and sea foam, the skies darkened. Ander kept looking skyward, then toward the horizon as if expecting a fleet of ships to appear in pursuit. At last he gave in and decided to steer for shore, but Scotland offered nothing but angry cliffs and unfamiliar coasts. What shallows and reefs lay ahead was anyone's guess and so they steered clear at the first hints of troubles.

Then the storm blew in.

It was as if Thor himself had awakened to their presence. A wall of black clouds gathered, and the wind gusted hard across the ship. It swayed dangerously close to capsizing, sending Yngvar and all the others scrambling for something to hold.

The roar of the wind now brought sheets of cold rain. Already late in the day, the sun vanished with all its light as if noon had been traded for midnight.

The wind hit the ship abeam, again nearly flipping it over like a bowl on the water.

"We've got to steer so the wind stays off the beam," Ander shouted. "She'll capsize for sure, otherwise."

Yngvar nodded, as if he had anything to say about what to do. He had never endured a true storm at sea. Even after a whole summer of crisscrossing between Ireland and Scotland, he had encountered nothing worse than a squall. Erik judiciously kept his ships off the water at any sign of bad weather. At the time Yngvar had considered it tedious, but now he understood the rationale.

If he had thought ships spoke through creaks and groans while sailing, in a storm, ships wailed with screeching wood and snapping strakes. The deck was full of sea water now, cold and foamy around his feet. He grabbed a pail and joined others in bailing. Ander worked with all his strength to keep a course that would not take them far off and would keep the wind from capsizing them.

A dozen men bailed in a frenzy. The rain lashed them and the wind shoved them along the deck. Waves and spray crashed over the rails to undo all their efforts at bailing. Bjorn was howling curses along with Thorfast, who seemed more likely to fall with a full bucket than anyone else. Alasdair worked steadily, keeping his head against the wind and throwing his share of water overboard.

Only moments had passed, but to Yngvar it seemed a whole day had blown away with the storm. It was relentless, wailing rage and spitting rain down into the darkness. Ander's steering had devolved into a battle against shifting winds. For long spaces he kept the winds streaming across the deck stem to stern, but then a sudden shift would hit abeam and men would grab onto anything and pray. Yngvar himself grabbed the rail and saw the ocean a hand's breadth from his nose more than once.

Thor had summoned an endless storm with endless water and wind. He did not throw his hammer, for no thunder broke the dominance of the wind's scream. Yngvar despaired of ever seeing a dry day again. But then the winds calmed and the torrents fell to a drizzle, then ceased altogether.

When finally Thor relented, the ship was swaying in a circle of blackness. No moon or sky revealed itself. No landmark showed in the night. They were blind.

Compared to the rage of the storm, the world had fallen into utter silence. Even the slap of water on the hull seemed gentler than ever. Ander had bound himself to the tiller, and only now untied his arm. In the madness Yngvar had not even realized the mast and yard had been taken down and stowed. It had been right over his head but he had so focused on bailing he never saw it. In the low light, men looked like lumps of seaweed spread out on the deck.

Not until dawn could they determine the extent of the damage. The cold and empty night yielded to a morning of weak light that barely defeated the heavy clouds overhead. The ship was taking on water, despite being freshly caulked. Whatever fresh water and mead they had aboard was ruined with sea water. Despite the violence of the storm no one had been injured.

"Thor just wanted us to know he was displeased," Thorfast said. "But not angered enough to kill us."

Alasdair pursed his lips, looking like a petulant child. "Perhaps God had mercy upon us. But why would he spare the men who killed his priests? I must think on this."

The damage had all been superficial, except for the slow seepage of water. Every ship took on water and bailing was standard duty. But this was worse and the ship was lower to the water line than ever.

Yngvar decided to gather the crew together. Men were still dazed and hopeless after the storm. They needed to hear a plan, even if he was making it up as he spoke.

"The storm has taken us off course," he said to the crestfallen men staring back at him. They either leaned against the rails or sat on whatever sea chests had not fallen overboard. "Sea water has ruined our short supply. But we are alive and we are not lost. We can survive this."

The men exchanged glances. Thorfast and Bjorn nodded encouragement. His friends would support him, even if they didn't know what he was about to suggest. They would always have his back, and it made him stand straighter for it.

"Ander, do you know where we are? I mean exactly."

"Of course not. There's nothing to see here. Not until I get some stars in view can I tell you where we are. I think we were blown north of our course."

"That's fine," Yngvar said. "Until that time, if we sail directly east, we will come to the coast of Norway. That is where we need to head now."

The crew leaned back and grumbled. Ander lowered his head at the suggestion, rubbing the back of his neck. Yngvar waited for the objections, which Ander led.

"Last time we approached the coast of Norway, we were hunted and nearly killed at sea. We're even fewer men now, and can't take that risk."

"But we can't wait to discover where we are and then search for inhabited islands. Norway is a certainty, but everything else depends on sailing skill and good weather. These skies promise more of the same weather. Thor warned us off the water last night. Next time he will have no mercy on us. And even if he did, we are without fresh water. We will die of thirst within days."

"You're asking us to be captured again," said one of the other men. His face was lined with worry, like every other of the crew.

Yngvar shook his head. "We may be taken in, but we have something now that they need. We have information on Erik Blood-Axe's plans. Reliable information. Whoever is on this coast would be a potential target of Erik's or a close neighbor of one. The jarls there will want to know. Hakon the Good will want to know. Rather than approach as a raider of a lost ship, I say we approach as men unafraid. We come to their aid, even if they do not realize it, and we will be welcomed for it."

Furtive glances were shared, and others stared at the deck. Ander folded his arms and stared off to sea.

"If we sail straight south, we could arrive in Northumbria," Ander said.

"And meet the same fate? We have a ship and not even twenty men to protect it. The Northumbrian's will take it from us, and we have nothing of value to trade with them. Besides, you only guess a straight line south will bring us to land."

"We'd eventually find Wessex and the channel." Ander's voice had fallen quiet, realizing that they had no time for such a journey. The ship was sinking beneath them and fresh water was out. They had to take the certain bet. Yngvar's task was to make them confident of success.

"Sail us east," he said to Ander. "Unless the crew votes for your southern approach."

No one, not even Ander, raised a hand for the journey south.

"Remember, we have what the Norwegians need, and can trade it for our safe passage."

No one seemed especially confident as they returned to their tasks. Thorfast and Bjorn both clapped him on the back.

"Do you think we might be rewarded for what we know?" Bjorn asked, his eyes wide with anticipation.

"Honestly, I don't know what they will do." Yngvar stared east, nothing but a flat gray sea ahead.

Once again, he was at the mercy of another, and from what he knew of these people, they loved war and murder as much as Erik. Whatever awaited them over that dull horizon was likely to be violence and doom.

They sailed directly toward it.

32

Yngvar had no hazel branch to wave, so he grabbed the driest cloak he could find and waved it from the prow. The branch was a universal sign of surrender, but he improvised. He had all shields placed on the racks and his crew assemble at the center of the deck. He alone hung over the neck of the prow waving until his arms felt about to drop into the ocean. Across the choppy water, two high-side ships glided with an imperiousness that made Yngvar wonder if they were escorting Odin himself.

Their hulls were dark, and their racks were ominously devoid of shields. Fat, square sails of white and red pulled the massive ships toward them. Yngvar's arms were still heavy from rowing, and waving a damp cloak only worsened it.

"How many men do you count?" Thorfast shouted to him.

"Enough to fill both decks. Were you thinking of giving a fight after all?"

"I wouldn't bother with numbers like that. I only fight when there's a challenge to be won."

The crew laughed, nervously and perhaps forced, but it brought a genuine smile to Yngvar. He nodded to his white-haired friend. Bjorn, standing next to him, frowned. He detested surrender and his repugnance couldn't be more obvious in his folded arms and bent mouth.

That too made Yngvar smile. His mad cousin probably would dive into a deck thick with enemy spears, and the gods would love him and carry him to glory. But not today.

The two ships flanked either side of their sinking ship. Though they had rowed and bailed ceaselessly, the ship had now sunk ever closer to the water line. Had they not made for Norway as straight as an arrow, they would have sunk at sea. That much had resigned his crew to their fates. It was as good as being blown ashore by the storm.

The enemy crew lined the rails, bows strung and arrows ready, but none were raised. A thin man with a beard as dark as night hopped up to the rail, steadying himself on the yardarm.

"Ho, strangers. Your ship is sinking beneath your feet."

By the gods, not another sarcastic bastard. Was this banter a custom in the north?

"And I thought the sea was rising," Yngvar shouted back. "My thanks for your keen observation, friend."

The ship pulled closer, and the boarding hooks were already in evidence along the rail. The other ship had slid across the opposite flank, staying at the edge of bow shot. It was both a precaution and a nod toward a peaceful meeting.

"Are we to be friends?" asked the dark-bearded man. "I think we shall be more like the victors and you the captured."

"Call us what you will," Yngvar shouted. "We have sailed far and with urgent news for your jarl."

Black-Beard paused at the claim. He spoke to an unseen man on deck, then turned back.

"What is my jarl's name?"

Yngvar shrugged. "I don't know him. He will want the news I carry. We surrender to you. So do what you must, but take us to your jarl straight away."

The boarding hooks and ropes flew from the other ship. Yngvar's crew helped the captors tie to their ship, attempting to demonstrate they did not want a fight. By the time Black-Beard had stepped over the rails to formally meet Yngvar, the enemy's posture relaxed. Bows lowered and shield were racked.

They exchanged half of Yngvar's crew to the other ship, and those left aboard under a new command were to continue bailing. The two ships escorted them to the coast.

It was as beautiful a land as Yngvar had heard described. The fjord was narrow and deep, flanked by heavy cliffs and mighty peaks all carpeted in green. The flat light made it easy to see how lush this land was compared with the barren landscapes of the Hebrides and Scotland. He inhaled the deep, earthy scents that mingled with the salt of the ocean. Gliding at peace through the fjord, he knew the satisfaction his ancestors had experienced in this place. How had they ever left such a magnificent land?

The coastal village where they disembarked was just like his father's. The people spoke with the same accent as his father, and their bright and curious eyes were the soft blues and hazels of his people. He was one of them, even if his mother had been a Frisian. Here was his true blood.

"Not much to look at, is it?" Bjorn said as they stood on the beach waiting for the rest of the crew to gather with them. "Couple a shitty houses, mountains, air as damp as a fat man's crotch."

"I'm not going to ask why you know how damp a fat man's crotch is." Thorfast now joined them, having finished the voyage on their ship. He rubbed his arms, which must have been sore from all the bailing. "I think this place looks peaceful. The people here seem safe."

"Well, with huge ships patrolling their coast, why not?" Bjorn's frown deepened. "Bastards probably don't know which end of the sword to hold."

Yngvar watched strong men leaping from their ships to join arms with family. These were not overprotected people, but simply recognized the weakness of Yngvar's own crew against their defenses.

Black-Beard found Yngvar once everyone had been assembled and all the ships were beached. "Your weapons are in our care for now. The jarl will decide whether they're returned to you."

The main settlement lay further inland, accessed by a forest track. After half a year in the barren lands of hard-scrabble islands, he enjoyed being enfolded by boughs of orange, red, and yellow leaves. They marched at a leisurely pace. Though they were captives, this felt nothing like being a prisoner of Erik Blood-Axe.

He felt more like an unwelcome guest that had inconvenienced his host.

The mead hall was old, settled upon a low rise where the trees had been cleared of stumps all around it. The thatch was still golden, indicating care was given to the structure. Guards stood by opened doors and welcomed their companions. They gave wry looks to Yngvar and the others, nodding as if they understood more than they shared.

Black-Beard led Yngvar into the dim light of the hall beyond. "Kar Gellirsson is the name of my jarl, since you could not name him earlier. He's a generous and kind man, but he's no fool. Choose your words wisely."

Yngvar tipped his head to Black-Beard's advice. He thought Black-Beard might have been called Haf by his friends, but with so many strange faces surrounding him he remained unsure.

The hall itself was a single room, and Jarl Kar did not seem to make this his residence. The long room was dominated with all the familiar accoutrements of daily life: a long hearth with glowing embers, looms and baskets stowed against the walls, tables and benches pushed aside when out of use, animal bones and scraps littered the corners of the room. Hirdmen were strong and proud, wearing their swords in the hall with peace straps tied. They regarded Yngvar with a mix of mirth and skepticism. They were all like grown uncles giving reproachful looks to their young nephews.

"Ah, Haf, I've not had a moment to prepare for you. Your messengers barely arrived."

The man who spoke must have been Jarl Kar Gellirsson. Yngvar could not imagine a less underwhelming appearance for a jarl. He was easily the shortest man in the hall and built like a fat pine cone. His long hair was as wiry wool that had been wet and then dried in the sun. It was a stale brown color, and gray mixed in it. His mournful, cloudy eyes rested in double bags of flesh and his jowls flopped loosely. A dark mole sprouted a hair at his cheek.

Yet Haf Black-Beard knelt before this man. "We captured these men at sea, my lord. They claim to have sailed far to bring you news, yet they could not name you."

Kar nodded, then waddled to his seat. The size of the chair swallowed him into shadow, but his smile was clear. He waved Haf to his feet and then gestured for Yngvar to approach. "So you've traveled far in a sinking ship to bring news to me. I'm impressed. What is your name?"

"Yngvar Hakonsson," he said, dipping his head in respect. "You will not have heard of me, but you will want to hear my news."

"So what is this news you've risked so much to deliver just to me?" Kar's dog-eyes glittered in the low light. He seemed amused, and Yngvar did not know why.

He glanced to Thorfast and Bjorn, then Alasdair. All of them watched him rather than the jarl, as if what he said next was more important than anything else. Perhaps it was.

"We have fled from Erik Blood-Axe."

Mention of Erik's name drew every eye and every scowl in the room. Kar Gellirsson sucked his teeth at the mention and grimaced as if he had stepped on a rock with his bare foot. The revulsion gave Yngvar pause. He had everyone's attention, but not in the way he had desired. He pushed on.

"We were Erik's hostages until we stole back our ship and escaped. In truth, we did not know where exactly we sailed. We knew the coast of Norway had to be warned. For Erik Blood-Axe has raised a fleet to attack his brother, Hakon the Good."

The reaction was not what he wanted. Kar's expression had shifted from amusement to interest to suspicion. He now looked down his fat nose at Yngvar, his baggy eyes hooded with doubt. He rubbed his chin with his thick fingers.

"Is that the extent of your news?" he asked. Yngvar blinked, then nodded. Kar glanced at the men surrounding him, a frown deepening into the lines of his cheeks. "Well, when is this attack coming?"

"He did not say when," Yngvar said. "But he will not delay. He has hired mercenaries to supplement his forces. They must be paid and he has no wealth to keep them all summer."

"You know the condition of his wealth, but not the timing of his battle plans?" Kar leaned back in his chair. "Now that's odd."

"Well, I guess at his wealth. We spent all summer raiding for slaves which he sold to pay for this attack. So it cannot be long in coming."

"How many ships will he bring? Will he bring them here?"

Realizing he must appear to be shrinking before the jarl, Yngvar stood straighter to impart more authority to his news. "I do not have the exact count, but he has thirty ships at his command. More can be taken from those sworn to him. His plans are to scour the coast and teach his brother a lesson. That is what he said."

"It's a long coast, if you haven't noticed. There are some places better to attack than others, and some places are hard to reach but would be fat prizes. Can you tell me if he has indicated anything at all?"

"We were not so close to him," Yngvar said. His cheeks felt hot and he wondered if his frustration was showing. "The very fact that he did not bother to pursue us tells me Erik is preparing to launch this attack soon. You should be ready to meet him, at sea if you can, for he would be easily divided and driven off on the water. Once ashore, his men would be emboldened to fight with no chance to escape failure."

Kar folded both his hands over his prodigious belly. He licked his lips slowly as he appeared to be reviewing what he knew against what Yngvar had revealed. "So you are escaped hostages? Where are you from?"

"We come from Frankia, and that is where we seek to return. My father is a jarl of some standing in those lands, and Erik was considering our ransom before we fled him."

Kar tapped the side of his nose with his finger, letting his gaze wander over the crew. "What would you ask of me, now that I've heard your warnings?"

"Let us repair the storm damage to our ships, then allow us safe passage to the extent of your power. We only seek to return home and leave this conflict behind us."

The hall remained silent as Kar narrowed his eyes at Yngvar and his crew. He continued to tap the side of his nose as he considered, then at last he leaned forward to speak.

"I don't know what to believe. Erik has sent spies before with similar tales."

Yngvar blinked at the assertion and his stomach tightened. Kar seemed to be convincing himself of his choice as he spoke, his voice growing louder and more confident.

"He sends men in poor ships, ones he cares not to lose, and gathers what he can from the jarls of the coast. You are exactly that."

"I'm no friend of Erik Blood-Axe," Yngvar said, the anger in his voice matching the suspicion in Kar's. He reached to pull over his shirt, but the erstwhile peaceful hirdmen charged at him with a half-dozen naked swords poised around his torso. "I mean only to show you how he treated me. Look at my back."

But the swords did not lower, and one cold tip dug into his abdomen. Kar remained frowning.

"Take them away until I know what to do," he said, waving his hand as if extinguishing a candle flame.

"Let me show you how he whipped me," Yngvar shouted. "We are not his spies. I'd kill him if I had the chance."

"So would I," Kar said. "Now get from my hall."

33

Yngvar spent his days at the door of the building where they remained imprisoned. The structure smelled strongly of sheep, though no traces of animals had been left behind. It was a simple prison of pallets, dirt floor, and a hearth. They had to urinate against the far wall, worsening the stench inside the dark single room building. Thankfully guards escorted men to latrines when needed, which had been more than Erik ever did. Still, Yngvar rested by the door and peered through the crack to see who was beyond. Sometimes the guards would speak to him through the door.

"You'll never fit between that crack, no matter how hard you try." Thorfast sat on a pallet beside the door. At least in this room there was enough space for all eighteen of his men to sleep on their own.

"No one is out there now, I think."

Bjorn, who sat opposite, stood up. "Really? So maybe we can break the door down and run."

"That idea doesn't get any better the tenth time you say it," Thorfast said.

Ander Red-Scar and the others mostly spent their time lying down and watching the ceiling. They had been three days into this imprisonment. Boredom and frustration were starting to build among the men. Alasdair, being the smallest of all, had taken been struck several times by men short on patience. It wouldn't be long before they were at each other's throats. One of the guards had been kind enough to leave them with bone dice. It had occupied their minds for a short time, but was not enough to pacify the growing restlessness. Bursting through the door might be their only hope before they killed each other.

"Well, I've been waiting for Yngvar the Great-Thinker to come up with a plan. But he's more interested in kissing the door than getting us out of here."

"We don't have many great choices," Yngvar said. "If we burst out the door, we'll be cut down before we get anywhere useful. Do you think we're going to steal a ship and sail off? We were lucky enough to do that once. The best we can hope is to flee into the countryside. Eventually we'll be rounded up again, but some might slip away. But how will a single man survive alone out here? Winter is coming, and I don't want to think of what that's like this far north."

Bjorn frowned and flopped back onto his pallet. Thorfast pulled his knees up to his chin and sat in silence. Yngvar felt the men staring at him. They had come to rely on him for daring plans that pulled victory from defeat. He had started to believe himself capable of it, too. Yet he was just a man, one who had a short run of luck.

"Wait, the guards are coming back," Yngvar said, pressing his eye to the gap in the door. Two men flitted in and out of his field of view until finally they were both poised before the door.

"Hey, where did you go?" Yngvar said, rattling the bolted door. The guard to his right answered, his voice muffled.

"I'll wager you'll be happy to know that Alrik Vigisson has arrived with news."

The name meant nothing to him, but the prospect of news raised his hopes. "What news? Has Erik's fleet attacked?"

The guards did not answer immediately. The one of the right eventually spoke. "I'm not sure I can tell you more. Kar will want to see you again, though, I'm sure."

Rather than speculate on what the guard meant, Yngvar sat down beside Thorfast. All eyes looked expectantly at him, but he said nothing. Why get anyone's hopes up when so much remained unclear? He simply closed his eyes and tried to clear his mind. An opportunity was forming, and he had to remain open to any advantage.

Not long after, the bolt on the door shook and light flooded the room. Guards in mail and shield entered, short swords drawn in case anyone thought of jumping at them. Unarmed and unarmored, Yngvar and his crew were not yet suicidal enough to attack, no matter what the enemy thought.

"You and three men you pick," said the lead man, pointing at Yngvar, "come with us."

Within moments Yngvar, Thorfast, Bjorn, Alasdair, and Ander Red-Scar were standing outside their prison and surrounded by a dozen armored men. No one protested Ander's inclusion. Maybe they considered Alasdair too small to be a full man. They did not threaten them, but just began herding them toward Kar's hall. No one spoke, and Yngvar searched his friends' nervous faces. He met each of their eyes and gave a short nod. This was the hand of the gods at work, he was certain, and he had nothing to fear. Kar would've killed them or enslaved them by now. Something else had stayed his hand.

Kar's ancient hall was surrounded by scores of men in chain shirts and glinting, dented helmets. Their low voices were like the hum of bees from a distance. The sun peered through dark clouds to cut their hard faces with deep shadow. As their guards led them through the mix, these men gave inscrutable stares as they passed. Inside the hall, more of their number filled wall to wall. The humidity and warmth of so many men was like a wall pressing against Yngvar's face. A thick haze of hearth smoke covered the room, and squat Kar Gellirsson sat on his chair at the far end.

Only another chair was placed next to his, and an older, stronger man sat upon it. Here was Alrik Vigisson, Yngvar guessed. Bulging arms coiled with gold armbands showed beneath the hem of a sparkling chain shirt. His hair was as light as Thorfast's, only of pure white versus the pale gold cast to Thorfast's. His mustache hung well past his beard and had gold beads tied into it. His hooded eyes swept the room to Yngvar the moment he entered.

"As requested, lord," said their lead guard after shoving through to the front. "These men claim they are from Erik Blood-Axe himself."

Kar's face went sour, as if he had bit into a rotten apple. The as-yet unnamed Alrik shifted in his seat to face Yngvar.

"You are their young leader?" Alrik's voice was warm and rough, equal parts kind grandfather and rabid wolf. Here was a man who could be a loyal friend and a fierce enemy. Yngvar felt it all from his voice and the power that radiated from his posture. He made Kar look like a bullfrog next to him.

"Yes, I am, lord. You must be Jarl Alrik Vigisson?"

Alrik raised a single brow, but did not acknowledge his name. "Describe Erik's fleet to me."

Yngvar thought carefully, closing his eyes to remember all the ships and their crews. He had spent an entire summer with most of these ships, and he had caulked many of their hulls. He had not thought at the time to make a careful accounting of what he had seen, and now regretted not having done so. He opened his eyes, and both Alrik and Kar were staring flatly at him.

"Thirty ships went to sea over the summer. Some remained behind. Perhaps then he would have forty ships at most. He did not have enough men to complete a full crew on each ship. So he would have less than eight hundred men."

"Does that match what you saw in his camp?" Alrik asked. He seemed unsurprised, but Kar was a shade whiter than he had been a moment ago.

"No, lord, he had less men than that. Perhaps half that number." Yngvar now began to wonder at his own count. He looked to the others for confirmation. Bjorn and Alasdair stared back as if they had never seen a single ship. Yet both Thorfast and Ander nodded in support. "It does not make sense, though."

"It makes sense," Alrik said. "Those other ships and men belong to other jarls. They joined him for his raids and left. Erik's true force is far less than what you witnessed."

"But to what end?" Yngvar said, now genuinely intrigued. "We were nothing to Erik. Why appear bigger to us?"

"He wants to appear bigger to everyone," Alrik said. He finally leaned back in his chair, folding his arms. "Do you think we have no spies among his number? He sailed all around us, making certain everywhere he went people were left behind to witness the greatness of his fleet. And how it would grow in the retelling. So, we here in Norway will quake at his name and fear to go to bed at night lest Erik's mighty fleet sweeps down upon us. But he is not so mighty. Not right now."

Yngvar lowered his head in consideration. He had never realized any of this, but it had made no difference to him. In fact, what difference did it make now? He raised his gaze back to Alrik.

"But he is mighty enough to sting this coast. He is no raider come to steal your flocks. He intends to burn and destroy, to teach you all a lesson. That is all that exists in the small, black heart of Erik Blood-Axe. And your spies have confirmed what I've told you. He is sailing now before the winter comes, before his mercenaries demand more than he can pay. For those other jarls will not join him in this madness."

Alrik gave a satisfied nod. "He acts with rashness uncharacteristic of the man who once called himself king of this land. You have captured his heart exactly, for he is nothing if not a vengeful man. He has sacrificed twenty sheep and twenty slaves to Odin. Our spies can tell us no more, as they have now returned to us. But what else would he sacrifice so much for if not victory in battle? He is coming and we will meet him at sea to break up his attack."

A smile overtook Yngvar's face. "So you believe us? Then you will let us go?"

"I wish to hear from the others first," Alrik said. He in turn asked similar questions of all the men Yngvar had taken, except Alasdair whom he ignored. Everyone described variations on what Yngvar had already said. While they answered Jarl Alrik's questions, Yngvar dreamed of facing Erik in combat.

Surely Fate had intended it. The Norns had blown his ship off course and directly into Erik's path. They were as unsatisfied with his fleeing as he was. His back was ruined from whipping not to mention the complete betrayal of Erik's oath. Had Erik not said it himself? *Should either of us be faithless, then let this oath be forgotten and forfeit the life of the trespasser.* The gods do not take the breaking of oaths lightly.

Of course, Yngvar would be the sword that brought the gods' justice to Erik.

When Alrik was satisfied, he turned to Kar for his questions. The frog-like jarl shook his head, his thick and frizzy hair too stiff to move.

"So you see we are true," Yngvar said. "We are not spies of Erik's. So you will free us?"

Alrik stretched and yawned, then extended a hand to Kar. "You are not my prisoners. Your fate is for Kar to decide. In my opinion you seem genuine enough. But Kar is more cautious than I."

"And that has served me well," Kar said, leaping to his feet. His stoutness was hardly impressive beside the power Alrik projected. He pointed at Yngvar. "This one is arrogant, and the others keep looking at him like they don't know what to say. I don't trust the lot of them. Keep them locked up until we return."

Yngvar's mouth opened to protest. Alrik's eyebrow raised again, but Yngvar had no chance to speak. Thorfast had stepped forward.

"Jarl Kar, you mistake his earnestness for arrogance. We all desire Erik's downfall, but none more so than Yngvar. He—"

"And this one speaks out of turn," Kar said. "Take them from the hall. I'll deal with them later. There's more important work to be done."

With that final command, the hirdmen closed around Yngvar and the others and they were marched back to their prison.

34

"So they've all left?" Yngvar asked, his eye pressed to the crack of his prison door. The single guard now only came to check on them three times a day. He gave his name only as Grettir. He was a young man, untried in battle with fresh red cheeks and a thin beard. Yngvar guessed only six months ago he might have appeared as green as Grettir. How much had changed over a single summer. Grettir was out of sight now, but Yngvar saw his shadow by the door as he checked it for any signs of attempted escape.

"You can answer me," Yngvar said. "Of course everyone is gone. But when did they leave? Has Erik's fleet been spotted? You must know something."

"They've been gone a day. You know what that means."

He did. Loki had scuttled Jarl Alrik's plans. Clear skies and fair weather seemed in the offering, but a terrible storm appeared by nightfall. If the ships were at sea, then they could have been scattered or worse. By rights the same would've happened to Erik's crew. But Loki loved mischief and wouldn't it be fitting to shove aside Alrik and leave a path for bloody-minded Erik to come ashore?

Grettir checked around the door, then asked through the crack. "The roof survived the storm? No leaking? And I'm not stupid enough to go inside to check myself."

"Someone's going to open that door sooner or later," Yngvar said. "I hope Kar's instructions weren't to starve us to death?"

A snort of laughter faded away as Grettir continued to circle the building. Yngvar glanced at the other men, who waited on their only relief from unremitting boredom.

"You won't starve," Grettir said, returning to the door. "There's enough of us to handle you all. Last night we couldn't come up here but for the wind. We'll make it up to you this morning."

"You're a good lad," Yngvar said. "If you let us out, I promise we will do everything to help you while the others are away. We'll even go back into captivity when Jarl Alrik returns. The men are going mad in here. There's no place to walk or stretch. The air is stale."

"And it's a sight better than being killed off as spies or made into slaves," Grettir said cheerfully. "So learn to find the light inside the dark. The roof looks fine. We'll be back with food."

Grettir left without anything more to add. Yngvar and the others settled into listlessness. The days of isolation and darkness were sapping any camaraderie the men felt toward each other. Even Yngvar, who loved both Bjorn and Thorfast like brothers, tired of their constant proximity. It seemed Alasdair alone was small enough to remain out of anyone's way. Yet even he had stopped speaking with Yngvar, preferring instead to huddle in prayer at the darkest corner of the room.

Yngvar was staring at the cold hearth ashes and Thorfast noticed. He rolled onto his side on his pallet. "If they had left us a hearth fire, we could've burned our way out of here. Or burned to death. Either way would be preferable to death by boredom."

"Stop talking about dying," Bjorn said. "You're always talking about dying in here. Did you know that? I'm sick of hearing it."

"Strange how you hear me say that, but can never listen to common sense."

"What does that mean?"

Yngvar saw the men stirring with the prospect of a fight. They were going to fan that spark of anger into a blaze, he was sure. So he tried to douse the fire now.

"No one get excited, or we'll be tearing each other to bits before long. We're hungry and bored, and we don't know what comes next."

"A great comfort, you are," said one of Erik's former crew. "They said if I followed you we'd be sure of success. Now look at me."

Yngvar ignored the jibe. "Here, let me use your bored minds to think through a problem that has bothered me."

Both Thorfast and Bjorn glared at each other, but both were willing to retire with Yngvar's offer of a diversion.

"If Erik has only half the men he showed to us, then he is in no real position to attack this coast. He can't win. At best, he can inconvenience his brother, and even then indirectly. I know Erik has spoken about having revenge on Hakon, but this is such a weak attempt. It will waste more of his resources than he can afford. A whole summer of raiding, and his only purpose is to squander his treasure on a failed attack?"

No one answered him. Several seemed indifferent to the question, others were considering his words. As expected, Thorfast was first to speak.

"The mercenaries are of no concern to him. He can raise more gold again and hire others. The gods favor a bold warrior. Maybe he believes he can win here."

Yngvar shook his head. "He is the son of a king and was a king himself. Kings thrive upon reputation. He knows that failures would not bring more warriors to his banner. He would not risk his reputation with half a force."

"How does anyone know what that mad bastard will do?" Bjorn threw his hands up in disgust. "Maybe he's out looking for a new man to bed his wife."

Yngvar had a thought, but it vanished when a knock came to the door. Expecting Grettir's cordial voice, he was surprised when Grettir was nearly screaming.

"A ship is coming. Not one of ours. And it's overflowing with warriors. Men in mail and shields off the racks. This is bad."

His rush of words sailed past Yngvar's understanding. What was he saying? Yet Thorfast jumped to the door, pressing his face to the crack.

"Then it is well you came to us, Grettir," he said. "You have here eighteen men who have seen plenty of battle. You let us out to fight by your side, and we will fling that enemy back into the sea."

"I don't know," Grettir said, his voice now almost a whine. "Kar said to keep you locked up and not fall for your tricks."

"It is some trick for me to call a ship from the sea to the shore, especially locked in here," Thorfast said. "I know you are afraid of mistakes, especially disobeying your lord. I would feel the same. But you must believe me, Grettir, your lord did not predict this. He would want you to make the right decision. How many men did he leave to defend his home?"

"Jarl Alrik took every fighting man with him. Just ten of us remain, and none of us have seen more battle than a squabble before."

Thorfast glanced back at Yngvar. His friend was looking to him to confirm that they could win this fight. Yngvar did not know how yet, but he had faced worse odds escaping Erik the first time. He nodded.

"We know what to do," Thorfast said, his voice soothing and clear. Yngvar admired how he easily responded to the changes in Grettir's mood. "Get us our swords and shields. Together we can defeat these bastards."

Grettir didn't answer, but lifted the bolt. Yngvar was nearly swept aside by his men seeking to get out of their confinement. At first Grettir leapt back and screamed, expecting to be overrun. Yet the crew only gathered outside the doors and waited for Yngvar to appear.

Parts of a plan formed in his mind, like the wooden pieces of a puzzle toy he had in his childhood. He drew from the tales of this father and grandfather. The songs of the skalds echoed in his head. All the while, his men surrounded him, overjoyed to be out in the air.

"Even if we die, it's under the sky," Ander Red-Scar said. He stretched his arms over his head as he smiled. None of the men seemed as if they were about to go into battle.

"So what do we do now?" Grettir asked. His face was waxy white.

"Weapons, you fool," Bjorn shouted. "Take us to our weapons."

Grettir led them a short distance to the main village. Women and children and the old were streaming toward the mead hall, the traditional place of safety. But they were only making their capture easier. Yngvar would have told them to scatter to every direction.

They were met by Grettir's companions, who could not believe what he had done. Yet Yngvar and all his men were so confident that it quelled their fears. In moments, they were led into the hall where their weapons were kept. They were given shields, plain round wood but sturdily built. In short order Yngvar and all were readied for battle. He had Gut-Ripper at his waist once more, and he rested his hand upon it's cool hilt as he addressed the assembled men outside the hall.

From the hill he could see across the pine trees to where the mast of the enemy ship showed in the fjord. He could not see the detail for the trees, but he knew they had anchored and were likely taking the ship's boat to come ashore.

"They're planning a quick raid," he said. "They're going to kill anyone who tries to stop them and they'll come for Jarl Kar's treasure. I'm sure he's buried most of it, but he must have some in his home. That's what they want."

Yngvar had everyone's attention. His eighteen men lined up with the ten young men Kar had left as a token force. They could keep the peace among the townsfolk and chase off bandits, but they had no hope against an organized raiding force. Neither did Yngvar's men, but none of them needed to hear his doubts.

"So we must give them what they want," he said. "Bring the treasure out here. Put your weapons down in a pile beside it. Show you have surrendered."

Grettir and the others squinted in disbelief. Yngvar's men merely listened, knowing he had more to offer.

"They will check the surrounding buildings for hidden attackers, but will find them empty. When they are satisfied, they will be seeing exactly what they expected."

"But what about you? And we'll be unarmed. This is madness," Grettir spoke up for the others, his voice rising with each word.

"And so they will be fascinated with the treasure, relieved that you are no threat and just weak boys. But we will be down the slope, behind them and in front of you. We will fall upon them while they fawn over their gold. They will turn and you will draw your daggers and plunge them into their backs. We will cut them down with sword and ax from the front."

"Daggers!" Grettir seemed on the verge of passing out.

"A final part of the plan," Yngvar said, improvising on the spot. "Is to stack spears at the door of the hall, one for each of you. A poor man's weapon, no one will mind them. But we will have a man hidden in the hall, and on my call he will deliver spears to you."

Yngvar watched the reactions from utter disgust to shock to admiration. Yngvar himself did not know if he was mad or if the gods were speaking through him. This plan seemed to come from nowhere.

"Hurry," he said. "There's no time for anything more. Ander, you take all the men around the flank and follow behind the enemy. Stay out of sight until I call for you. Alasdair, I have a job for you. Grettir, hurry up with the treasure, and hide your daggers at your backs."

Whether anyone believed him or not, at least acting in charge got men to take orders. Yngvar plucked Alasdair aside and led him toward the hall. "They'll mostly be interested in the young women. You will get up in the rafters and hide. You are the smallest one. When you hear me call, you will bring out the spears set by the doors."

"This sounds like a dangerous plan," Alasdair said as they entered the hall. "But I trust God is with us. We are defending against raiders."

"We are raiders," Yngvar said. "But I will accept your god's aid if it kills enemies for me."

Inside, the women and children huddled at the far end. A man was already stacking spears beside the doors. Yngvar divided the groups to be less conspicuous. He then hefted Alasdair into the rafters while the women watched. "Here's where being small is a great aid. You steady up there?"

Alasdair nodded and folded himself into the shadows over the door. No one would look up there. Yngvar looked to the women. "None of you betray him, and he will save your men outside."

His heart raced as this plan unfolded. Grettir and his companions surrounded a large wooden chest with a heavy lock. They were busy setting their swords in the grass. They stared at him as he ran past, pointing at a nearby pine he would climb. His stomach burned with fear for these men. They were taking a huge risk in disarming themselves.

Grabbing a low branch, he hauled up into the tree. He scrambled higher, remembering how he loved this as a child. Once he was as high as he dared, he crouched against the rough trunk. The noise of the raiders was clear. They were proceeding through the outer village, bursting into emptied homes. Some lit fires and black smoke rushed skyward to malicious shouts. Yngvar had done the same during the summer, but had not experienced the thrill these men did. They worked their way to the center, where Grettir and his men huddled together.

Yngvar counted twenty enemies. That meant ten more back on the ship. They were in mail coats and iron helmets, round shields of bright red and white slung over their backs. They carried axes and swords. No bows or spears that he could see, which relived him of his worst fear. He did not want to be shot out of his perch. Their faces were carved from long days at sea, etched with lines of storm and battle. They burst into laughter upon finding Grettir and the others. Their leader, a predictably muscular brute with an ax slung over his shoulder, stepped forward and spit on the ground.

"Worms that you are," he said. "Won't even give us a good battle. Do you prefer to die as women?"

Grettir looked directly up at Yngvar. He thought his bowels would open up, such was his fear of being discovered. But the giant enemy was fortunately more interested in the chest.

"You want us to believe this is all your treasure? Ha! We are not so foolish to think a village of this size is not richer than this." The man nodded toward the chest, and two of his companions approached it. "Still, it is a wise offering. Check the hall, make sure there are no surprises."

Commands dispatched, the enemy split up to check the hall and surrounding buildings while a core force remained with Grettir. That had been arrogant, Yngvar thought as they divided themselves. Had Grettir's men been desperate, even unarmed they could have seized the attack. Yet it also showed the enemy believed they had defeated their opposition.

Yngvar could not see where Ander and the others had gone, nor did he dare adjust himself. The enemy were right below and any movement would alert them. He had to trust Ander and the rest were in position now. The screams of girls from the hall told Yngvar that Alasdair remained hidden. Poor Grettir and his companions blanched at the shouts, and the enemies laughed at him.

"We'll be enjoying their company tonight. So get used to that sound."

The enemy regathered, each one confirming they had found nothing. Grettir again looked up at Yngvar as if pleading for him to spring the trap. But the enemy needed to be more off balance still.

"Open this chest," the strong leader said. When no one had a key, he began to batter the lock with his ax. Finally it broke open and they gathered around to stare at Kar's treasure.

Yngvar inhaled, drawing the pine scents to his lungs, loosing needles into his hair and shirt, then let out a bellow that would have shaken snow from the mountaintops.

"Attack!"

He drew Gut-Ripper and leapt out of the tree. He plunged down on the rearmost man, slamming him to the ground. A quick stab directly into the enemy's side and the chain links crunched. Blood flowed and the enemy screamed. Yngvar leapt at the next man, his face alight with glee.

Everyone turned on him. Twenty shadowed, angry faces. Their weapons were ready and Yngvar finally realized he was alone against them.

But Grettir and his men reached to their backs, pulling daggers and charging the enemy.

A sword too long for this close combat shot up against Yngvar, who turned it aside with his stouter blade. He used his free hand to punch the assailant in his face. His hand flashed with pain as it rammed into cheekbone.

Suddenly others came streaming around the building. At the

front Bjorn was red-faced and sprinting with an ax held high. The rest trailed his charge.

"Behind us," the enemy leader shouted, and any man who still faced Grettir had now whirled about.

Bjorn slammed his ax down on an enemy shield, destroying it with a single blow and sprawling the man on his back. Yngvar laughed, then saw Alasdair fumbling out of the front door with a sheaf of spears. He looked like an old woman carrying a bunch of firewood too large to handle.

The melee was short and fierce. Once Yngvar's crew joined and Grettir's men retrieved spears, the killing began in earnest. Completely surprised and surrounded, each enemy warrior looked to himself. It was an error remedied too late. The leader could not call his men to shield wall, and so they fought in small pockets.

Gut-Ripper was red, and Yngvar danced away from anyone who had a better reach. Instead, he fell on enemies already tangling with another and used his short blade to finish them.

He leapt over a dead foe, intent on aiding Thorfast who backed away from a flurry of strikes by a larger opponent.

But the man on the ground was not dead.

He grabbed Yngvar's leg and sent him sprawling.

Gut-Ripper bounced out of his grip. The man on the ground, his face nothing but bright red blood that flowed out of his cut scalp, wasted no time in plunging his dagger at Yngvar's exposed gut.

35

Yngvar twisted away from the dagger, sitting up to grab the weapon with both hands. The blade scored his side, dragging hot fire across his flesh. His attacker was a nightmare enemy, a red skull of flowing blood. His beard was sopping with gore, lying flat over his neck. The man roared in fury, the whites of his eyes standing out in the glistening red of his face. His breath stank of blood as he roared. He tried to drive deeper, letting go of Yngvar's leg to use both hands on his dagger.

He tried to yank his leg back, but the attacker flopped onto his leg to pin him as they both struggled with the gleaming knife. Its tip dripped Yngvar's blood as it shook between them.

Then a spear lanced across Yngvar's shoulder and drove into the eye of his attacker. The shaft plowed deep, making the lone eye of the red-skulled man nearly pop from its socket as he screamed in agony. Both hands grabbed the spear, but he flopped to the side and groaned his final breath.

"Dear God, I've killed a man." Alasdair stood over Yngvar, a spear in both his white-knuckled hands. His face was splattered with blood, but where the skin showed it had turned to ash and his lips were white. He started to tremble. "Will I go to hell for this?"

"If you do, it's not because you killed a man," Yngvar said, pulling his leg from beneath the dead man. "It'll be for saving my life."

The tremendous noise of combat—the screams of agony and fear, the clank of iron, the thud of butting shields—all of it had subsided. Bodies were scattered everywhere over the grass. A body hung over Kar's chest, blood running down its side. It was as if the man sought to carry away the treasure into death. Spears lay broken on the ground. Shields were scattered like old plates. A helmet sat in the grass, blinking with sunlight striking off its curves.

"We've won!" Bjorn shouted, followed by an animal scream. He hefted his blood ax into the air with one hand, and in the other he lifted an enemy head that drizzled blood over his naked chest. Somehow, he had lost his shirt.

Cheers went up from Grettir and his men. Yngvar leapt to his feet, looking to where Thorfast had been. An enemy was facedown in the dirt, but Thorfast was gone. His heart pounded as he ran to where they had been fighting. Nothing of his friend's possessions had fallen here.

"I'm fine," Thorfast said. "Thanks for your concern."

Thorfast was splattered with blood, but otherwise unharmed. He frowned down at Yngvar's abdomen. "Is that serious? Your guts aren't going to pop out, are they?"

Yngvar shook his head, then gave Thorfast a slap on his shoulder. He had to count the dead and the living.

He combed the small battlefield. He found Grettir sitting dazed on the grass, a gash on his nose that leaked dark blood. Yngvar patted his head as he moved on. It seemed he had taken the worst injury of all his men. Ander Red-Scar met him, his face flush with the rush of battle.

"That was a trick worthy of your ancestors," he said. "They really thought the day had been won without blood, and look how they paid for it."

Yngvar's chest warmed at the compliment. "I'm glad it succeeded. But there are ten more men on that ship, maybe more."

His men were rousing from the stunned moments after a victory, where the defeated lay gasping in the dirt and the victors staggered in disbelief at their own fortunes. But until the ship departed or was captured, they were still not safe. He called them together.

"Bring me one survivor, if any. The rest—" he paused to survey the dead strewn at his feet. He curled his lip at them. They were raiders and had earned their graves. "The rest, you will cut off their heads and carry them down to the beach. Show their companions what fate awaits them here. Either they bring battle or leave us."

"Lord," Alasdair said, standing beside Yngvar and still clutching his spear as if it could never again be wrested from his hands. Yngvar was not sure if he was being addressed or Alasdair had invoked his god.

"It is grizzly work. You'll need a strong stomach for it. But we need to frighten the enemy from our shores." Yngvar scanned the men, finding many who would not look at him. Ander nodded. Bjorn was already at the task, hauling a corpse into position for a chop of his ax. Others joined.

Yngvar turned aside. The sickening chop of metal on flesh and bone curdled his stomach. He was glad such noises never reached his ears in battle.

"Your prisoner," Thorfast said, appearing with two other men who dragged an enemy between them. It was their leader. His chain shirt had been pierced at the chest, and the blade had stabbed deep. His breath was ragged and wheezing loudly. No doubt, his lung had been punctured, and if he did not bleed to death first he would eventually drown in his own blood.

"Are you part of Erik Blood-Axe's fleet?" Yngvar asked without preamble. He drew Gut-Ripper and touched the point to the man's neck.

His bravado was gone and his head hung to his chest as he remained suspended between the others. Yet he refused to answer.

"You overestimate your position," Yngvar said. He slid the tip of his blade down to the man's chest wound and fit it into the puncture. The man gasped and flailed with the pain. "You are dead. You know this. I can send you to the feasting hall with honor." He twisted the blade slightly, so that the wound gaped open and a horrible sucking noise filled the air. "Or I can make you suffer and die like a pig. So just answer me."

"Yes, the storm blew us off course." The man's voice was weak but surprisingly clear. He barely lifted his head, though.

"Where is Erik? Why is he coming to this coast?"

"I don't know where he is now. Some ships turned back when the storm came. We were to row all night and attack at dawn."

"So the attack broke up, and you don't know where Erik went. What was his objective?"

"I don't know." His voice was a bare whisper now and his head sunk lower. "The main attack was a feint. Erik was taking us else-where. I don't know more. South, we were to sail south. Now kill me. Torment me as you will, but this is all I know."

"How many were to sail south?" Yngvar pressed the blade again but the enemy barely winced. He pushed deeper, finally eliciting a groan.

"Five ships."

Yngvar and Thorfast exchanged looks. This man had no more to offer, so Yngvar pulled Gut-Ripper from the wound. He looked at the two holding him erect.

"Let him to the ground and put a sword in his hands." When they had done as asked, Yngvar laid the blade against the man's neck. He looked up now, his hazel eyes barely opened. A fierce light still glowed there and his red teeth were clenched in hate.

"We will battle again in Valhalla." Yngvar sawed across the enemy's throat, then let him drop dead to the ground.

The world seemed quieter. He did not know what to think at having killed a helpless man. Fortunately, the situation did not indulge him.

"The ship has turned away," Bjorn said, happily trotting back from the shore. Had it been so long? Yngvar felt like his interrogation had been minutes, yet he confirmed Bjorn's words. The mast of the ship was clear above the trees and heading out to sea.

"So Erik is feinting to the south," Yngvar said. "But why?"

No one answered. They all stood around the dead enemy leader, his scarlet blood pooling beneath his face. He was not going to answer any more questions. Yet he had shared the limits of what he knew. Erik would not tell his common warriors his plans, at least not more than they needed to know.

"Does trimming the great beard mean anything to anyone?" Thorfast's question shook Yngvar from his thoughts. He stared at Thorfast in confusion.

"Did you get hit in the head?" Bjorn asked. "Why are you talking like that?"

"No, I've been thinking since before the attack. Like Yngvar said, why is Erik throwing his resources at a battle he can't win. Now this one," Thorfast nudged the corpse of the enemy leader with his foot, "said the whole thing is a feint. Why?"

"To draw away strength from where he intends to attack," Yngvar said. "But five ships, even filled to the gunwales, that's less than two hundred men. He's not even going to establish a winter camp here. Jarl Alrik must have three times that number under his banner."

"So he doesn't plan to stay. He's here for some reason of his own. He was just driven out of these lands, right?" Thorfast scanned the growing circle of onlookers surrounding them.

Now Grettir, no longer dazed and the cut on his nose crusted over, spit on the ground. "And glad to see him gone. He was hated by all."

"Right, and some played a larger role in driving him out than others, is that not also right?" Thorfast asked.

"Revenge," Yngvar said, feeling his neck hairs stand up. "He's doing all of this to extract revenge on someone instrumental in his downfall."

Thorfast's white hair shimmered as he nodded. "And so I heard in my conversations with his men that he planned to make sure the great beard got trimmed before winter. I heard that more than once, and from his hirdmen. They laughed like men drunk on murder."

"Jarl Ketil Ragnarsson rules the south," Grettir said. "He's halfway to the border of Agder. He has a magnificent beard, and he's quite proud of it. He also was an open enemy of Erik's when he was still king. He dealt him a hard blow before he fled, sinking one of his ships with a good amount of treasure upon it. I hear Jarl Ketil sent men who can swim into the fjord to retrieve all of it."

"But why feint here?" Bjorn asked. "Makes no sense."

"If I'm not mistaken," Yngvar said. "I would call Jarl Alrik the hersir over the many jarls of this coast. But Jarl Ketil must be too far south to be called upon for this battle. Erik wants his way with Ketil and risks no pursuit or reprisal from his fellow jarls. He will storm Ketil's hall and trim his beard by taking his head. Erik could pay a man to poison Ketil's mead, but that would not be his way. He would want to feel Ketil's blood on his face. Plus making fools of his former jarls would please him. This is all for his pride and lost treasure."

The thought of Erik so close, without a massive army to defend him, set Yngvar's pulse racing. He owed Erik revenge, both for his back and for attempting murder. Here too was a chance to gain fame and honor as the man who killed the hated Erik Blood-Axe. He would be famous throughout the world.

He glanced at his companions, faces still flushed from battle and enemy blood still upon their flesh. He could not risk their lives for his own goals. That was how Erik himself behaved, and Yngvar would never put himself on footing with that scum. Yet the glory would be shared, and the rewards as well. A mighty reward would be given for Erik's head, he did not doubt.

"We must warn Jarl Ketil," he said.

The faces surrounding him all appeared astonished. Thorfast blinked rapidly, then looked down at the chest of Kar's treasures. Yngvar smiled.

"Grettir, your lord's gold is a sore temptation," Yngvar said. "You have laid it at the feet of my men, who came north seeking riches such as these. Now we have them."

Ander and the rest of crew stared with furrowed brows and folded arms. Yngvar, however, shook his head.

"But I gave my word to aid you," Yngvar said. "And while I am no oath-holder of these men, I will not steal from you and I will ask my friends to follow my example. For there is greater treasure and glory in aiding Jarl Ketil. Think of what riches await us if we are the ones to bring down Erik. What would King Hakon pay for his brother's head?"

Grettir swallowed, then spoke in a cracking voice. "It's well known Erik's bounty would be worthy of a king. I think that's one reason he wanted to clear the area. Look at how many answered Jarl Alrik's call. If they smelled him close by, none would give up their search for him."

"And we are the only ones who know his true goals," Yngvar said. "I do smell gold—and blood."

"Yet here is treasure easily taken," said Ander. Yngvar squared with him. He did not sense defiance from the older man, but instead recognized his leading Yngvar to fully convince the others.

"Easy to take, and impossible to carry," Yngvar said. "There is one ship in the fjord and it is ours. Were it not beached it would be at the sea bottom by now. So where do we go with our stolen treasure that Jarl Kar cannot find us? Do we hide in the mountains? Men cannot eat gold in the winter, nor any other time. What gain do we have in stealing this? But Erik is worth ten times whatever sits here, and it will be rightfully ours."

Heads bobbed in agreement, and Ander gave a thin smile as he inclined his own.

"Then we make haste for Jarl Ketil. We will need wagons and horses to carry all of us. Grettir, you will have to bury your jarl's treasure and then guide us. We will need every man here."

"We're going as well?" His eyes were as wide and desperate as a fish thrashing on a dock.

"You are, as will every man we can find between here and Jarl Ketil," he slapped the shaken man on his shoulder. "Certainly you do not want to remain behind as a coward? We are heroes riding to glory, and you should be among our number."

Cheers went up, and Yngvar smiled as he imagined his revenge.

36

Yngvar bounced along in the wagon, standing behind the driver like he was sailing from the prow of a warship. But wagons were no warships. The lead wagon barely held a dozen men, and its gray wooden slats threatened to fly apart at every ditch or stone in the path. The horses could only be goaded to travel so fast and had to be rested and fed. Their feed consumed space in the wagon. It was a constant battle to push these animals, but the trails were not as well traveled.

He glanced over his shoulder, where two more wagons each drawn by two horses carried the rest of the men. Grettir and the rest of Kar's men were in one wagon and another was filled with glory seekers picked up from settlements along the tracks. They had perhaps forty men now, a full ship's crew and then some. They bounced along the track, dappled light splattering over them as the column raced beneath branches full of yellow and red leaves. At times it seemed they would all shake out and scatter over the grass.

"I hate wagons," Bjorn said, tucked into the corner beneath Yngvar. "My ass is battered just from sitting here."

"But yet you can still complain," Thorfast said. "Nurse that anger for Erik."

"I can't wait to see his head spinning through the air," Bjorn said.

255

"Erik is a fearsome enemy," Alasdair said. He was small enough to sit on the edge of the cart without falling off, though he waved like a wheat stalk whenever the cart hit a rut. "You should not make light of him. I will pray to God for protection against Erik's evil."

"Just don't pray in the path of my charge," Bjorn said. "And ask your god to give me a good, clean strike at that bastard's neck."

Yngvar leaned over the driver's shoulder, a young and inexperienced man like most of the others who had been left behind by their oath-holders. "How much longer? We were to arrive last night, yet here it is morning and it seems we will be driving until dusk."

"Not much longer, lord," the driver said. "We are going up to follow the cliffside paths that overlook the fjord. The horses are struggling to pull us higher. It's what you asked to do."

The constant drive uphill made Yngvar feel as if he would stumble out the rear of the cart. But he had wanted to survey the area first. It would not do to pull up to Jarl Ketil without first giving him warning. The fjord cliffs would be perfect for this scouting. Unfortunately, most travelers never took these paths, making them rough to traverse. The carts creaked and thudded as they rolled across mostly untraveled ground.

Yngvar felt the cart leveling off. It was somewhat like being on the open sea, where you learned the feel of the waves and how they moved your ship. He stood higher to get his first glimpse over the rise. His hands went cold.

Black smoke was a thin smudge in the gray sky.

Worse still, black dots of birds circled lazily in place where the smoke dissipated.

"We're too late." Ander spoke quietly from the rear of the cart. He recognized the signs as well. Erik was already upon Jarl Ketil.

"Maybe too late to aid Jarl Ketil," Yngvar said. "But we might be just in time to catch Erik."

Once they came to the cliff edges, the lead driver stopped his horses. The beasts were panting and slick with sweat. The driver immediately jumped down and began speaking softly to them. The rest of the men leapt out of the wagon, Yngvar leading the way. He stood at the steep cliff edge, looking southeast toward the smoke.

The fjord was knife thin and nearly pincered off by cliffs at the entrance. Directly below, rocks sat in greenish water, but from the water's surface they might be less easily seen. It was a treacherous fjord that required skillful navigation.

His eye traveled up the glistening water now reflecting the iron gray of the sky. The distant beach had four ships beached there. They were mighty ships of dark wood and high sides. Yngvar had spent all summer sailing beside them. Their white-and-red-striped sails were furled on the mast, ready to drop and speed these ships away from pursuit. From this point, he could not see much farther into the settlement. Trees and the land itself obscured his sight. But he could see the tips of yellow flames where the smoke rose. Erik had torched whatever he found and was still occupied inland.

"What do we do now?" Thorfast asked in a quiet voice.

He shook his head, not entirely certain. Throughout the day it had taken to travel this distance, he had come up with a dozen mad ideas. He was expecting to have to convince Jarl Ketil of the danger and then make plans accordingly. He had not expected to be Ketil's relieving force. The men he had taken with him were simply to shore up a shield wall that would have been fronted with Ketil's more experienced warriors. Now, he counted battle-hardened men on one hand.

"Do you feel it?" Yngvar asked. He looked at both Thorfast and Bjorn, who had come to his side and were equally dejected at their prospects. Neither of them responded to his question.

"I feel it. This is what we left home to find. This is the adventure we've craved. Only a desperate few, inexperienced men to face down a despicable foe and great treasure in the offering. Whatever happens today, it will be as glorious as anything our ancestors ever did. It might be more so. We came to a battle not just for gold but for revenge and for honor. We came here to pluck a blight from this world. However the coming battle ends, we will be cheered in Valhalla until Ragnarok begins the world again. We left home to become heroes, and so we are."

"So we are," Thorfast said with a smile.

"Heroes we are," Bjorn said.

"The right choice is to turn back now, before we're seen." Ander Red-Scar stood behind them, frowning at the distant fires. "But then we would return home poor."

"And as cowards," Yngvar added.

"Better to die in glory than be named a poor coward," Thorfast said.

"I'll never be called either," Bjorn said.

"Then we need a plan that will take us home wealthy and famous," Ander said. His frown shifted to Yngvar.

If Yngvar had prepared for this, he could have burned Erik's ships and trapped him in a land where he would eventually be killed. But not only was he unprepared to burn ships, he would derive no satisfaction or reward for it. He wanted Erik's head, and by extension Gunnhild's too. The death of her husband would destroy her hedonistic life. Folding his hands behind his head, he stepped away from everyone to think of what he could do.

He stared idly at the rocks below and the white foam of waves crashing over their exposed tips. He guessed seals would sun themselves here and entire communities of birds made their homes in the cliffs. Ketil's people probably climbed these cliff faces hunting for eggs. This narrow strip was an entire world unto itself, a community of predators and prey.

The narrow strip.

Erik's ships would have to pass directly below this point to navigate around those rocks. He remembered stories of adventures recited in the hall on long winter nights, of how a handful of men defeated entire armies with their cunning traps. Of course, this was how to destroy Erik.

He turned to the crowd at his back. They were mostly young faces, unscarred and thin-bearded, mixed with the harsher older faces of Ander Red-Scar and his companions. He had enough for what he planned, though the trick was in timing and luck. The gods would have to love him before he could hope for victory.

"We cannot help Jarl Ketil," he said. "If he has survived, then it is well. But Erik will not turn back without his prize and so we must not count on the jarl's forces. It will just be us against three times our number. If any man wishes to turn away now, I will not call him a coward. He is, in fact, wise. We willingly run toward what must be death."

A few of the younger men at the rear glanced at each other, as if daring themselves to flee. Yet everyone held, and Yngvar let go his breath.

"But I've no wish to die yet, and so I have a plan. Erik has greater numbers, but we have surprise working for us. He is burning his enemy's home and reveling in victory. In doing so, he has lowered his shield before us. There is one thing that will drive Erik mad beyond reason, and that is to take what is his. Four ships are beached below. I will bring Ander for his skill at the tiller along with thirty men to make a full crew. We will steal his ship. Not one of his ships, but Erik's own. I know which one it is. He will return and find us sailing away with it, and of course he will give chase. He will pass right below here. I will be committing my life and the lives of those who sail with me to the hands of the men who remain atop this cliff. While I am stealing Erik's ship, you will be gathering rocks and logs, anything heavy enough to kill a man and break a deck. Throw these wagons overboard. Anything at hand. Let the first ship after mine pass, otherwise, the rest will have time to avoid your trap."

He paused to be certain the men were understanding his plan. He also took the moment to scan the faces for those he would take. He had to leave someone here who could organize these men and make certain they did not run off before time. None of them could be trusted except for his own, but they would be the best fighters. Even leaving one man behind would not be enough to prevent the others from running off. He had to trust his life to strangers.

"Lord, who will remain here?" Grettir asked carefully, but Yngvar heard the hopeful note in his voice.

"Ten men who can be trusted not to flee. All gold will be shared equally with everyone. By all means flee if you see we are killed, but do not abandon us until that moment. Thirty men will be trusting their lives to you, and you will earn the rewards as well as if you were on the deck of that ship with me."

Grettir nodded, and rubbed the crusted cut at his nose. "You were good to your word with me. I will stay and I will guarantee that Jarl Kar's men will not abandon you."

Yngvar gave a slight bow of gratitude. "A mere ten of you will tell stories of how you killed six times your number and not be lying. Break those decks for us, and it will make us all wealthy."

He turned to Thorfast and Bjorn then smiled. "For gold and glory."

37

"Waiting is a mistake," Bjorn said, slapping his palm against the hull of Erik's ship.

"I've explained this already," Yngvar said, summoning all his patience. He stood in the surf, sinking into the beach sand as cold waves washed over his naked feet. He scanned the gentle slope, across a stretch of knee-high, brown grass that swayed in the wind. Distant smoke and flames flowed into the sky as before, except now he heard shouts and screams and the occasional clang of weapons.

"Explain it again," Thorfast said. "And maybe Bjorn will pay attention. Or so we hope."

The majority of Yngvar's men stood in the weak shadow of Erik's high-sided ship. Only a dozen were aboard, Ander Red-Scar among them, and they would steer the ship and help the rest board once it was launched. From their humorless eyes, Yngvar realized more than Bjorn needed reassurance.

"Erik has many horrible traits, but stupidity is not one of them. If we launch the ship before he arrives and sail in circles waiting for him, then he will know we are bait for a trap. It must appear as if he is just catching us in the act of stealing his ship. And he must not know

I am here, or he will certainly know this is a trap. So we wait for signs of his return."

"But he's not returning," Bjorn said.

"Nor is he leaving any place to rest in the Ketil's lands." Yngvar pointed back at the smoke. "He's burning it to ashes. So they will return to the ships. And this delay is in our favor. It gives more time for the men on the cliff to build their trap."

The sea slapped the hull and seagulls cried from distant rocks. They waited longer than Yngvar had hoped. He could've stolen all their ships as well as Jarl Ketil's two smaller ships beached farther away. Erik had not left a single guard behind.

"We've been seen," Ander shouted from the ship. "They are coming."

Yngvar's heart flipped in his chest. "Let's get this beast launched. Hurry now!"

Glancing over his shoulder, he glimpsed a vague line of pale men at the top of the slope. He threw his shoulder into the prow of Erik's mighty ship and pushed.

They had already worked it free of the beach while waiting for Erik. The hull slipped easily into the ocean, with dozens of hands to push it back. A horn sounded behind him as they were wading out into the gently rolling waves. A more distant horn followed it.

Lines flung down from the ship, and men scaled the high sides and jumped the rails. Yngvar was halfway up when Alasdair reached down and pulled him aboard. His young friend stumbled back and landed on the deck. Yngvar could not help but laugh, as did anyone who saw it. Alasdair himself turned red, but smiled as well.

He went for his boots, which everyone had removed and set on deck prior to launch. No one wanted to fight with boots full of sea water. Bjorn had finished wearing his boots when he hefted his ax over his shoulder.

"When did you decide to fight with an ax?" Yngvar asked.

Bjorn's face reddened as he mumbled his answer. "I don't have as much trouble drawing an ax as I do a sword."

Thorfast whirled on him as if he had caught him stealing. "You mean, you can't forget to unhitch your peace straps with an ax like you do with a sword."

"I get excited. I can't help it." Bjorn scratched the back of his head while Thorfast and Yngvar laughed.

The rest of the crew were not as jovial. They scurried to arm themselves and recover their shields. Others obeyed Ander's commands as he wrestled against the tiller to turn the ship. It slewed hard to the side and most men lost their balance. Yngvar, who was in the midst of putting on his last boot, fell with the sudden jolt.

"They're not happy," Thorfast said, holding onto the rails. "We've got their attention."

Yngvar pulled himself up on the rail and saw the men streaming down the slope. They had dropped whatever chests and sacks of loot they had carried, and were now just at the beach. Yngvar was surprised at the distance they had already covered.

"We don't want to outstrip them too badly," Yngvar said, turning back to Ander, who still fought the tiller with his teeth clenched. He shook his head, unable to speak as he struggled in the hard turn.

"The wind favors us," Thorfast said. "We should be able to elude them in this fine vessel. You've seen how it flies over the waves."

"I have," Thorfast agreed. Yet he had not spent much time studying the ship he had just stolen. This was a king's ship, and built as such. Forty men could easily sleep on its deck. The high sides would defeat attackers from a lesser ship. A thin rowboat long enough for twenty men rested beside a sunken hold at the center where the mast was set. This was filled with casks and sacks, most likely Erik's supplies. A sealskin tarp covered most of these items. He imagined Erik had plans to fill this hold with Jarl Ketil's gold. It made him smile to think he had defied Erik that much already.

Ander grunted in relief as the ship turned straight. More horns blared and angry voices carried clearly across the water. At last from among the crowd of men flowing onto the beach, Erik's banner showed. It was a small triangle of white cloth with a red sword emblazoned at the center. Its tassels swayed as its bearer ran alongside what must have been Erik. From this distance, he was nothing more than a larger blur among others.

At last able to answer, Ander shouted from the tiller. "You said not to make it look like we're bait. So should we delay and make it seem like we wish to be caught?"

Yngvar waved him off. Of course, to slow down would be suspicious, and he had to keep Erik in a state of fury. Men glorified fury in battle, but Yngvar thought it a drawback. If a man cannot think, he can be played like a harp by those who can. If he kept his enemies blind with anger, they would walk into any trap he set for them.

The ship raced across the narrow fjord, its square sail full and tight. Men crowded the prow and watched for dangers as they closed on the exit to the open sea. Yngvar stared at the cliff face. His hands trembled with cold. He saw no one up there, but from this vantage he probably would not. He hoped they had not become lax during the long wait for action. He had an even chance against a single ship, but no chance at all against all three.

Shouted warnings came back as Ander cut close to the rocks at the exit to the sea. Yngvar trusted him, and instead looked past to his pursuers. One ship was in the lead, with two others trailing behind. The fjord rocks would mean they would have to stagger themselves to pass through, and therefore slow them down. They were also gaining, as they chose to row as well as rely upon their sails. The long oars shined as they rose and fell. Yngvar smiled, for their exertions would tire them before the fight.

They slipped out into the open sea, and a cheer went up. The waves were choppier on the open water, and lashing two ships together for a battle would be difficult. Now silence came over the crew as they all went to the bow to watch their trap. Yngvar still did not see anyone atop the cliffs.

"They've not left us," Thorfast said quietly. "I think Grettir is an honest man, don't you?"

"Fear of death goes a long way toward destroying a man's honesty," Yngvar said. "I just wish we could see them, but then so would Erik."

The first ship slipped through the rocks, a wide margin ahead of the other two, which were not rowing as hard as the lead. The first ship was undoubtedly Erik's, for only he would push his men before a battle. The other two captains had more sense to conserve their strength. That lead ship, its red and white-striped sail fat with wind, cut the water with a palpable fury as if it were a fist punching through each wave.

"Here it goes," someone shouted.

Yngvar looked to the cliff and saw the dark shapes there. The first ship was just passing beneath when a wagon backed up just above it and dumped a load of rocks.

Dozens upon dozens of rocks large enough to be seen from a distance hurled over the sides, crashing on the deck of the unsuspecting crew below. He heard wood thump and crack and men scream in shock and anger. But those rocks were only the opening salvo.

The wagon went over as well, breaking up against the cliff as it fell. It clipped the rear of the first ship, sending its prow flipping out of the water. Yngvar saw crewmen falling overboard. The next wagon dumped logs and rocks on the second ship. These slammed and bounced off the cliff as they scattered over the second ship. Much of it plunged into the water, but one large trunk fell like a spear through the second ship. The hull broke apart like a child's toy, and men were leaping off to grab whatever debris would let them float.

Yngvar cheered along with everyone else. They laughed and cursed Erik for a fool. The lead ship sped along, uncaring or unaware of the destruction behind it. With the rearmost ship sinking, the men on the cliff concentrated on the remainder of the first ship they attacked. More stones and logs fell, but these were ineffective or missed completely. The ship had not sunk. It wandered off course like a man staggered by a punch, but it was still sea-worthy. Though the ship steered closer to the cliff—perhaps the steersman had been killed—the debris hurled down was not enough to sink it. Soon the stones stopped falling, like a waterfall drying up before their eyes.

The cheers lulled as they realized they might have a second ship to fight.

The lead ship was nearly upon them.

Then something huge fell from cliff. Yngvar could not understand what it was, for it was not shaped like a log or rock.

Yet it crashed into the deck with resounding crunch of wood. The ship lurched and bowed at the impact, and more men jumped for the water. A second object fell, and finally Yngvar comprehended.

"They killed the horses," he said. "They're throwing them down the cliff."

The second horse landed on the deck, and now he did not doubt that ship was sinking. It was already listing to one side and the crew was jumping away to the rocks or into the water.

Nothing else fell from the cliff. Yngvar saw the men leaping and waving their hands, but could not hear their victorious shouts.

"Stop!" Bjorn screamed at the distant scene. "Don't kill any more horses!"

Thorfast turned on him. "Those horses gave us a chance again."

Bjorn's face was red. "Horses aren't like people. They don't deserve a death like that."

He was oblivious to the astonished faces surrounding him as he stepped out of the bow and back toward the prow. He readied his ax, taking imaginary swings at enemies.

"I'm pretty sure he's eaten horseflesh like the rest of us," Thorfast whispered.

"It's nerves before battle," Yngvar said. "We all have our ways. Bjorn's thoughts get confused. You joke overmuch. I—well, I don't know what I do."

"You stare at men like they are ghosts to be walked through. You fight the battle in your mind before the first spear is thrown. That's why we're following you." Thorfast patted him on the shoulder. "And while this quiet moment between friends is touching, I believe a blood-mad lunatic is pulling his ship up right behind us. I think he wants our heads."

Turning around, the lead ship was now upon them. Its oars withdrew into its hull, like a monstrous turtle pulling into its shell. The dragon head upon the prow snarled as the dark ship slid closer, a bristling patch of shining spears lining the rails.

"Take in the sail," Ander shouted. Across the choppy water, the enemy ship did the same. Boarding hooks spun and flung out as the ships drew side by side. Erik did not want to destroy his own ship, and so seemed to be taking care to approach carefully.

Erik Blood-Axe towered at the front of his men, his golden hair and rigid face flecked with dried blood. His chain armor gleamed. As his fur cloak fluttered behind him, he stood high on the rail as the ships joined together. He was too distant for a spear and neither side had archers, or else Erik would have fallen dead for his bravado.

"You would steal my ship," his voice boomed across the water. "That takes some balls. Too bad I'm going make you eat them before I flay you alive. Who leads this doomed crew, so I know whom to personally kill?"

The hooks bit into the rail wood. Erik's crew hauled the ships closer, groaning as the waves rocked them back.

Yngvar stepped forward, lowering his unadorned wooden shield so Erik could plainly see him.

"You tried it once before, you coward, and failed." He drew Gut-Ripper then pointed it at Erik, the green pommel gem winking lustily in the thin light. "Today you die by my hand."

The storm that crossed Erik's face could've blown their ships to the roof of the world. He snarled and raised his ax. "Kill them! Kill every last man!"

38

Erik's men jumped screaming across the gap between ships, not waiting for the final tie-off to bring both together. They were as a wave of axes, swords, and spears behind a wall of round, brightly painted shields. The scars of battle were clear upon them. Some shields were already cracked or chipped, others bore remnants of arrow shafts. The enemy thumped to the deck to be opposed by Yngvar and his men. One fool barely cleared the rail, and Yngvar rammed him overboard with his shield.

The war cries from both sides threatened to deafen Yngvar as he continued his challenge of Erik. "Come to me, coward. Or do you only fight men who are bound?"

Erik glowered at him, but despite his rage he was patiently guiding his men where to attack. None of his orders were audible, and Yngvar's hands grew cold thinking Erik could actually have a plan. He wanted him raging mad and out of his senses.

As if in answer to that, Bjorn gave a roar like a wounded bear. He was a year younger than Yngvar, but he stood taller and was far stronger. He stood out from his companions by a head or more. Long-hafted ax poised overhead, the worst possible way to grip an ax in battle, he charged at the enemy just gaining the deck. Yngvar did not want to see his cousin impaled on enemy spears, but his reckless charge made it seem he wished to die.

Bjorn screamed and swept his ax low. The first enemy to face him tried to drop his shield, but was too slow. His left leg sheared away below the knee and he collapsed like a felled tree. Bjorn's red blade now arced up, hacking away the exposed shield arm of the next man in line. The enemy made no sound, but blinked as his shield clattered to the deck with his forearm still laced through the straps. Finally, Bjorn's ax collided with a third enemy's head. Yngvar didn't even see how, but the blade struck from under the chin and broke through to the man's nose. This one fell back screaming into his companions.

The deck around Bjorn was clear, but he did not intend to stay out of the press. He sought new enemies.

"Everyone," Yngvar yelled. "Follow Bjorn!"

His men shouted encouragement as his cousin hacked his way through enemies clamoring to stop his ax. Shields cracked, limbs flew, and blood sprayed. Throughout it all, Bjorn howled and roared his fury.

Now Erik had leapt from his place to face Yngvar himself. Erik's men gave him a wide berth, understanding he meant to fight Yngvar alone.

The world narrowed down to this single spot on the deck. Erik's ax was low at his side, and his shield of red and white guarded him well. His eyes flared with hate, peering from beneath his helmet and over the rim of his shield.

"You're older," Yngvar said. "You're slower. And you're dead."

He struck with speed that surprised himself. Gut-Ripper slid beneath Erik's shield, but he quickly knocked the blade down. Erik was too close for his ax to be of any use, and so he shoved Yngvar. His strength was such that Yngvar could not resist and so stumbled back, his own shield held against the blow he expected.

Recovering his stance, he braced but no blow fell across his shield. He slid toward Erik's shield side, hoping to avoid an attack while he repositioned for his own. Erik circled him cautiously. He did not waste his strength on a strike that would've gained him little. It was a wise choice. Sweat already poured down Yngvar's brows as he circled around their patch of deck. He was dimly aware of the chaos around him, but remained focused on Erik.

"Come on, old man," he said. "You think to cut off my balls? We'll see who will be gelded."

Erik narrowed his eyes. He was neither old nor easily goaded. He kept straight on with Yngvar, never letting him get on his shield side. For his part, Yngvar wanted to pin his shield arm and stab beneath it with his short sword. The stout blade would eviscerate Erik, even through his chain shirt. But Erik had more experience, and Yngvar's sweat came in part from realizing he faced a man with patience and hatred in equal measure.

He feinted quick jabs that Erik lazily struck aside. His face never changed from the rigid lines of anger and concentration. His glare transfixed Yngvar like a spear through his heart.

Suddenly Erik was closer. His ax flicked out, hooking Yngvar's shield and yanking it down.

The rim of Erik's shield slammed into Yngvar's nose bridge. It did not break, but white streaks of pain filled his vision and he fell back. Another tug and his shield stripped from his arm. He had lost his grip in the sudden flash of agony.

When his teary vision restored, Erik smiled at him across the deck. Yngvar felt cold air on his arm where his shield had been.

"Not just for cracking skulls," Erik said, adjusting his grip on his ax. "You should see your face, young warrior. You realize now I'm playing with you. But this battle needs me and I tire of you. You were a boring opponent. A man of no consequence. It is an insult to kill you, but I do as I must."

"Does it bother you that you can't satisfy her?" Yngvar put both hands to Gut-Ripper. He could not recover his shield without losing his head. "Perhaps your son will look like me. I lay with her enough that she must be full with my child now."

It was Erik's tender spot. He roared and struck for Yngvar in a savage blow.

He dove to the deck. Erik's ax swiped above his scalp, shaving hairs from his head. The world slowed to nothing.

Gut-Ripper punched forward.

The blade drove through Erik's right calf, piercing the thick ball of muscle and sawing against the bone.

The former king of Norway screamed and fell across Yngvar's body.

His moment to kill Erik was now, but Gut-Ripper was stuck in Erik's leg. It broke from his grasp.

Men surrounded them now. Blood from someone drizzled hot across the back of Yngvar's neck. The weight of Erik's body lifted from him.

Yngvar scrambled away in time for the enemy blade to stick into the blood-slick deck.

He kept rolling, then sprung to his feet. He had no weapon. Two men carried Erik between them as he screamed in horrific pain. Gut-Ripper remained in his leg, it's green pommel gem blazing in the wan light as if it were a cat's eye at night. A third man, the one who had tried to kill Yngvar, walked backward to defend Erik with his shield. They carried him to their ship.

All around, the enemies were breaking for their ship. Erik had fallen and they had been broken.

Yngvar's heart leapt. "Don't let them flee! Erik is wounded. Kill him! The bounty!"

Bjorn was standing on something, as he was waist high over the press of battle. He was like a red demon and his ax harvested blood and flesh all around him. Corpses and arms still gripping their weapons littered the deck. Thorfast's white hair was clear in the dark melee, and he fought next to Bjorn.

It was victory.

Until a half-dozen torches spun over the battle and landed in the hold.

For an instant, Yngvar did not understand. Then the casks there caught flame.

A ball of fire whooshed into the air around the mast. The kegs apparently were full of oil and not well sealed. Erik's men must have known this and so sabotaged their own ship.

Flames spread to the sail and mast in the high wind. A wall of fire extended between Yngvar, who had rolled to the opposite side of the deck, and the rest of the battle. It was like a blazing curtain.

Before he could do more, a black shape leapt through the fire. The hulking brute's cloak smoldered, making him seem like a fire giant that had just crawled from a volcano.

The enemy roared and sloughed the burning cloak. He carried a two-handed ax.

His clear eyes gleamed with madness.

Hrut shrieked and raised his ax, as enraged as Bjorn was on the other side of the fire.

Yngvar had no weapon. His feet slick with blood and sea water, he slipped as he dodged Hrut's strike. Crashing to the deck, he turned in time to see the flattened, bruised nose in the face of his worst nightmare bearing down on him.

39

Yngvar rolled away from Hrut's maniacal strike. The ax crashed into the deck, splitting the boards like kindling wood. A weapon. He had no weapon, and Hrut allowed him no time to seek one.

The giant roared and charged again. Yngvar dove to the side and tried to grab Hrut's legs. He jumped out of Yngvar's grip.

Across the fire, now spread everywhere with the high wind, he saw men carrying the row boat to the side of the ship. Erik's own ship had cut off and was already pulling away. They risked fire jumping to them. Already glowing sparks were flitting on the wind.

"I'm going to kill you," Hrut screamed as he struck again.

Well, of course that was obvious. Yngvar skittered back, now too close to the fire that it blazed against him. Hrut did not need any goading to go mad with rage. He had run straight off that cliff into a world of blind madness long ago.

The swipes came ragged and one after the next. Hrut was as strong as a horse and as tireless as a plow ox. If one strike even clipped Yngvar, he would lose a limb to it.

"Your jarl has abandoned you," Yngvar shouted as he stumbled back. Again, more fire sent him nearly running back into Hrut. "Save yourself."

"You fucking dog-shit! You must die!"

It was like a slow dance between roaring fire and the whistling crack of Hrut's ax. Despite the danger, he felt a cool flow to this duel. His men were leaping overboard. He glimpsed Thorfast's white hair as he stared across the flames. He raised his sword, then slipped overboard. Yngvar hoped it was into the rowboat below.

Someone screamed his name. Young Alasdair was being bodily heaved overboard. Yngvar couldn't see who did it.

The ax clipped his shoulder, neatly cutting the cloth but not scratching his skin. How had he pulled back in time? Were the gods with him?

Hrut's raving was incoherent amid the roar of fire and the screams of men. The ship groaned and creaked. Smoke stung his eyes and filled his nose with an acrid scent of oil. Through the gray smoke, Erik's ship slipped ahead. The bastard had gotten away. Yngvar hoped Gut-Ripper infected him with bending sickness. That was a horrific death, and Erik deserved it.

The smoldering cloak was at Yngvar's feet.

Hrut glistened with sweat and blood. Yngvar suddenly realized the giant enemy's chain shirt was torn at his abdomen and the waist of his pants were stained dark with blood. So Hrut had been wounded, perhaps mortally, and so cared only to take Yngvar with him to the feasting hall.

"You stupid brute," Yngvar said. He ducked in time with another strike. For all his experience, Hrut was like a child with a toy ax. Yngvar snatched up the burning cloak. It singed his hands, but he handled it gingerly.

He sprung up and flung it over Hrut's face.

It covered him, smoke flowing out from all over. Hrut reeled back in horror, snatching with one hand to knock it off.

Yngvar barreled into him. His face crushed against the hot links of chain mail, gouging his cheek.

His right hand punched into the hole in the mail, and he drove it through into the puncture wound.

"You picked a terrible way to die," Yngvar hissed.

His hands were deep in hot guts, almost hot enough to burn. He grabbed something soft then yanked out.

Hrut fell back, his purple and gray intestines unraveling from beneath his mail shirt. Yngvar's hand was thick with blood and fluid. As he watched Hrut gurgle and collapse to his knees, trying to hold his guts back into his body, Yngvar vomited down his shirt. He staggered away, letting Hrut die out of sight.

He turned into flames. All sides were on fire and the deck was now closer to the water. Dying men groaned on the decks and some screamed as they caught fire. Yngvar's skin was taut with heat. The wind fanned these flames all over. He could either burn alive or drown.

A lick of fire made the choice for him. A burning rope broke and slapped across his back. It burned fiercely, and he ran for the rails.

The cold water was soothing. All sound became thick with echoes. The moaning of the dying ship was louder beneath the surface. Every snap and pop was dull thunder. Air rushed past his ears in a playful gurgle. He was weightless and refreshed. He had a lungful of air. He could enjoy the moments before terror and death.

He tried opening his eyes, but the salt water burned. He could see nothing but milky gray. Other things floated through the water with him, debris or dead bodies. He wasn't sure.

Now he felt arms welcoming him. Had Brandr, who died in the sea's cold embrace, and his Uncle Gunnar, who had been committed to the waves he rode in his youth, come for him? It made sense and it was good to be welcomed to death by family.

He was rising up as his lungs began to burn. They were taking him to Valhalla, or perhaps handing him up to Valkyries.

Breaking the surface, the surreal world of coldness and death shattered. Distant screams and closer shouts assailed him. He gasped reflexively, spluttering cold, salty water that was level with his chin.

"I have you, lord."

Yngvar blinked through the salt stinging his eyes. Alasdair struggled to hold him in the water. The poor boy seemed to be drowning himself. His eyes were bloodshot and wide with terror.

"Get him up here." It was Thorfast's desperate command. Strong hands latched onto Yngvar's shoulder and lifted him onto the side of the rowboat.

It rocked wildly, and though men seemed to have braced for it, everyone still shouted in terror. At last, they clawed him onto the tight boat, where he rested between Thorfast and Bjorn. Both were red-faced and dripping sweat.

The ship rocked again, and Alasdair slipped aboard. He spit sea water over the side as Ander held him by his waist. He had stripped off his shirt, so that orange flames of the burning ship reflected off his wet flesh.

"I guess you couldn't hear us?" Thorfast asked.

Yngvar shook his head. "Sorry, got distracted."

"We were telling you to wait for us," Bjorn said. "We were coming to meet you. But you seemed to want to fight that foe."

Yngvar smiled weakly. "I would not say I wanted to."

The rowboat was packed with survivors, but not all thirty men remained with him. He wasn't certain all of these men were those he had taken to battle. Losses in such a close fight were unavoidable. He hoped his men died in combat and were not currently burning in the wreck of Erik's high-sided ship.

Erik! He sat up, spotting the fallen king's dark ship racing toward the horizon.

"Be glad he doesn't come back to finish us," Ander said. "Until we get to land, we're helpless on this boat. Damn thing might capsize in a good wind."

"He's got Gut-Ripper stuck in his leg," Yngvar said. "I loved that sword."

No one spoke but paddled toward the shore. The battle was ended, and Erik had survived. Yngvar had not done what he had vowed to do.

But he had given Erik a memory he would never forget.

And he believed the gods had marked them to fight again. After all, he would have to retrieve his sword one day.

40

Yngvar sat beneath the high table of Jarl Kar's hall. Thorfast was at his right and Bjorn was to his left. Opposite the table, Alasdair picked the bones of his meal for the last bit of flesh. Ander Red-Scar was already flushed and boasting loudly to the rest of the men at the table. The feast had only begun, but the story of Erik's defeat had to be told and retold to every man packed into the hall. Outside, warriors fresh from their so-called battle were eager to press inside to hear the tale. But Yngvar expected the casks of ale set out there would keep them waiting as long as needed. He was tired of retelling the story.

Yngvar smiled at his former slave. He was like a puppy with a bone. They had not eaten this good in many months, and the roast fowl had been the most succulent Yngvar had ever experienced. Yet Alasdair took it to the extreme, licking his greasy fingers when no more satisfaction came from the bones on his wood plate.

"You never told me where you learned to swim," Yngvar said. "It's a rare skill."

"My Da thought I should know something useful," Alasdair said, picking through the bones a final time. "Then he sent me to the priests to learn more useful things. I think he actually sold me, if truth be told, lord."

"Will you stop calling me lord," Yngvar said. "You've saved my life more times than I care to think about. We are equals."

"Of course, lord." He plunged a wing bone into his mouth while everyone around him leaned back laughing.

Ander had finished repeating his story of the battle to the men crowding his shoulder. As everyone had done since returning, he extended his hand to Bjorn.

"But here's the reason Erik's men fled. This one is a mighty berserk! The bear-god filled him with rage and he killed three men with three swoops of his ax. He carved a hole through the enemy and made them so fearful that they pissed themselves. You should have seen him."

Bjorn lowered his head and mumbled incoherently. To Yngvar's surprise, his cousin did not covet the attention heaped upon him. For all their childhood, he seemed to want attention and glory, but now that he had both it made him uneasy.

Yet there could be no doubt, the ferocity of a single man had broken the enemy's will. His father had told him stories of such men. One mad bastard could turn the tide of battle, just as one coward could start men fleeing. Warriors fought as individuals but acted in accord with a single will. Bjorn had proved the old tales.

"They seem to forget who came up with the plan every time they tell this story," Thorfast whispered. "You need to be sure your name is not lost in all this."

"Nor yours," Yngvar said. "Your silver tongue and big ears have kept us alive all summer."

"No one remembers words," Thorfast said, his mouth imitating a frown. "They remember deeds."

"I'll not forget who carried me out from Erik's grasp, nor who devised the whole plan to escape him." Yngvar threw his arm around his best friend. "We are all together in this. None of us alone would be alive without the other. Let me toast you."

He grabbed his mug. He learned since returning as a hero that his mug would never remain empty. He held it up to Thorfast, who grabbed his own.

The crowded hall turned toward them, and Yngvar was suddenly exposed to all with expectant smiles. Yngvar panicked, realizing a key moment had arrived and he had no words to describe the complex emotions he felt.

His friend winked at him, still keeping his mug raised. Thorfast the Silent knew the right words.

"This toast is for all of us who dared the open seas. For Yngvar and Bjorn—and me—who left home as children and became men. For Alasdair who lived as a slave and became a hero. For Ander Red-Scar and those who stood loyal to their lords even in their deaths and prevailed against lies and fear. It was a long year. A year of blood. A year of hopelessness. But we prevailed. We are the descendants of the wolf, from Ulfrik to Hakon to Gunnar to Aren. We do not lie down to die. We know only victory."

The hall cheered and every mug and drinking horn spilled foam as they raised high. Yngvar slammed his mug against Thorfast's. His eyes were wet and a lump formed in his throat.

"Fine words and all true," Bjorn said, then joined his mug to theirs.

Yngvar endured the back-slaps and congratulations that flowed from that moment forward. His whip scars throbbed with a dull ache, but he blurred it with drink and smiles. Thorfast's words had raised the spirits of a hall full of hungry warriors who had experienced nothing but humiliation and frustration. They had gone seeking battle and glory, and found neither.

For Yngvar had learned that Erik's feint was never serious. The storm had scattered his ships, but it was of no consequence. None of them engaged Jarl Alrik and Kar's fleet. They fled at the first chance, leading them on pointless chases until Alrik determined Erik had been lost in the storm. He had guessed the enemy was confused without a leader and so fell back. Of course, they learned the shocking truth when they found Yngvar and his band recovering in Kar's hall.

Along the high table, Jarl Kar sat with his hirdmen. Kar's sad eyes and stiff mane of hair made him look like a dog that had been caught shitting on a bed. It was an ungenerous comparison, but Yngvar was still not fully over being locked up for Kar's suspicions. At his right, in the seat of honor, the regal Jarl Alrik stared wistfully at the back of the hall. Had Thorfast's colorful words inspired him to recall his own adventures? He worked one thick hand through his white beard. His mustache was limp with the ale that had soaked it, and the gold beads tied into it seemed about to fall.

Finally, to Yngvar's greatest surprise, Jarl Ketil Ragnarsson sat beside Alrik. He was as muscular as Alrik, but much fatter. His famous beard was raggedly shorn to his chin, and a terrible cut at his neck showed how close he had come to death. Apparently, Ander Red-Scar had the sense to board Erik's ship and untie the captured jarl from the mast. He had been stripped naked, though Yngvar never saw it himself. Tonight he was clothed in a clean, gray shirt and brown pants. He had not stopped smiling since Yngvar first met him on the journey back to Kar's hall.

When the evening feast had worn on and the humidity of the hall became unbearable, Yngvar felt sleepy. Yet no feast could end while the jarls were still awake, and all three were as excited as if they had truly won a great victory. The night might carry on well past Yngvar's capacity. Alasdair was already beneath the table, sleeping in a curled-up ball.

Jarl Kar suddenly jumped up on his bench. His hirdmen began beating the table for attention. Despite the late hour, most men had not succumbed to their drinks. The hall gradually silenced as Kar's pine-cone-shaped body wavered on the bench. He belched, then addressed the hall.

"It is time I add my words, such as they are, to this feast. I doubt I can match the poetry of ... of ..."

"Thorfast," said Thorfast. The hall filled with laughter and Kar's face reddened.

"Of course, it's the drink." More laughter followed and he waited for it to die down. "I owe a public apology to these brave men. I doubted their intent, and in so doing I almost cost the lives of my people and lost my treasure as well. Were it not for them, I hate to think what could have happened. And of course, Grettir, you and your fellows proved you are brave men. You were wise enough to defy me when it was to everyone's benefit. I am humbled to have you in my service. I've done little to deserve such capable men. But the gods see fit to bless me with the greatest warriors in all of Norway."

Cheers were met with good-natured challenges from Alrik's men. Grettir himself stood straight and lifted his chin. Yngvar nodded at Kar's words, for they were noble and respectful. They brought honor to all who heard them. What a comparison to Erik's jealousy and spite.

"Since the gods have decided that I must lose my treasure, or at least what I was unwise enough to keep in a chest—I'll have to fix that later—I am sharing it out in equal measure to all of you who defended it. That is right. Old Kar the Closed-Fisted will hand over his treasures to the men who dared their lives to protect it. For what is gold if it is covered with the blood of noble men? I would rather have you alive and gather gold again some other day."

The cheers shook the walls. Thorfast and Bjorn both looked at Yngvar between them. He folded his arms and smiled. "Uncle Gunnar did not lie to us, did he?"

Ander Red-Scar was nearly in tears, hugging his companions for the joy of it. Alasdair was now awake and rubbing his eyes, the only calm face among the crowd.

Jarl Ketil stood and tapped Kar's leg. It nearly sent him falling over, to the delight of everyone. With a nod, they exchanged places. Yngvar wondered at the creaking bench, for Jarl Ketil was a bear of a man. His rough shorn beard flayed out beneath his chin, but he still patted at it reflexively though it was no longer there.

"I've my own words for these men." Ketil didn't seem sure who to look at, but he settled on Ander. After all, he had rescued the jarl. "I was defeated and stripped naked. But your planning saved my life. I must be honest, I have much gold to pay out in blood money to the families of those slain under my protection. And Erik carried away a good portion of my wealth. But what I cannot grant to you in gold, I will grant to you in land. This I can give and I will give. For those with the freedom to choose, I ask you to come to me at any time, and you shall have a farm and flocks such as I can give you. But for those who carried me from humiliation, I must do even more. I will find what I can award you, and do so gladly."

Ander bowed and the tears on his face glittered in the hearth firelight.

At last, Jarl Alrik spoke. He did not stand on a bench. He did not need to call for silence. Men respected him enough that he needed neither to command their attention.

"Yngvar Hakonsson, Bjorn Arensson, Thorfast the Silent, I know these three names now. Your stories have all been told, and I expect there are others to tell still. You are brave men all. Yet Yngvar, you faced Erik Blood-Axe in combat and lived. It is no small feat. I respect such a man. I admire your courage and cunning. I need men such as you. You did not kill Erik, so I cannot pay his bounty. You did not save my life nor my fortunes. But it takes no effort to see the gods have marked you all for greatness. I would have your service, and grant you my deepest respect and honor. I would offer the same to all your men. I am not far removed from King Hakon himself, and I would expect he would offer you the same. But I am the lucky man here, and so I offer you this first. I know you want to return home. If that is any man's wish, I will grant it. I will place you on a ship of my own and sail you to your homes. But I urge you to consider serving me. Tomorrow, you may tell me your decision. Tonight, let us drink until no man remains standing!"

The hall resounded with cheers. Yngvar, however, did not know what to think. He looked at Bjorn and Thorfast, and both seemed as torn.

They spent the night subdued until at last sleep claimed them.

The next morning, Yngvar was up early. Most men were piled around the hall. The place buzzed with snoring. Thorfast was already awake as was Alasdair. Only Bjorn and Ander remained asleep. With a nod from Thorfast, they each woke one of them. Then they went out of the hall.

Tents spread out everywhere where men slept off their revels. Yngvar led them to where they could be alone among a smattering of small pine trees.

"Well, what do you think?" Yngvar asked. "We've been trying to go home all year."

Thorfast shrugged. "I'm no jarl's son. There's no inheritance for me to claim. I've left home and I'd prefer to stay gone. At least until my mother gets settled with the idea."

"My father don't care where I am," Bjorn said. "I feel bad for Uncle Hakon, though. He was kind to me."

Yngvar tilted his head and closed his eyes. He did not need to think of his choice. His eyes snapped open immediately. "I feel bad for my father, too. And mother. But this is our time, not theirs. This is our adventure. This is what we left home to find. It's right here, in the land of our ancestors. I don't want things handed to me. I want to grab them myself. Here we are heroes and have a name. At home, people still think I'm a spoiled child to be married off to the hag-daughter of a petty jarl. Now that I am wiser, I am prouder of my father than ever before. But he's had his life. I want mine. I'm staying."

"Well, I guess we worried for nothing then," Thorfast said. "Bjorn and I were planning to tie you down until you agreed to stay on."

"He ain't lying," Bjorn said.

"I'll stay with you, if you don't mind, lo ..." Alasdair's mouth bit off the final word, drawing Yngvar's laugh.

"Mind? I dare say I might not live long if you abandoned me."

Ander sighed, and he put his arm on Yngvar's shoulder. "You've shown me more in this year than your uncle did in his whole life. You're a match to the legend of your grandfather. You might do better than him one day. I'll be waiting to hear. But many of us have families back home. We promised to bring them gold. They probably think we're dead. But home will always be Frankia for some of us. I wish I could stay on with you. I really do."

Yngvar placed his hand over Ander's. "I know it. Will you bring word to my father of what happened?"

"You know I will."

"And tell him that his brother accepted his apology and that he loves him and waits in the feasting hall. It's important he knows this." Ander nodded gravely. Yngvar paused and licked his lip. Then he pulled Ander aside, away from the others who looked on with raised brows. He whispered close to Ander's ear. "And would you tell Thorfast's sister, Kadlin, that I'm earning my fortune but that I'll be back for her. She just needs to wait a while longer."

Ander laughed, patting Yngvar's shoulder. "I wish you luck with that. I'll deliver the message, though, you can depend upon it."

"Good!" Yngvar clapped his hands, then turned back to gather his companions together.

"Descendants of the Wolf," he said to Thorfast. "I like it."

Arm in arm, they strode back toward the hall and toward a future of bold adventure.

AUTHOR'S NOTE

Our story opens in Western Frankia in 935 CE. By this time, Hrolf the Strider, known better to history as Rollo, had died. His son, Vilhjálmr Langaspjót (William Longsword) had been ruling after his father since 927. The region known as Normandy had already secured two additional land grants since the initial agreements reached in 911. Normandy was nearing its final shape. It was a tumultuous period, despite our fictional hero Yngvar believing the world had become too peaceful for a man to earn a name in Frankia. In fact, William had faced an early revolt from other Normans who felt he had grown "soft" and too "Frankish." A few years of peace would follow, but more struggle and political intrigue would scourge Normandy soon after.

Yngvar Hakonsson, his father, and all his companions are completely fictional. They call themselves "descendants of the wolf." Considering Yngvar's grandfather was named Ulfrik, which means Wolf Leader in Old Norse, this makes perfect sense. As readers of the first series know, Ulfrik helped Hrolf secure the lands of Normandy after the siege of Paris in 885. Such a man would've been a hero to the local Normans and one many bold young men would want to emulate.

The focus of our history and the characters that shaped it must necessarily change now that Yngvar has traveled to Norway. We now leave Frankia and Normandy behind to look north once more.

Erik Blood-Axe is perhaps one of the most famous men in Norse history. His name is writ large across the sagas. The moniker, Blood-Axe, conjures dynamic visions of a berserk Viking. But despite all of this, Erik's real history is not well documented. What we do know of him must wait for later volumes of this story to be told. For his history has now become intertwined at least in part with our fictional characters'.

Erik was the favored son of Harald Finehair, who was the first ruler of a "united Norway." In fact, Harald controlled mostly the west and southwestern coastal jarls. However, he never had all jarls under him at all times. In any case, Harald was an active man and is said to have fathered twenty sons. Reality was likely closer to eight. The two we are most concerned with are of course Erik and Harald's youngest son, Hakon.

Erik ruled concurrently with Harald until he died at age eighty. During this time, Erik was killing off his brothers to ensure his succession to his father's authority. Erik may in fact have been the oldest son, but birth order did not determine inheritance. That was mostly decided by who proved to be the strongest. In our story we have Erik called Blood-Axe, but he was probably not called this until many generations later. However, it's easier to recognize him by the name he is famous for, so it is left in the story. Erik's rule was despotic and cruel, and he heavily taxed his subjects. This not only created hostility to his rule but impoverished his jarls. It takes little imagination to realize how that would play out for Erik's reign.

In the meantime, Hakon the Good (again, a name granted to him much later in history) was fostering in Wessex under King Aethelstan. Sources say he was only fifteen when he returned to Norway, having heard of his brother's deeds. He sought to challenge him for the throne and won by simply showing up. He promised to repeal hated taxation laws and thereby won the support of all the jarls. Erik was chased from Norway without a fight.

This is where our characters enter the historical stage. Yngvar has arrived shortly after Hakon's rise. Erik and his wife Gunnhild have fled to the west, where they set up a base of operations. Erik was significantly less bold than a nickname like "blood-axe" would suggest. He never fought Hakon, and he crawled off to a life of piracy. Quite a far fall for one from such a bold lineage. Gunnhild is maligned throughout the sagas for cruelty, sexual appetite, cunning, and a raft of other insulting qualities. She is also said to have been a beautiful woman. From what we can surmise, Erik feared his wife and the mighty "blood-axe" may have been more like a hen-pecked husband than our stereotypical ideal of the Viking warrior.

Much more turmoil is in the future for the northern way. If Yngvar and his companions seek adventure and battle, they will have it in the years to come. Erik will prowl the region as a pirate and more. Hakon has the love of his people—for now. He is still young. There are other players yet to take the historical stage who will bring strife with them.

Yngvar and the descendants of the wolf have yet to face their greatest challenges.

I hope you enjoyed this book. If you would like to know when the next one is released, please sign up for my new release newsletter on my website. I will send you an email when it is out. You can unsubscribe at any time, and I promise not to fill your mailbox with junk or share your information. You can also visit me at my website for periodic updates.

https://jerryautieri.wordpress.com/

If you have enjoyed this book and would like to show your support for my writing, consider leaving a review where you purchased this book or on Goodreads, LibraryThing, and other reader sites. I need help from readers like you to get the word out about my books. If you have a moment, please share your thoughts with other readers. I appreciate it!